Valour *and* Vanity

Valour *and* Vanity

Mary Robinette Kowal

A Tom Doherty Associates Book

New York

VALOUR AND VANITY

Copyright © 2014 by Mary Robinette Kowal

Reading Group Guide © 2014 by Tor Books

Edited by Liz Gorinsky

A Tor Book
Published by Tom Doherty Associates, LLC
175 Fifth Avenue
New York, NY 10010

www.tor-forge.com

Tor® is a registered trademark of Tom Doherty Associates, LLC.

The Library of Congress Cataloging-in-Publication Data is available upon request.

ISBN 978-0-7653-3416-9 (hardcover)
ISBN 978-1-4668-0839-3 (e-book)

Tor books may be purchased for educational, business, or promotional use. For information on bulk purchases, please contact Macmillan Corporate and Premium Sales Department at 1-800-221-7945, extension 5442, or write specialmarkets@macmillan.com.

First Edition: April 2014

Printed in the United States of America

0 9 8 7 6 5 4 3 2 1

For Glenn and Pat

Always laugh when you can, it is cheap medicine.
—LORD BYRON

Valour *and*
Vanity

One

In Like a Lion

It may be stated with some certainty that travel can be trying even to the steadiest of characters. Thus it was with some trepidation that Jane, Lady Vincent, found herself on a tour of the continent as part of her sister's wedding party. Her last visit to the continent had ended abruptly when Napoleon had escaped his exile and reigned terror on Europe.

The troubles she faced with this tour had been of the prosaic sort: which carriage to take, how to arrange their party's quarters, and, most of all, how to manage her mother's nerves. Those nervous complaints had been a constant companion on their meandering course across Europe. Jane was relieved that they were now in the Free Imperial City of Trieste, where she and her husband would separate from the rest of the family. She would miss Melody and Mr. O'Brien, and had become quite fond of his parents, Lord and Lady Stratton. Of course she would be sorry to say farewell to her father, but no amount of tender regard for her mother could quite subdue her relief at their impending departure.

Fair weather had favoured them, and their last morning in the city had been filled with balmy breezes off the Gulf of Venice, which gave glad tidings for the voyage that they would shortly take to Venice and from there to Murano.

Jane climbed down the worn steps of the old Roman amphitheatre in the heart of the city, following her husband to where the stage had once lain. The sides of her bonnet shielded her from glimpsing the modern buildings that surrounded the open-air theatre and allowed her to maintain the conceit that she stood in part of the Roman Empire.

As she walked, she kept her gaze trained upon Vincent's back.

Though it was at least three years out of fashion, the blue coat of superfine showed off the breadth of Vincent's shoulders to great advantage. His brown hair curled over the top of his tall collar. Even with his high crowned hat, the wind dishevelled his hair further than his usual wont. When he made an effort, he could cut as fine a figure as any gentleman of Jane's acquaintance, but she much preferred the ease of his natural carriage.

Vincent paused at the base of the stairs and consulted the letter he was holding. "Byron says that the glamural is under an arch to the right of the stage."

Jane lifted her head and peered around, looking for the old stage illusion. Trieste had so many ruins from when it was part of the Roman Empire that no one in the town paid them much heed, but Lord Byron's letter to Vincent said that this faded revenant of glamour was worth viewing. As the ruin was but three streets from the docks, it seemed a natural excursion to make before departing.

The sides of the amphitheatre rose around them in a gentle slope that took advantage of the natural hillside. Remnants of old brick pilings showed where the back of the stage had once stood as a colonnade. Now there was nothing there to prevent them from seeing the street, which ran just on the other side of a row of remaining column bases. A few slabs of marble still graced the ruins, a vestige of their former glory. "Do you think he meant a whole arch or a fragment?"

Vincent scowled at the page, holding it in both hands to steady it against the warm breeze. "I am uncertain."

Jane took a few steps toward one of the marble remnants, which stretched higher than the others. As she did, part of a brick arch came into view. Movement flickered within it for a moment. "Here, Vincent."

He hurried across the cracked paving stones, folding the letter as he went. "Well spotted, Muse."

Jane and Vincent slowed as they reached the arch, as though their movement might disturb the illusion that had been spun there. In the shadow the remaining brick cast across the ground, the ghost of a lion stood, tossing its head. The glamourist who had created the illusion had rendered the lion with the precision of one who had actually seen such a beast. As faded as the illusion was, the folds of glamour that sketched it remained robustly alive. The mane was "torn and fray'd," with almost no fine details remaining, but still moved as though it belonged to a real lion. The beast bent its head and opened its mouth in a silent roar. The skeins that would have provided the sound had long since decayed back into the ether.

Jane sought Vincent's hand in wonder. He took it, as silent as she in appreciation for the artistry of the long dead glamourist. The lion swished its tail and stalked back and forth beneath the narrow confines of the arch. Its feet passed through rubble, but the illusion did not break. Sometimes he roared before stalking, sometimes after, and once he sat down and bathed a foreleg.

"What an amazing creature. So vital after all these years."

"How . . . how do you think it is done?" Jane furrowed her brow, trying to understand the techniques involved. By her understanding of glamour, creating this illusion should have required weeks of effort, but stories written of the Roman theatre indicated that the glamours were refreshed with each production.

"I am confounded, truly." Vincent let his hand slip free of hers and crouched to study the glamural more closely. "The folds of glamour that remain are too fragile for me to feel comfortable subjecting it to a closer inspection. I am astonished that it has survived this long. Perhaps it uses *amarrage en étrive*? Though that would not result in this variation . . ."

Jane squinted at the glamour, but without teasing the threads apart, it was impossible to tell how it had been created. Her husband was quite correct that the ancient folds were likely to tear if handled. She hazarded a guess based on what she could see. "If it were doubled or nested?"

"Possible." He rested his hand on his chin as he studied the lion. "Look at the power in its movements."

"I could almost believe that it was a recording, if it were not fully rendered." The techniques to record sound in glamour were well understood, but comparable efforts with images were less satisfactory. Vincent had experimented with a weave that he called a *lointaine vision*, but it resulted in a view of the subject from only one perspective. The lion was fully fleshed out no matter where one stood.

"It has not repeated a cycle of movement once, has it?"

Jane shook her head and then, recognising that he was not watching her, pronounced her agreement. "Individual gestures, but not complete patterns. And I must own that I am relieved that you cannot sort out the effect any better than I can."

"No surprise there. You have always been better than I at understanding threads."

Though Jane would not admit it aloud, his praise of her skills still warmed her, even after nearly three years of marriage. It should no longer be a concern, but she sometimes still felt the shadow of his education with the celebrated German glamourist, Herr Scholes. "I will accept your compliment, only because I know that you have always refrained from looking at others' work."

"Not always. Recall that I first learned glamour by unstitching my sister's lessons." Vincent stood and stepped back to study the arch. Lost in abstracted thought, he walked through the arch to the other side. The lion roared as he passed by it, almost as though it had felt his movement. He put a hand on his hip and placed the other over his mouth as he stared at the lion. Finally, shaking his head, he dropped his hand. "It is a wonder."

"Perhaps Herr Scholes will know." Jane walked around the arch, not wanting to pass through the illusion, even though it could do no harm. She supposed it was a testament to the artist that the lion could still cause her a sense of disquiet.

"Or perhaps this is a technique that only one glamourist has ever known, and it is lost to history."

"Such as our *Verre Obscurci*?" She took his hand. This was the tragedy of glamour: It could not be removed from the place where it was created. An accomplished glamourist could tie the folds of light off to keep them from vanishing back into the ether, but even that would fade and unravel over time. To move a glamour required exerting precise control over every thread that created it and maintaining each thread's exact relation to every other thread. Two years prior, Jane and Vincent had discovered a way to record glamour in glass, the *Verre Obscurci*. It would not help save the lion, because the technique required glamourists to cast their folds through molten glass, but it did suggest a future in which great works were not confined to a single space.

He grimaced and squeezed her fingers. "I sometimes wonder if we are right to pursue it. Perhaps glamour is meant to be ephemeral." He gestured to the lion. "Then I see something like this and wish for a way to carry it with me."

"I cannot think that—"

"Jane! Vincent!" The voice of Jane's younger sister pulled their attention to the street. Melody walked towards them, arm in arm with Alastar O'Brien. Even a glamural of cupids could not proclaim the newly-weds' love more thoroughly than the glow of delight that seemed to surround them. It would not surprise Jane if they soon announced to her parents the impending arrival of a grandchild. "I thought we would never find you. Then Alastar remembered Vincent speaking of a glamural and Roman theatres, and la! Here you are."

Vincent released Jane's hand, stepping back to a proper distance. His natural reserve had diminished with Melody and Alastar, thank heavens, but he was still less easy when in a group.

Jane moved forward, smiling, to give him a moment. "I thought you were at the Roman baths with Mama."

"We were, but then Mama was telling another lady that you were off to visit Lord Byron, and then that lady mentioned his poem "The Corsair," and then Mama could think of nothing but pirates, and now she is certain that you will be killed at sea." She tossed her head, and sunlight caught on her spectacles and made them flash. The lenses did nothing to diminish the power of Melody's beauty. In the Roman ruins, her blond curls might well have been part of a glamour of some goddess. "We came to warn you that she is at the dock waiting."

Jane closed her eyes in aggravation. Her mother had been the one to suggest taking ship to Venice after one of Mrs. Ellsworth's many correspondents spoke highly of the beauty of the trip, even going so far as to recommend the *Ophelia*, for which they had obtained passage. Sadly, it did not surprise Jane to discover her mother's mind had changed, and yet, of all things, what she had most wished to avoid was a scene with her mother upon their departure. That is why she had arranged to say their farewells at the hotel that morning. "Thank you for that."

Mr. O'Brien straightened his spectacles. Beside Vincent he seemed slight and scholarly, though he was a well-proportioned man. "The truth is, we shall miss you terribly when you go. You have made everything . . . so much smoother. I do not know if I shall—that is, Melody tells me I need not be concerned about her mother's nerves, but— Well."

Used to her mother's histrionics, Jane was not often perturbed by them, but it was all too apparent that Mr. O'Brien wished he and Melody were coming with them rather than continuing to tour with their parents.

Vincent rubbed the back of his neck and offered the tight compression of his lips that was his public smile. "She is enjoying herself. Truly. You do get used to it."

"I suppose we should get on with it, then." Jane took Melody's arm for the walk to the docks and let the gentlemen lag behind so that her husband could explain to Mr. O'Brien how to cope with the hysterics that had so often accompanied them on their journeys. Though Jane esteemed her mother, she had to own that Mrs. Ellsworth sometimes had more sensibility than sense, a fact that Vincent had struggled with a great deal in the early days of their marriage. It was a silent relief to see that her husband had found his place, and a comfort to see him sharing that with the newest addition to their family.

She had methods of her own for managing her mother's expansive feelings, though today that had not worked so well as she might have liked. They arrived amid the bustle of the docks far too soon. Even at a distance, she could discern a familiar voice. With a sigh, Jane steadied her bonnet against the stiff breeze across the harbour.

"Lady Vincent! Sir David!" Mrs. Ellsworth's voice cut

through even the clamour of the docks. She insisted on using their titles, no matter how much Jane or Vincent protested. She was so proud of being able to say, "My daughter's husband, Sir David Vincent, the Prince Regent's glamourist" at every possible opportunity that it seemed cruel to deny her the fun.

Melody giggled. "You see."

"You do not need to tease me. You will have her full attention soon enough." Jane released her sister's arm and went to meet their mother. "Mama, you should not have left the baths on our account."

Her father, Mr. Ellsworth, had his hand at her mother's back as though he were supporting her, but she walked with all the swiftness of a governess in pursuit of a small child. Jane was very much the focal point of her march across the docks. She was only thankful that Mr. O'Brien's parents did not feel the need to indulge her mother's humours. This threatened to be exactly the overwrought farewell that Jane had wished to avoid.

"You must not go!" Mrs. Ellsworth came to a stop in front of them with a hand pressed to her bosom. "Charles, tell them they must not."

Jane's father cleared his throat. His thinning white hair fluttered under his hat and, in the morning light, seemed almost like mist. "My dear. Your mother wishes me to tell you that you must not go."

"You could make more of a protest than *that*. Lady Vincent, Sir David. I implore you to not take ship."

"Mama! They must take ship. It is an island. One does not simply walk into Murano."

"Just so, and Lord Byron is expecting us in Venice." Vincent offered a bow to her mother.

This was the reason they had given for separating from the honeymoon party, though the truth had more to do with the glassmakers on the neighbouring island of Murano. That they were going there to work would have required explanation, and Mrs. Ellsworth was not given to discretion. If they told her that they had created a way of recording glamour in glass, the entire continent would know. Thank heavens that Lord Byron's extended stay in Venice provided them an excuse to visit. The invocation of a lord was usually more than sufficient to distract Mrs. Ellsworth. Alas, that seemed not to be the case on the morning in question.

"But last night, one of the serving men at our hotel told one of the maids, who told our Nancy, that there were pirates on the Gulf of Venice. And then today! In the baths! A woman spoke of barber sailors!"

Mr. O'Brien was taken with a sudden fit of coughing. He turned that pink of embarrassment so peculiar to those with red hair. Clearing his throat, he said, "I believe you mean Barbary corsairs, madam."

"There, you see! Mr. O'Brien knows that there are pirates."

"I am afraid that I do not." He removed his spectacles and polished them with a handkerchief.

Melody's spectacles flashed in the light as she tossed her golden curls. "La! We have said as much before. The last of the corsairs were defeated by the American fleet. These waters are quite as safe as any."

"Oh—oh, it is too much. Sir David, I implore you. After all that Jane has suffered already . . ."

Jane stiffened at the implication that Vincent had been the cause of any of the events of the last year. The words were simply careless, but she could not let them stand. She took a step closer to her mother, as though her proximity could protect her husband from Mrs. Ellsworth's words. "What I have 'suffered' has been by my choice alone. I will thank you not to suggest that Vincent had any fault in it."

Mrs. Ellsworth's mouth formed a small O of astonishment.

Jane pressed on. "While I am grateful for your concern, we are in no danger. The passage via the *Ophelia* will be quicker than the overland journey, and we have told Lord Byron that we are coming. You would not wish us to be disrespectful to his lordship, would you?" It would be of no use to remind her mother that taking ship had been her suggestion.

Mr. Ellsworth patted her arm. "You see, my dear?"

Mr. O'Brien stepped forward and joined Jane's father in soothing Mrs. Ellsworth. "If I might . . . The Barbary corsairs, even when they were sailing, were on the Mediterranean. This is the Gulf of Venice."

"Oh, but—" Mrs. Ellsworth's newest protestation was cut short by a cabin boy, who ran up to Vincent and bowed. In rapid Italian, he asked pardon for interrupting and let them know that Captain Rosolare wished them to board.

Vincent thanked the youth in Italian. Turning back to the party gathered on the dock, he offered a bow. "We must take our leave."

The next few moments passed in a jumble of heartfelt farewells. Mrs. Ellsworth abandoned her attempts to prevent them from leaving, though she did make extravagant use of her handkerchief. After so long travelling together, Jane had to admit to some melancholy at separating from the rest of the party.

But it was with great relief that she followed Vincent up the gangplank and aboard the ship.

The departure from Trieste had the familiar rhythms of any sea voyage, as sailors called to each other in voices that seemed brined from their time at sea. Ropes, thick as Jane's wrist, got tossed from dock to ship as they cast off. For a moment, the *Ophelia* seemed to lumber as a tug pulled it away from the dock; then the sails rose, catching the air with their flutter till they filled.

The time aboard passed with more speed than Jane anticipated, as she stared over the water and relished these idle moments with Vincent away from the constant requirements of her family. The salt air carried her tension across the waves.

It seemed they had but just left Trieste when the captain announced that they were already half-way to Venice. She sat with Vincent in the bow of the ship, using a coil of rope as their bench. The ship skipped over the brilliant cerulean waves, tossing the salt spray back into their faces. The remnants of the nuncheon they had packed in Trieste sat between them, the crumbs of a pastry sharing space on oilcloth with dried figs.

Vincent lifted a silver travel cup of wine and peered at it. "One wonders what wine Homer was drinking when he spoke of the wine-dark sea."

"Certainly a vintage no longer known, if it matched the sea." Jane inhaled the sea air, pressing her ribs against her short stays. "That colour. I cannot imagine a glamour that could re-create something so vibrant."

Forgetting for a moment the effect of travel on glamour, she reached into the ether and pulled forth a fold. The ship's motion pulled the glamour out of her fingers before she could make even a single twist. It rippled like a film of oil before vanishing back into the ether. Jane blushed at her foolishness. It took enormous energy to work glamour while walking even a few steps, and here she had tried it on a moving ship. The inability to work glamour at sea was what had given Lord Nelson the advantage against Napoleon's fleet during the blockade.

"Do that again." Vincent set his cup down on the deck. His gaze took on the vacant stare of someone looking deep into the ether.

"Have you an idea?"

"Merely a curiosity, which might become an idea later."

"You intrigue me." Jane reached for the glamour again. It slid through her hands so that she almost could not catch it in the first place. She lost control of the fold. It tickled under her fingers and sprang free. Jane laughed in surprised delight at the rainbow, which spread and shimmered in the air.

"I have not had the opportunity to see glamour dissolve like this. Only read the theory." Vincent reached into the ether himself. His fingers hooked on a fold, tightening. Then it sprang free. The coruscating colours flowed back in the ship's wake. He turned to watch it, and a slow smile spread across his face.

He reached for the glamour again, snatching wildly like a kitten reaching for a feather. Again, it tugged free of his fingers.

Vincent threw back his head and laughed. Giggling, Jane joined him.

She could only imagine what the Prince Regent would say if he could see his favourite glamourists essentially blowing soap bubbles with glamour. There was something delightful about the sheer wildness.

Jane pulled out another fold and spread her fingers as she released it, fracturing the rainbow into a half dozen pieces. "Look, the way you release it affects the shape of the . . . of the oil film."

Vincent grinned. "Apt name. Perhaps an oil of light?"

"Oiled glamour?"

"Glamoil?"

"Perhaps not."

He laughed and curved his hand so that the glamour slid over his palm in a patchwork cord of undulating light. "I recall Young experimenting with using multiple glamourists to try to stabilise the glamour."

"Did it work?"

"Not even a little." He pulled another thread, which evaporated as readily as its predecessors. "I wonder what would happen if we brought our *Verre Obscurci* aboard a ship. It worked when carried."

Jane considered. The sphere they had created bent light in the same twists as a glamourist's hands but did not require a glamourist to hold it steady. "That shall be something to try, if we can fashion a new one."

The lookout shouted from the crow's-nest, his words snatched away so that only his tone reached them. The ship's crew suddenly sprang into action, raising sails as the boat became an explosion of canvas. Jane looked toward the horizon in front of them. "Not Venice, so soon?"

"No." Vincent stood slowly, looking behind them. "It is absurd that my first thought is a desire to keep this from your mother."

The look of dread on his face made Jane turn in her seat. A ship sailed toward them. Even to her untutored eye, the cannons upon its decks were obvious. "Is that . . ."

"A Barbary corsair. Yes."

Two

Corsairs

Jane stared at her husband for a moment. Her breath felt as though it had been ripped from her body like glamour on a ship. "Pirates."

Vincent gave her a small, tight smile. "May I ask you to go below, Muse?"

"You ask me to go below as though you are not coming."

"I have some skill with weapons and might be of use in repelling the boarders." He squinted at the ship behind them. In the few moments since it had first been spied, it had visibly gained on them.

"You do not mean to fight. Vincent, tell me that you do not." She knew that he had more than just a familiarity with weapons. His father's insistence on perfection in all the accomplishments required of gentlemen meant that her husband was more skilled with the sword than most of his peers.

"They take slaves." He gave a grin that was half grimace. "I must defend you or your mother will never let me hear the last of this."

Amidships, the captain directed his crew to try to increase their speed. The first mate, a slender young man with dark curls, raised his hands and bellowed to the other passengers, who moved about the deck in a circling, confused mass, very much in the way. *"Signore e signori, devo chiedervi di andare sotto coperta per la vostra sicurezza."*

For a moment, Jane was so astonished that she could not understand his Italian, for all that her music-master had insisted that she master the language in order to sing it properly. Then her senses restored themselves, and she understood him to say, "Ladies and gentlemen. I must ask you to go below deck for your safety." No doubt he also wanted to get them out of the way of the crew.

Jane stood and gathered their nuncheon into an untidy bundle. She loathed the idea of leaving Vincent exposed on the deck, but was forced to acknowledge that she would only be in the way. "Very well. Promise me that you will be careful. Or at least as careful as one can be while holding a gun."

"Likely a sword." Vincent escorted her down from the bow. "I doubt any member of the crew will give a pistol to an unknown person. A sword, though . . . the captain will have arms for just such an event."

"It disturbs me that you know this." Jane tried to keep her tone light to mask her fear as they hurried across the deck.

"The benefits of a thorough education. They shall fire the

cannon twice in warning. Do not let this distress you. They want the ship as a prize, so will be unlikely to harm it."

"But the passengers aboard . . . You said they took slaves."

"They . . . yes. They do. I would wish that unsaid."

"But it would be no less true if you had been silent." She gave a breathless laugh. "I hope I shall not have reason to be thankful that I am so plain."

Vincent stopped at the ladder leading below deck. He turned her toward him and rested his hands on her shoulders. "I love you, Jane."

The use of her Christian name, rather than his pet name, almost undid her resolve. That, more than his talk of swords or guns, told her how very serious the coming encounter was.

She stood on her toes and kissed him in answer. His hands tightened on her shoulders, and he replied with a fervour that he had only ever shown in the privacy of their own home, heedless of the crew members around them.

Vincent stepped back, cheeks flushed. "Now. Go below, and I shall see you after."

Clutching the cloth with the remnants of their nuncheon, Jane followed the other passengers below deck. There, a sailor led them down a dark, narrow passage to what must be the captain's cabin.

As he locked the door to secure them, Jane pulled off her bonnet. The cabin had a single berth affixed against one wall and a broad table with chairs enough for a dinner of eight. Windows looked out the side of the boat to provide illumination as well as a view of the sea. In the distance, they could see a dark smudge along the horizon. The Italian coast was so close to hand.

If they could but outrun the corsairs, then they would be safe.

The cabin was occupied with the other passengers on the ship. Two gentlemen stood in tight conversation in one corner and only glanced round as Jane came in. The younger of the two raised his eyebrows in astonishment. Jane ran a hand over her close-clipped hair. She had been travelling with family so much that she had forgotten that it would seem strange to other people.

The other inmates consisted of three women and their children—two daughters approaching marriageable age and three boys, one still in leading strings. One of the older women knelt with her head bowed in prayer in front of a gilded crucifix, which the captain had affixed to one wall. Her hushed voice tumbled out in Italian at a rate too fast for Jane to make out.

Another woman had taken a seat on the captain's berth with two girls on either side of her. Were it not for the looks of terror on their faces, they would have made a pretty picture in their dark curls and simple travelling dresses. One of the little boys sat at the woman's feet, playing with a toy soldier. He was no more than two, the same age Jane's child would have been if she had not—she pushed the thought aside as indulgent, and continued her examination of the room.

The other two boys had their faces pressed against the window, clearly trying to see the corsairs. Their faces were bright with the elation that comes of ignorance. To them, this was nothing but a game. Their mother stood behind them, hand pressed to her mouth as though to keep herself from speaking.

She looked round as Jane entered, saw that she was merely another woman, and went back to studying the sea.

The older of the gentlemen broke off his conference and crossed the room to her. He walked with a slight limp, assisted by a fine ebony cane. His hair had silvered, but aside from that, he still had the bearing of a younger man.

He addressed her in Italian. "Madam, please make yourself easy." He frowned and looked past her to the door. "But where is your husband?"

"Sir?" Jane replied in the same language.

"I saw you on deck. He is a glamourist, is he not?"

"I—Yes." She did not need to make the point that she was Vincent's creative partner—in this moment, the error was a trivial concern. "He stayed above to assist the captain in repelling boarders."

The gentleman winced. "I see that my conception of artists is an ill-founded one. Most would not choose to stay, I think."

Jane raised a brow. "I do not believe that is a motivation confined to artists."

He offered her a small bow. "A fair point, madam. It is likely, however, that his valour will be unnecessary. We are not far from the coast, and the captain will outrun them."

"But if he does not?"

He raised his cane. Twisting the head, he withdrew it enough to allow a peek of the shining steel blade encased within. "Then . . . that would be unfortunate. But there is no need to worry about that which might not be." He pulled a chair out for Jane. "Please, madam."

Jane took the seat he offered, though a part of her wanted

to join the woman who was praying. After seeing her settled, the gentleman took his leave and returned to his conference with the other man. The younger man had a dissipated look, which sometimes afflicts young men of fashion. He held a satchel and fidgeted with its catch as he stared out the window. He, too, looked as though he wanted something useful to do.

In many ways, the only one who was not waiting for someone else to take action was the woman who prayed. She was at least making a direct appeal instead of fretting idly. Their course had been set the moment the corsairs had spotted them. The only hope now was that they might outrun the pirates and reach the safety of the Venetian coast.

Jane pushed her chair back and crossed the room to kneel in front of the crucifix. Perhaps prayer only provided an illusion of control, but Jane was too accomplished a glamourist to deny that illusions could provoke emotions. That same perception allowed her to see beyond the curtain of bravery to the fear in her husband's eyes. The truth was that Jane had no way to sway the resolution of this battle. She could only pray that they reached safety in time.

She could only pray that Vincent was not injured.

So Jane bent her head. She clutched the topaz cross she wore beneath her fichu and prayed. The ship swayed around them, rocking her on her knees. Overhead, footsteps sounded as men ran back and forth preparing to meet the corsairs. She listened to the footfalls, trying to ascertain each time if one of them were Vincent's. When she finally did hear him walk overhead, she wondered how she could have thought any other set was his. She recognised the steady tread as surely as the beating of her own heart.

When she had read of pirate attacks in "The Corsair," by Lord Byron, they had seemed a swift and brutal thing. The author had left out the interminable period before the arrival of the corsairs, the period of tense waiting in which hope built that they might reach the coast in time.

The frantic pace overhead gradually slowed, and the entire ship seemed to hold its breath. They all waited as the minutes turned towards an hour and then past it, and still the ship fled with the wind.

This was not how Jane and Vincent's life was meant to be. They were supposed to create art for princes and explore the boundaries of their craft. They had left London to escape the intrigues there and the undesirable excitement of political unrest. Attack by pirates belonged to another's life. Oh . . . her mother would be in a state after this. Assuming they lived to tell her.

Jane lifted her head and looked to the window to escape her own thoughts.

The woman there had her hand on her younger son's shoulder now, and had joined in staring out the window. The smudge of land was larger. How Jane wished she could see the pirate ship behind them.

If they had outrun the ship, then someone would have come to say so. Jane closed her eyes again. If she stared at the land, she would go mad wishing that they were on it.

A cannon boomed over the water.

Jane flinched at the sound. One of the other women shrieked, and the younger of the two girls began sobbing in Italian. "They shall sink us, Mama!"

A moment later, the cannon sounded again, distinctly closer, but there was no answering crash of wood splintering beneath a cannonball. Jane wet her lips. She said, "They are warning shots. They do not wish to harm the prize."

The girl continued to sob as though she had not heard Jane, but her mother gave Jane a grateful look and smoothed her daughter's hair, whispering to her.

Jane got to her feet, unable to remain still any longer. Her knees ached from kneeling, and she staggered as she stood. At first she thought it was due to stiffness from being still so long, and then she felt the ship shudder again.

The corsairs were boarding. Shouts of alarm sounded, only slightly muffled by the stout wood of the cabin. Gunfire sounded in volley after volley, amid savage cries. Jane snatched up their nuncheon and emptied the contents of the oilcloth on the table. Taking the travel cups, she tied them into a corner of the cloth, thinking to use it to club someone. It weighed so little that she abandoned the effort.

She lifted one of the chairs and tried its weight. Senseless—senseless to think that would keep them from being taken should the worst occur, and yet she could not sit by and do nothing. She had faced Napoleon's army and would not be cowed by barbarians.

The gunfire overhead ceased almost as abruptly as it had begun. No more than five minutes could have passed. A set of footsteps sounded in the hall—not Vincent.

If they were safe, Vincent would have been the first down the stairs. Jane turned toward the door, the chair held ready.

The handle of the door rattled, but the lock stood firm. The older gentleman who had spoken to her earlier finally drew the sword from his cane and came to stand in front of Jane. "Behind me, madam."

The door crashed open, splintering around the lock. In the opening, a corsair lowered his booted foot. Behind him stood a cluster of other pirates, equally alarming. There could be no doubt as to what he was. A long tunic striped in yellows and reds flared around the strange ballooned trousers of a Turk. His curved scimitar preceded him into the room. Jane had seen drawings in *Punch,* but had always thought they were wild exaggerations for the purposes of attracting readers.

Faced with this new reality, she acted on instinct and tried to weave a *Sphère Obscurcie* to hide behind. For a moment, she thought that it would work with the ship standing still in the water, but the waves tossed them, and she lost her grip. The glamour evaporated into an oiled rainbow.

The corsair shouted at her and sprang forward. With a sweep of his hand, Jane's chair flew to the side. Before she could draw breath, he had her arm twisted behind her and the scimitar pressed against her neck. Jane shivered. His breath stank of beer and was the least noisome part of his person.

"Drop your weapons," he said, in heavily accented Italian. He tightened his grip on Jane, lifting her on to her toes to assert his point.

"Sir, release the lady." The gentleman wet his lips and stepped forward, sword held at the ready.

One of the others stalked into the cabin and, with a single twist of his scimitar, disarmed the man. With the next stroke, he clubbed him upon the head. The gentleman dropped to his knees, stunned but not unconscious. He struggled to rise.

The scimitar felt as though it would stop Jane's speech but she forced the words past. "Sir—please. No more. Do not resist them."

He nodded and stayed on his knees.

"Good." The pirate who had struck him gestured to the others. He issued some order in a rippling language that Jane did not recognise. In response, his men herded the small group of passengers out the door.

At every step, Jane was certain the blade at her throat would slide across her skin. The fichu of lace seemed inadequate to the task of protection. The corsair relaxed his grip only when they came to the ladder leading back on to the deck.

Jane was under no illusions that he was any less vigilant for this relaxation. She climbed the ladder without protesting or attempting to spring away. Where would she go?

After the dim confines of the passage below, the sun stung Jane's eyes. She winced, wishing for an idle moment that she had not left her bonnet below—but of what import was that? Propriety, and her complexion, were matters for another day.

As her eyes cleared, she peered around the boat. The corsairs' captain strode up and down the deck—his height made him obvious, even if his bearing did not. He wore a long moustache on his otherwise clean-shaven face. The ends hung below his chin and accented his shouts with their movement. He carried a brace of pistols tucked into his waistband. The wind whipped the ends of his bright sash through the air like blood in water.

A group of sailors sat along the rail, guarded by corsairs who held pistols at ready. Vincent lay crumpled next to the sailors, as though he had been tossed there like a rag doll. Utterly limp.

Jane darted forward, only to be snatched by the corsair

behind her. Now she twisted in his grasp to no effect. He shook her and raised the scimitar. Jane struggled to control herself. It would help no one if she were to be made an example.

With an effort, Jane steadied her breathing and pointed to Vincent. "My husband. Please?" The pirate grunted and walked her across the deck. He growled something to his fellows, of which Jane only caught the word, "Glamourist."

With a shove, he hurried her the last several feet toward Vincent. Jane stumbled on the hem of her dress and dropped to her knees beside her husband. She lay a hand on his chest.

Through his waistcoat, the strong beat of his heart gave her a relief beyond measure. She could now look at him for injury. Blood clotted the hair at the back of his head, but he appeared otherwise unharmed. Jane undid his cravat and loosened the high collar of his shirt to give him more air.

With the cravat, she dabbed at the wound on the back of his head, heedless of what went on around them. He groaned and shifted at her touch.

Jane lifted her head and looked to the closest sailor. "Have you any spirits?"

He looked at her without comprehension, so Jane repeated the question in Italian, and then her poor French. He continued to stare at her without any sign of understanding. A hand appeared on her right, holding out a silver flask. Jane turned to thank the person for the offer, and discovered it was the older gentleman from below. The other passengers had also been herded to the rail to sit with the sailors, and the pirate who delayed her had apparently only been committing another small act of cruelty.

"Thank you." She poured a small measure of liquor on to

Vincent's cravat and spared the gentleman a glance. "Are you injured, sir?"

"My vanity only." The gentleman shifted to lean against the rail. They had taken his sword cane, and he stretched his leg out gingerly in front of him now.

Jane granted only a nod of acknowledgement, for the greater part of her attention was fixed upon her husband. Dabbing carefully, she cleaned the blood away as best she could. When he stirred again, she passed the flask under his nose, in lieu of smelling salts. Vincent coughed and his eyes fluttered open.

"Thank God." Jane replaced the lid on the flask and returned it to the gentleman. In English, she said, "Vincent? Love. Can you hear me?"

"Muse?" He lifted a hand to his head. "I fear I have overdone glamour again. The room is spinning wretchedly."

"Not glamour this time." For a moment, she was caught in the memory of the excess of glamour that had nearly killed him. The vision of Vincent's heels drumming the floor in a seizure almost overwhelmed her. She pressed his free hand in hers, as she had not been able to then. "Our ship was set upon by pirates. You have sustained a blow to the head."

His eyes widened at that. Vincent struggled to raise himself to his elbows, but fell back. "Pirates?"

"Barbary corsairs."

He looked past her, brow creasing. "Dear Lord."

"You were very valiant and tried to resist them."

"Rash is more accurate." He rolled onto his side. "Help me sit."

Jane eased him into a sitting position. "Have a care. You have quite the lump."

"It seems more bearable if I am sitting." But he sat hunched, with his head held between his hands as though it would burst.

Jane sat beside him, rubbing the base of his neck, which was all the comfort she could offer in the circumstances. The pirate captain paid them little notice at first, seeming content to leave them along the rail. The other passengers had been assembled with the sailors. The young man from below insisted, to every corsair that passed him, that he was a nobleman and must be released at once.

They paid him no mind.

In short order, the corsairs pulled each passenger up and searched them for valuables without regard for age or sex. The captain stood behind them holding a rough canvas bag into which the valuables were deposited. With some he discussed ransom, and, when the terms were agreeable, he sent them to stand beside a boat. Vincent squinted at the action as though he had trouble focusing. "Muse . . . they may separate us. If they do . . . I will come for you, no matter what happens."

"And I you."

He lifted his head and offered something that was almost a smile. "That I know."

When the pirates came to them, Jane stood, and they took her wedding ring, the topaz cross at her throat, and the brooch that fastened the lace fichu about her neck. The captain took the lace as well and tied it around his own neck, laughing. Even with her cooperation, he still took the opportunity to lay his hands all over her person. Jane kept her gaze fixed on Vincent.

A muscle pulsed at the corner of his jaw, and his complexion slowly turned a furious red, but his brown eyes steadied her.

When the pirate released her, Jane stepped swiftly to the rail. Her skin crawled beneath her clothes, and she wished, very much, for a basin of hot water and a stiff brush.

The pirate barked at Vincent, clearly telling him to stand. Vincent rose to his knees and seized the rail to pull himself to his feet. His face turned an alarming green as he rose. Closing his eyes against the motion of the ship, he swayed in place. Jane steadied him as best she could. She wrapped her arm around his waist and tried to get her hip under his weight.

The corsair rattled out another sharp line of command.

Jane's temper snapped. "He is injured. Can you not see that?"

"I am well enough for their purposes." Vincent slowly straightened, though she was not at all certain that he could remain on his feet much longer. With care, he emptied his pockets, giving over his watch and its seal, his pocketbook with the monies for their journey, down to the last florin. The pirate dropped each item into the rough canvas bag. Vincent looked past him to the group by the lifeboat. "May we offer a ransom as well?"

The captain sneered and spoke in Italian that was heavily accented, even to Jane's ear. "You—you are British and your country is notorious for breaking their treaties. You are strong, and will fetch a good price."

The older gentleman from below limped clear of the group by the small boat. "One moment, sir. May I speak with you?"

Pursing his lips, the captain's eyes raked the gentleman up and down as though calculating his worth. "For yourself?"

"About ransom for those women and children who require it." He hesitated. "And for this lady's husband."

"That is an expensive proposition you make." The captain nodded to one of the young girls. "She would fetch a pretty price. Are you certain you can afford it?"

"I am Giacomo Sanuto, a senior officer at Banco de Giro. I assure you, I can." His words were bold, but a trickle of sweat ran down his temple. They began to haggle, numbers flying so quickly that it seemed the pirate captain had more than a little experience with this. Signor Sanuto matched him, though, and they had soon come to an agreement of three hundred pounds per woman and one hundred per child.

The pirate turned then to Jane and grunted. "This one is distinctly unpretty, and I'm not likely to sell her. One hundred and fifty pounds."

Jane could not bring herself to be injured by the comment on her appearance. Signor Sanuto nodded with clear relief at the figure, though it had been her allowance for a year before she married Vincent. "And her husband?"

"He's strong. The captain of this ship tells me he is a glamourist, so useful, too. One thousand pounds."

Jane gasped. Signor Sanuto swallowed. "But he is English, as you noted, and they are notoriously intractable. Five hundred."

"Nine hundred."

"You are not allowing for his injury, I think. He will require care before being fit to work. Surely knocking that off his price would be fair. Seven hundred and fifty?"

The captain stroked his long moustaches. "Done." He turned to one of the pirates and rattled off a command in his native tongue.

The pirate pulled them from the rail and added them to the group of passengers waiting by the ship's boat. Vincent offered Signor Sanuto his hand. "Thank you, sir. When we are ashore I shall make arrangements to reimburse you."

"Please do not trouble yourself." The signore shook his head. "It was the Christian thing to do, and I doubt that an artist has anywhere near that figure."

"While I do not generally care for titles, I want to reassure you that you will be repaid. I am Sir David Vincent." He cleared his throat. "I am the Prince Regent's glamourist."

The gentleman's eyes widened. "I am glad they did not know that, or they should have asked a higher price for you."

"Still. We are in your debt." Jane offered him her hand. "I cannot thank you enough."

"Do not thank me until we are safely in Venice."

Three

Noble Influence

The port office in Venice was vast and echoing and stank of fish. In the distance, the great clock in Piazza San Marco chimed, the two mechanical Moors atop it striking the bell eleven times. Each gong reverberated through the office, reminding Jane of how long their small boat had been adrift at sea. By good fortune, they had been picked up by a sailing vessel and carried into the port, but all of them were weary and sunburnt. The victims sat in different parts of the hall talking to various clerks who were attempting to manage the consequences of the pirate attack.

The clerks used crates, which were awaiting registration and approval as extemporized office furniture. The space was never meant to handle this sort of event. Jane shifted on the hard wooden crate she had been offered as a seat and stared with some envy at the folding chair that had been produced for Signor Sanuto. It had no padding, but even something with a back would be welcome. The voyage in the small boat had done no good for Vincent's dizziness, causing him to empty his stomach repeatedly into the ocean. He now sat sagged on a box, facing one of the port's clerks. Jane was not certain that he was wholly conscious.

For what seemed as though it were the fifth time, she finished the recital of their story. Being required to do so in Italian made the entire process that much more trying.

The clerk slicked his lank hair back from his face. "I am sorry, sir and madam. But without your papers, I cannot allow you into the city."

Jane made every endeavour to keep her voice level. "But I have explained that they were taken by the pirates. We have nothing."

"So you have said." The clerk shuffled papers on his desk. "If there were someone who might vouch for you, it would be a different matter."

They had come round to this again. Jane repeated what she had already told him. "We were to stay with Lord Byron."

"So you have said. It is a pity that his landlord reports that he has left the city."

"He is expecting us," Jane said, with less patience than she had before. "The landlord must be mistaken."

He picked up the note that had come in response to their request for assistance from Lord Byron. "No. No . . . Signor Segati is quite clear. He has gone to an assignation in La Mira."

Jane tried to put on her most reasonable tone, the one she used for calming her mother. "If you could simply release us, then we could apply at his house ourselves. He has surely left instructions with his staff."

The clerk simpered. "Ah, but who then would pay the entrance fee you owe?"

Jane rubbed her brow. Across the room, she saw the mother with the daughters stand to leave. The woman met her gaze briefly and offered a small wave; then she was gone.

They had arrived safely in Venice, but were now destitute. The pirates had taken all of their funds, and it would take a month or more to contact their banker in London. When Vincent had handed over their funds aboard the ship, Jane had been in too much shock to fully comprehend the consequences. If Lord Byron was not in town to vouch for them, she hardly knew what they would do. They were utterly without resources. Jane had expected that there would be some sympathy for their plight, but there had instead been this endless round of questions from a man who seemed to have no power save that of keeping them in this drafty room.

"Is there a British consul in Venice?"

"Of a certainty."

Jane waited for him to draw the connexion, but he simply looked at her coolly. "Then may we not speak to him?"

He looked puzzled. "Ah—but he is a good friend of Lord Byron. Surely you know that, as you are yourselves such friends of Lord Byron's. They are gone together to La Mira."

Jane sat back on her box, astonished and annoyed. "How might you know that?"

"It is common gossip, madam. I do not wish to shock you,

but it is well known that Lord Byron keeps a mistress in every port." He slicked his hair back again. "You must understand that invoking his name is . . . well. It raises certain questions about your character."

Jane's mouth dropped open. "My character? Sir. I have been waylaid by pirates. Are you now implying that it was somehow my fault? Because if you are, allow me to assure you that when our circumstances are altered, as they will no doubt be, I shall not forget your treatment of us."

He drew himself up in his chair. A strand of hair escaped and trembled along his nose. "I do not take kindly to veiled threats, madam."

Nor had he taken kindly to reason, but Jane managed to hold her tongue about that. She glared across the room and saw Signor Sanuto rise to leave as well. His back was to them, but she could tell that it bore none of the frustration that she felt. A manservant had arrived for him with a new walking stick and a greatcoat, which made Jane feel her own grime all the more. Signor Sanuto was shaking hands with his clerk, laughing, even. She let her breath out slowly and tried again with the man assigned to them. "Please tell me what we might do to be allowed to leave here."

"Well. You are without your papers, but I might overlook that irregularity, for certain considerations."

Vincent ground his teeth audibly together, proving that he was at least a little awake. In English, he said, "I thought we had left the pirates at sea."

Jane put her hand on Vincent's arm, though his words exactly matched her feelings. "As we are without funds, would you accept a promissory note?"

"Here we return again to the fact that you are unknowns in our city." He shrugged and held up his hands, as though to say that the decision was not in his control.

Signor Sanuto put on his greatcoat, on the point of departing. Jane knew one person in this city. She stood. "Signor Sanuto!"

He turned round at his name and frowned; then he limped across the vast room toward her. His infirmity seemed more pronounced on dry land.

Vincent sat up. "Jane, we cannot ask him for money."

"I do not intend to."

The signore came within speaking distance. "Lady Vincent. Is something the matter?"

"I do hate to impose, again, but our papers were on the ship and this gentleman needs someone to vouch for our identity."

Very quietly, he said, "Why are my friends being detained after the trial we endured today?"

"Signor Sanuto, sir! I was only—" Flushing, the clerk cleared his throat and drew a paper toward him. He began to scribble upon it with sudden focus.

As he did so, the signore turned to Jane and Vincent. "My apologies. I did not expect that you would have such difficulties. I believe we have the confusion straightened out."

The clerk cleared his throat again. "Sir David? May I ask you to sign a few papers, please?" His attitude was so markedly improved that Jane had to wonder with whom they had allied themselves.

Vincent excused himself and went to the desk, leaning heavily against it. Jane took his place at Sanuto's side. "I owe you thanks once again."

Signor Sanuto smiled. For a moment he reminded Jane of

her father when he presented her with a gift. "It pleases me to be able to help. Speaking of which . . ." He leaned down to whisper. "Your husband is not well, yes?"

Jane shook her head. "I'm afraid he is concussed . . ."

He grimaced in understanding, put a finger to his lips and straightened.

Vincent returned, folding a paper and placing it in his coat pocket. The circles of fatigue under his eyes were deep, and he seemed as though he were barely able to stand. "Our entry papers are in order. Thank you, sir."

Jane placed her hand on Vincent's arm to steady him. "Yes, thank you."

"It is the least I could do." Signor Sanuto looked down and tapped the floor with his walking stick. "May I do more? Would you stay with me at Ca' Sanuto? The truth is that my family is away, and our palazzo is too large for one person. After the events of today . . . Well, I would not like to be alone tonight. If you do not mind going to Murano, that is. It is a small town, another island like Venice, but just a short gondola ride away."

Jane did not hesitate or pause to consult Vincent. She did not want to chance a trip to Lord Byron's home only to be turned away, not with Vincent in the state he was in. It would be different if they had funds and could seek a hotel, but they had no resources at all. "Thank you. That is very kind."

Vincent made the small whine that sounded as though he were imperfectly holding his breath, which so often indicated that he was conflicted. It was clear that his pride did not like this solution, but he did not object. "Yes, thank you. In fact, we have business in Murano."

"Good. I have but one favour to ask."

"Of course."

Signor Sanuto clapped Vincent on the shoulder. "I only ask that you sleep in tomorrow, so that I might do the same."

Vincent offered one of his rare public smiles. "I think we may assure you of that."

Jane had no trouble making good their promise to Signor Sanuto. She woke as the sun came streaming in through the large windows of the bedroom the signore had provided for them. The light revealed details lost in her fatigue of the night before. The ceilings rose to at least twelve feet and were adorned everywhere with delicate plasterwork reminiscent of waves. Shells and seahorses completed the theme, reminding her that Venice was once known as La Serenissima, the Bride of the Sea. Murals that were a mixture of paint and glamour adorned the walls to make each seem vibrant and alive. The furniture, while in an older style, displayed exquisite marquetry and had no doubt been in the family for generations.

Rolling to her side, Jane studied Vincent. He lay sprawled on the feather mattress in the nightshirt that their host had provided. His broad chest rose and fell in deep slumber. His cheeks still had the red of too much time in the sun, but some of the unhealthy grey tinge had left the space under his eyes.

She snuggled closer, intending to take comfort in his presence for only a few moments, but when she opened her eyes again, the sun had risen nearly to noon. Stretching, Jane could not restrain a sigh of contentment.

"Awake?" Vincent's voice rumbled with disuse.

Jane tilted her head back to look at her husband. His eyes were still hooded with sleep, but he looked remarkably improved. "I am. How do you feel?"

"Better." He rolled onto his back and pressed both hands to his face. "My head aches still, but I suppose that is to be expected."

"I am only grateful that it was no worse."

Vincent caught her hand and pressed it to his lips. "When I think of all the ways in which it could have been . . . I should have listened to your mother."

Jane laughed and kissed him on the cheek. "If we listened to Mama every time she was frightened of something, we would be guarding for wolves and wearing flannel with liniment around our necks, even in summer."

"True. And yet—"

"Please do not torture yourself in this manner." Jane pushed herself to a sitting position. "I propose that we count our blessings that it provided us with the opportunity to meet Signor Sanuto—who, I might add, we should pay our respects to before it ceases to be morning."

Jane padded across the marble floor to the lounge. She had received the loan of clothing from the closet of Signor Sanuto's wife—who, he assured her, was "such a good creature that I am certain she would join me in urging you to make use of her closet." She had borrowed a day dress of sturdy muslin. The dress itself was a simple round gown, but the fabric was sprigged throughout with small flowers. The peach sash seemed exactly calculated to please her. Vincent had taken the use of a clean shirt. His coat had been brushed and mended till it looked new, and hung waiting for him on the back of one of the chairs.

As she undid the ties on her borrowed nightdress, she said, "Do you know that when we were in the captain's quarters, I thought Signor Sanuto a coward for staying below. I am quite ashamed of that now."

"He is older and has a limp besides, probably attained in the war." Vincent stood and winced, steadying himself against the bed. "Also, I believe that his was the better choice. I was hit so early that I do not even recall the pirates boarding."

"What? No tales of valour? No stirring epic with which to delight Lord Byron? With whom I am quite vexed, I might add. Did he not say he was looking forward to our visit?"

"Yes, but where women are concerned, Byron is not entirely his own master." Vincent scratched his chest and stretched again. He paused in the middle of his stretch as the last of the ties on her gown came free. "I have a certain understanding of that, in this moment."

Jane raised her eyebrows, heat flooding her cheeks. "Oh?"

"Indeed." He crossed the room and brushed her hair back from her face. "Our host did ask us to sleep in. I should hate to forswear that promise."

"With your injury? You astonish me."

"I very much hope to." Vincent picked Jane up and carried her back to bed.

When they exited their bedchamber, they discovered that their host had been called away in the morning and would not have been at home even if they had emerged when they first awoke. His staff, however, made them comfortable, and said that the signore had urged them to make use of the palazzo. It was a glorious structure, filled with rare antiques and art by the best painters.

They had been offered a light repast on the balcony by their host's cook, Letizia, a delightful older woman with hair still dark in spite of her years. She had left them with plates of dried figs, olives, and pastries, and a shining silver bell should they require anything else. The sunlight rippled upon the canal and reflected back upon the boats that plied the water.

It was easy to loose oneself in watching the gondolas speed back and forth on their various errands, and though Jane knew that it was no more unusual than the street traffic in London, the novelty made it charming. The houses, too, with their marble entrances straight to the canal, seemed the most delightful of prospects.

Signor Sanuto arrived later that afternoon as Jane and Vincent were sitting on the balcony overlooking the canal. Their host's gondola, with the traditional low profile, had been polished until it shone. Inlaid silver picked out the details in the wood.

The signore stuck his head out of the black coffinlike cabin on the low boat, hallooing them from the water in Italian. "I shall be up in a moment. It is good to see you."

The gondola turned into the water entrance to the palazzo, sliding from view to allow their host to step out of the water directly into his home. Not long after, he appeared in the parlour and limped towards the tall glass doors to the balcony. Jane rose to meet him as he walked outside, leaning heavily on his cane with his limp much exaggerated. "Signor Sanuto, are you well?"

"I was about to ask the same of you, my dears." He smiled at them, but the skin around his eyes seemed pinched.

"We are well, thank you." Jane urged him to sit and laughed. "I am afraid I must offer you your own refreshments. Your cook has been so good as to lay out this nice table for us."

"I would take a little wine and enjoy the afternoon with you. Letizia is wonderful. She has been with the family since my father's time." He shifted in his seat and winced. "I have been thinking of you all day and feeling dreadful to have abandoned you here."

"I have never felt so comfortable in my life." Jane did the honours as hostess and poured a glass of the excellent amarone that Letizia had set out. She must have known her master would want some, for she had laid out three glasses.

"That is exactly what I wished to hear." He accepted it and saluted her. "Now. Tell me what brings you to Venice. We do not see so many Englishmen since the Republic fell."

Jane hesitated, trying to decide what to say. The reason they had given her family—that of visiting Lord Byron—was only an excuse, required by her mother's want of discretion. They had therefore agreed to tell no one of the glamour in glass unless absolutely necessary. Vincent, in particular, after seeing how his *Sphère Obscurcie* had been turned into an instrument of war, was loath to share the knowledge that they had come up with a way not only to record glamour but also to move with it. And yet their host had been so kind, so very generous, that she felt they could trust him. She glanced to Vincent. He had a small furrow between his brows and gave the slightest of head shakes.

No. Well . . . she would discuss it with him in their chambers that evening, but for the moment she would stay with the same tale they had told her mother. "We were to visit Lord Byron, but . . . I am afraid he has left town unexpectedly."

He tilted his head to the side as if wondering about her hesitation. Jane saw with dismay that he had attributed it to something else. He thought she was hinting for an invitation to stay longer, and his next words proved her guess to be correct. "Ah—and you have nowhere to stay without him. Then you shall stay with me until he returns."

"Oh, we do not want to impose. That was not my meaning—" But, they did not, in fact, have anywhere to stay. "I only . . ."

"It is only that you have already been so generous." Vincent leaned forward with such a severe expression that Jane wished she could tell Signor Sanuto that he was not angry, only uncomfortable at accepting charity. "On that subject, I am afraid that I will need to ask for your help once more. You said you were with a bank. Might we make arrangements through that institution to reach my banker in London?"

"I am only too happy to arrange a line of credit so that you are not in distressed circumstances."

"I had intended it as a means to repay you."

The signore demurred. "It is unnecessary."

Vincent set his jaw. "I cannot let this pass. You must accept something."

Signor Sanuto appeared ready to match Vincent in stubbornness, but finally shook his head with a sigh. "If you are truly troubled, then make a donation to Santa Maria degli Angeli in my name. It is to my faith that you owe your freedom, not my pocketbook, so that is the best way of repaying any debt." He straightened his leg and winced with an audible gasp.

"Sir! Are you hurt?" Jane reached for the bell to call someone to aid him. He had suffered just as much the day prior as they had, without the benefit of rest. It was thoughtless of her to make him play the host also.

"I am well." He held up one hand to stay her. The other hand rubbed his knee. "Apologies. It is an old wound from when the Republic fell to Napoleon. Fatigue sometimes causes it to seize, and I am afraid I twisted it at the bank today. They are doing some construction in my office, and I slipped on plaster. Felt the fool. But . . . I am getting old, and I am not so steady on my feet with this stick."

Jane could not forget how he had lost the other walking stick, in defence of her and her imprudent thoughts of resisting. Privately, she decided that they would not only make a very substantial contribution to his church, they would buy him a new walking stick besides.

She rose, smiling. "Then, shall I entertain you? In the boat you had said you wished to see me work glamour. You have me now at your disposal." She had seen a piano in the palazzo and could easily play a little to amuse him.

His face lit up for a moment, and then he shook his head. "But you are tired. Yes, I would very much like to see your work, but my curiosity is not so insatiable as that."

"Then let us show you a *tableau vivant*." Vincent rose to stand beside Jane.

She turned so her back was to Signor Sanuto and whispered, "Are you well enough?"

"I have a headache, nothing more. See?" Vincent wove a

Sphère Obscurcie so that they vanished from view. He followed it with a similar weave to mask their sound. Neither weave was as quick as his usual, but still fast enough to cause Signor Sanuto to jump in his chair and gasp. She never tired of the response from people witnessing Vincent's technique for the first time. Most glamourists needed months of careful work to create a glamural detailed enough to mask anything, but with this simple weave, it was possible to vanish instantly. Small wonder that Wellington had taken advantage of it in the war against Napoleon.

But while these illusions usually cost Vincent no effort, his breath had sped with those simple folds.

Jane shook her head at her husband. "I was going to offer to play the pianoforte with the accompanying glamour."

"We could show him Cupid and Psyche. You like that one."

"When you are in best health, yes. Recall how long you had to work to master the wings. Vincent. Be reasonable, please."

"What about Zeus and Io?"

"I cannot be comfortable with the theme of that myth." Jane crossed her arms over her chest.

"Then what do you suggest?"

"I suggest that you do not always need to be the master glamourist. I suggest that you sit down. I *suggest* that you wait until you are well."

A muscle pulsed in the corner of his jaw. "I thought I had established my health this morning."

"Very well." Jane dropped her arms. "Then let us do Cupid and Psyche, since you are so confident in your health."

"Good."

One day his stubbornness would be the death of him. Biting her tongue, Jane pulled folds of glamour out of the ether and wrapped them about herself in a quickly rendered sketch of Psyche. She twisted a skein to create the unlucky oil lamp in the young Greek woman's hand. Carefully, she added a suggestion of flame above the lamp. In a fully realized glamour, this would be no more than the foundation to more detailed work atop it, but part of the charm of a *tableau vivant* was in the looseness of the glamour, in much the same way that a quick pencil sketch could sometimes capture a subject's essence more fully than the finest oil painting. It was about the gesture. She posed her Psyche in the moment of discovery, pulling back with wonder and the dawning horror of what she had done.

Vincent sat on the balcony and posed as Cupid waking. The winged god emerged around him in powerful swathes of glamour, but Jane could hear his breath already, while her own pulse was only a little accelerated. As soon as the wings appeared in the glamour, Jane reached for the knot that had tied the *Sphère Obscurcie* in place. "Ready?"

"Yes."

She untied the knot and they became visible in an instant.

Signor Sanuto sat forward in his chair, eyes widening in wonder. In spite of her fears for Vincent, it was a beautiful tableau. Psyche held the lamp toward her husband, chiton fluttering about her legs as the flame of the lamp flickered. Cupid stared up at her, with his wings captured in the act of unfolding. The glamour completely obscured Vincent's clothing and replaced them with the sculpted figure. Even in his weakened condition, the artistry of his work was apparent. It reminded Jane that while anyone could work glamour, it was the same as saying that anyone could paint. Pull a thread from the ether or hold a paintbrush, yes, but to achieve the emotion, the sense of betrayal and longing that her husband could wring from a few swiftly placed folds, required a rare talent.

And then Vincent lost his grip on the glamour.

The wings warped and trembled with colour before vanishing into the ether. The strands unravelled and the rest of the weave came undone. A trailing thread evaporated into an oiled rainbow before disappearing entirely.

Jane released hers as soon as she realized what was happening. With the discipline of long practise, she let the threads slide from her grip back into the ether. The illusion vanished smoothly.

She had never seen Vincent drop a glamour in public before. It had happened on occasion when they were working on a large installation and he pushed himself to the limits of what his body could withstand, but never in performance. His face was flushed with effort and clear humiliation, but at least he had not fainted.

Signor Sanuto clapped, seeming not to notice the peculiar end to the *tableau*. "Bravo! Brava! Wonderful."

"Thank you." Jane stepped forward to draw attention away from Vincent.

"I particularly liked the flourish at the end when Cupid whisked away into darkness. It quite took my breath away."

Jane inclined her head to hide her expression. That was a . . . gracious way of viewing Vincent's gaffe. She cleared her throat. "If there are any glamours around the palazzo that you need refreshed, I should be happy to take a look at them."

"Perhaps I might commission you. That would be something, eh? A glamural by such celebrated artists, favoured by the Prince Regent of Britain." He rubbed his knee again. "Now, unfortunately I have a few more items of business I must attend to before dinner. If you will excuse me?"

"Of course."

He rose and limped off the balcony. The fact that Vincent did not rise to see him out made Jane certain that his distress was greater than he would admit. She waited until Signor Sanuto had gone inside. "Vincent?"

"You were right."

"Oh . . . love. I am sorry." She knelt by him and felt his brow. It was not fevered, but his cheeks were still flushed.

"Everything is spinning." He clenched his hand into a fist and pounded his knee. "I hate this."

"I know." Jane ran a hand down his back, trying to soothe him. His pride was wounded quite as much as his head, and only time would heal either.

Four

A Suitable Circumstance

The next day Signor Sanuto seemed in sounder health, but his knee was clearly troubling him, so it was approaching noon before they were able to take their host's gondola from Murano to Venice, where Banco de Giro was situated. Vincent was nearly silent the entire ride, and held the rail of the small boat as if it were tossing on a much larger sea, though Jane found the crossing to be quite easy. When she inquired if he was well, he merely said that he was thinking. She let him "think" in silence, but resolved to limit their water excursions until his head was clearer.

At first blush, the main island of Venice was all that had been promised in travellers' tales, with its long graceful canals, arching bridges, and sun-dappled buildings. The walks along the canals were filled with people from every continent, reminding Jane that Venice had once been the centre of an empire. Moors, Jew, Arabs, and Armenians mingled among the Venetians and gave Jane happy memories of London. Only as they walked through the town did Jane begin to note the signs of poverty everywhere. Napoleon had sacked Venice, leaving the fabled city with none of its former wealth. The magnificent palazzos often had cracked façades or empty window boxes where there once would have been flowers.

Signor Sanuto led them across a footbridge and down a small lane that opened on to a piazza filled with the seemingly incessant pigeons. Banco de Giro faced on to this piazza and showed none of the signs of decay that were evident in other portions of Venice. A long gallery shaded the main entrance with a series of graceful arches. Inside the building, marble floors echoed with the hushed passage of men of business. Heavy wood tables glowed with polish and gave the dim impression of a library devoted exclusively to the study of money.

This impression was broken only by the workers who were drilling into the masonry wall above the steps. A length of canvas stretched down the stairs and puddled on the floor to catch the dust. They had installed wall sconces above the first half of the stairs and were at work on a third near the first landing.

Their host took in the mess and sighed. "Yesterday, I complained about the plaster dust on the floor when I slipped, and the canvas is apparently their solution. I shall be so happy when this is over."

"What is the work they are involved in?"

"Gaslights. It is the newest thing, and should make it easier to see, but the process of having them installed has been unpleasant."

Jane nodded in understanding. "The Prince Regent has them in Carlton House. They are astonishingly bright."

"That is the chief argument in their favour. Well, I am afraid my office is upstairs, so we shall have to go by the workmen." Signor Sanuto led the way across the bank, nodding to a clerk here and a businessman there. "I do wish it were not so unpleasing, though."

"I could mask it for you." Vincent nodded to a clear section of the wall. "Set up a repeating pattern to hide the workmen while they are about their business."

Signor Sanuto started up the stairs, with a little sigh. "Having seen your work, I wish I could take you up on that, but alas. We have a strong room here, and with the glamour laid upon it to prevent theft, our policies do not allow any other illusions in the building."

He gestured toward a seemingly blank wall, which stood behind the banking counter. Jane expanded her vision to the second sight and saw that the blank wall was actually constructed of glamour. She had heard of strong rooms before, but had never had the opportunity to see one. The glamour concealed the entrance to the bank's vault, as well as a variety of corporal alarms. A thief who did not know the correct entrance would sound one of those alarms. At first glance, the illusion appeared to be a tangled mess that would have appalled Vincent's sense of artistic integrity, but those interwoven strands concealed glamourous alarms. Attempting to undo the folds to see the corporal truth beneath them would be

Mary Robinette Kowal

surpassingly difficult. It was an ingenious combination of the tangible and the illusory.

Continuing, Signor Sanuto said, "At some point, I should ask you to take a closer look. We have had some trouble with—" His foot snared on the canvas and his bad leg went out from under him.

Jane reached for him, but Vincent was there first. He caught Signor Sanuto, staggered down a few stairs, but somehow managed to keep them both upright. The cane bounced and rattled down the remaining stairs, rolling across the floor until it stopped against a clerk's desk. For a moment the room was silent; then a flurry of men ran across to assist them.

It was clear that their host could not put weight on his bad leg. Still, he drew himself erect, leaning on Vincent, and unleashed a torrent of Venetian on the workers. It sounded, to Jane's ear, very like Italian, but was entirely its own tongue. She could gather nothing from the local language, except through his tone. Though Signor Sanuto's voice never raised, his face became quite red and a vein throbbed in his neck. He pointed at the canvas, and waved his hand as though to indicate the entire mess.

The most senior of the clerks came up the stairs and gave a low bow, speaking Venetian in deeply penitent tones.

Signor Sanuto clapped Vincent on the shoulder as he replied.

The clerk nodded, and then came to stand on his other side. Together with Vincent, they assisted him back down the stairs to the main floor. Jane hurried in front of them, trying to stay out of their way. Had he fallen, he could have been grievously injured. If Vincent had slipped as well . . . It did not bear thinking about. He *had* caught their host.

She bent and picked up Signor Sanuto's walking stick from where it had fallen, feeling of no other use.

Since Signor Sanuto seemed incapable of managing stairs, the clerk escorted them to a nicely appointed room on the main floor for patrons who wished to examine the contents of their vault in privacy. Signor Sanuto was lowered into a chair at the large conference table. He winced as he stretched his leg out in front of him.

He changed back to Italian for their benefit, and gave them a rueful smile. "I believe the balance between us has been restored. I would have taken a nasty fall were it not for you." He grimaced and rubbed his leg. "Please, have a seat and we shall take care of our business."

Jane started. "But you are injured. Surely you must want for a doctor—"

"Who will tell me that my knee is ruptured, as it has been for over a decade. This has aggravated it, but done no new damage. Please believe me. I have had time to become used to the vagaries of the injury. I used to be quite the good dancer."

The door to the room opened and they were joined by the senior clerk, who bore a lap desk and an envelope bulging with papers. Signor Sanuto thanked him in Venetian and proceeded to organize the papers, in spite of Jane and Vincent's protests. "I have work to do today, so I would need to set up shop in here regardless, because I will not be able to manage the stairs. Tending to your accounts"—he held up a hand to stop Vincent who had drawn breath to speak—"Truly. I appreciate your concern, but will feel better to have some work that I can accomplish. The rest of my tasks today will not be so easy. So . . . here."

Signor Sanuto's efficacy was impressive. It took only a few moments for him to have Vincent sign the agreements. Though Jane had no direct experience with banking, she could nevertheless see that Signor Sanuto had done everything in his power to expedite the process. He had established a line of credit at Banco de Giro for use with local merchants, as well as arranging for them to be given a supply of coins for their immediate needs.

Vincent took fifty pounds out of the purse they had been given and offered Signor Sanuto the coins. "You had said that a donation to your church was welcome."

Signor Sanuto smiled and looked chagrined at the same time. "Yes, but truly, there is no need."

Jane put her hand on the table to offer her support to Vincent. "Please. With thanks for our deliverance."

"How can I refuse a lady? The Abbess will be most grateful."

"And you must also allow us to repay you."

He hesitated and straightened his papers, with a frown. "A thousand pounds is less than it costs to clothe my wife and daughters, but for you? And I mean no offense by this: For you it is not an insignificant sum, am I correct? Prince Regent or no."

"It is a matter of honour."

Signor Sanuto pressed his hands against his eyes and sighed. He lifted his face a moment later with some apparent pain. "And you will not allow me to claim that you saved my life today?"

"Perhaps," Jane said, "but you saved two."

Their host smiled. "You British and your debts of honour." Sighing, he pulled a paper toward him and wrote on it for some moments. "This is a promissory note against funds you hold in England. If you are quite certain, deposit this with the clerk as you depart, or wait until you are ready to leave Venice, or after you are back in England. Or not at all, which would be my preference." He did not flaunt his wealth again, but the implication remained clear that he could afford the ransom and they could not.

Vincent took the paper and added his broad, masculine signature to the bottom. "Thank you."

Jane offered Signor Sanuto her hand in appreciation. "Can we not convince you to go home and rest?"

He shook his head and waved at the papers in the envelope. "I have all of this to attend to. I shall see you tonight. Dinner, perhaps? Or the opera . . . I shall have to see what is playing."

"I think you and Vincent will get on well, because you have a familiar stubbornness."

Laughing, Signor Sanuto bowed from his seat. They took their farewells and stepped out to the hall, leaving him bent over the table with his stack of papers.

Vincent turned the paper over in his hand and tilted his head toward Jane. "Well, Muse? It is your money, too."

"Of course, we must."

Nodding, he strode across the room to the nearest clerk and handed him the paper. "Will you see that this is deposited?"

"With all due speed, sir." The clerk looked the paper over and added his stamp to it.

Vincent heaved a sigh as he stepped away from the desk.

"Relieved to no longer be dependent?"

"Very much so." He straightened and rolled his shoulders. "And now, I propose that we see if Byron has made arrangements for us so that we no longer need to trouble our host."

The apartments that Lord Byron had taken were not far from Banco de Giro. Though they no longer had the directions, Vincent recalled that they lay just west of the Piazza, over the shop of a draper. Fortunately, Lord Byron was a notorious enough figure in Venice that they had little trouble in discovering precisely where the "English poet" lived.

The building had once been magnificent, but, like so much of Venice, now displayed the fallen splendour that had overtaken the islands when Napoleon had ravaged them. The owner had carved it into separate suites and rented those out to people like Lord Byron. It was difficult to look at the exterior and not compare it to the grand palazzo of Signor Sanuto.

Vincent frowned at the refuse in the street. "One wonders what led him to apartments such as these."

"Perhaps it is grander on the interior?"

"Or his finances are in worse condition than I thought."

"Are his estates troubled, then? I had thought it was the scandal with Caroline Lamb that caused him to leave England."

"Mm . . . Byron thrives on scandal, I think." Vincent knocked upon the door. "But funds? Even when we were in school together, Byron was always out of pocket."

"Oh." Jane had no time to give further response before the door opened.

A young woman with large dark eyes and a graceful figure stood framed in the door. Her hair hung loose around her shoulders and her gown was . . . insufficient. She did not offer them a welcome, but merely raised one brow in question.

Vincent offered her a short bow and spoke in Italian, "Good afternoon, madam. Is this the residence of Lord Byron?"

She snorted. "Yes. But the bastard is not home."

Jane's eyes widened at the vulgarity of the woman's language. Surely the phrase carried the same meaning in Italian as in English.

Clearing his throat, Vincent nodded, as though it were a discussion of the weather. "I see . . . Did he leave any instructions regarding Sir David and Lady Vincent?"

"Instructions? What do you take me for?" She spat upon the walk. "I am not his housekeeper. I know nothing of you, or your wife, or where that bastard has gone. Try Mira to see if he's with his slattern there."

Jane took Vincent's arm, quite finished with this encounter. "Thank you for your time."

The woman snorted again and stepped back into the house, shutting the door behind her.

"Well." Vincent rubbed the back of his neck. "That is unfortunate."

"Indeed. I wonder at his invitation, if that is the sort of household he keeps. I feel that I should be doubly grateful to Signor Sanuto now."

They turned their steps back toward the main piazza with Vincent in a brown study. He shook his head as if clearing it of thoughts. "Shall we interview glassmakers?"

"That is why we came to Murano." Jane took his arm.

"But we should also purchase some clothes. His wife's dresses are lovely, but—"

"But one more form of debt." Vincent raised her hand and kissed it. "You are monstrously clever for finding a way to convince me to shop."

"An attack by pirates might have been a bit extreme, but I do what I can to make sure you are respectable."

"A task that I do not envy." They left Lord Byron's apartments behind and set out to explore Murano.

The gondola ride from Venice to Murano reminded Jane again of the ethereal wonder of the island city. Seen from a distance, it was easy to imagine it in its era of glory. The buildings came right to the edge of the water, so it seemed as though Atlantis had reemerged from the deep. Every kind of stone imaginable graced the structures in an exuberance of masonry. Glamour enhanced the effect by creating seascapes that extended up the sides.

The only unhappy moment was when a fast-moving pleasure boat created swells that their gondola bounced over. It pitched and heaved about as if they were at sea.

Vincent sagged against Jane, closing his eyes. He pressed his lips tightly together and swallowed convulsively. A light sweat stood on his brow.

"What may I do?" She felt his brow for fever. Vincent was not prone to seasickness under normal circumstances, but he had a decidedly green cast.

His voice was hoarse as he replied. "Forgive me. It has

been some time since I have been badly concussed. The motion of the ship—"

He broke off and leaned out the gondola's small window, demonstrating the effects with more vehemence than comfort.

Jane passed him her handkerchief, and did her best to not fuss over him. He would be mortified enough as it was, without feeling as if he were a burden. "I would rather that you were unfamiliar with the symptoms."

"As would I." He took the handkerchief and wiped his mouth.

She ventured, "We can wait until you are well to visit the glassmakers."

He shook his head, though his eyes remained closed. "Please do not worry. Once we are on land, I will be well."

"You will not be in any fit condition to work glamour."

"As we discovered yesterday." He pinched the bridge of his nose and breathed slowly. "But we will not be working glamour today. I would rather spend my recovery making progress in those areas that I can."

"You are only seeking a way out of shopping for clothes."

He gave a hint of a smile with the small compression of his lips. "You know me too well."

Jane sighed. He was right in that. She knew him too well to suppose that she could convince him to spend the afternoon resting. Still, she would keep watch on his health. She could not entirely trust his judgement in the matter.

Indeed, when they arrived at the dock in Murano, Vincent preceded her out of the boat and turned to offer his hand, as though his complexion did not have an unnatural pallor.

She accepted his aid and stepped up onto the dock beside him. "Are you certain that you do not wish to return to Signor Sanuto's home?"

"Quite. I shall feel better for walking." True to his word, his countenance improved as they strolled along the canal to the glassmaker's district.

Jane considered before she asked the question she most wanted to know. Vincent was so often private about the life he had led before he disavowed his family that she sometimes hesitated to ask about his youth, particularly after meeting his father. She felt the urge to protect him from the memories he had walled away, and yet she wanted to know everything about his life, even the parts that were sometimes difficult to hear.

They stepped onto one of the bridges arching over the canal. "Do I dare ask how often you have been in this condition?"

Vincent tucked his chin into his collar in thought. "Three? Perhaps four times, but one was so mild it barely counts. And let me assure you, Muse, that this is not severe."

"You now require me to ask what severe is and how you know?"

"Severe means that I cannot stand without toppling and am confined to bed for a week. It means seeing everything in double and forgetting great swathes of time. But I was also only twelve, so one must allow for that."

"Good heavens. Twelve? And so severely hurt? Were you thrown from a horse or did you run into a tree with mad exuberance?" She posed that question, preferring it to the more likely scenario.

"My father hit me." His tone was easy. His pace did not falter. The sun continued to shine as they crossed the bridge. "He caught me working glamour. Again. I have been told that what actually caused the concussion was that I hit my head on the hearth's andiron when I fell. I do not remember. Certainly his usual blows were not enough to have caused it."

"Oh."

"He was contrite while I was confined. I do remember that, though the rest is patchwork." He gave a shallow laugh. "I suppose it was unusual enough to remain fixed in memory."

This revelation was why Jane so seldom asked about his life as The Honourable Vincent Hamilton, third son of the Earl of Verbury. She hated the silence that followed as he burrowed into old wounds and explored the pain over again. She did not like to be the cause of reminding him how he had lived before he had remade himself as David Vincent.

Vincent straightened his head as they reached the foot of the bridge. Surveying the street, he said, "I believe we turn left here for the Nenci Glass Factory. My notes are, sadly, aboard a pirate ship."

"That is what I recall as well." She let him change the subject and accompanied him down the side of the canal. The houses were pressed one against the next without space for gardens, but the island felt alive even so. Bird-cages frequently hung out of windows, filling the air with the twitter of canaries or the cooing of doves. Window boxes dripped a profusion of blossoms in purples and golds.

But the true life was in the glass. Animals, chalices, and candlesticks gleamed in the shop windows, the sunlight seemingly on the verge of bringing them to life. A little girl stood pressed with her nose against a shop window, looking at a glass terrier within. She put Jane in mind of Melody as a child. Shaking her head, Jane pulled her gaze away and looked to the next shop.

Strands of beads in chalcedony, aventurine, and gold-flecked glass hung like unformed glamour in the window. One shop seemed to have nothing but ranks of mirrors. In the midst of this sparkling profusion, the haberdasher stood out.

The soft wools and linens in the window welcomed her attention. A copper basin displayed a selection of fine canes. Jane paused. "Vincent . . . ?"

He looked around and sighed. "Oh. Might we not visit the glassmakers first?"

"I was thinking of the canes, honestly. As a gift for Signor Sanuto."

At that, he brightened. "That is an excellent suggestion." He turned his path toward the door.

"But as long as we are here . . ."

"I continually forget that you are wicked." His show of affliction was made less convincing by the twinkling of his eye.

Within the store, they were greeted by a smart man of middle years with a tailor's apron over his coat. His gaze took in Vincent's jacket and Jane could imagine the tally he was making. *Three years out of date, fine work when new. Recently mended. Buckskin trousers, much worn. Excellent Hessian boots. A gentleman of means, but not in the fashionable set.* Aloud he only said, "How may I be of service?"

"I need to order some clothes." Vincent scowled at the nearest bolt of cloth.

Though he had been raised as a young man of fashion, Vincent so hated what he saw as pretence that Jane took pity upon him and spoke to the tailor. "We were recently robbed while travelling, and my husband needs to replace his wardrobe. If we could arrange for three fine cambric shirts without frills, a blue coat appropriate for day wear, and one for evening. He will also require a new pair of buckskin trousers and breeches for evening."

The tailor produced a small tablet and the stub of a pencil from his apron. He jotted notes, nodding.

Vincent had wandered deeper into the shop and was rolling a fold of fabric between his fingers as though it were glamour. "Also a greatcoat. Black, preferred." He held up a bolt of a soft sorrel. "And I should like a waistcoat of this."

"Very good. And the other inexpressibles? Should the gentleman require those?"

Vincent compressed his lips. "I am wearing all the clothes I possess, so, yes."

"That is unfortunate. Should you require gloves, then, as well?"

"No, thank you." Though it was possible to work glamour with gloves, it was difficult to control the fine details, so most professional glamourists eschewed gloves. This was something that Jane had yet to accustom herself to.

The tailor seemed perturbed at this, so Jane said, "We are glamourists."

"Ah." He nodded, discomposure clearing with the explanation. "Then may I suggest a light linen coat, such as one might wear on a summer excursion? It would be more comfortable with the exertion of glamour."

"Excellent suggestion." Vincent moved to the next bolt of fabric. "Where is your cloth for cravats?"

"Here, sir." The tailor lead Vincent to a selection of fine muslin, linen, and silk.

Having now committed himself, Jane's husband proceeded to examine the fabric with all the attention to detail that he brought to his work. He considered the weight of the fabric, the way the textures worked together, and their utility. Jane settled into a chair to one side to enjoy the spectacle of her husband shopping for clothes.

At times, the varnish of the Right Honourable Vincent Hamilton smoothed the edges of her husband's taciturn nature as his early training reasserted itself. Unlike the times when he had been forced to assume the role of a young gentleman of means, here his natural love of art seemed to express itself in appreciation for the art of tailoring. As he relaxed in discussion with the tailor, his headache seemed quite forgotten. One might almost think he was enjoying himself, though not enough for her to try him with shopping for her own wardrobe.

When he had done, the tailor asked him to remove his coat for the purpose of taking his measurements. Jane appreciated this quite as much as the rest of the day. The tailor slid his hands over Vincent's back to smooth the fabric. Jane saw the moment of hesitation when he brushed the scars there. The tailor was a consummate professional, though, and only that momentary pause and the slight widening of his eyes told of his surprise. She knew all too well how apparent the bumps and welts of flogging must be, even through fabric.

Even so, her husband was a tall man with the broad chest of a professional glamourist. With his arms spread wide for the tailor to take his measure, the power of his figure was all the more apparent. If she thought she could dissuade him from visiting the glassmakers this afternoon, Jane would have suggested they return to the palazzo straight away.

That he had not forgotten their purpose was apparent when he shrugged his coat back on. "Thank you, sir. My wife and I have some other errands, but I can stop by this evening for the first of the shirts."

"No need, Sir David. I will have my shop boy run it to you if you give me your direction."

"Thank you." Vincent wrote down the details for Signor Sanuto's house for him.

As he was occupied with writing, Jane stood and addressed the tailor. "I was wondering if you happened to have a sword cane in the shop."

"Nothing suitable for your husband's height, I am afraid." He led the way to the display of canes. "A nice ebony, perhaps?"

"This is for a friend of ours. About your height, I think."

"Ah. In that case . . ." He pulled out a cane that bore a striking resemblance to the one that Signor Sanuto had lost. Twisting the handle, he drew the sword that was held within. "Would this suffice?"

"That is the very thing." Indeed, Signor Sanuto may have acquired his at this shop.

"Shall I send it with the other items?" The tailor took a cloth from his pocket and wiped the steel clean of smudges before returning it to the shaft of the cane.

Vincent said, "Should we take it with us, Muse?"

"I think so."

Nodding, the tailor wrapped it in brown paper, tied with a bit of twine. "Is there anything else?"

Jane cleared her throat and looked to the window so that her bonnet would prevent her from seeing the tailor's judgement. "Yes. It is rather irregular, but I shall also require a pair of buckskin trousers."

"Ah—planning ahead for Carnevale."

Jane turned her head with astonishment. Even Vincent made a sound of surprise. She had been prepared to tell a story about a fancy dress party, when the truth was that she would not be able to wear muslin so close to a glassmaker's furnace. To have the notion of a woman in trousers accepted so easily was beyond her expectations.

The tailor pulled a piece of paper from his tablet and scribbled a name upon it. "The usual course is to have your measurements taken at the *modista* of your choice and then I make them to fit. Signora Bartalotti does lovely work, and we have cooperated before."

Jane dropped a curtsy in thanks. This would also solve the problem of how to replenish her own wardrobe without taking further advantage of Signor Sanuto's kindness.

With the formalities completed, the Vincents returned to the street, cane and a small package of stockings and other inexpressibles in hand.

Sighing, Vincent shook his head. "You understand that I am committed now to two more visits."

"It did not seem such a hardship as you made it out."

"The man knows his craft, so that makes it easier."

"Hm." Jane arched her eyebrow at his evasion. "Was there any trouble with our letter of credit?"

"None at all." He rubbed his hair. "It was deuced uncomfortable to be without resources."

"Do you think we will have any trouble without our letters of introduction?"

"I hope not." They turned off the main street and went in search of a glassmaker.

Five

Interview with a Glassmaker

Without their notes, which had been lost with the ship, it took the Vincents some time to find one of the glass factories. Working from memory and directions from a street performer, they eventually made their way to a narrow street, little more than an alley. It led towards a little courtyard formed where two of the buildings were set back from the street. A pair of stable doors led out of the building to their left. The small sign over the doors said PIETRO NENCI: VETRI D'ARTE ALL'INSEGNA DI S. GIOVANNI— PIETRO NENCI: ART GLASS UNDER THE BANNER OF SAINT GIOVANNI.

Vincent tried the door, which was locked. He knocked on it. Some moments later it opened, and a slender young man with a heavy leather apron stepped out. Jane caught a glimpse of the glowing yellow maw of a glass furnace through the door before the man pulled it shut behind him. He addressed them in Italian, clearly recognising that they were not local.

Vincent replied in the same language, "Could Signor Nenci spare a moment? We have a commission we wish to discuss with him."

The young man seemed entirely indifferent. "Who is calling?"

"My name is Sir David Vincent." He hesitated as though considering adding more of his credentials, but checked himself. Though they had originally carried letters of introduction from His Royal Highness the Prince of Wales, Vincent had a natural modesty that would prevent him from claiming the acquaintance without proof.

Shrugging, the young man left them and slipped through the door again, opening it only wide enough to enter himself. He left them standing in the street.

Nearly a quarter hour passed before a stout man in the rough linen of a labourer opened the door and stepped out into the street. He, too, pulled the door shut behind him. "Yes?"

"I am Sir David Vincent. This is my wife, Lady Vincent." He paused, waiting for the man to introduce himself as well, but the glassmaker simply scratched the stubble on his chin. "We want to commission you for a project that is somewhat unusual in nature."

"Leave a drawing with my assistant, and we'll get back to you about price."

"The unusual aspect requires us to be present while it is being made."

Nenci squinted at them and scratched his chin again. "Happy to make any design you want, but you can't watch."

"It is crucial that we—"

Nenci barked in laughter. "Bold, aren't you. No." He turned to go.

"Pardon?"

Barely turning his head, he replied, "I don't take kindly to spies trying to steal my trade secrets."

Vincent inhaled sharply. "You have mistaken our intent."

"Have I? You are English. We've already lost enough trade to you and those cursed hacks in Bohemia who think they can drop in and 'observe' without us understanding what they're after."

"We are glamourists. We are here to conduct an experiment that—"

Nenci stopped and wheeled on the spot. "You think a story like that will fool me?"

Jane stepped forward to give Vincent a moment to govern himself. "I assure you that it is true. If you would like, I can exhibit my abilities." She reached for the ether and sketched a rose in the air.

The glassmaker snorted. "Is that supposed to convince me? Any young lady can do as much. My own daughter covers half the house with her glamours."

Vincent seemed to expand as he drew an angry breath. His hand moved as he reached for the ether, but no glamour followed. He let the breath out as if the glassmaker had punched him. Jane laid a hand on Vincent's arm to soothe him. Even if he were in best health, no exhibition could possibly sway this man.

Face pale, Vincent took a step back, spun on his heel and walked away.

Jane turned to follow him, calling back to the glassmaker. "Thank you, sir. It seems clear that our funds are best spent elsewhere."

"Good luck with that. There are only three other glass-makers in Murano who work in blown glass. They'll all give you the same answer."

Jane hesitated in astonishment. "Only three others? But the guidebook—"

"Was written before the Fall. Do you know why there are only four of us? Because of lying thieves like you." He wheeled around and stomped back into his shop. The door shut, and this time there came the unmistakable sound of a lock being engaged.

Jane hurried after Vincent. The tails of his coat flapped be-hind him as he strode down the narrow street. "Vincent, wait."

He checked his stride and stood in the middle of the street, head down. As soon as she gained his side, he began walking again. Spots of red burned high in his cheeks.

"What happened? When you—"

"When I could not catch hold of the glamour? Just that." Vincent's mouth twisted.

"But you could see it?"

"Yes. Yes, I could see it. I could touch it. I failed to have the requisite control to manage it."

Jane sighed with some relief. If he could still see and touch it, then the blow had done no permanent damage. "It will just be a matter of time."

"It is worse than it was."

"Only because you are more tired, I think. The boat ride across . . . You must give yourself time."

Scowling, he turned on to the main street. A flurry of nuns in black and white passed them. Vincent stepped to the side to allow them to pass, and then continued on.

Jane took his hand. "Where are you going?"

Watching the canal, he pulled free of her grasp to rub the back of his neck. "To try another shop."

"Shall we return to Ca' Sanuto, instead? It will not hurt us to wait another day or so."

"And give Nenci time to talk to the other glassmakers? Even if I am useless—"

"Stop. Was I useless when I was"—Jane forced herself past the words and the memories attached to them—"when I was with child and unable to do glamour, was I useless? No. As you so often reminded me."

Vincent found her hand and squeezed it. "I am sorry."

Shaking her head, Jane returned the pressure of his fingers. Some activity would do him good. Part of what had driven Jane mad when she was increasing was the forced inactivity. Vincent was prone to brood as it was, and so defined himself as a glamourist that an afternoon spent at home would likely make him more miserable than not. "No need for apology. Still, you are correct that we should not give Signor Nenci an opportunity to prejudice the other glassmakers against us."

Vincent agreed, and they continued on by the canal. Yet each glassmaker they visited gave variations on the same refusal to allow them to watch the glass being made. Their manner was not so blunt as Signor Nenci, but the denial was just as steadfast.

Footsore, Jane and Vincent made their way through the streets to Signor Sanuto's, rather than chancing Vincent's equilibrium in a gondola.

"Muse, I am at a loss."

"We could . . . we could return to Binché." It was a location with painful memories for both of them, but nothing else there was harmful. "We had success at the La Pierres' glass factory. And the Chastains would be happy to see us."

He nodded, walking on in silence past Venetians who went about their shopping, carrying baskets of fish or produce. The occasional tourist blocked the walk, gawking at a display of glass. Vincent sighed, and then again, with resignation. "We had discussed that, but the quality of the crystal is better here."

"I do not think it will be good enough to get a glass that works without full sunlight."

"But it might." Vincent scrubbed his hand through his hair. "That is the rub of it. Not knowing. Wanting to try the better glass."

"What of Bohemia? It is where the fashionable glass is coming from these days."

"In some ways that worries me more. It seems more likely that the technique would slip out there. I want to keep this close, until we have a better understanding of how it works, what it can be used for . . ." He rubbed the base of his neck again, grimacing. "Perhaps we should return to the house."

It was not like Vincent to give up, but after the trouble they had experienced getting here, she felt that a certain sense of dismay was entirely appropriate.

* * *

The walk through the streets of Murano, with its graceful courtyards and the grand palazzos overlooking the canals, should have delighted Jane, but her thoughts could not keep away from the flat refusal of any of the glassmakers to listen to their proposal. Then, too, there was the unlooked-for expense of the pirate attack. Though she would have spent any amount to keep Vincent safe, the fact was that removing themselves to Bohemia, in the hope that the glassmakers there would be more receptive, was more than they could afford at present. As it was, when they finished here, they would have to return to England and begin accepting commissions again at once. They had possessed the necessary funds for this trip, but the trouble with travelling so far from home was that one needed to bring along all of the money one might require. Planning for an extended stay in Murano, as they had been, had called for the proverbial "deep pockets." Were it not for the kindness of Signor Sanuto, they would have been in sore straits indeed.

At times, Jane missed the relative simplicity of her life as a gentleman's daughter, when she had to worry about nothing more than what gown she was going to wear to dinner. But to give up her art would be impossible; she loved the challenge of exploring their craft. But in this moment, faced with a difficult problem, a part of Jane very much wished that she were still a little girl who could go to her papa to fix everything. The rest of her mind was turned toward finding a solution to their problem.

Vincent, too, seemed lost in preoccupied thought as they

strolled back through the streets to Ca' Sanuto. She suspected that the crease between his brows was only partially from their failure to engage a glassmaker. It must drive him mad to have so much difficulty with glamour due to his current state.

When they arrived back at the palazzo, they found a message asking them to join their host on the balcony for an apéritif. Signor Sanuto sat on a chaise lounge that had been carried outside for his use. A pillow lay under his injured knee, and a table with a silver bell sat within easy reach.

At their approach, he turned his head. "My dears! I am glad you are home."

"Thank you. We were beginning to feel that, aside from our present company, no one was happy to see an Englishman here. Speaking of presents . . ." Jane slipped the cane out from under Vincent's arm. "We have a small token for you."

She was rewarded by seeing their host's face soften as he recognised the shape. "You did not . . ." He stripped the paper away and revealed the ebony length. A twist of the handle revealed the sword within. "You did."

A suspicious moisture brightened his eyes. Signor Sanuto looked at the canal and cleared his throat. "Lady Vincent . . . Sir David—though I regret the circumstances, I am most pleased to have met you." He slid the sword back into the sheath and tried the length of the cane. "Just right."

"It was Jane's idea."

"You have married a remarkable woman."

"Believe me, I am well aware of this." Vincent looked at Jane, not their host, as he replied, and his expression was filled with a tender regard that stopped her breath.

Signor Sanuto pulled a handkerchief from his pocket and

passed it under his eyes quickly, before making a show of shining the wood. "I well believe that. Now"—he looked up, smiling—"I hope that I may count on the pleasure of your company until your friend returns. Then I will relinquish you to his prior claim."

Jane and Vincent shared a look of the sort which comes with knowing perfectly the mind of "the partner of her life." A rise of the eyebrow, imperceptible to an outsider, replied to by the smallest inclination of the head, comprised the whole of their visible conversation; and yet, within that, they discussed the sincerity of Signor Sanuto's invitation, the fact that he was a man whose company they enjoyed, and the reality that neither of them had a desire to remove themselves to a hotel in service to notions of propriety that had no bearing here. In truth, Jane rather thought she would prefer to remain here even after Lord Byron's return.

Vincent bowed to Signor Sanuto. "We are at your service. Thank you."

"Excellent. I am so very glad." He gestured to the chairs that had been drawn up on the balcony. "Join me, please."

"How is your leg?" Jane took the nearest seat, while Vincent moved to the parapet and looked out over the canal.

"Provoking, but otherwise improved from this morning. I shall need to be gentle with it for a day or so, and then it will be quite all right." He shook his head. "I am only happy that my wife is away, or I should not be allowed to leave the house for days. Weeks, perhaps."

"My mother also worries incessantly."

"She is usually right, though. And I will confess, it is

sometimes pleasant to have my daughters fuss over me." He took a sip of wine. "Have you any children?"

"No." Jane turned away and reached for the bottle on the table. "More wine, sir?"

Vincent turned from the view. "Has your family had the palazzo long?"

Signor Sanuto raised his eyebrows, but in no other way showed surprise at their barefaced attempts to change the conversation. Jane bit the inside of her lip. It had been a harmless question, or at least not a question intended to harm. It had been nearly two years since her miscarriage, and she should be beyond the point where the want of children would cause her discomfort, yet she was grateful to Vincent for stepping into the conversation.

Vincent led Signor Sanuto on a discussion of the palazzo and the history of the family, including several doges over the years. Pouring wine for Vincent and herself, Jane rejoined the conversation, and they spent a happy quarter hour discussing the various points of historical interest in the structure. Vincent sat in a chair by Jane and sipped his wine as they chatted. The conversation drifted, as it often does, to broader points of history, and then to more particular points. They learned about the ferro on gondolas, which gave them their distinctive prow, and that the English word "ghetto" derived from the Jewish Quarter in Venice, which was called the "ghèto."

Signor Sanuto paused mid-story and raised a finger to his lips. He nodded at Vincent. Jane's husband sat in his chair, but his head had sagged forward and he had clearly fallen asleep. Most of the wine remained in his glass, which he held loosely in one hand, so she thought that it was the lingering effects of the blow to his head more than anything else.

Jane whispered, "Forgive him. He has had a trying day."

Signor Sanuto nodded his head. He beckoned her closer. Moving as silently as she could, Jane rose and came to perch on the edge of his chaise lounge.

In a low voice, their host said, "What happened to distress him, if I might inquire?"

And here they came again to their secret. Jane did not feel quite right about dissembling, but with Vincent asleep, she also had no opportunity to ascertain his feelings on sharing the nature of their visit. She chose to offer the same initial explanation they had given to the glassmakers. "We had hoped to commission a glassmaker, but no one wanted to work with us."

"Who did you try?"

"All the glassblowers. We started with Signor Nenci."

Signor Sanuto rolled his eyes. "Oh, *him*. He is notorious for being suspicious even among glassmakers. I am not surprised you made no progress there."

"They all seemed to think we were English spies."

He winced. "It has been hard for them. Venice used to be funded almost entirely by our glass industry, but now . . . it is a poor remnant of its former glory, and much of that can be laid directly at the feet of apprentices who came to learn and then left with the craft. The glassmakers have earned their right to be suspicious. Perhaps . . . It occurs to me that I might broker an agreement for you. Sometimes such things are easier done if handled by a local."

"You have already done so much."

He shrugged. "You were badly treated when you arrived, and I want you to return home with many happy stories of Venice. It is no trouble. I am accustomed to bargaining."

"I have the direct benefit of that." Jane turned to regard Vincent, whose face was slack and exhausted. "Thank you. That would be most obliging."

"It is no trouble."

"There is one more thing." Jane hesitated. This was no more than they were telling the glassmakers. If Signor Sanuto were to help them, he would need to know this much. "We are curious about the interaction of glamour and glass. Because of this, we need to be involved in the process of making the commission. Do you think you can arrange this? It seemed to be the point that most concerned them."

Signor Sanuto rubbed his mouth, considering. "And you must be present."

"Indeed."

"They are notoriously private."

"So we have experienced."

"There is a newer glassmaker, Signor Querini, a client of our bank. He is not as established, but perhaps more willing to take a chance because of it. Shall I speak to him?"

"That sounds ideal."

"Very well. Are there any details that may help sway him? If I can convince him that there may be additional profit—"

Jane shook her head. "We are exploring this for our own education. We would, in fact, prefer that no one be aware of our work."

"I see . . . Well. Consider it done." Signor Sanuto nodded toward Vincent. "I wish I could help him in other matters."

* * *

There was a delay of some days while Signor Sanuto arranged for a meeting with Signor Querini, the glassmaker he recommended. This allowed Jane time to visit the *modista* and acquire a small wardrobe of her own.

Vincent's head also had the opportunity to clear, so that by the time of their appointment with the glassmaker, he pronounced himself quite fit. Jane withheld judgement, noting that he rubbed the base of his neck more than his usual wont. Still, it was the only outward symptom of discomfort, and he was steadfast in his assertion of health. Indeed, in the gondola ride from the palazzo, he gave no hint of illness.

Signor Sanuto had them disembark at Calle Angelo dal Mistro and climb the short wooden flight of stairs from the canal to street level. He waved Vincent's help away and hauled himself up using his cane and the railing embedded into the side of the canal. At the top, he consulted a piece of paper with the glassmaker's direction written upon it. "This way, I believe."

They walked to the next street, when he stopped and shook his head. "My apologies. It is the opposite direction."

Jane gave him a smile. "The number of times I have been lost in Murano, it makes me feel better to know that a native also gets turned round."

He flushed a bit, but nodded. "This is not a part of the island I often visit. After a certain point, one tends to make the same familiar rounds and allows the knowledge of the other areas to fade. Ah, here is the street."

From there he led them down several twists and turns, until Jane was certain that they would walk back into the canal, but he at last brought them to a small unmarked door in the side of a low stucco building. Signor Sanuto knocked on the door with the head of his walking stick.

After only a moment, the door opened and an enormously fat man poked his head out. His face lit up. "Signor Sanuto! Welcome, welcome . . . and these are your friends? Come in. Please come in. Mind the step. Mind your dress. So much soot—I should have warned you. We try, but the furnaces, you see. So much soot."

The furnaces had been apparent from the moment they stepped through the door. Two large brick ovens dominated the far side of the glass factory and made their presence known through the heat they pushed across the room. Each had a glowing oven in the side filled with molten glass. The furnaces were operated by a number of men, who went about their work with dedicated focus.

"Please, have a seat. Here." He had a few chairs drawn up to a roughly constructed desk covered with samples of glass and a few scattered work orders. "Now, what can I do for you? Signor Sanuto has been so kind as to suggest that I might be suitable for your commission, but there were some aspects that were not quite clear. He says that you wish to be present?"

Vincent nodded. "We are experimenting with the effects of glamour on glass. The object itself is simple, only a sphere, but we need to be present while the glass is being worked."

Querini frowned and tugged on his little finger. "We? Signor Sanuto only said anything about 'a glamourist.' That's one. 'We' is two."

"My wife and I."

"A lady can't go anywhere near a furnace. There's Signora Caspari, but she only makes beads, and that's just a small furnace."

"We have worked with a glassmaker in the Netherlands. When we did . . ." Jane shifted in her seat, suddenly embarrassed to admit this indiscretion in front of Signor Sanuto. "When we did, I wore buckskin trousers, and plan to do so again."

"Worked with another glassmaker!" He broke off, plump cheeks mottled red, and turned to Signor Sanuto with a torrent of Venetian.

Wincing, their host held up his hands in a placating gesture and uttered words that were clearly intended to be soothing. Jane bit the inside of her cheek. She had quite forgotten the suspicious nature of the other glassmakers, and had intended only to reassure the man that she was aware of the dangers. Vexed with herself, she lowered her head and let her bonnet block out the sight of the conversation, which was quickly becoming an argument.

Vincent took her hand. He leaned over and murmured. "You will worry a hole in your new gloves."

She smiled, but it did not soothe her much. She held his hand, occasionally catching the sound of her name or Vincent's in the midst of the flowing Venetian. Then the conversation shifted, and she suddenly recognised numbers.

They were close enough to Italian for her to identify them, but what had caught her ear was the rhythm. Signor Sanuto had begun haggling.

Jane lifted her head. Querini was standing in front of his

bench with his hands set upon his wide hips. By the look of concentration on his face, he was not going to give ground easily. Neither, it was apparent, was Signor Sanuto.

Then the same number repeated. One hundred. Both men said it; then said it again, and then nodded.

Signor Sanuto let out his breath in a huff and turned to the Vincents, rubbing his hands as though his next task was to get them to agree to the same bargain. "Signor Querini has agreed to work with you for a weekly rate, rather than per item. He is requesting one hundred pounds a week in exchange for the education that you will be getting, in addition to the cost of the glass itself."

Vincent frowned. It was far more than they had paid M. La Pierre back in the Netherlands, but they had come to Murano because of the quality of glassmaking. Still, it was more than either of them had expected.

Signor Sanuto's mouth twisted as though he had tasted something sour. "He would also prefer for you to work at night, after their regular work is done, so that there is . . . there is no interference with his regular workers."

By which Jane took him to mean that they would not be able to steal any of the glassmaking secrets, since there would be no one else in the factory save them.

"Because it is after their regular hours, he will only be able to work for four hours a day, and then only every other night, with Sundays off."

Four hours. Three days a week. That meant he would be receiving nearly eight pounds for each hour of work. Jane's father had tenants who paid that much for their lodging for the year. It was a scandalously high sum.

"Might I have a moment to speak with my wife?" Vincent's words were precise to the extreme. He stood, brushing his hands off on his trousers.

"If you will pardon us." Jane also rose, and together they stepped out into the street.

Vincent shut the door behind them with a great deal of care, but Jane could see the muscles clenching in the corner of his jaw.

"A moment, please, Muse."

"Of course."

Vincent stalked down the street, trailing a string of mutters in German, French, and possibly Latin, and stopped in front of a blank wall. He flung out his hand and snatched the ether, pulling a thread of deep red and wrapping it around him. Random colours and shapes appeared from his efforts, roiling in a visible expression of his outrage. The mass bore no resemblance to the delicate work of which he was capable, but if art was to be judged for its ability to convey emotion, then this laid forth a clear picture of a man pushed to his limits.

Jane had half a mind to join him. The audacity of the man's proposal. It was as though he knew that they had no alternative—which, upon reflection, he probably did, through having spoken with the other glassmakers. Vincent stood panting with effort at the end of the street and wiped the glamour away. He came striding back, with his chin tucked deep into his cravat. He wore a scowl such as he had in the days when she first met him. She had become so unused to seeing that expression that it made her recognise how accurate his friends had been when they said that marriage to her had lightened him. He was still a gruff and often grumbling bear, but he was no longer angry.

He strode past her, holding up a finger to indicate that he needed another moment. He gained the far end of the street, spun, and repeated the circuit. By the time he had begun his return, his pace had slowed and his head had lifted. His brow remained lowered, but the danger that he might bite someone had greatly diminished.

"Better?"

"No. And now I have a piercing headache as well. D—ned concussion. Only work at nights? We shall get nothing done."

Jane shared his indignation, but practise dealing with her mother had given her an extra store of patience. "It is far from ideal, and it means that our progress will be slow, but it will happen."

He stabbed his finger toward the glass factory. "That man is taking advantage of us."

"I know. I feel the same."

"You seem calm enough." Vincent ran his hand through his hair and clutched the back of his head with a groan.

"I am vexed, but I see little alternative save to leave. We had no luck on our own, and Signor Sanuto has managed to convince one glassmaker to work with us. Only one." Jane bit her lip and looked at the ground. She shook her head, irritated to be forced into this. "Do we have a choice?"

Vincent's sigh was more growl than anything else. "No. No, I suppose not. And we can afford it, if we are very disciplined with our time."

"Agreed." Jane lifted her head, bonnet framing her husband

against the length of the street. "It will be worth it, though. Once this is all over, we shall look back and laugh."

Vincent's tension eased from his face. "You are a wonder. How do you remain so calm?"

"You have met my mother, I believe."

He rewarded her with a chuckle. Still laughing, they re-entered the glass factory and accepted Signor Querini's terms.

Six

Memories in Glass

The day between the negotiation and their first appointment with Querini passed slowly. Jane availed herself of the pianoforte in the music room at Ca' Sanuto and worked on a piece by Rossini that had not yet made its way to England. The glamour noted in the score complimented the piece with waves of purple and blue that seemed to ripple from the instrument. It was an exceedingly simple interpretation of the piece, but the practise was good for her.

Vincent sat on the sofa, playing with a small glamour of a lion that he created and dissolved repeatedly. He scowled more often than not.

Jane paused only once in her music to ask, "How is your head?"

"Fine." Occasionally he rose to check the

clock on the mantelpiece, though its ticking was audible through the gaps in the music.

When he pronounced it time to depart, Jane closed the pianoforte with relief. She went to their rooms and put on the gentlemen's clothing she had ordered. She had not worn trousers since the year prior, with the coldmongers in London, and she had forgotten how importunate the cloth was between her thighs. Still, it was the best option for working with glass and did offer her a greater freedom of movement than her skirts.

With her short cropped hair and plain face, she could pass for a gentleman, but being *seen* to wear trousers still made her feel undressed. She picked up her long cloak and threw it over her apparel. With the addition of her bonnet, she felt as much a lady as she could with cloth bunching around her legs as she walked. Jane had to resist the urge to pluck at the confining fabric.

Signor Sanuto's gondola took them through the canals to the landing closest to Querini's. The sun had set, and the combination of shadows on the water with the reflections of lamps made it appear as though Murano floated in the sky. The streets that twisted back to the factory were even darker than the canal, and Jane slipped her arm through Vincent's to keep from stumbling. This was one of the many times that she wished that glamour cast actual light instead of little more than illusion.

Vincent knocked at the door, and a young man opened it. He stepped back, beckoning them in. During the day, the glass factory had been lit by a series of tall windows and skylights. At night, the red glow of the oven defeated the candles scattered about the room.

The young man had dark hair that blended with the shadows and a strong hooked nose. He nodded to them. "Signor Querini will be but a moment. May I offer you something to drink while you wait?"

"No. Thank you."

The glassmaker lumbered out of the shadows. "You've met my apprentice, then. Good, good."

"We have not yet been introduced." Vincent inclined his head with stiff formality.

"Oh . . . this is Biasio." He made no move to introduce the Vincents, so Jane did the honours.

The apprentice flashed her a grateful smile in return. "May I hang up your cloak?"

"Thank you." Jane removed her bonnet, handed it to him, and then untied her cloak.

"By the blessed Virgin!" Querini's eyes popped open as he stared unabashedly at her legs.

Jane's face heated. She handed the cloak to Biasio, who kept his eyes studiously averted. "I did say I was going to wear buckskin trousers."

"You look like a man. This is unholy . . ." Querini tugged on his little finger and walked in a circle. "I am going to hell for this."

Hanging up the cloak, Biasio laughed. "I think it is no different than a masquerade, Master Querini. My own sister borrows my clothes at Carnevale."

Muttering, the glassmaker shook his head. "A woman should look like a woman, and a man should—"

"My wife's attire is not why we are here." Vincent shrugged off his own coat and rolled up his sleeves. "We have a limited quantity of your time. I would not like to waste it."

Grateful to Vincent, Jane followed his example and rolled up her own sleeves. "Agreed."

Still muttering under his breath, but in Venetian now, the glassmaker pulled a leather work apron over his shirt and tied it around his substantial belly. Producing a pocket handkerchief, he dabbed the sweat from his face. "What is it you wish to make."

"A sphere of *cristallo*."

"That's it? Just a ball?"

"A perfect sphere." Vincent rolled his shoulders. "I shall need you to hold it quite steady as we cast glamour into it. The glassmaker we used in Binché—"

"I know what I am about, sir. You do not need to instruct me." He took up his long blowpipe and gestured to Biasio. "You. Make certain the fire stays even."

Jane went to the far side of the oven, heat from the furnace soaking through her shirt and causing it to cling to her back. She stood beside Vincent as the glassmaker thrust the blowpipe into the molten glass and gathered a gob at the end of it. Stepping back, he began to blow. He rotated the pipe quickly.

Vincent raised his hands and stopped. "I need the glass to be steady."

Querini pulled the blowpipe from his mouth. "You said you needed a perfect sphere."

"Yes."

"So I have to turn it, or the glass will droop."

"Yes, but the end is bobbing too wildly for me to approach." Vincent shook his head. "I need the glass to remain steady, so please try not to let it move around so much. I will accept the imperfections this introduces."

Grumbling in Venetian, Querini knocked the cooling gob of glass from the end of the pipe and gathered a fresh ball. Vincent stepped as close to it as was safe and spun the weave for a *Sphère Obscurcie* around the glass. They had decided to try this pattern again because they knew that it worked in glass. Since the shape of the fold itself was spherical, it mimicked the shape of the glass. Jane's job, as Vincent laid his folds, was to match his glamour with a gossamer skein of cold to enhance its path through the glass.

Using this method, they had been able to record a glamour in glass once before. As the ball of glass spun, they tried to match its movement and to lay the strand of glamour into its surface. It required careful coordination between the glassmaker and the glamourists to be able to settle the glamour into place.

Vincent grimaced. "No. Lost it."

Querini lifted his head from the pipe in question.

Jane tried to provide a balance to Vincent's gruffness. This would go more smoothly if the man were willing to work with them instead of merely tolerating them. "Again, if you please, sir."

He shrugged, cleaning the pipe off, and thrust the end back into the furnace again. He pulled it out of the glowing orange mass and held it again to his lips. The tube wavered before either of the Vincents could get the glamour aligned with the crystal, much less wrap it into place.

The air burned Jane's lungs as she spoke. "Do you have a stand of any sort? We need the end of the pole to be kept perfectly steady."

"Those are for amateurs." Querini snorted and shoved the

blowpipe back into the oven. "I can make a perfect sphere without one. A perfect sphere."

Jane wiped the sweat from her brow with the back of one hand. "I do not doubt it, but for our purposes, the steadiness of the pole is as important as the shape of the sphere."

He glowered at her for a moment before rolling his eyes. "Biasio! The Y-stand from the corner next to the tempering oven."

"Yes, sir." The apprentice ran across the room, grabbed a Y-stand, and hurried back with it. He placed it in front of the furnace at Querini's direction. His motions suddenly seemed familiar, but Jane could not think of where she had seen him before. She supposed that it was only the similarity of circumstance: He looked nothing like Mathieu La Pierre, but perhaps he reminded her of him simply by virtue of being a glassmaker's apprentice.

Querini settled the blowpipe on the stand with a muttered grumble. The contrast between working with him and with Mathieu was sharp. The Belgian apprentice's enthusiasm and the way he joined in an attempt to better the work had made the discovery a delight. Even when the heat from the furnace had made Jane increasingly ill—

No . . . No, it had not been the heat. She had thought that at the time, but that was only because she had not yet realized that she was with child.

Vincent lay in the thread for the *Sphère* before Jane was prepared. Her memory had distracted her, and when she tried to follow his movements, her alignment was poor. Again Querini thrust the blowpipe into the furnace and again pulled it out.

Jane bit her lip and tried to focus, but her thoughts kept turning back to Binché and how ill she had become. She should not have been working glamour at all back then, let alone something that required so much energy. Lord help her, she had thought it was only an excess of glamour making her so ill. It was laughable that a *child* had not occurred to her until the doctor had arrived.

She lost the thread again. "Sorry." Her heart raced under her shirt. The heat made it so hard to catch her breath. "Again, please." In the interval, Jane pushed her hair back from her face. Her hair had been long when they were working in Binché. She had not cut it until Vincent had been taken. She should be cooler here with the short hair, but she could not breathe. But surely that was only her fancy. It was no hotter here than it had been in Binché.

Jane's hands shook as she reached for the glamour. She should not be tired yet, but the threads seemed to slip through her fingers. Vincent growled as yet another attempt dissolved. It was the past. She tried to push her struggling sensibilities aside. She had not known what would happen, and if she had—if she had, she would have made the same choices again. Still. That keen sense of relief when she had miscarried, and the self-loathing that came with it—

She almost lost the thread of cold again and bore down too hard on it. The sudden change in temperature caused the sphere to crack.

Vincent shouted and ducked. Querini jumped, dropping the blowpipe.

Jane stood where she was as pieces of crystal flew across the room. It was just like in Binché.

In an instant, Vincent had her by the shoulders, turning her from the furnace. "Jane? Are you all right?"

She nodded, but could not form words on the first try. "Apologies." Her breath hitched, and she forced it down. Was she so fragile as to be undone by a memory? This was not Binché. She was not with child. "I misjudged. It will not happen again."

Vincent ran his thumb along the line of her jaw. "Jane . . ." He wet his lips and glanced to Querini. "I think we should take a short break."

"No, no . . . I am fine now."

Querini snorted. "You'll kill someone—"

"Sir." Vincent's voice snapped through the room, like glass, and Querini fell silent. Jane felt as though she had a bonnet and could only see directly in front of her. He put an arm around her shoulder and drew her away from the furnace. "What is the matter? Are you tired?"

She shook her head. "No . . . I only—it is—" She did not want to say it aloud and remind him of what she had done. The choices that she had made. Jane pressed her fingers to the bridge of her nose, closing her eyes. He was her husband. He deserved her honesty. "I am reminded—I am reminded of our time in the Netherlands."

"Oh, Muse . . ." Vincent pulled her into his arms and held her there, with his chin resting atop her head. Jane leaned against him, feeling his heart beat through her body. "Let us go home, hm?"

"No. I do not want to. I should—this should not upset me so." It was only a memory.

"You have stopped me from working at times that I resented it, but had to acknowledge that you were correct."

She counted his heartbeats, with her eyes squeezed tightly shut until she could trust her voice. "And you think I should stop?"

"I think we both should. Let us walk, and then come back after we catch our breath. Or tomorrow. Please? In exchange, I promise to stop without grumbling the next time you ask me to. Or, at least, without *much* grumbling."

Jane laughed, because she knew that he would want to hear it. "With that offer, how can I decline?"

Vincent released her and called across the room. "We shall take an early evening."

"You're still paying for a full day."

Vincent held very still. "Then I expect you to wait."

"Vincent . . ."

"If it were me, Muse, what would you do?"

She lowered her head. He was right. She was in no fit condition to work. Vincent took her hand and led her gently outside, away from the furnaces and the heat, but the memories followed her. Without speaking, Vincent shifted to pull her arm through his and hold her closer as they walked. A cricket chirped from behind a wall. The water of the canal splashed as an oar settled into the water. Someone laughed inside a nearby house, and in the distance, a woman practised an aria, her voice haunting around the corners of Murano.

Jane leaned into her husband, feeling his warmth against her side. "I am sorry we had to stop."

"You should not be." He rubbed his thumb over the back of her fingers. "I had expected it to be me that would need to be pulled away."

"Yes, well . . . you seem quite fit."

He shrugged. "I am not. I tell you that I am, and it *is* little enough of an affliction that I can ignore it, but after working glamour, my head aches. The room still pitches sometimes when I stand too quickly. But I spent so long being told that I was not allowed to work glamour that when I cannot—or even *should* not—I grow resentful."

"At least you have reason. *You* were injured."

They turned on to a bridge over the canal. Vincent tightened his grip on her hand. "So were you."

Jane's breath caught. There was no doubt about the "injury" that he referred to. The miscarriage. Jane held her jaw clenched against tears. She cast her gaze down to the water and followed the path of a gondola. Its dark shape made a void in the water, rippling the stars in its wake. "Two years ago."

"I . . . I do not think you allowed yourself time to . . . We came back to England, and as soon as your body allowed, you threw yourself back into your work. Our work. I should own that I did the same." Vincent stopped her at the summit of the bridge. "I do not think we allowed ourselves time to grieve."

"Do I have the right?"

"You lost a *child*, Jane."

"One that I did not want." She still watched the gondola, but she could hear Vincent suck his breath in.

"I wish you would stop blaming yourself."

"Who else should I blame? Napoleon? Lieutenant Segal? The horse that ran off the road? My mother, for the weakness of my womb?"

"Me?"

Jane's head snapped back around of its own accord. In the reflected glow of the city, Vincent's face was soft, his brows upturned with vulnerability. "How can you—no. You cannot blame yourself for being captured."

"I can blame myself for not leaving when you urged me to, when all reason told us that war was coming. That is not what I meant, though it would be reason enough." He shook his head, biting his lip. With something like a laugh mixed with a sob, Vincent tilted his head back and addressed his words to the sky. "But before that . . . because you resented me for wanting a child."

He had been so happy when he learned she had conceived, but they had never spoken of their plans or even raised the question of children before then. Jane lifted her hand and brushed it across his cheek. "I do *not* blame you for wanting a child. Or for getting me with one. I participate in *that* willingly enough."

Vincent smiled and lowered his gaze to her. "You do."

In silent accord, Jane and Vincent turned to begin their stroll again. Even in the dark, even speaking in English with no one to overhear them, it was difficult to talk of this subject, but Jane pressed on. If she waited, the words would close up inside her again. "When I was little, I always played at having a family with my dolls. I used to beg for a baby sister. Then Melody arrived, and Mama became so ill. I did not understand at the time, or more probably was not told, that the birth had nearly killed her. She has . . . she has been truly ill, and I think she was not always so nervous. I was her third confinement."

"I did not know."

"It is why, I think, that she frets so over us. I . . . I suspect there were times that I was unintentionally cruel in begging for a sister."

Jane felt more than heard Vincent's sigh through the places where they were touching.

"We had a nurse, but I had played at babies so long, and was so in love with the idea of having one of my own, that I treated Melody as though she were mine. I carried her everywhere my parents would let me, and Mama was inclined to be indulgent. In many ways, as much as Melody was my sister, she was also a daughter to me."

"That would, I imagine, be enough to cure any desire to be a mother again."

"I never resented it—or rarely." Jane shook her head and leaned it against him for a moment. "The resentment grew as Melody got prettier and I did not. By the time you met me, I had resigned myself to the life of a spinster."

"Which still confounds me."

"You are very sweet. But . . . but even you were first drawn to Melody, were you not?"

Vincent's voice was low. "That is not fair, Muse."

"I am sorry." She tilted her head up to kiss his cheek. "The point being, I had given up. I had shut away thoughts of being a mother, and then, when I met you—when I *married* you—those thoughts did not return, because we had the work. And I thought . . ." She had told him this before, during the months that they had been in recovery in Brussels before returning to England, but it was still hard to admit. "I thought you loved me because of what talent with glamour I have."

"But you know that is not it. I love you because of your passion, your curiosity and wit, and because you inspire me every day, every moment I am with you. And I do think you are beautiful. Not fashionable, not handsome, not insipidly pretty, but full of beauty. You find the beauty around you and reflect it for me to see. You are yourself and"—his voice broke—"you are my Muse."

They had stopped walking at some point in his declaration, and Jane rose onto her toes to meet him. Standing by the bank of the canal, they kissed. The space where one began and the other ended folded together like two strands of glamour weaving a single image. Jane felt nothing but the warmth of her husband, his fingers in her hair, and the tender shape of his lips against hers.

A gasp sounded in the canal behind them. "Are those men kissing?"

Jane and Vincent released their hold on each other. For a moment, Jane looked down at the passing gondola before recalling her attire. She had forgotten her bonnet and cape when they left the glass factory.

"I am wearing trousers." They had been so *present* when she first put them on that she was stunned by how quickly she had grown accustomed to them again.

"And I find them very becoming. But perhaps we should walk apart. For propriety's sake." Vincent raised an eyebrow and glanced down at her trousers with a slow smile. "If you would walk in front of me, I shall follow from behind."

Jane swatted him on the arm. "Rogue."

"Muse."

Heedless of the gondola in the canal, Jane resumed her

hold on her husband's arm as they walked. He cleared his throat. "Do you want children?"

"I do not know if that is a question about which we have much choice."

"Well . . . there are—um . . . measures." Vincent cleared his throat and tugged at his cravat. "To prevent conception, I mean."

Of course he would know about such things. She bent her head to watch the cobblestones as they walked. It was not, she feared, a matter of preventing conception. "I meant . . . It has been two years. We have not been shy in our affections."

"Ah." That single, voiced exhalation was filled with the weight of his understanding. Her first—and her only—pregnancy had been within four months of their marriage. Then the miscarriage, and since then . . . nothing.

"I do not know if there was some damage, or if it is the glamour." Jane lowered her voice, even though they were alone. To speak of this so directly was embarrassing, but the fact was that most doctors agreed that the exertion required to work glamour could harm an unborn child in the same way that running might. In Jane's memory, she ran through a field of rye and felt a stitch in her side. She rubbed at the remembered ache. Had it been then? She shook her head to clear the memories. "My time has always been somewhat irregular, but when we are working heavily on a extensive project, it stops altogether."

"I did not know that." His voice was hoarse with suppressed emotion. "We could stop working for a time. If you wanted to try."

She did not miss the fact that Vincent had said *we*. His art was his life. "I do not know if I want to give up our art."

"It would not be forever."

"How long would you be willing to stop? A few months? A year? Two?" Beside her, his pace slowed. She could feel him turning the thought over. "Let us say that there is nothing wrong with me that a cessation of glamour will not cure. Then we have a child. What then?"

"We can leave them with a nanny."

She raised an eyebrow at his use of the plural and its suggestion of multiple children, but did not comment on it. The larger issue still lay before her. "But is that right? To have a child and then ignore him?"

"Most of my childhood was spent with nurses or tutors."

"We had tutors and nurses, too, but my parents were always there and involved in raising us. I cannot imagine having a child and travelling as much as we do. It would have made me sad, as a child."

"You had parents who loved you."

"Yes." Jane shuddered, recalling again the relief she had felt upon her miscarriage. "My parents wanted children very much. My fear . . . my fear is that I do not want to cause a child to suffer the isolation that you did."

"I think there is little chance of that."

"No?"

He laughed. "No. Melody did not feel abandoned, did she?"

"I was not a professional glamourist, then."

"Should I offer to remain home during the child's early years and let you go out to earn our living?"

"Be serious, Vincent."

"I will be, in a moment. My point is that there is no reason that you cannot continue to work. Mrs. Kauffman was one of the founders of the Royal Academy of Arts, and her marriage did nothing to stop her from working. I had the privilege of taking a review of portraiture with her during her last visit to London, the year before her death."

"Did she have children?"

He hesitated and shook his head.

In some ways, the trousers made it easier to discuss feminine matters with him, as though they were something unconnected to her. Still, her voice hitched as she pressed on. "I would have to stop working glamour for nine months. Perhaps more, to conceive again."

"We have done very little work on this trip. After we finish here, we will be travelling for some months more. We could go to visit Herr Scholes and discuss theory. Show him the glamour in glass . . . But I am putting pressure on you. I am sorry."

"No . . . no, this is helping. I do not want to give up our art, nor do I want to be an absent mother."

He drew breath as though to speak, but paused instead, giving Jane time to work through her thoughts. Did she want a child? If it were possible to have both a family and her art, would she want that? With her first pregnancy, she had thought she would have to give up glamour and possibly Vincent . . . Jane's stomach hurt with the memory. It had not been the child that she resented but everything she thought she would lose. And if she could have both? "I do not know what I want."

"You do not need to know now."

"I am thirty-one. We cannot wait too long to decide."

"I am very clear about what *I* want." Vincent raised her fingers to his lips and kissed them. "I want you to be happy."

They had turned on to Calle Dietro Gli Orti. Ca' Sanuto lay at the end. Jane traced his lips with her fingers. "Then take me back to the glass factory."

Seven

Canals and Monkeys

Their work at the glass factory went more smoothly after they returned. To the best of their knowledge, they appeared to have laid the strands accurately for several *Verre Obscurci*, though it was impossible to tell if any of them worked until they cooled first. More significantly, Jane and Vincent had worked well together. She still thought of their time in Binché, but not with the same fear.

For the moment, they must wait to know if they had succeeded. Working at night as they were, it was impossible to know if the glamour in glass were working since it required full sunlight to make anything invisible. Until the glass cooled in a tempering chamber, they could not take one out into the sun to be certain. Depending on the temperature, it could take two to three days to cool enough to be moved without risk of cracking. Jane well remembered the frustration of waiting for that in Belgium.

Exhausted, but cautiously pleased, they returned to Ca' Sanuto deep into the night. Letizia had left out a cold supper in their room, which Jane was almost too tired to appreciate.

The following day, they had no work planned at Querini's. What had seemed an imposition was now something for which Jane found herself grateful. She and Vincent spent the morning refamiliarizing themselves with each other, emerging only when it became necessary to find something with which to break their fast.

Their second visit to the glass maker's factory went more smoothly, but the glass from the first visit was still too warm to take home. Jane had to restrain herself from expressing her frustration. The weather was cool, so it was naturally taking longer than she wished.

Over the next days, they settled into a routine of sleeping late into the day to conserve their energy for the time in the glass factory. Signor Querini, for all his bluster at the beginning, worked steadily and without complaint.

His apprentice, Biasio, turned out to be a glamourist whose skills seemed chiefly employed in creating draughts to stoke the fire. Rather than grumbling, though, the young man seemed utterly captivated by their work.

One evening during a pause, he brought Jane a glass of water.

She sat on a chair outside the glass factory enjoying what little breeze came down the alley. Her fingers ached from the tight, delicate work they had been doing, and she wanted the energy to stir the air more. Smiling at him, she took the glass gratefully. "Thank you." It was exquisitely crafted of *cristallo*, with the stem in the shape of an aventurine-laced dolphin. "What a lovely glass."

He blushed. "I made it."

"Did you?" She took a sip of the water. Her shirt clung to her back with sweat.

Vincent lay on the ground beside her, heedless of the dirt, with his arm flung over his face. His breath had slowed from the ragged pace of the end of their session. He might almost be asleep. They were planning on attempting an interwoven glamour next, to see if the glass could reproduce more than one effect.

"May I ask a question, Lady Vincent?" The young man's toe dug into the dirt.

"Of course."

"The glass . . . is it—are you making a record of the glamour inside the glass?"

Vincent stirred and lowered his arm, looking up at the boy.

"That is . . . I was watching your folds, but they are so slight that I couldn't see what you were weaving."

Jane lowered her glass. "Did you look at the spheres?"

He nodded. "They have faults in them. But . . . but I don't see that they do anything."

"It is just an experiment." Vincent sat up. "Nothing more."

If Signor Querini was jealous of his techniques, they could be jealous of theirs. Privately, Jane saw no harm in answering the apprentice's questions, but if he understood what they were after, then Querini would as well.

That evening, Querini reported that their first attempts at the glass spheres were finally cool. The Vincents wrapped them in velvet and took them back to Ca' Sanuto. Jane thought that she would not be able to sleep, wondering if the spheres would work in the morning. She curled up next to Vincent, cradling her head on his shoulder. He turned his face toward her, but, in the next moment, gave a paltry snore like a kitten sleeping. A moment after that, Jane was asleep as well.

In the morning, she awoke to an empty bed. Vincent sat in the window of the palazzo, with his drawing-book on his knee. "Do not move, please." A stub of a pencil worked across the page.

She blinked sleepily at him, content to lay in the bed for the moment and be his model. He still wore his nightshirt, unbuttoned at the throat and exposing the spot where his neck curved into his shoulders. His hair stood out from his head in a mad tangle. Though a line of concentration creased his brow, his countenance had none of the exhaustion that still claimed her limbs. "Feeling better?"

Still focused, he nodded, adding another scratching of shadow to part of the page. "You?"

"Tired." She let her gaze drift to the spheres wrapped in velvet. "Are you going to let me up so we can try them?"

The corner of his mouth curled in a smile. He made one more mark and set the drawing aside. "Yes. It was all I could do to not look while you slept."

"You could have woken me." She sat up, stretching.

"I tried." He stood, holding out his hands to her. Without

effort, he lifted her to her feet, and then planted a kiss on her forehead. "So I hope you appreciate how very good I was in not peeking at them."

"I am proud of you." Jane went to the window and pulled the curtains back fully. The light showed that it was earlier in the day than they had been rising this week. She turned to face Vincent, who stood by the desk. A beam of sunlight stretched across the room, lighting the gilding on the mirrors and catching in their surface. Biting the inside of her lip, she nodded to him.

Vincent unwrapped one of the spheres. As the cloth fell away from the glass, Jane found that she had stopped breathing. For a moment, it lay in the shadow still, but then the sunlight caught it.

Vincent vanished. Jane gasped.

"May I take it that it worked?" His disembodied voice sounded on the edge of laughter.

Jane nodded. Even knowing what they were attempting, even having seen it work before, she could not help but be filled with wonder that the sphere worked. Without either of them touching so much as a strand of glamour, the glass remembered the pattern that they had created in the glass factory. The twist of glamour had marked its passage through the glass and left a record there that light followed as willingly as it obeyed a glamourist's hands.

The desk had vanished as well, which meant that this *Sphère* was somewhat larger than the previous one they had created. A *Sphère Obscurcie*, in the hands of a glamourist, was a thin twist that reflected light back outward. Spun at a gossamer weight, it hid everything within it from sight while bending around objects that intersected its perimeter so that they remained visible, such that the floor would stay in view but the desk would not. A *Verre Obscurcie* was the same effect, captured in glass.

"We have done well, love." Jane tilted her head, studying it. "Shall we test the size of this one or look at the others?"

The desk melted back into view. "Test this, I think." Vincent's voice was closer.

Jane waited till he appeared. "Hold."

He halted with a grin. Jane answered his smile. She was fully within the *Sphère*'s influence now, and could see everything within it clearly. Vincent stood perhaps seven paces in front of her. She took a step back, and he vanished again.

Forward once more into the circle. "This is larger, is it not?"

"I believe so." He rolled the sphere in his hand. "I wonder how large we could make one."

"Is it dependent on the glass, or the weave we encase?"

"Shall we look at the others to see if we can find an answer?"

The rest of the morning was spent in happy examination. Not all of the spheres had been successful, but they had managed to create four of the *Verres Obscurcis* in various sizes. The effect appeared to be related to the size of the glamour when they wove it, but with such a small sample, that was by no means certain.

After a morning spent studying the spheres, Jane declared the desire to do something in celebration. At Vincent's suggestion, they took a gondola into Venice with the intent of spending the rest of the day as tourists before returning to work with the glassmaker. The Basilica Di San Marco, with its mosaics and glamours, was to be a principal destination. They engaged a gondolier and set off. Jane leaned back in the little cabin with Vincent's arm around her. The gondola slid into the Grand Canal, which was full of traffic. She watched her husband out of the corner of her eye and was pleased to note that he showed no ill effects from being on the water.

She was able to relax, then, and enjoy the sights as they followed the canals of Venice. Pleasure craft vied for space with merchants floating rafts of goods to their warehouses. Gondoliers slipped through the spaces between, ferrying passengers about the city.

In the midst of this, a man swam towards them.

Vincent sat up. "Is that—?" In a moment, he had the door to the cabin open and had clambered out onto the bow of the gondola. It rocked with his movements, but did not seem to trouble him. Jane slid forward on the seat, unable to discern what had caught his attention, until he raised his hand and waved. "Byron! What the devil are you doing?"

In the middle of the Grand Canal, Lord Byron stopped and treaded water. "Vincent? I should have thought that was obvious. I am swimming." He glanced over his shoulder. "Racing, actually, but I seem to have left the others behind. Still . . . I should continue on."

Vincent turned to their gondolier. "Can you accompany this gentleman without interfering with his movement?"

Jane could not hear his response, but a moment later the gondola turned and began to pace Lord Byron, who changed to a sidestroke, which kept his head above water.

He carried on his conversation as though they were in a drawing room. "I expected you weeks ago. What held you up?"

"We have been here for almost two weeks. Your landlord said you had left town."

Byron cursed with an easy fluency. "Signor Segati must have realized that I have been seduced by his wife. This is the first time he has interfered. I am sorry that you were the recipient of his mischief."

"We may have met his wife as well . . . Are you still in her favour?"

"Ah—oh. You arrived on *that* day. Truly, I am sorry. She is sweetness embodied at all other times."

Jane had her doubts about that.

Vincent cleared his throat. "I take it she said nothing about us?"

"Truth be told, she said that some friends of mine had come begging. I should have realized that it was you, but—well . . . we had to repair our relations, and that is always such a sweet duty."

"Fortunately, there was no harm done. We—we had the opportunity to meet a local gentleman on the way here and have been staying with him."

"Speaking of 'we,' is that the famed Lady Vincent I see behind you?"

"It is." Vincent turned with a rakish grin. "Jane, may I present Lord Byron."

Jane climbed forward to sit in the door of the gondola cabin. "How do you do, sir."

"Generally very well, I have been told." Water cascaded down his arm as he pulled himself through the canal. It imperfectly veiled his form, which appeared to be dressed in nothing more than—Oh. He appeared to be dressed in nothing at all. The saucy look he gave her reminded Jane of why he had been called "mad, bad, and dangerous to know."

Jane averted her gaze, finding a sudden need to examine the horizon. He laughed. "She blushes! Oh, well done, Vincent. Well done. I like a woman whose feelings are not hidden behind artifice."

He began to recite:

I like the women too (forgive my folly!),
From the rich peasant cheek of ruddy bronze,
And large black eyes that flash on you a volley
Of rays that say a thousand things at once,
Heart on her lips, and soul within her eyes,
Soft as her clime, and sunny as her skies.

In spite of her best efforts, Jane's gaze was drawn irresistibly back to the celebrated poet. Had he just invented that verse while swimming in the Grand Canal? Based on what she had heard of him, she would not put it past the man.

Vincent cleared his throat. "Please recall that you are speaking to my wife."

"I have not forgotten." Barely slowing his pace, he splashed the water and sent some spray at Vincent. "Why do you think I am flirting? There is something to me very softening in the presence of a woman, some strange influence, even if one is not in love with them, and a married woman comes without complications. But my apologies, madam, for the manner of our meeting, as well as for my manners. Come to call, and I shall be on my best behaviour."

In this moment, Jane was at once strangely charmed by him, and also quite grateful that they were staying with Signor Sanuto. "Not your *best* behaviour, sir. How should I recognise you then?"

He laughed, not at all offended. Looking ahead, he pointed to a gondola moored at the end of the Grand Canal. "That is the finish line. Once there, we shall go back to my apartments together. You can send for your things."

Vincent hesitated and looked back to Jane, who gave a minute shake of her head. "I think . . . that we may be settled with Signor Sanuto. We have business in Murano, and that is where he lives."

"I suppose that is just as well, as I am leaving town in the next day or so. Whenever I can make up my mind to actually go, which is so difficult sometimes to put into action. In this case, however, there is a young lady who has quite caught my attention, and I feel compelled to pursue her."

He had no shame in his nature, it seemed. Jane asked, "To La Mira?"

"Heavens, no. That affair was over last month, when the lady threatened to jump into the canal and then did." He shook his head. "No, this young lady is in her appearance altogether like an antelope. She is a famous songstress— scientifically so; her natural voice (in conversation, I mean) is very sweet, and the naïveté of the Venetian dialect is always pleasing in the mouth of a woman. Now, if you will excuse me." He lowered his head and began to swim in earnest, moving away to the gondola marked as the finish line.

Vincent drew back into the cabin and whispered, "When he gets out of the water, do not stare at his feet. The right is a club, and he loathes having attention drawn to it."

Do not stare at his feet? The man was without clothing. Jane had no intention of watching him *at all* when he emerged from the canal. She resolutely kept her eyes on her gloves as he hoisted himself out of the water and into the gondola.

Vincent leaned closer to her. "It is safe to look now. He has a blanket wrapped round him." That made her blush even more deeply, yet Jane lifted her eyes. Lord Byron sat in the prow of his gondola with his feet out of sight. Bending down, he lifted a bottle of champagne from a bucket of ice. "Look what I have won. Join me?"

The interior of Lord Byron's apartments was in better condition than the walls outside had suggested. Tall ceilings with friezes and gilt murals surrounded moth-eaten carpets, which lay over vast marble floors. In places, the walls had been replaced by glamour to mask crumbling plaster. Other holes had been papered over to keep draughts and rats out.

Yet the rooms were comfortable and had clearly been designed to be lived in rather than simply viewed. Lord Byron had set his own stamp upon the space with his collection of oddities picked up in his travels. Key among these was his ménagerie of animals. Dogs roamed the palazzo freely, lounging on sofas or curled in front of the hearth. A monkey sat perched atop the valance spanning a great window overlooking the canal, and another hopped on to Lord Byron's shoulder the moment they entered the palazzo.

The little grey creature remained there as they entered the drawing room, and Lord Byron reached up to scratch the fur under its little chin. He walked with a slight roll that nearly masked the lameness in his right foot. As much as he collected animals, the poet appeared to collect people as well. He nodded to several individuals as they passed through the palazzo: a man in a gondolier's uniform read with his feet up on a coffee table, an odd young man in a fez fiddled with a lock on a door, a young woman in half dress ate bonbons on the balcony, and another man wrote at a desk.

Lord Byron patted a bulldog who rose to meet him with stumpy tail wagging. "Moretto, were you a good boy today?"

"He only ate one of my papers, but he also made off with *il dottore*'s shoe." The man at the desk rose, setting his quill down as he did. He was a compact man with an aquiline nose and dark hair brushed forward around his face.

"He did bring it back, to be fair." *Il dottore*, the man with the fez, continued to examine the lock. "How did the race go?"

"I won, of course." Lord Byron flung himself down on a sofa, putting his feet up on the cushion. "Mingaldo was miles behind and hallooing for a boat. Utterly knocked up. He says he was undone by bad shellfish yesterday."

The man by the desk *hmm*ed, and then crossed the room to Jane and Vincent. "I am John Hobhouse, at your service."

Vincent made the introductions, since Lord Byron seemed disinclined to do so. Jane offered Mr. Hobhouse a curtsy.

"Oh—introductions. So tiresome." Byron tilted his head back and called to the young woman. "Marianna, are you not going to kiss me, my sweet?"

"You did not kiss *me*." She continued to watch the water, fanning herself peevishly.

He shrugged and scratched the monkey again. "How are you finding Venice?"

Jane sank on to the nearest sofa, shooing a cat away to make space for Vincent. "To be honest, we are spending most of our time in Murano, but what I have seen of Venice is lovely."

"The view of the Rialto—of the piazza—and the chant of Tasso are to me worth all the cities on earth." He paused, considering. "Save Rome and Athens. Perhaps. And the women. God help me, but I love the Italian women."

Mr. Hobhouse settled in a chair across from them. "And how was your journey in?"

Vincent smirked. "Unpleasant, to be honest. We were set upon by corsairs."

Various exclamations resulted from that statement, ranging from a simple "Good Lord" to "Inconceivable," and finishing with Lord Byron's "Stap my vitals!" Byron had sat up with the monkey clinging to his collar. Face alight with interest, the poet leaned forward with his elbows on his knees and hands steepled in front of him. "Corsairs, you say. I thought you were coming from Trieste."

"We did. Mind you, your directions on where to find the glamural were not as clear as they could have been."

"What care I for that? Tell me of the corsairs."

Vincent's face coloured and he rubbed the back of his head.

"To tell the truth, I took a blow to the head and remember little of the events. Jane saw them, though."

"Unlucky that." Lord Byron turned his burning interest to her. "Well, Lady Vincent, you shall have to be my muse, then."

She darted a glance to Vincent. "I am not certain I am equal to the task." Her husband was glaring at Lord Byron, but broke off when she laid a hand on his knee. Jane affected a manner lighter than she felt. "They were much like the corsairs that appear in *Punch*'s illustrations. Long moustaches, winding turbans, and striped trousers like a commedia player's."

Vincent put his hand on hers and squeezed. "Show him."

She bit the inside of her lip, but nodded. Jane had not wished to remind him of his difficulties with glamour by being free with it. It was, however, well suited to the task. With quick strokes, Jane drew the captain of the corsairs in front of her. It was not a fully realized rendering,—more like the sketch that a dressmaker would create to display an idea for a new gown. She had him brandish his curved scimitar, and gave an added flourish by having his long moustaches blow in the breeze.

Byron frowned as he stared at it. "Is this accurate, Vincent?"

Her husband nodded. "While much of my memory was victim to the attack, I had the opportunity of some minutes to stare at the captain. Jane's rendering is precise in its detail."

"Off Trieste, you say? What happened in the attack?" Lord Byron turned his attention back to Jane.

"I did not see any of the attack itself, as I was below deck with the rest of the passengers. They brought us above deck

Mary Robinette Kowal

to ransom us later, but the fighting was done by then. They put us in the ship's boat and then sent us back to land."

"Vincent? Have you nothing for me?"

He shook his head and spread his hands. "I remember sending Jane below. Then she woke me after the attack. Even that is full of dark holes in my memory."

"He is the only passenger who stayed above."

"I beg your pardon, madam." *Il dottore* had abandoned his work with the lock and now stood behind the sofa. "Not pirates. You think you were attacked by pirates, but you were not."

"I assure you, we were."

The odd little man shook his head and tapped the fez upon his head. "Corsairs, excellent haberdashery choices, fez beneath the turban, but not for this captain of yours. Also, corsairs in the Gulf of Venice? And dressed like that? Not unless they were on their way to the theatre. To perform, I mean." He looked suddenly as if he had said too much, made an awkward gesture with his hands and spun on his heel to return to the business of the lock.

Lord Byron nodded. "I must agree. When I wrote *The Corsair*, it was not without some research. I would not say that I spent time as a—enough. Suffice to say that what you describe is not a corsair attack. To ransom you, they would have taken you to a secure location and then sent a message. How should they have been assured of the funds if they let you go?"

Jane's mouth worked without finding words. She swallowed, trying to make sense of what he said. "But we *were* attacked."

"Were you?" called the Doctor, looking over once again. "A blow to the head? To the *back* of the head?" Vincent's face paled, and his hand rose to his scalp. He had been attacked from behind.

Eight

A Ring of Intrigue

Jane looked from *il dottore* to Vincent, trying to grasp this new possibility. "Are you suggesting that the blow was on the back of his head because one of the crew struck him?"

"Was anyone else injured?"

She had not thought of it at the time, but there was a curious absence of blood in her memory of the deck. "Signor Sanuto—he was hurt when the pirates came down to where the passengers were. In fact, he was hurt defending me."

Vincent started. "Defending you? Jane— you did not tell me they had threatened you."

"I—you were ill and the danger was past, so I did not wish to worry you." She blushed. "There is little enough to tell."

"And yet I would very much like to hear it."

His expression confounded Jane. It was a mixture of hurt and anger, yet she did not think the anger was directed toward her.

Reluctantly, very reluctantly, she related the whole of what took place in the passenger cabin when the pirates had stormed in. Vincent became quite still; then he abruptly stood and walked away from the sofa to stare out the window. His hands were knotted in fists at his side. Lord Byron turned to watch him go, a brief smile colouring his face. He leaned closer to Jane. "He loves you very much, in case you were unaware."

She coloured at his presumption, to comment thus on their marriage. "I—yes, thank you."

"While he collects himself . . . It seems to me that if the pirate attack was indeed not real, then Signor Sanuto must know that."

"But how could he? He was below with me."

From the window, Vincent said, "Because he paid the ransom."

Of course, if Lord Byron was correct about how the pirates worked, then Signor Sanuto would have to have been aware. "But perhaps . . . If we grant that these were not corsairs, might they not be a different sort of pirate? Perhaps the Venetian variety accepts ransoms in this manner?" But even as she said it, Jane could see that the method made no sense.

All previous elation about the *Verres* faded. The group spent some time debating and turning over the possibilities till Jane felt quite ill.

* * *

When they departed, Lord Byron put his gondola at their disposal, with the prompting that his invitation to share his lodgings still stood. The Vincents' trip back to the palazzo was spent in silence.

When they arrived back at Ca' Sanuto, the stairs to the upper floor seemed longer than they had before. Jane dreaded the conference they were about to have with their host. Vincent's brow was pulled down very low, and his shoulders rode hunched within his coat. They found Signor Sanuto in his study with work candles pulled up next to his desk and his leg braced upon an ottoman with pillows piled beneath it. He looked up from a ledger when they entered and smiled. "How was your day?"

He seemed so happy to see them that Jane wondered how they could doubt him.

"We have been busy." Vincent tucked his chin into his collar and took a seat opposite Signor Sanuto. Jane sank into the chair next to her husband. Her heart raced inside her stays as though she were managing a large fold of glamour. "We spoke with someone today who suggested, with reason, that the pirates who attacked our ship were not corsairs."

"Not corsairs?" The signore sat back in his chair, face slipping out of the candlelight. "They certainly looked like corsairs."

"Perhaps too much. Then there is the subject of the ransom . . ." Vincent's voice caught. "How did they collect the money?"

"Ah." Signor Sanuto twirled his quill in his fingers, staring at Vincent for a moment, and then at Jane. She could only watch with aghast fascination as their host's face struggled with emotion. His jaw clenched, and twice he appeared to draw breath to speak. At last he sighed and sat forward, placing the quill in the inkpot. Lowering his leg, he began to rise and winced. "Sir David, would you be so kind as to shut the door."

Vincent stood slowly, not taking his eyes off Signor Sanuto. "I will require some explanation."

He nodded, not looking at either of them. "The door, please."

Striding across the room, Vincent shut the door firmly and turned to face Signor Sanuto. Their host still sagged in his chair, but the sound seemed to recall him somewhat. Reaching to the side, he pulled open a drawer on his desk and extracted a paper. With his mouth in a thin line, he placed the paper on the table, sliding it toward Vincent. It was his promissory note. "This is why I did not want to accept your funds when you attempted to repay me. I stopped the deposit."

Jane could find no other meaning. "You knew. Knew that they were not pirates."

"I did." He placed another item on the table. A small woman's ring. Jane's wedding ring. "And I could think of no way to return this to you without revealing that I knew."

"And our other property? And those of the other passengers?"

"Some have been restored, where possible. Most . . ." He held his hands out helplessly. "It is the part of the—the cost that I most regret, because those paying it did not agree to do so. It was . . . necessary."

"But why?" Vincent remained by the door, perfectly still. "Why stage a pirate attack? What could demand such elaborate measures?"

Signor Sanuto sighed and sounded old for the first time since they had met him. "There are things you ask me that I cannot answer. Stories that are not mine to tell."

"We must have some answer, sir."

He rubbed his brow. "Let me try. Let me try to speak of things that are common knowledge to see if you can draw the picture. Venice was a republic for one thousand years. Until only ten years ago, in fact, when Napoleon intimidated the council into disbanding our country. It should never have happened. Since then, we have been handed to the Hapsburgs as though we were nothing more than chattel. They have been trying to wring every drop of wealth that they can from Venice. They tax us heavily. For instance, the glassmakers cannot bring in the materials that they require for modern techniques. Their work stagnates."

"This does not account for anything that occurred."

Nodding, Signor Sanuto straightened the pages of his ledger. "What if . . . what if you knew of papers aboard a certain ship that could affect the fate of your homeland? What would you do?"

Jane frowned, feeling as though the conversation had taken a familiar turn. "Are you suggesting that you are a spy?"

He gave a dismal smile. "My answer to that would be the same if I were or if I were not." Leaning forward, he tapped the promissory note with one finger. "Suffice to say that I had good and sufficient reason to decline your offer to repay me, and even more reason to feel guilty for your injury."

Vincent snorted and rubbed his hair, in the gesture Jane recognised so well as an attempt to order his thoughts.

"It was . . . it was a surprise that not all of the passengers went below deck. The plan—I should dissemble, but—" He bit his words off with a groan. "I paid the captain to surrender without contest. The running, shouting, and gunfire was all feigned for the passengers. No one was to be hurt." Grief seemed to add its weight to Signor Sanuto's age. He rose painfully and limped to where Vincent stood. He held out the promissory note and the ring. "I had not expected such valour."

Stiffly formal, Vincent took them both, turning the ring over in his hand. "It seems little valour was required."

Signor Sanuto shook his head. "*You* were prepared to fight. I was prepared to lie."

The tenor of the conversation was so familiar to Jane. It put her in mind of when Vincent had been working for the Crown and unable to tell her. If Signor Sanuto were being open with them, if he had been engaged in work that he could not discuss, then Vincent, of all people, should understand those difficulties. Her husband's continued anger must rise from the shock, the injured pride that he had been taken in so completely, compounded by the fact that the blow to his head had nearly taken away his ability to do that which he valued most.

Jane stood slowly and smoothed the folds of her dress. It came to her that it was no wonder Signor Sanuto had been so free and easy with his wife's wardrobe when they first arrived, since he had been the instrument for losing theirs. "Does your wife know?"

He shook his head, looking deeply penitent. "I beg that you not tell her when she arrives. She would not understand."

"I did. When I was in her position."

Vincent's head came up at that, but their host was focused on Jane and did not see his surprise, nor the understanding that began to soften his features. Signor Sanuto shook his head. "You are a remarkable woman, Lady Vincent. I hope you understand that not all women are so . . . steady in their thoughts."

Jane recalled her own mother, whose feverish nerves had been her constant companion. "Truly? None of the women in the cabin were overcome during the attack, save one who might be excused by her youth. If you trust your wife in other matters, then you might consider if you can trust her with this."

"I wish . . . I truly wish that I could. It is no comfortable thing to keep secrets from those one holds in regard."

"I am well aware of this." Vincent wiped his face with his hand. "Our friend Lord Byron has returned. We shall remove to his apartments tomorrow."

"Oh." The signore's shoulders fell. "I should—yes, of course you will want to stay with him."

They took their leave with careful civility—Jane more civil than Vincent—and retreated to their rooms, where Vincent closed the door carefully behind them. He folded the promissory note and tucked it into his coat pocket.

Then Vincent took Jane's hand, very gently, and raised it. Without taking his gaze from her face, he slipped her wedding ring back on her finger. Tears filled Jane's eyes at the tangible reminder of how fortunate she was. Vincent rubbed his thumb over the ring, smiling. "That is better."

"Very much so." Jane took a breath to relieve some of the tension that continued to build within her. "I wonder at him, taking the trouble to recover it. And when—and why? There is so much I do not understand."

"I am confounded as well." Vincent lowered her hand and proceeded to pace the length of the room. He scrubbed his face with his hands as he walked. "You want to stay here."

Wondering how he could tell, Jane undid the buttons on her blue walking dress. Each button on the dress reminded her that it was new and that she had possession of the dress solely because her other clothes had been taken in the supposed pirate attack. "I am not certain."

"But he lied to us."

"Not when we asked him directly."

Vincent bent his head, and his pace slowed somewhat. "True."

"And you should know what it is to hold a secret that you cannot share, even if you should wish to do so."

He nodded. "I dislike it."

"As did I. It is discomfiting to know that one has been deceived, even if there were no other harm. But . . ." Jane removed her walking dress and laid it over the back of the chair. "But . . . he has certainly sought to make amends."

"I suppose he has." Vincent dropped into a chair and ran his hands through his hair. "Aside from hitting me upon the head—"

"—I am certain that was not him."

"Aside from *causing* me to be hit upon the head, he has been a gracious host. I will grant that."

"But . . . ?"

"I cannot help but wonder . . . Staging a pirate attack. What could have been so valuable?"

"I cannot hazard a guess. For myself, I am satisfied enough to know that he did not try to dissemble when we inquired, though the temptation must have been strong. That he stopped our funds from being deposited in his account and returned the note speaks well of him, too." Jane came to sit on the arm of Vincent's chair, dropping a kiss upon his forehead. "I think this does not sit easy with him, either."

"No. It does not look to." Vincent stretched his long legs out in front of him and leaned his head back against his chair with a groan. "Why can nothing be simple?"

"Allow me to offer one exceedingly simple reason to *not* remove to Lord Byron's."

He raised his eyebrows in question.

Jane placed a hand to her bosom and sighed over-dramatically. "I fear for my virtue."

It brought a laugh, short-lived though it was. That slight ease in tension gave her a measure of confidence that his anger would pass. One thing remained for Jane to puzzle over: Was it possible that Signor Sanuto wished them to remain because he had some need for their glamour in his endeavours?

By mutual agreement, the next morning Jane carried the message to their host that they would remain if he would still have them.

He sat upon the balcony taking his morning coffee. His shoulders sagged in relief. "I am glad. So very glad. I have grown to have a great regard for you and your husband."

"You have been very kind to us"

He winced and turned away. "Say rather that I have done you harm and am trying to make amends. It is little enough to invite you to stay in our home."

"And to help us with the glassmakers? The trouble there had nothing to do with you."

"I suppose not. Coffee?" He lifted the pot and offered it to her. When Jane nodded her acceptance, he poured. "Is your work going well?"

Jane accepted the cup he handed her. "Indeed. We have been quite successful. So you see, you have that accomplishment to claim some part in."

He laughed and shook his head. "It is good of you. But I can hardly claim an accomplishment when I have not the smallest understanding of what you are attempting."

A *Verre Obscurci* might well help him with the troubles that he had hinted at the night prior. It had certainly been essential for them. Jane smoothed her skirts. "Perhaps we can show you someday. For now, though, Vincent is very private when we are working on a new project."

"He does seem so, yes."

"Please do not take his upset too much to heart. He will soften once he has some distance and time for consideration. It is the shock, I think, more than anything."

"Of course. Still, I am glad that you have had some success, and will, as you suggest, count that as a small victory of my own." He hesitated and then set his cup down. "Your husband is a very skilled glamourist, is he not?"

"Though I am biased, he is the best I have ever seen."

He nodded as though he had expected that answer, but kept his gaze fixed on his cup. "You say nothing of your own skills, which are not inconsiderable, I believe."

Jane blushed and looked toward the canal. She had a recognition of her own talents, and though she understood that she was, in fact, quite good, she was not accustomed to acknowledging it. "You are too kind."

"Merely practical. Lady Vincent, though I have no right . . . I should like to consult with you on a matter."

She held very still, wishing that Vincent were present.

Signor Sanuto turned the cup in the saucer as if he could read his fortune in the coffee grounds. "Is there any chance that . . . Would you help me pick a present for my daughter's birthday?"

"Certainly. I should be very glad to." And yet Jane was absolutely certain that Signor Sanuto had been about to ask her a very different question, one which involved glamour and pirates.

Nine

A Strain of Friendship

The easy friendship that had begun to develop between the Vincents and Signor Sanuto was strained by his disclosures, but this was to be expected. They continued to stay with Signor Sanuto. Several times it seemed as if he were on the cusp of saying something about his cause that then turned to a different topic.

In truth, though, they did not see much of their host the next week, as they were occupied at the glass factory in the evenings, which was when he was at home from the bank. When they were not engaged at the glass factory, they called on Lord Byron.

Jane found Byron to be as mercurial as his reputation had promised, and also as brilliant. As much as she was uncomfortable in the house he occupied, Jane found the conversation stimulating. Their topics ranged from politics to poetry to music to glamour and all the ways in which they intersected.

They were not expected to be at the glass factory on the last evening that the poet was in Venice, so they spent it with him. A conversation on the topic of inspiration led by leaps to the role of muses, and then to the theft of fire and to Prometheus.

As if to exhibit the effect of inspiration, Vincent leapt up and pulled handfuls of glamour around himself. The form of Prometheus coalesced around him, with deft strokes that showed no sign of his injury. Jane, seeing what he was about, also rose and cloaked herself in a *Sphère Obscurcie* to weave eagles, which swooped down to pluck the liver from his side.

Compared to the necessary precision of the work that they had been doing with the glass, it was a pure joy to work so unfettered. Her breath quickened as the eagle soared aloft, but it was no strain to hold the threads. Jane took a breath and made the eagle dive again—no easy task—and was rewarded as Vincent answered her efforts by opening the hand of his creation and having fire appear within it.

They held the spontaneous *tableau vivant* for a span of some moments, Jane's heart beating quickly with excitement as much as from the effects of glamour. In silent accord, they released their threads at the same moment and reappeared out of the dissolving glamour.

Those few assembled guests applauded, calling out approbation for particular elements. Then Lord Byron sat forward in his chair, pushing aside the young woman draped over him, his eyes intent upon Vincent.

Many are Glamourists without acclaim.
Yet what is Glamour but to create
From naught but illusory light; and aim
At an ephemeral life beyond our fate,
And be the new Prometheus to attain,
The noble fire from Heaven, and then, too late,
Finding the pleasure given repaid with pain,
And vultures to the heart of the bestower,
Who, having lavished his high gift in vain,
Lies to his lone rock by the sea-shore?
So be it: we can bear. —But thus all know
Who chance to behold an o'ermastering glamour
One noble stroke with a whole life may glow,
Or deify the ether till it shine
With beauty so surpassing all below,
That they who kneel to Idols so divine
Break no commandment, for high Heaven is there
Transfused, transfigurated: and the line
Of Glamour, which peoples but the air
With Thought and Beings of our thought reflected,
Can do no more: let the glamourist share
The palm, he shares the peril, and dejected
Faints o'er the labour unapproved—Alas!
Despair and Genius are too oft connected.

The room fell silent. Jane put a hand to her chest, overwhelmed by the remorse that his poem conjured. As much as anything else, she felt desire—a desire to create a work that could move the observer as much as his words had inspired her. It was perhaps only the repetition of the work with the glass, but in that moment, she felt that their experiments were mere irrelevant technique.

"I should probably write that down." Lord Byron laughed and picked up his glass of champagne. He drank it all, and turned to the young woman who had been draped over him, giving in to a more immediate impulse.

Jane recalled that evening when their next appointed time to work with Signor Querini arrived. Though the work with the glass was tedious, their control over the effect improved with each effort and they could more accurately predict the size of the finished glamour.

The attempts to create other patterns proved less effective because there was little time before the glass had cooled too much to take the pattern of glamour, but, even so, the results interested Jane. They produced one glass which, in sunlight, displayed a partially sketched tulip floating above it. If they could master this technique, then perhaps some day glamours like the lion at Trieste could be recorded in their entirety instead of fading away with the passage of time.

After finishing one evening at the glass factory, they arrived at Ca' Sanuto so late that all the windows were already dark. They had been unable to return with the glass from their previous session until it had finished tempering, so in the morning Jane turned her attention to the spheres from earlier efforts. On their days off, she and Vincent had been attempting to write an account of their discoveries about working with glass. Jane's eyes were crossing with the difficulty of expressing in words the concepts involved in the glamour they had been working. She cleaned her quill, thinking about how to explain the relationship between the entry point of the glamour in the glass and the shape that resulted.

Vincent put his hands on her shoulders and leaned down to kiss her on the neck. "We have been at this for nearly two hours, Muse."

"Is that why my back is stiff?"

"Likely so." He picked up her quill and applied his pen-knife to its tip. "May I tempt you away? A walk might do us both good."

Jane nodded and cast sand over the page to blot the ink. "Likely so. I feel as though my brain were pudding."

"Pudding. Hm . . . What sort of pudding? Plum?"

"Suet, I think." Jane pushed her chair back and stood, stretching until the straps of her short stays dug into her shoulders.

"Salty. I would not have expected that of you." Vincent squinted at the pen and tried the tip with his thumb.

"I shall blame any saltiness in my language on you."

He laughed and closed his penknife. With a sidelong glance at Jane, he set the pen and knife down upon the table. She was fairly certain that they were done writing for the day. "I have my doubts about your salty language. Will you demonstrate?"

Jane blushed; then her colour heightened with annoyance that she was blushing at all. This was her husband, after all. She cleared her throat. "You have said nothing of whether you like your pudding with . . . gravy?" Her skin fairly burned, but she could not restrain a giggle.

Vincent chuckled with delight and picked her up, spinning her. "That is *not* salty."

"It is!" Jane squeezed his side with her fingers.

Twisting away, her ticklish husband yelped with sudden laughter and almost dropped her in his hurry to set her down. "No, truly. It is not."

"It is." Her fingers sought his sides again.

Vincent folded in half, twisting away from her, with his arms tight to his ribs. She found ways past his defences, and he fled across the room in breathless mirth. The corners of his eyes bent in tight wrinkles of amusement as he snorted in response to her efforts.

Something in the distance crashed, with the sound of wood splintering. Startled at the noise, Jane stopped her pursuit. Vincent stepped away from her, frowning. "Was that in the palazzo?"

"I am uncertain." Jane tilted her head, listening for further disturbances.

A man shouted, clearly inside the palazzo. Heavy footfalls, of more than one person, echoed off the marble below. Vincent held out his hand to Jane. "Will you wait here, Muse?"

"No, of course not."

"There are days when I wish you were not as stubborn as I am."

"Then your wish is granted every day, because no one could be as stubborn as you."

He snorted as she followed him to the door of their apartments. Still, Jane stayed back when he cracked the door to peer out. The shouting continued, but now some words were clear. "Search," and "escape," and—most chilling—"Sanuto."

Vincent's breath hissed out of him. "Whatever business he was caught up with has found him."

"Or not. It sounds as though they are searching."

Nodding, Vincent put his eye to the door again. His face had the same worried frown that she felt on her own. "At least one man is in a policeman's uniform."

Jane waited until he pulled back from the door and eased it closed. "What should we do?"

"I do not know. We know things, told to us in confidence, that we should not, and yet . . ." Vincent knotted his hand in his hair before continuing. "If they are here, it seems to me that he is probably not at the bank. Perhaps he got word of the search and has fled?"

"Or is unaware, and about to walk into . . . whatever this is."

Outside, the noises of the search continued. At least four men called to each other as they went through the palazzo. It would only be a matter of minutes before they reached Jane and Vincent's apartments. Jane turned to look at the cabinet where they had stored the *Verres Obscurcis,* wrapped in velvet.

Vincent gazed at the same cabinet, as if he had a similar thought. They could use them to hide upon the balcony. The day was sunny enough that the glamour caught in glass would make them invisible.

Jane took a step away from the door. The events reminded her so much of being in Binché that the urge to hide became very strong. She crossed the room and pulled open the drawer in which they kept the *Sphères.*

It was empty.

"Vincent!"

He crossed far enough to see the empty drawer. Whites

showed all the way around his eyes. He cursed softly, turning away.

The footsteps in the hall approached their door. Vincent set his shoulders, walked to the door, and pulled it open. "Good afternoon. May I help you?"

The man in the hall wore a policeman's uniform. His long black coat flared around white trousers as he spun. He took a step back in surprise at Vincent's appearance. With a rattle, he drew his sabre and pointed it at Vincent. The *polizia* called over his shoulder in Italian. "I have them."

Jane pressed her hands to her chest and willed her heart to slow down. For his part, Vincent stood very still with his hands out from his side. Matching him, Jane used her gentlest voice to ask, "What is happening?"

The *polizia* said nothing, merely kept his guard up. Moments later, the other three policemen they had heard arrived at the door. One of them stepped forward and rudely felt at Vincent's waist for a knife or sword. Finding nothing, he turned out Vincent's pockets and removed all the coins, loose ends, and bits of paper that a gentleman might carry. He seemed disappointed to find nothing more dangerous.

A fifth man walked slowly up the stairs, dressed in the severe uniform of a Venetian chief of police. The *capo di polizia*'s feet made almost no sound in their thin kidskin boots.

He stopped at the top of the stairs and raised an eyebrow. "David Vincent?"

"The same."

"You are charged with trespass, fraud, intent to commit fraud, forgery, and impersonation of a nobleman."

Jane gasped. "You are mistaken, sir. We were invited here by Signor Sanuto."

The man's gaze turned toward her, but his face remained coolly smooth. "There has not been a Signor Sanuto in over fifty years. The line ended when the last male heir died of syphilis. If you are going to choose an alias, I might suggest one that is not so easy to discover."

"An alias? But . . . but, no. Signor Sanuto is the man who lives here. He is a senior partner at Banco de Giro. We went to the bank with him and took out a line of credit. You may ask them."

"The same bank you are accused of defrauding. Really, madam, I must thank you for incriminating yourself in this manner." He took out a small pocketbook and a pencil. Wetting the lead on his tongue, he began to write.

"*Capo*, sir." The *polizia* who had searched Vincent held out a folded piece of paper.

The *capo* took the promissory note that Signor Sanuto had returned to them and raised his eyebrows again as he opened it. "Another forgery? Really. You have been industrious."

Jane took a step toward him. "But we—"

Vincent turned his head. "Jane."

The weight in his voice stopped her. His face was still and composed. In his youth, before Vincent had cast off his family name, his father had made him study law. Jane could see her husband pulling that part of his past forward and wrapping it around himself like the strands of a *tableau vivant*. With this character assumed, Vincent turned to face the *capo* with his hands still held out from his body. She could not see his face, but she could hear the grave courtesy in his voice.

"Sir. I believe that my wife and I have been the victims of a swindler. Might we have the privilege of showing what evidence we may in our favour?"

The *capo* stared at Vincent, his pencil held above the page. "This is an interesting manoeuvre. I admit to curiosity." He folded the note book and tucked it back into his pocket. "Very well. What do you have to offer me?"

"We met a man calling himself Giacomo Sanuto while we were taking a ship to Venice. The ship was set upon by pirates—"

The *capo* barked a laugh. "There are no pirates on the Gulf of Venice."

"I have been made aware of this." Vincent inclined his head in the smallest of bows. His voice grew tighter and more formal. "Be that as it may, we were taken through the customs office at the port, as were the other passengers on the boat. Even if Sanuto has arranged for there to be no record of him, then one of the passengers will be able to confirm that he was aboard."

The *capo* gestured to the officers. "Bring them, please. Gently." He gave Jane a mocking bow. "I have no wish to have you escape, but neither will I be needlessly cruel."

Jane wished to say something clever, but knew not how.

Jane and Vincent were loaded into a small boat with the *capo* facing them for the ride across the lagoon to Venice. Jane kept her hands folded on her lap and tried to maintain a tranquil countenance, though her mind was anything but composed. As soon as Lord Byron pointed out the disparity with the ransom, they should have left Signor Sanuto—she did not even know what name to curse, since that was clearly an assumed one. Whose clothes had Jane been wearing? It was a trivial question, but Jane found herself fixing on it rather than the larger concern. If she let her mind approach too near the question of what would happen to them, she felt close to panic.

Vincent sat by her side, with a space between them so that the officers did not think them about to try anything untoward. His hands, likewise, were clasped in front of him, but his head was bent in thought. A muscle clenched repeatedly at the corner of his jaw.

The boat drew up in front of a tall brick building with a grassy plot in front of it and steps leading down to the water. Porters ran to and fro pushing carts piled with goods. Clerks walked the steps, noting the ships tied up there in their tally books. Jane did not recognise any of it.

"Where are we?"

"The port offices." The *capo* raised his eyebrows in surprise. "That is where you said you wished to go, is it not?"

"But this is not . . . this is not where we were taken."

Vincent raised his head. He studied the building and then half-turned towards her. "I was not fully conscious, so it is up to you, Muse."

She felt the sound of her pet name as though it were a steadying hand upon her back. Jane drew herself up and attempted to rally her senses. "We were taken to a warehouse. The exterior was red, and it stank of fish." Jane closed her eyes, trying to recall their arrival. "When we came in, Piazza San Marco was to our left, and the building faced the lagoon on the far side of the Grand Canal."

The *capo* stared at her, a slight frown creasing his otherwise unyielding mask. Nodding slowly, he directed the crew to attempt to find the building that Jane described. They rowed along the canal and she sagged in her seat when the building appeared. A part of her had feared that Sanuto would have somehow spirited it away.

They tied up to the dock in short order. Vincent followed the *capo* out of the boat and reached back to help Jane up to the dock. His hand was on hers, warm and comforting. Never had she been so glad that her husband eschewed gloves. She took comfort from the pressure of his hand against hers.

Then the officers forced them apart. Her skin tingled where he had held her, as if they were still connected. Jane's breathing slowed and steadied. As shocking as this was, they would be all right. They had faced greater hardship than this.

The *capo* opened the door to the red warehouse and ducked inside. Vincent and Jane followed him, with the officers close behind. It took a moment for Jane's eyes to adjust to the dim interior.

It still stank of fish, but the crates and boxes were gone. In fact, the space was empty of everything save a broken cart in one corner piled with a torn fishing net.

There was no evidence that it had ever been anything except a warehouse.

Ten

Want and Abundance

The *capo* took them next to Banco de Giro.
It was in the building Signor Sanuto had taken
them to, but the bank had no knowledge of
him. They did recall the incident when an older
gentleman had slipped on the stairs, but he had
said that he was an agent of Vincent's. That
was when the forgeries began.

Without comment, the *capo* had loaded
them back into the boat and returned with
them to Murano, where the bulk of their creditors remained. The station house he took them
to sat off Murano's Grand Canal and had a full
complement of *polizia* standing outside. The
badge of the Kingdom of Lombardy-Venetia
was emblazoned on the wall over the hearth.
Light from an enclosed courtyard shone merrily

through the windows on to a large desk, as though to mock them.

The *capo* slid a paper across the desk. "Is this from your banker?"

Vincent picked it up and looked more ill than he had since they had been at sea. His skin turned grey, and all the vitality seemed to suck out of his skin. "It is." The paper in his hand trembled slightly as he handed it to Jane.

It took her a moment to understand the substance of the letter.

My dear Sir David,

I have received your letter of 9 September with some dismay. While it is fully within your rights to withdraw the funds that you have placed with us at any time, I had hoped that we could continue . . .

"All of it?" Jane stared again at the letter, trying to will the words "placed the whole of your account" to mean anything other than what it did. She looked again at the date of the letter that their banker said he had received. "This is the day we arrived here."

Vincent's mouth twisted in a grimace. "The clerk in the—in what we thought was the customs house had me sign and date several papers. I have no doubt that one of them was used to forge a letter to our banker."

"That letter"—the *capo* beckoned for Jane to return it to him—"is the thing that makes me believe you might be victims of this as well."

Jane sat up, feeling the first rush of hope since the police arrived that morning. With each new discovery, Jane had become more stupefied. She felt only shame that she had been so duped by events that were, upon reflection, perfectly evident. "Sir, we are—"

"I said, *might* be victims." He gestured to the other papers on his desk. "The line of credit you established with the tailor was a forgery and has your signature. Likewise, you owe money to the dressmaker for Lady Vincent's wardrobe—again, with another forged line of credit. Signor Querini is owed payment for his work for you. The owner of the house in which you have been staying is also demanding a fee for rent, plus damages for your time there and the clothing you wore—which, I might add, we have witnesses for. You might simply be a swindler who was caught, and this letter is your cover story. I have no proof, after all, that you really are Sir David Vincent."

How many ways had they been fools? Vincent could be excused because he had been sorely injured, but she? She had been too trusting. Some part of her wondered if this were even a real *capo*, or real police station, but the material evidence they provided was too strong to be denied, much as she might wish it.

Vincent addressed the floor. "As we have explained, our papers were taken from us aboard the ship."

"Yes. The 'pirate' attack."

"What of the British consul?" Jane asked. "He can vouch that we are who we say."

"If he were here. Mr. Hoppner is, in fact, the first person I attempted to contact when these trespasses came to light. He is, alas, out of town."

"With Lord Byron." Vincent scrubbed his face with both hands and gave a wretched chuckle. "Of course. May I ask how you were made aware of the crimes?"

The *capo* tapped his pencil upon his note book. "We received a hint." He shifted in his chair. "This seems an elaborate scheme for the small amount of money that your banker transferred. Would they have had reason to suspect you had more?"

The small amount of money? They had near five thousand pounds saved. But when Jane reflected on what it must have cost to arrange the pirate attack, it did seem incredible that they had made the attempt. "Perhaps they were after the other passengers' funds as well?"

The *capo* said nothing, merely gazed at Jane so coolly that she had the sudden suspicion that there were no other passengers. Vincent suppressed a curse and bent his head again.

"You have thought of something, sir?" The *capo* raised his eyebrows.

"Merely comprehending the situation." Vincent knotted his hands together so tightly that his tendons stood out. "What will you do with us?"

The *capo* sat back in his chair and pressed the pencil to his mouth, as though using it to quiet himself. He sighed and lowered his hands. "That is the question, is it not?" He gestured to the papers on the desk. "I do not think that you are anything but naive victims in this, but you owe upwards of two thousand pounds to various creditors. Have you family you can apply to for aid?"

Jane's throat was dry as she answered. "They are travelling. They were bound for the Dalmatian coast when we parted."

"And you, sir?"

"My family and I are estranged." Vincent made his small noise of protest, near inaudible even to Jane. It was as though he had imperfectly held his breath and a small stream of air leaked out as he thought. He straightened. "I can write to the Prince Regent and request an advance on a project we will be creating for him. And meanwhile, I am—we are both—professional glamourists. Tomorrow I shall seek employment to pay our debts."

"From whom?"

"I—I have not yet had the opportunity to explore that."

"And have you any credentials? Letters of recommendation?" The *capo* remained placid, yet Jane could feel his disapprobation as clearly as if he had stated it. "I think you will find it rather more difficult than you might expect."

"Difficult or not, what choice do we have?" Jane said.

The *capo* grunted, but betrayed nothing else of his thoughts. He then removed some sheets of paper from his desk and slid them across to Jane and Vincent. "I expect you will want to write some letters."

"Thank you, sir." Vincent rose to take the paper and looked at it, frowning.

Jane shared his concern. Letters within England were often expensive, but the cost was paid by the recipient. To send a letter between countries required either asking an acquaintance who was travelling to that country or paying for the service. They had no resources in either regard.

"Have you recommendations for a courier?" Jane was not certain why she asked, since they could not afford such a thing. And yet, what other choice did they have?

"Write your letters and instruct the replies to return here. I will send them for you." It was an exceptional kindness. Or was it meant to grant control over their correspondence? The *capo* leaned back in his chair and steepled his fingers in front of him. "Meanwhile, though I would be fully justified in putting you into debtors' prison, I shall not hold you. However, because you might still prove to be swindlers, you may not leave Murano until your debts are cleared. It is too easy to catch a ship from Venice. I will circulate your descriptions to our gondoliers, to ensure that you remain here. I shall also require you to report daily until such time as your debts are repaid." He gestured to the officer who had searched Vincent's pockets. "*Gendarme* Gallo will receive your report."

It was more fair than Jane had any right to expect. They thanked him profusely, but all the while Jane wondered how they would manage. They had no funds and no friends at all. The only resources they had were the clothes upon their backs, and even those they owed money for.

Jane and Vincent stood on the street in front of the station house for a moment, both of them too stunned to do much more. They had been released, but released to where? They were not allowed to leave the island of Murano. Even if they could gain entrance to Lord Byron's apartments, those were in Venice. Jane took Vincent's hand, for her own comfort as much as for his.

He looked down with some surprise from wherever he had been lost in thought. His skin still had an unnatural pallor. He squeezed her hand. Jane began to walk. She knew not where she was going, only that she did not wish to remain in front of the station house any longer, lest the *capo* decide that he had made a mistake and imprison then after all.

"Why did you curse when he asked us if the swindlers might have thought we had more money than we did?"

"Because our glass would have . . . It could be sold to a military bidder."

A chill spread from the base of Jane's stomach. "How? I mean, how could they have known?"

"Sanuto. Pretending to be a spy. It played exactly upon my sympathies. He had to have known about my work for the Crown."

"That is common knowledge, though, after the trial. Or rather, it is known that you were an agent for the Crown, but not what you did, and certainly nothing about the *Verre Obscurci*. Unless—do you think . . . Mathieu?"

Vincent shook his head. She could just hear his hiss of distress over their footfalls. "I think it was me."

"But you—when Napoleon's men had you . . . you said nothing." He had been flogged. She had watched from a hill, unable to do anything, as they tried to beat the information out of him.

"My desk. Recall?"

Jane gasped with the recollection. When Lieutenant Segal came for Vincent in Binché, he took the travel desk that her husband had carried. It had contained their notes about the glass and their efforts with it. Scanty, to be sure, but enough to see what they were considering. She let her breath out slowly. "And I wrote out more notes just this morning, which they must also have."

Vincent cursed again. "We should never have stayed with Sanuto."

His vehemence stung, reminding her that she had been the one to urge that they remain at the palazzo. She protested, "How could we have known?"

"But we did, the moment that Byron pointed out the inconsistencies in the pirate attack. I should have known—I *did* know—and should have urged us to leave."

"Is the fault mine, then? Oh yes—yes, I can see that." The sarcastic words rose in response to his implication, and her own sense of guilt. "*I* urged you to be forgiving. So it is then my fault that we are in this state."

"I would not have said so, no."

Jane stopped, pulling her hand out of his. Just barely did she manage to check the angry words that flew to her lips, and lock her jaws tight around her response. Vincent halted a few paces further and bent his head. He held his hands out from his sides in a gesture that spoke eloquently of his helplessness.

When he spoke, his voice was rough. "Jane, I am sorry. That was uncalled for, and not true. I trusted him, too. By his design."

With care, she said, "Allow me to suggest that attempting to discover which of us is more at fault will not help us with our present situation."

He rubbed his face, before lifting his head. "Thank you for your patience, Muse. I am . . ." He clenched his fists and stared at a flower box in the closest window, as though it demanded all of his attention. "I am distressed. Being in debt reminds me too much of the days after I first cast off my family name. My father predicted that I would wind up in penury, performing on a street somewhere." He forced a laugh that fooled Jane not at all.

Thought of in those terms, though, it was not at all surprising that Vincent was struggling with his sensibilities. Jane was distressed as well but did not have Vincent's history with his father to add to the burden of feeling. Yet she had allowed her emotion to carry her tongue as much as his had.

Jane reclaimed his hand. "I am anxious, too. My only hope now is that we do not discover that I have inherited my mother's nerves."

"That seems unlikely." He tucked her hand under his arm and resumed their walk. Most of the day had vanished to answering questions and then raising others.

Indeed, the remaining questions focused her attention on the parts of Murano that she habitually let her gaze glide past.

The beggar sitting at the base of a bridge. Children in much-patched clothing playing in a doorway. A juggler tossing balls for a few coins. And the pastry shop. Every time they passed a shop redolent with the smell of baked goods, her gaze would drift to the sticky rolls, her stomach would clench in hunger, and she would remember that they had no money at all. The officer who had turned Vincent's pockets out had left them with nothing.

How had the *capo* thought they would make their way in this state? It was not his concern, so she supposed that he did not trouble himself with such questions. Jane tried to think of what they should do to attend to their immediate needs. She had never been on the receiving end of charity, though her family had always made certain to take care of the poor on her father's estate. But she could hardly expect a gentleman's daughter to suddenly appear on her threshold with a basket of produce and eggs. They wanted even a threshold.

Lady Stratton, the mother of Melody's husband, often went on charitable errands, but Jane had no notion at all where the lists of those in need came from. In her own household, her father had assembled the list from . . . somewhere. There must be, then, a way to apply for aid. The vicar in their neighbourhood did much charitable work. There were poorhouses enough, though her only knowledge of them was through fiction. They could not be as awful as Mrs. Radcliffe's novels made them appear, but she found herself reluctant to seek one. Even if they were not full of bugs and squalor, she and Vincent would be separated, and that could not be borne at the present moment. "I think . . . I think we need to find a church."

"Eh? Why?"

"Because they are used to dealing with the poor and will know where we can sleep tonight."

He seemed to hold his breath for a moment. "Of course. That makes good sense."

"And yet you hesitate."

"Only because I find myself unprepared to trust anyone who is kind."

Murano had churches in abundance. The structures seemed part of the fabric of the island, though they varied widely in style from a fifteenth-century convent to a modern structure built no more than fifty years prior. None of them were Anglican. Jane's feelings with regard to Catholics had changed considerably over the course of the last year, so it was not a question of *if* they would seek aid at a Catholic church but of which one. The Vincents needed only to turn another corner to encounter additional choices.

Though neither would admit it, there was a certain amount of fear involved in begging for the first time. And there was nothing else that Jane could name their task. The first church she felt comfortable approaching was a humble structure save for its glorious stained glass, which seemed essential in the Murano churches. Of all the churches they had seen, this one reminded her somewhat of home, with a vine clinging to the stucco walls of the church's clock tower.

After the brilliant afternoon light, which had reflected off the displays of glass on the street, the dim interior gave a soothing welcome. Jane felt her shoulders soften a little. Vincent, too, seemed to walk easier in the interior of the church. Along the walls, candles burned under small altars to Mary and saints that Jane did not recognise. The crucifix that hung at the front of the church had a gentle glamour about it so it shone as if with its own light.

Scattered on the pews, a few old women and one man with the curved spine of the very elderly sat with their heads bowed in prayer. Jane looked around for any sign of the vic—no, of the priest, or for someone who could tell them where he might be found.

Fortunately, the priest was instantly distinguishable by his long black cassock. He appeared to be in his middle years, with a slight belly and very red cheeks. His hair had once been brown, but had faded to the colour of nothing. At the sound of Vincent's boot upon the stone floor, the priest turned round. His eyebrows raised in a slight question, as if wondering why these two people, who were not part of his congregation, had arrived.

Vincent dipped his head in lieu of touching his hat. In Italian, he said, "Good afternoon, Padre. We are . . . we are in need of advice and possibly aid. If you have a moment?"

"Of course." The priest tucked his hands over his little belly and waited.

Gesturing to Jane, Vincent hesitated. She could see him trying and disposing of several sentences before he said bluntly, "My wife and I have been robbed and have no money for lodgings. Do you know of a place where we might stay the night?"

The priest frowned and shook his head. He looked to Jane with some sympathy. "Lost it all gambling, has he?"

Vincent flushed a deep red. Jane put her hand on his arm to still his chagrin. "No sir. He has over-simplified, perhaps. We were victims of a swindler, but I assure you that this was not my husband's fault."

The priest shook his head again, clearly not believing her. His gaze darted to Vincent and then back to her. "I have heard many such tales as yours, from gentlemen who found the pleasures of Venice to be more expensive than—"

"I do not lay wagers, sir." Vincent's voice was low and sharp.

The priest raised his eyebrows and turned his attention again to Jane. "How long have you been in Murano, madam?"

Jane took a breath to calm herself. They had few places to turn, and they needed this man's help. "We have been in Murano these three weeks."

"And you have made no acquaintances in that time?"

His scrutiny of their situation angered Jane, and yet made her feel unaccountably embarrassed, as though they were at fault for having been robbed. "We were, the entire time, with the gentleman who misled us. The English consul is not in residence at the moment, or we would apply to him for assistance."

"And the *capo di polizia?* Did you report this to him?"

It would be more accurate to say that he had reported it to them, but Jane inclined her head.

"And what did he say?"

Vincent flecked a piece of lint off his sleeve. "He blamed us for being fools, quite as much as you do. Were I left to my own devices, I would sleep outside tonight, but my wife—" His breath sounded suddenly unsteady. "Are you able to help us, sir? Please."

Stomach knotting at his distress, Jane reached for Vincent's hand. His palm was slick with sweat, but cold.

"Of course." The priest pulled a small scrap of paper and a lead pencil out of his pocket. He scribbled on it for a moment. "If you will take this to Signora Celsi, we can arrange a bed for your wife. It will be a roof over her head, if not what she is accustomed to."

"And my husband?" Jane twisted her wedding ring, an idea slowly coming to her for if there were no lodging for Vincent.

"He is able-bodied and male. Venice's charities are intended to provide means for those who cannot fend for themselves. Women, children, and the lame or ill."

"Then I thank you for your time and charity." Jane curtsied, without taking the paper.

"Jane. Truly. I can sleep outside one night."

"No."

Vincent took the paper from the priest. "Thank you, sir. If you will excuse us—"

But the priest had already turned back to attending the small altar. Stepping out into the courtyard again, Jane was surprised to see that the sun had not yet set. It seemed that the interview with the priest had taken a lifetime. Vincent exhaled heavily.

"I feel much the same." The energy that they had given to banter on the way to the church had dissipated, and left Jane feeling flat and painfully aware that they had been taken from the palazzo before breaking their fast. The tightness of her stomach contributed to her general anxiety.

"I have slept out of doors before. It will do me no harm."

Jane linked her arm through his and encouraged him to step away from the church. "But it will harm *me*. I have read too many novels and cannot shake the idea that if we are separated, we shall not see each other again."

"Ah, but true love will always triumph. Is that not what the novels say?"

"Yes, but we are in the land of Romeo and Juliet."

"What a happy thought *that* is." He tilted his head back to study the sky. "Jane, stay in the church lodgings. It looks to be a dry night so do not worry. It is only one night."

"Are you certain of that? Because I am not. Even if we find work tomorrow, do you have reasonable expectation of receiving payment on the same day?"

"I—No. So then it is more than one night. Still, that is not so—"

"No." Jane stopped them in front of a shop. "I read the newspapers. People who sleep on the streets are killed, and I will not—you cannot ask me to—I cannot abide the thought of you doing so, not when we have another choice."

"All right. What do you propose?"

"We sell my wedding ring—" Jane raised her hand to check the objection that rose instantly to his lips. "I spent two weeks without it and was no less married to you. When our funds are restored, we can repurchase it. Meanwhile, it will offer us the opportunity to find some lodgings and keep us from being so desperate that you are actually contemplating sleeping on the street."

Vincent's face undertook a clear struggle to restrain strong emotions. He turned—first his face, then his body—away from Jane as though to hide the effort of retaining his composure, until his turn brought him to face the store she had stopped them in front of. A pawnshop. He stood as one transfixed. "I—I cannot."

"And I cannot take shelter knowing that you are outside. So we are at an impasse."

"Jane, I made a vow to provide for you. Your father trusted me with you. To sell your—" His voice broke as if he were incapable of completing the thought.

"We made vows to care for each other. And as for my father, he will understand fully."

"I do not know that *I* do."

She hated adding to the distress of the day, but she was also quite certain that she was right. The ring was a symbol—and an important one, yes—but it was not their marriage. That needed nothing outward to cement it. "Do you love me?"

"You know I do."

"And did you love me when I did not wear your ring?"

"Why must you use logic?"

She ignored his weak protest and pressed her advantage. "Further, you gave me this ring. Considering your theory that a husband's role is to provide for his wife, it can be argued that selling this ring is, in fact, an extension of the care that you provide for me. Also, it gives me an opportunity to fulfil my own wedding vows to love you for richer, or for poorer."

"I had thought we already lived through the 'for worse' portion of our vows." Vincent gave a sigh that was closer to a groan. "It is difficult not to feel that I have failed as your husband."

"You have not. Sanuto took many things, but not my faith in you. Do not let him take your faith in our marriage."

"Ah, Muse . . ."

He let her steer him to the pawnshop and only hung back a little as they entered. When it came time to negotiate with the pawnbroker, Vincent proved to be a shrewd haggler. While the sum they arrived at was nowhere near the worth of the ring, it still managed to be respectable enough to allow them to secure a furnished room above a grocer. The remaining coins were tucked away for the day when they would repurchase the ring.

The room was up two narrow flights of stairs, nestled under the eaves of a roof. The plaster of the walls was largely intact, and the linens on the bed, though worn, were clean. A single table stood crammed between the bed and the wall, with a chair tucked under it. Across from it, a small hearth provided a draught for the room. Their wardrobe consisted of five wooden pegs on the wall. That comprised their furniture.

When they were at last in the room, with the door shut and the single candle lit, Vincent stood in the gable at the window. He stared out across Murano. "Well . . . at least we do not have to tell your mother that we were attacked by pirates."

Eleven

An Accomplished Lady

Jane startled awake.

Beside her Vincent gave a strangled cry, as if a scream were escaping from his dreams. It had been months since his sleep had been disordered, but not so long that she did not immediately recognise his state. Jane half sat, and pressed a hand against his chest. A fine film of sweat covered him, and his heart beat against his rib cage. Moonlight through the window showed a hard line between his brows.

"Vincent?" She rubbed his chest, trying to wake him gently. "Vincent. It is a dream."

He tensed; then his eyes dragged open and the tightness eased out of him. Vincent sagged under her hands. He wet his lips. "Thank you."

Jane curled against him, resting her head on his shoulder, and he shifted to wrap his arm around her and pull her closer. She put one hand on his fore-head to try to smooth the creases that remained there. "The old nightmares?"

"A variation, I think." He closed his eyes and sighed. "That feels pleasant."

"What was it?"

She felt his shrug under her cheek. "I could not find you. And . . . a ship? No. Perhaps a warehouse . . . It is fading already. It does not matter."

"Can I do anything?"

He shook his head, rustling the pillowcase. "You do enough already." Vincent took her hand and kissed it. He rolled onto his side with his back to her and pulled her arm around him, cradling her hand against his chest.

With her other hand, Jane traced the visible scars on his back, left from his encounter with Napoleon's men. The scars left by Sanuto were not visible, but were no less deep for it.

Neither of them slept well. Even apart from Vincent's nightmare, every time Jane rolled over, it seemed that a different piece of straw in the mattress found its way through the ticking. The bed, too, was not quite wide enough for both of them to lie prone: one of them must always be on their side or tucked under the other. When the sun rose, so did she, and so did Vincent.

Her stomach growled to announce that it was awake as well. They had been so tired upon reaching their room that seeking food had seemed an overwhelming task. Today, though, she would have to find something for them. Jane stared at the small grate in the hearth and rubbed her hair in consternation. She had never cooked anything more than toast and water for tea.

Well . . . as they had neither bread nor a kettle, she would not be making either of those enormously complicated dishes. She turned to the chemise that she had worn the day before and began to dress. As she slipped it over her head, she wrinkled her nose at the sour smell. Jane realized that she had no notion of how to launder it. Frowning, she said, "I am beginning to wish that I had somewhat more practical accomplishments."

"Hm?" Vincent stood by the window, buttoning his trousers. "You are very accomplished."

"Music, glamour, painting . . . but I do not know how to cook or to do the washing, which, you must admit, would be more useful in our present circumstances."

"Glamour has proved useful thus far in our marriage."

"True, and probably will be so again." Today, they could begin to try to find work. Jane had no notion of how to go about that, since all of their commissions in England had come from referrals or people already familiar with Vincent's work. It had never occurred to her to wonder about what his early career was like. She had only known him after he established himself. "When you first started as a glamourist, how did you find work?"

"Hm? Oh. I had recommendations from Herr Scholes and J. M. W. Turner of the Royal Academy. Prinny, too, once he heard what I was about, though that came later."

"And today . . . without letters of recommendation, how should we proceed?"

He pulled his waistcoat on. "We? I thought to do this alone—not because I think I am more able, but because for small jobs it is unlikely that anyone would require two glamourists."

"And you are a man."

"This is not a matter of masculine pride."

"I meant that they will take you more seriously. For all that glamour is considered a womanly art, the only professionals are gentlemen, as with dancing and painting."

Vincent opened his mouth and then closed it again. He snorted. "Do you know, I had not realized that. But of course it makes sense, because women are not required to have a profession in the way that men are."

"I think that may be true for women of gentle birth, but certainly we have seen maids enough. To say nothing of cooks, dressmakers, and milliners."

"True . . ." he said slowly, as if considering her words. "But, our partnership aside, it is still more natural for a woman to remain at home."

Jane sighed, rubbing her forehead. Under other circumstances, she would be very tempted to give him a copy of Mary Wollstonecraft's *The Rights of Women.* In the moment, though, she felt unequal to the task of explaining the thesis. "When we are back in England, I have a book I should like you to read. For the moment . . . you have a valid point that you are more likely to find work as a glamourist than I am."

"I won a point? I shall have to record that."

His humour cheered her more for its attempt than for the joke itself. Jane shook her finger at him, then came to help him with his cravat. It was wrinkled and had lost most of the stiffness of its starch, so though Jane tied it as best as she could, no one could mistake Vincent for a young gentleman of fashion. "I am going out with you, however, to see if I can find some employment of my own."

"Muse, you do not need to—"

"Yes, I do."

Vincent stopped arguing, though he did shake his head. He was smiling as he did, so Jane let it pass. They climbed down the narrow stairs and stepped onto the street. By mutual agreement, they made their way toward the main canal, where most of the larger residences and businesses were situated. As they walked, Vincent explained that his plan was to go door to door and attempt to demonstrate his abilities in lieu of a letter of recommendation. In truth, he said, even with a letter, he still almost always had to display his talents.

Then he slowed and pulled her to the side, toward an aged church of brick, which sat close to the canal upon a wide green lawn. "Is that . . . is that the church that Sanuto wanted a donation for?"

The stone engraved above it said SANTA MARIA DEGLI ANGELI. Jane tried to recall, but had only heard the name in one conversation. "Perhaps?"

"Huh. I had expected that it, too, would not exist." He rubbed his hair into a wilderness. "I wonder if they know. Or, for that matter, if they are involved."

Jane spied a nun working in a small vegetable garden by the side of the church. Without being entirely certain what it would accomplish beyond gratifying her curiosity, Jane walked up to the iron fence that stood around the church grounds. "Pardon me—"

The nun looked up and favoured her with a smile. "Yes?"

Jane had a moment of surprise that beneath her wimple, the nun had the clear brown complexion and lively dark eyes of a mulatto. She wore a heavy canvas apron over her habit and had a basket of vegetables by her side. Wiping her hands on the apron, she approached the fence. "May I help you?"

"This is an odd question, but do you know a Signor Sanuto?"

The nun frowned and shook her head. "I am afraid not, but I rarely leave the convent aside from taking the children to the park. You could ask Sister Aquinata. She has family here and may know people that I do not."

"Oh. Are you not Venetian?"

"Rome before this, but Vienna originally."

"*Ich habe einige Zeit in Wien verbracht,*" Vincent said, and offered her a bow. "*Sie sind ein langer Weg von zu Hause aus.*"

The nun's face lit up at the sound of her native tongue. Though Jane could not understand the conversation that followed, she knew that Vincent had spent time in Vienna when he studied with Herr Scholes. It seemed that they were sharing fond memories about the city, and some introduction must have occurred, because Jane heard her own name at least twice.

After a few moments, they returned to Italian, and the nun was introduced as Sister Maria Agnes. "My apologies, Lady Vincent. With the Hapsburgs in power, German is spoken more frequently here than it used to be, but it has been too long since I have had the pleasure of meeting someone who has been to my home city." She wrinkled her nose and lowered her voice to a collusory whisper. "We are supposed to withdraw from the world when we take our vows, but I can never quite let go of my love of home."

"I am in full sympathy with a love of home."

"Well, come in. I will introduce you to Sister Aquinata, and you can ask her about the gentleman. Although . . . Sir David will have to wait outside. Convent. You understand?"

Jane squeezed Vincent's hand. "If you want to go on, I will meet you back in our room later."

He smiled gratefully and took his leave of Sister Maria Agnes. The nun gathered up her small basket of produce and led Jane to an opening in the gate, which she unlatched so that Jane could step onto the cool green grass. Chattering merrily about Murano and how much she liked the gondolas, the nun kept up a happy string of conversation that pulled Jane along in her wake. She led the way past a small yard in which little girls skipped rope and played under the watchful eye of other nuns. Turning around a corner created by a vine-covered wall, Sister Maria Agnes led Jane into what appeared to be the convent's kitchen.

The nun set her basket down and whisked off her apron. While most of the women had the dark look of Venetians, there was a freckled redhead, and two Africans. As Sister Maria Agnes peered about the room for someone, Jane was overwhelmed by the smell of bread baking. A half-dozen nuns worked with their sleeves rolled up to knead and bake dozens of loaves.

The warm yeasty aroma had more of heaven in it than any perfume. Jane's mouth watered at the thought of the fragrant loaves. Their deep brown crusts had a powdering of flour, even after coming out of the oven. The ones that waited to be baked sat in plump, pale rows on the broad wooden table. When she was finished here, she would have to buy a loaf of bread. And perhaps some cheese.

Sister Maria Agnes saw the direction of Jane's gaze, but misinterpreted the reason. "We contribute to relief for the poor, so most is for that, and the rest is for the orphan house."

Jane pulled her gaze away from the bread. "It must be gratifying to be doing such good works."

"Mostly. Like any occupation, there are times when it can plague you. But the trials are the Lord's way of making you stronger, or at least that is what the Abbess says. Ah—there is Sister Aquinata." She waved, as though to beckon her fellow nun over, but then darted across the room to her. Jane hurried after her and was soon in front of a tall, round nun who wore a flour-splashed apron over her habit and an additional smudge of flour upon her ruddy nose.

"Sister Aquinata, Lady Vincent here is looking for a gentleman that she thinks we might know. What was his name?"

"Signor Sanuto. But he might have used a different name, or he might not have come here at all."

The nun cocked her head and stared into the middle distance. Then, with a shake, she said, "The name is unfamiliar. What does he look like?"

"He has silvering hair and—here." Jane reached for the ether and began a very rough sketch of Signor Sanuto's face in the space between them. Her breath and her heart sped, with a jump in tempo that surprised her. Spots of grey swam at the edges of her vision. Jane continued to work, knowing full well that this was not enough glamour to make her faint.

Then the spots grew darker, and more numerous, and Jane knew that she was wrong.

Jane woke moments after she fell in an ungraceful heap upon the floor. Sister Maria Agnes was still bending down to her, with deep concern. The room spun, but Jane pushed herself up into a sitting position so as not to cause the nuns further alarm. "Forgive me, that is ordinarily well within my limits."

"Sit, sit." Sister Maria Agnes patted Jane's shoulder as if that would somehow heal her. "Water, please? Will someone bring a glass of water?"

"Truly, I am perfectly well." More than anything else, Jane was vexed with herself and somewhat embarrassed. "It is only that I have not eaten since . . ." She broke off, frowning. The night before last? Her mind went to Vincent at once, wondering how he must be faring if he were performing glamour right now.

"Since when, dear?" Sister Maria Agnes helped her up and into a chair that another nun brought over.

Jane rubbed her head, trying to get the spinning to stop. Was this what Vincent had felt like with his concussion? "Night before last, I think."

Sister Aquinata snatched a warm loaf off the table and thrust it at her. "Then you must eat."

"Thank you, but I could no—"

"Yes, you can, and you will." The nun folded her arms

across her ample chest and scowled at her. "I have seen more than my share of half-starved girls come seeking shelter. I know the look. So you will swallow your pride and my bread and you will tell us why you have not eaten for the past two days."

Jane took the warm bread, her hands moving of their own volition. "Only a day and a half." The crust of the fragrant loaf dimpled beneath her fingers, releasing a more intense perfume from its interior.

"And this man had something to do with it, I suppose." The nun nodded toward the glamoured portrait of Sanuto, which Jane had somehow tied off before falling. She did not have a memory of that, but did feel a moment of absurd pride at the mark of her training.

She nodded in answer to the nun's question about the portrait and tore off a small piece of bread, trying to be delicate in her movements. The interior was soft and warm. When Jane took a bite of the simple rye bread, it was the best thing she had ever tasted. Her entire body relaxed round the flavours of sweet sunshine, warm earth, and comfort. She closed her eyes in appreciation.

"Is he your husband?"

Jane's eyes opened with alarm. "No! Oh, no. Not at all. Sister Maria Agnes met my husband."

"I did! Charming man. Studied in Vienna." The nun announced to no one, and everyone.

"This man—he—" And then Jane began to tell the story, in bursts and fragments at first, growing steadier as the gentle attention of the nuns surrounded her. They did not leave off their bread making, but she felt their concern nevertheless.

As she spoke, Sister Aquinata pounded the bread she was kneading with a vehemence that was mighty to behold.

At one point she slammed the dough down on the table. "Do you mean to say that this man used us? Used *our* church to get even more money from you?"

"It does appear that way." Jane had, by this point, eaten a good quarter of the loaf of bread.

"Humph." Sister Aquinata spun away and then returned with a glass of milk, which she slammed down on the table. It sloshed over the sides, a puddle. "Drink that, and then continue."

Jane felt rather like when she was younger and her governess would insist that she take a tonic, except that what Sister Aquinata was offering was delicious instead of vile. Still, she was not a woman to be refused. Taking a sip of the milk, Jane organized her thoughts and then continued the story. She told them everything, leaving out only the nature of the glass spheres that she and Vincent had been working on.

When she was done, an older nun, who had been among those listening and making bread, wiped her hands on her apron and came to stand in front of Jane. Her face was severe, covered by a canvas of wrinkles, and a thread of white hair had escaped from its habit. "You are English, am I correct?"

"Yes, madam."

"Your Italian is very good."

"The credit belongs to my music tutor, who was from Padua. He insisted upon perfect pronunciation."

"You are a glamourist?" When Jane nodded, the nun asked an unexpected question. "Have you ever taught?"

"Only my sister. I have done some small glamour instruction with young girls in the neighbourhood, but have never engaged in a formal course of study." Jane could not fathom where this line of questioning was going.

The nun turned to look across the kitchen. "Sister Maria Agnes?"

The German nun who had first helped them dipped a curtsy. "Yes, Reverend Mother?"

The nun who had questioned Jane about teaching seemed to be the Abbess of the order, and yet she was in the kitchen working with the rest of them. "Do you still need help with the choir?"

"Do I—?" The nun looked confused for a moment, and then glanced at Jane. "Oh—oh, yes. Yes, I do."

Nodding, the Abbess turned back to Jane. "I can pay you fourteen shillings a week, plus a loaf of bread per day. You will assist Sister Maria Agnes with two classes daily, one with the younger girls and one with the older. Are the terms agreeable?"

Jane was not fooled for an instant about their need for a music teacher. Their generosity, simple and direct, made all of Sanuto's duplicity obvious by contrast. "You do not have to do this. You have been more than kind enough already."

"My dear . . . I am not certain if you have noticed this, but we are nuns. This is something that I feel absolutely certain we must do. Besides . . ." The Abbess winked at Jane, an expression that was totally unexpected beneath her severe habit, but which made it clear that the wrinkles she had acquired were from smiling. "Sister Aquinata has been shooting me such looks this past half hour that if I did *not* help you, then one of us would be doing penance for the next week."

"Then, thank you. I accept your generous offer."

A whoop went up from Sister Aquinata and no fewer than three other sisters.

"Good. Do you have any questions?"

She looked around the low, cosy kitchen and at the sisters who were so industriously at work. "Will you . . . will you teach me to make bread?"

Sister Aquinata broke into the first smile Jane had seen from her. "I knew I liked you. Come. Get an apron."

Jane spent much of the day at Santa Maria degli Angeli helping with the baking and then with some mending. The sisters had offered much useful advice on how to face some of the obstacles that lay before Jane and Vincent, ranging from where to find used clothing in good repair to how to make a simple dinner of roasted squash. She had expected them to be so full of piety that laughter would be foreign to them, but it was quite the opposite.

The nuns had sent her home with a small bundle of bread and cheese as an "advance" against her salary. The loaf, wrapped in a piece of cotton sacking, was one she had shaped herself. She had a delicious pride about the warm round of bread. She climbed the stairs to their room, holding her skirt up with one hand and the bread with the other.

Letting herself into the room, she was struck again by the smallness of it. Without standing on her toes, Jane could touch the ceiling at its highest point. And as small as the room was, it seemed to echo when Vincent was not there. The sun was low in the sky, but it was to be expected that he might still be out. She hoped that it was because he had found a commission.

Jane set the bread on the little table, leaving it wrapped in the cloth to retain as much warmth as possible. She wished that Vincent were back so she could share it with him. It was absurd to be so pleased about it, but having a tangible object that she had made with her own hands made Jane feel somehow more at ease. The next weeks would be difficult, but she now had more confidence that they would survive than she had last night.

She paced to the window and looked out. Where was he?

Jane walked the four steps back to the table and felt the bread. Cooling, but still warm. She walked again to the window.

This would never do. She was pacing, and for no reason other than that she had nothing with which to occupy herself. No book, no newspaper, no needlework, and no music. Jane was not well suited for idleness.

Well . . . if nothing else, she could use glamour to mask the meanness of the room, and at least keep her skills in good order.

Vincent arrived long after dark. She heard the unmistakable sound of his tread as he climbed the creaking stairs. Even before he entered, she could tell that he was exhausted. Jane lit the candle stub from the night before—their landlord had said that candles were their own responsibility—and winced at the sudden flare of light.

Vincent paused outside the door. She heard the exhalation

of his breath; then he opened the door briskly, with a smile. "Good evening, Muse."

Jane stood and helped him off with his coat. "I have some bread and cheese, if you are hungry."

"Thank you, that would be most welcome." He lowered himself into their single chair, as though his joints ached. "How was your day?"

"Very good. I spent it with the nuns at Santa Maria degli Angeli." She unwrapped the loaf of bread, now long cold, and slid it over to him. "You have to tear it, I am afraid."

He gave a little grunt of understanding and tore a piece off the end. His broad hands somehow managed to make even such a seemingly coarse act seem graceful. "Did they know Sanuto?"

Jane shook her head, sitting on the bed to face him. "But they were incensed at how he had used their name to—to swindle us." It was still hard to admit, even among themselves, that they had been fooled so easily.

"I stopped in at the tailor's. He was naturally surprised to see me and said he had never heard of Sanuto. I think he was telling the truth, but . . ."

"It is hard."

"Yes." He bit into a piece of the bread and closed his eyes with the same look of veneration that she had felt, which meant, Jane suspected, that he had not yet eaten anything. Vincent wiped the crumbs off his fingers and reached for the cheese. "This may be the best thing I have ever eaten."

"I made it."

He looked up, brows rising in surprise.

"Well, I mean, Sister Aquinata made the dough. I merely

kneaded it and shaped the loaf. She says that she can teach me to cook while I am here. And . . ." Jane took a breath, suddenly nervous that he would mock her pitiful fourteen shillings a week. It was so little compared to the fees they commanded as glamourists. It would buy a few pairs of gloves in her old wardrobe. "And they have offered me a job teaching music. Fourteen shillings a week. It is not much, but I thought that it would help, and it is only for a few hours a week. Plus a loaf of bread every day."

"That is—that is good news, Muse." Vincent broke off a piece of cheese and another piece of bread. His brows had pulled a little closer together.

"And you? How was your search?"

His gaze remained fixed upon the bread and cheese, tearing the bread into smaller and smaller pieces. "Murano is a small town, and though there are some tourists, there are no grand families whose homes need embellishment."

"Oh."

"Tomorrow I shall approach businesses. For now, though, I am very grateful for your fourteen shillings." He reached across the table for her hand and squeezed it. "And your bread." Vincent had not, however, seemed to notice the glamour she had cast upon the room to make it somewhat more agreeable. He remained sunk in silent contemplation.

Twelve

Lessons and Learning

Sister Maria Agnes had a brilliant contralto that could have graced the professional stage. Turned to the service of God, Jane thought that it would be difficult for anyone to deny a divine hand at work, but the little gardener nun seemed blissfully unaware of the exceptional quality of her voice. With such an example, Jane confined her role, at first, to accompanying her lessons on the pianoforte rather than singing.

However, it became quickly apparent that their roles were reversed when it came to teaching the strokes of glamour intended as embellishments for the music. Most, but not all, composers hired a *Sténocharmeur* to create visual elements of glamour to accompany their music, in much the way they might work with a writer for the libretto. It was never very detailed work, as it was confined to quick strokes between musical notes and in the rests. The line of notation ran above the musical staff, with indications about the type of fold to draw from the ether or the proper stitch to create a given effect.

Jane now sat at the piano with a cluster of eleven girls, ranging in age from twelve to sixteen. Open on the music rack in front of her was an arrangement of J. S. Bach's *Jesu, Joy of Man's Desiring*. "Now, you see here that the score has a *pastille* and a *planche* with a rising line following it. That indicates that one should draw out a lightweight fold from the foundation elements of glamour that we laid before the song began. And here, the *pastille* with the vertical bar means to twist it about the fold of white we drew earlier."

The girls nodded dutifully, although Jane saw more than one frown at the fold of white that glowed above the piano, pinned to the visible realm by virtue of being wrapped around the thumb on Jane's left hand. She had, she suspected, jumped beyond their understanding. "Look . . . You see how the thread is hooked behind the first joint of my thumb and I hold my hand with it slightly bent? This is to keep the thread from slipping back into the ether. Glamour, unless tied off or held, always wants to dissolve back into its natural state. The *Sténocharmeur* who designed this illusion assumes that you know this technique and so does not note the additional twist needed to wrap the thread around your thumb."

Sister Maria Agnes nodded in agreement. "Indeed, glamour is not possible for a violinist, for example, as they can never let go of their instrument. Well, most violinists. We shall exclude Paganini, who is, by all accounts, exceptional."

"Is it easiest for singers?" Lucia, a lively girl of twelve, frowned in concentration as she dipped her hand into the ether.

"It depends on the singer and the song," Sister Maria Agnes said. "Working glamour has a significant effect on your breath, and one must have impeccable form to do both well, which is why it is so important to listen to Lady Vincent's instruction. This is also why we have a separate glamourist choir that works in concert with our singers during services." She rested her hand on the shoulder of a young lady who was paying rather more attention to the end of her braid than the pianoforte.

The girl, Elizabeta, startled and dropped her braid. "But it is *hard*."

"Of course. All things are hard when you first begin, but become less so with practise. Practise, however, is more fun when it is a game." Jane pushed the bench back from the pianoforte and pulled out a bundle of looped cords. She selected one and wrapped it around her fingers. "We call this a cat's cradle in England."

Elizabeta said, "Cat's cradle?"

For a moment, Jane had thought that Elizabeta had spoken in English, then recognised that she had spoken the words "believe the chains" in Italian. Only then did Jane understand that Elizabeta had said *both* things, in a manner of speaking. In Italian, the girl had named the game *catene credile*—"believe the chains."

Jane laughed in delight at the understanding. "Do you know, I had not realized where the name of the game came from. Indeed, glamour involves stitching chains of belief for the observer. I assume, then, that you all know how to play this. It is a game, but also an excellent way to practise the movements of glamour without taxing yourself. Who will play with me?"

Lucia let the glamour dissolve off her hands and stepped forward. She took the crossed strings between her thumb and first finger and wrapped them around the other strings, in the familiar pattern. As the string slipped from Jane's hands to hers, Jane pointed at Lucia's fingers. "Do you see how she naturally flexes her thumb to keep the string from sliding off? It is the same movement that we were discussing before. And this . . ." She took the string from Lucia in the next pattern and paused as she started to twist the threads. "See? It is very similar to a *tordre le fil.*"

She let Lucia move the strings back to her own hands, then nodded to the other girls. "So, please, take some string and find a partner."

As the girls separated into pairs, Jane had the satisfaction of seeing Sister Maria Agnes applying herself to playing the game with Lucia with the same diligence as their pupils. More than the fourteen shillings a week, the satisfaction Jane gained from teaching was helping her bear their time in Murano. She just wished that Vincent could find a similar satisfaction.

The night was nearly moonless, and their room sunk in shadows. Curled into a tight embrace against Vincent's back, Jane ran her fingers over the hair on his chest. She traced the contours of his ribs and slid her fingers lower, but he caught her hand and brought it back up to his chest.

Jane kissed the back of his neck. "I am cold."

"Would you like me to put more wood on the fire?"

"No—I was hoping . . ." She lifted her head up a little to look toward his dark form. "Someone reminded me that to-day was October the seventh. I had forgotten, myself, but—"

"Our anniversary." Vincent sighed and pressed her hand tighter against his chest. "I am sorry."

"I thought, perhaps we might celebrate? Here?"

"Oh, Muse . . . forgive me." He had given variations of this answer every time that she had proposed anything relating to their marital duties.

For her own part, Jane would be content—mostly content—with simply being close to her husband, but Vincent had always been a man of healthy vigour, and this listlessness concerned her. "Might you . . . need a release? Perhaps you would feel more at ease."

He rolled onto his back, sheets rustling around them, and ran a hand down her face. "I never want to treat you as simply a release."

"I would not mind."

"I would. If I cannot be fully with you . . . It would distress me." Vincent wrapped his arm around her, pulling her closer. In the cool room, he was like a glass furnace, radiating heat. Jane snuggled closer, drawing one leg up over his. Vincent jumped a little. "How can your feet be chilly even through stockings?"

"I did warn you that I was cold."

He chuckled a little at that and kissed her forehead. "After three years of marriage, you would think that I would know what happens to your feet in winter."

Jane tried again, shifting to encourage him. "There are ways to warm them."

Vincent's breath halted as though he were holding it, and for a moment she thought she had succeeded in engaging his attention. Exhaling slowly, he turned to kiss her on the forehead. Then he rolled onto his side again, staying close to keep her warm. "I love you."

Jane pressed her cheek against his back, bit her lip, and did not cry.

Vincent met Jane at the convent after she finished teaching, as he sometimes did. He stood in the shadow of the building across the street, leaning against the wall. After two weeks of searching, she had hoped that he might have had some success today, but apparently not. After calling on all of the families of means in Murano, few though those were, Vincent had visited the merchants, working his way through the shops methodically in the hopes that one of them would be interested in having a glamourist enhance his store. From there, he had begun pursuing other occupations.

What had begun to worry Jane was not that he had difficulty finding employment but that his interest in finding Signor Sanuto seemed to be turning into an obsession. When he was not speaking to merchants about work, he was making inquiries about Sanuto's activity.

When he stepped into the sun, the light caught in the bristles on his cheeks. He ordinarily went clean-shaven except for his side whiskers. The stubble that was beginning to fill in the space between them was a mixture of colours ranging from the dark brown of his hair to red and—to Jane's surprise—white.

Jane crossed the street, smiling at him. "Your beard makes you appear to be going grey."

"Eh? Oh . . . yes, well. I thought if I looked less of a gentleman I might have some success finding a job." He rubbed his cheek ruefully as they walked. His tone was light, painfully so. "Today I attempted to acquire a job hauling bricks for a mason. I was declined. Apparently, I have the hands of a gentleman and am unsuited for 'real work.'"

"I wish you would not distress yourself. While it is not to my liking, the wages that I am receiving are enough to keep us until we hear from my parents."

"Telling me that your parents will pay for my mistake is not the consolation that you might think it is."

"Or the Prince Regent, or—"

"But we will still be in debt."

Jane hesitated, uncertain how to comfort him. The size of their debt confounded her as well, but she was equally certain that this was but a passing hardship. Unpleasant, yes, but not permanent, and not threatening. If it became truly necessary, they could use the coins saved from the sale of her wedding band to supplement that income, though Jane did not think reminding Vincent of that would be a comfort. "My time teaching takes up little of my day. I could seek additional employment."

"That is not my point. I should be contributing, not asking my wife to support me."

"As a labourer?"

"All work is noble," he said with the air of someone who repeated a sentiment in the hopes of believing it.

"Yes, but—"

"But—as it happens, your concern is groundless." He fished in his pocket with an unmistakable jingle. He held out his hand and showed Jane a handful of coins.

"You found work!"

"Of a sort, yes."

"Doing what? For whom?"

"Glamour. A merchant."

"Of a sort! Here you were looking for work carrying bricks, and you have found employment in your field." Jane scolded and took his arm. Why did he not seem pleased, if he was working as a glamourist? She frowned as a thought occurred to her. "You are not working as a coldmonger, are you?"

He shook his head, grimacing. "Though I did inquire about that once."

"It is dangerous."

"I know. But I am not a coldmonger, Muse."

"Then why are you not more excited about having work?"

"Well . . . I do not know if it will continue."

It did not seem possible that his confidence had been so shaken. "Of course it will, once he sees how good you are."

"I would prefer not to think about what-ifs." He paused for a moment as they passed a Pulcinella puppet booth. They had to stop talking due to the piercing voice of the hand-puppet player. Jane was surprised that he had not been stopped as a nuisance—it had to irritate the local merchants. But the hand-puppet booth had a small circle standing in front of it watching the puppets with great enthusiasm as Pulcinella beat up Scaramuccia. In spite of herself, Jane was strangely tempted to stop and watch the brightly coloured figures battle.

When they were past the puppet show, Vincent said, "I have been thinking of late about Querini. What do you think he would say if we approached him without the *capo di polizia* with us?"

She pretended not to notice that this contradicted his assertion that he preferred not to consider "what-ifs." She answered, "He would say nothing about Sanuto's whereabouts, I am certain."

"No . . . Truly, I do not think we shall find Sanuto."

"And yet you continue to look for him. Am I right that half of your day is spent trying to find a hint of where he has gone?"

He scowled at the canal. "You are not wrong."

"What reason would he have for remaining on Murano?"

Vincent sighed. "I must do something."

"I know." Jane took his arm and turned him toward the glass district. "So let us go ask. Why wonder about what-ifs when we can find an answer?"

"I cannot imagine that he will be happy to see us, no matter if he is involved or not."

"To be certain." A thought occurred to her. "Perhaps we should not begin by asking after Sanuto. Perhaps we can speak to Signor Querini about having you assist at the glass factory in exchange for some reduction in what we owe him. If it does not interfere with your work as a glamourist, that is."

Vincent snorted. "There is little chance of that. But I have neglected to ask how your day was."

"Satisfactory, thank you. I made good progress with the elder students in understanding *tordre le fil*, so Sister Maria Agnes decided to treat them to a tour of the scriptorium. The manuscript Sister Franceschina and the others are illuminating is a beautiful project. I wish you could see it." Now that he had found his own work, she felt less awkward about relating her news. "I have also been asked to contrive the music for two Sundays hence. It is only a children's choir, I know, but it is the first group performance I have ever been given charge of—unless you count Michaelmas pageants at home, which I do not."

Vincent frowned. "Do you think we will still be here in two weeks?"

"I—well, I hope that we will have had some relief by then, to be certain. But, even if we do go, Sister Maria Agnes can conduct them in my absence." She peered at him. "Did you have a chance to stop round at the *polizia* station?" He had made it part of his daily rounds to visit the station house to report that they had not left Murano and to see if they had received any mail.

"Nothing has arrived."

"Well . . . it has only been three weeks, so I suppose that is not surprising."

"I had hoped to hear from Byron, but—well."

They turned on to the narrow street that led to Querini's glass factory. As they walked down the twisting passage, Jane had a sudden fear that the glass factory would have vanished. It was with immeasurable relief that she saw the small sign over the door. Vincent released her arm and set his shoulders. "Ready?"

"Yes."

He smiled without any mirth and knocked upon the door. After a moment, it was opened by a young man who, for a moment, Jane thought was Biasio. However, he had only a general build and colouring in common with the apprentice. "May I help you?"

Vincent inclined his head. "Would you be so good as to tell Signor Querini that Sir David Vincent and his wife would like a moment of his time?"

"You're—? Um . . . Wait here." He backed away from the door, eyes quite wide, before he shut it hastily. There followed the unmistakable sound of a bolt being shot as he locked the door.

Jane had not heard the corresponding sound of the door being unlocked when he had first opened it. "Well. I suppose Signor Querini has spoken of—"

Within the glass factory, she heard, quite clearly, Signor Querini roar, "What!" From there, his voice dropped to a mutter, which, though incomprehensible, was constant, and grew steadily louder as the glassmaker approached the door. Jane found herself stepping back involuntarily as the bolt snapped back.

Vincent stood his ground, head high. The glassmaker threw the door open and stood framed in it against a vivid, glowing background of molten glass. "You! Have you brought my money? My money, sir! Hours I spent, wasted, working in the night. In the night! For what? Well? What have you to say? Hm?"

"We are without funds, but I thought—"

"Then why are you here? Why do you waste my time?"

Jane could imagine, rather than hear, her husband's teeth grind, but when he spoke, his voice was admirably calm. "I had thought to offer to work for you in recompense for our debt."

The glassmaker stared, his mouth gaping. He snapped it shut. "Doing what?"

"As you know, I am a glamourist of some skill."

"All I ever saw you do was wave your hands and make useless spheres. Glamour? Glamour makes pretty pictures. What do I need of those?"

Jane said, "It can also create a breeze to help the furnace or cool the workers." Though, to be fair, he had Biasio for that.

Behind Querini, his workers gradually stopped what they were doing and turned to watch. Lit in the orange glow of the ovens, they seemed like supernatural creatures come to labour on the earth. Jane looked among them for Biasio, but the apprentice was not immediately visible.

"Thank you, no. No, I have no need of that. No. Nor of you. Either of you. I only want my money."

"And might I not do something else? Work the bellows? Some apprentice labour?" Still, Vincent's voice was utterly calm.

"Teach a foreigner my craft? Bah! Never again! Bad enough that I let you into the factory to work. Do you know what that has cost me? Do you? The other glassmakers are furious. Furious, I tell you. And for what? Hm? For what?"

"We will pay you, sir."

"Will you? In the meantime, what am I to do? What? Your funds were to have paid for—" Suddenly, he looked furtive rather than angry. "Bah! You are wasting my time."

Jane stepped forward, peering intently into the interior. "Where is Biasio?"

"Who?" He wiped his mouth.

"Your apprentice, Biasio. The one who worked with you on our project."

"I don't know what you are talking about. Biasio? I never heard of such a person!" He stepped back, shaking his finger at them. "You are thieves! And liars! Do not bother me again."

With that, he slammed the door. The sound bounced off the narrow alley and left a reverberating question in its passing. Why was he lying about Biasio?

Thirteen

Tearing the Cloth

Though it was now obvious to both Jane and Vincent that Biasio must have been involved in the theft, it was less obvious how much Querini had known. The furtive look in his eyes had been coupled with a certain amount of fear. It was hard to say if it was fear of being caught by the authorities or fear of reprisals for speaking to Jane and Vincent.

Though they had no more discoveries, the speculation alone served to distract them both from time passing as three weeks turned to four, which was the earliest they could hope to hear from the Prince Regent. But at the end of that time, they still had no word from England.

Jane's family would just be reaching Prague, so it would be another two weeks before there was any hope of a return letter, longer if there were early snows in the passes. From Lord Byron, they had no word at all.

Vincent had written to Byron's landlord, separately, not quite trusting that the *capo* had actually sent the letters. The landlord had been good enough to return a reply that, yes, Lord Byron was away and that, yes, if they came to Venice he had instructions to let them use the apartments. They showed the letter to the magistrate, but he declined to allow them to leave Murano.

November continued to pass with still no word from family, Lord Byron, or the Prince Regent. The concern that they might be gone from Murano before the choir performed had so little foundation in reality that Jane was able to contrive another service with them. Vincent went out every day and came home in the evenings, often with his shirt still sweat-dampened from his labour.

His spirits, however, remained subdued.

As Jane was returning home from the convent, the day was a fine autumnal one favoured by the golden light so beloved by the artist Titian. She turned her path from her usual walk through the streets to stroll along the canal and then to the broad square where the larger pleasure craft moored. The Pulcinella booth was often there, and Jane thought she might take in the show before returning to their lodging.

The view of Venice, so close, was particularly fine that afternoon. High, white clouds gave just enough punctuation to the sky to make its blue more brilliant. The Pulcinella booth had a small crowd in front of it, laughing with delight. A smaller crowd had gathered at the opposite side of the square to watch another street performer, but Jane had eyes only for the puppet show.

She was halfway across the square when a dragon rose above the other street performer's audience. Its roar echoed across the pavement and stopped her progress. The audience applauded the glamour, although one little boy ran screaming across the pavement, to the amusement of all save his mother. The dragon vanished, fading from view as artfully as it appeared. She could not see the glamourist beneath the figure, but she knew his work as intimately as she knew her own.

Vincent was busking.

This was the glamour that he had been doing. The merchants for whom he had been working.

He had not lied to her directly, but he had certainly done everything in his power to make himself appear to be employed by *someone*, rather than entertaining on the street. Jane was more than a little vexed that he had hid it from her. She would have liked to have watched him work. Perhaps she could even have helped.

But why had he not told her? As he himself said, all work was noble. So why had he hidden it from her?

As she watched, an enormous bridge appeared overhead, complete with water and buildings on either side. The rapidity with which it appeared made Jane suspect that Vincent had built the scenery in advance and hidden it within a *Sphère Obscurcie* until he needed it. Now a workman, rendered in silhouette, walked on to the bridge for the opening scene of the famous shadow play *The Broken Bridge*.

Even knowing Vincent's strength and power as a glamourist, Jane was still impressed by what she saw. To make a figure move was more than many glamourists aspired to. It was difficult to manage the innumerable threads that composed a figure, even in miniature. What Vincent did now was doubly difficult.

First, the figure was larger than a man. He was rendered in only black, to be sure, but with such exquisite detail that even his hair seemed to move as he raised his pickax over his head and brought it down upon the bridge.

Second, Vincent was working the figure high over his head. The farther from a glamourist the threads stretched, the harder it was to control them, and the greater the strain upon the performer. She had seen him lay folds of glamour upon the ceiling of a ballroom, but those had been layers of stationary fabric, which he could tie off when he needed to rest. This? This was nothing short of a marvel of endurance and artistry.

He brought in the second figure, the Traveller, who wished to cross the bridge but was stopped by the hole in the middle. Though Vincent focused his attention on one figure or the other, the fact that he was managing two of them, and at this scale, filled Jane with no small amount of concern. She had seen Vincent work past his limits before.

The Traveller said, in perfect Italian. "Excuse me sir, is this the road to Venice?"

"Naw. This here don't go nowhere but to the canal. Tra-la-la."

He had adapted the play from its London environs to the locale and the changes, small though they were, brought laughter from the crowd. The shadow play continued as the Traveller tried to cross the river, only to receive increasingly rude responses from the Workman. When the end of the play came and the Traveller kicked the Workman into the river, Vincent caused the illusion of water to seem to splash over those watching. They jumped and shrieked, then laughed when they realized how they had been taken in.

Applauding, people tossed coins into a hat upon the pavement. As the crowd dispersed, Jane could see her husband at last. His coat lay draped upon a stone bench behind him, and he worked in his shirt sleeves and waistcoat, with the collar open at his throat. The fabric clung to his skin, and sweat plastered his hair to his brow. A bright flush of effort lit his cheeks, and even from where she stood, Jane could see the great gasps of air he was taking in. Vincent bowed to his audience, pausing to answer a question from one and receive a compliment from another. As he stooped to collect the money in his hat, he saw Jane.

The flush on his cheeks vanished as if he were stricken. For a moment, all animation in his features froze. Vincent looked down, and then continued to collect the coins that his performance had garnered. A performance that would be worthy of Carlton House in London, and he had received a few cents for it.

She could imagine the thoughts that must go through his head. *My father predicted that I would wind up in penury, performing on a street somewhere.* All work was noble . . . but to be a street performer, given his history? This was why, even as he brought in funds, his spirits remained low. It must be destroying him.

Vincent stood, pocketed the money, and pulled out a handkerchief to wipe his brow. Other than the brief moment in which he had made eye contact with Jane, he gave no sign that she was there. He addressed his audience with a ready smile that was as much an illusion as anything crafted of glamour. He appeared to be soliciting requests for a *tableau vivant*.

Jane sat down on a bench on the opposite side of the square and watched Vincent work. His routine, she could see, was clever in the way it was constructed. By moving to a smaller scale intended for close-up viewing, he was able to calm his breath without a substantial break in performance. Also, the tightly packed group of observers drew the attention of passers-by, so he gradually accumulated an audience of some dozen people.

But still more people walked past without noting the glamours that he raised above them. Some stopped, but not many. Still, as the audience grew, so did the size of the illusions he crafted, until he ended the set with another shadow play. This time, he performed *The Haunted Inn*, in which a merchant finds increasingly disturbing and amusing ghosts at the inn where he has taken lodgings. In the final scene, a haunted bed chased the merchant down the street. Vincent made the illusions appear to vanish into the distance.

With a bow, he thanked his audience and stood, head down, as the passers-by continued on their interrupted errands. Jane had watched, as transfixed as any of the other members of the audience, though she wanted to stop all those who had walked past without taking note of Vincent's extraordinary work.

How could anyone fail to recognise the exceptional nature of his craft? Yet scores of people had strolled past without even turning their heads.

Across the square, Vincent shook himself, then stooped to pick up the hat. He tipped it to pour the coins into his hand, not troubling to count the money before putting it into his pocket. He stood slowly, with clear effort. Vincent held still in an attitude that she recognised all too well as that of a glamourist waiting for the grey spots in his vision to pass. She had done the same countless times herself, after far less strenuous work than this.

Jane started across the square, fearful that he had misjudged his limits, but Vincent turned to pick up his coat. He shrugged it on as casually as if he were preparing to go on a hunt at a country estate. Head still down, he walked across the square to meet her, setting his hat upon his head as he did.

"Good evening." Vincent glanced back toward where he had performed, but avoided looking at her. "I did not lie. The crowd is mostly composed of merchants."

Jane fell in beside him as they turned their steps to home. "It is quite a good show."

He snorted.

"The shadow plays in particular astonished me."

"Jane, I would—may we talk about something else?"

"Of course . . ." She began to tell him of her day, but found herself tailoring her stories to leave out the work she was doing contriving the glamourist choir and to focus instead upon a particularly troublesome student. Vincent grunted or nodded in response whenever she paused. To someone who did not know him, he would have seemed fully engaged, but Jane could see that he wore a mask as carefully controlled as the figures in *The Broken Bridge*.

He listened to her, nodding at the appropriate moments, but his attention was turned inward. When she paused in her recital, he said, "I spoke with one of Signor Nenci's apprentices."

"Who?" The change in subject caught Jane off guard, and she did not recognise the name.

"The glassmaker we first approached about the *Verre Obscurci.*" The breeze had dried the sweat on Vincent's brow, and he walked with his hands tucked into his pockets. "Querini used to be an apprentice of Nenci's. I wanted to see if I could learn anything."

"I take it you did." Jane raised an eyebrow. "And are you now going to drag it out to fill me with suspense?"

He smirked, shaking his head. "Querini had only recently started his glass factory, which we knew. The apprentice said that it was a matter of some curiosity as to how Querini could have afforded to start the studio. He boasted at first about a 'large commission,' but the apprentice did not know what it was."

Jane gave a shiver that had nothing to do with the wind. "Likely us."

Vincent nodded. "He had also never heard of Biasio, and given the tight-knit nature of the community, that seems . . ."

"Unlikely, at best."

"Exactly, unless Biasio was hired by Sanuto to steal the *Verre Obscurci* technique." Vincent walked a few more feet before continuing. "There is one other thing of note. Querini announced his intention to set up his shop only a few weeks after we wrote to Byron asking him if we could visit."

"After we wrote, or after Byron received the letter?"

"Both. The timing is such that someone in London could have read our letter and written here, or someone here could have read the letter after it arrived at Byron's."

"Surely you do not think that Lord Byron is involved." Jane's stomach turned at the thought. "He was the one who warned us about the pirates."

"It is not in his character as I know it. But he was in dire financial straits when he left England." Vincent shook his head. "Still, I think it is more likely to be someone who had access to his mail. Mr. Hobhouse, for example, or Marianna, or even *il Dottore*."

The next thought that occurred to Jane made her wince. "And then there is the timing of his departure."

"Yes, that is quite convenient as well." Vincent stared at the ground as he walked. His brow was contracted, as if the very thought pained him.

Jane went twice more to see Vincent perform, until it became clear to her that it troubled him to have her watch. Though he made an effort to hide the fact that his spirits were depressed by being a street performer, neither would he hear of stopping. In truth, as they moved farther into November, Jane had good reason to be glad of the coins that he brought home.

Murano had been a delight in the late summer, with its golden light reflecting off the canals and the tumult of flowers in the window boxes. The autumn, though, was cold, grey, and dreary. Their little garret had a draught that would have overwhelmed a larger fireplace than theirs. In spite of Jane's efforts to find the holes and patch them by shoving cloth into the spaces between plaster and the window or pasting paper over the cracks, the room was perpetually cold. With their combined efforts, they were able to afford wood for the hearth in spite of the scandalous price it fetched on an island with no trees. Like most of their food, the fuel for the fire came from the mainland.

As the season went on, the crowds that watched Vincent became scarcer, as well. Grumbling at the fickle nature of the Crown, Vincent sent another letter to the Prince Regent, and Jane sent another to her parents, since by this point they should have left Prague and be en route to Copenhagen. More than once, Jane thought of using the coins from the sale of her wedding ring, but those were set aside to recover the band, and Vincent would not hear of spending them. She was grateful for the work the nuns had given her, else they would have been cold *and* hungry.

She was therefore vexed when she realized that her "flower" had arrived. Before, it had never been more than a minor inconvenience and an excuse to spend a day or two reading in her room. Now, though, Jane could ill afford to spend the day at home as it would affect her wages at the convent. She tore a length of stained muslin into rags with more force than was strictly necessary.

"What is the matter, Muse?" Vincent paused in the process of pulling his boots on.

Jane stared at the cloth in her hands. After three years of marriage, surely he knew what the signs were. Though, to be fair, her monthly time had always been somewhat irregular due to the toll that glamour took upon her body. Even when her time arrived, there were usually only two days in which it was not possible for the cloth to contain her courses. And of course Jane usually had a maid who would prepare the cloth for her.

She sighed and ripped another piece of cloth to size. "It is my time of the month."

"Well, that is good news."

"Good news? How is it good? I cannot work today."

"Why not?" A moment later, he looked anew at the cloth and reddened. "Ah. Ah, yes. I see."

"And even if that were not the case, I can assure you that this is not a time of delight for me." She tore another strip from the cloth. "Why should you think it is good news?"

"Because, it means you are not—" He shook his head and drew his boot the rest of the way on. "It does not matter. I am sorry that you are uncomfortable."

Jane gripped the cloth in her fists. It meant that she was not with child. Given their straitened circumstances, of course Vincent would think that it was good news.

He stood. "Is there anything I can do for you?"

Jane forced her fingers to relax. "Would you be willing to stop by the convent and let them know that I will not be able to be there today or tomorrow?"

"Of course." Crossing the room, he stopped to kiss her on the forehead. "Shall I stop in later to see how you are?"

She shook her head and stacked the rags into a neat pile, but waited until Vincent left before attempting to make herself somewhat more comfortable. Without a book to pass the time, this would be a long and unpleasant day.

* * *

Jane sat by the window, where the light was best and picked out the stitches in her other dress. She had played with glamour for a while, but, having reached a point where she was too winded to continue, she had decided to remake the dress for some variety. The years spent in needlework in her parents' drawing room had some practical application after all. Jane would never have guessed that while embroidering chair seats.

The door downstairs slammed, and she heard the unmistakable sound of Vincent climbing the stairs. He ran up them two at a time. Something had happened. Jane put her sewing aside and stood as he flung the door open.

His face was wind-reddened from his run and his hair looked as though an owl had mauled it, but he was smiling. "We have a letter. A parcel, in fact."

He was smiling. Jane found herself unable to speak, could only clasp her hands against the incongruous desire to meet his smile with tears. She swallowed. "From?"

"Your sister. I have not opened it. Thought you would kill me if I did." From his coat pocket he pulled a small parcel, wrapped in brown paper and glued shut. "Thought it would kill me to wait, so I ran. Must have seemed a madman."

"The light is better by the window." Jane pushed her sewing aside to make room for him and took the parcel. It showed the wear of its journey, with water stains at the edges of the paper and a great smear of mud along one side. She had expected her father to reply to their inquiries, not her sister. Turning it over to tear it open, she paused. The return was from Vienna, but her family had already visited there. They should be in Copenhagen now.

Wetting her lips, she pulled off the paper. Inside was a cloth bound book and a letter.

Vienna

7 October 1817

Jane, Lady Vincent

My dearest sister,

You must be surprised to see that we have returned to Vienna instead of continuing on to Prague as we had planned, but I have had a Happy Change in circumstances, which I am certain that you might guess at, and made the Mistake of intimating that to Mama, who can now think of nothing but my health, and she was set for us to return to England, if you can imagine that, but Alastar—the dear—convinced her that Vienna would do as well since he has so many friends here from when he was abroad with his parents, which includes a Doctor of Good Repute, who attended the Empress Marie-Louise during her lying in—is that not a Wonder—and he shall attend me as well!

Oh, Jane! I am the Happiest of Creatures! Alastar is beside himself with Joy, as are his parents, who are being so gracious and attentive. I trust that you are enjoying yourself in Murano and wish that you would leave off your work and come join us right away, because I know how long travel takes and it will be a month before you receive this and another month before you could possibly arrive, but I should very much like for you to be here. My confinement is not until February but you know I should be easier to have you close by. You are such a steadying influence.

I include an anniversary gift for you from a Favourite

Author of mine, although I understand that she passed away this year, which is Decidedly Tragic, still her volumes remind me of us at times more than I am entirely comfortable with, but I do so enjoy them. For your Vincent, I have something as well, but it shall not travel so nicely, so you both must come to collect it. There, if that does not tempt you, I do not know what will!

With all my fondness and a heart overflowing with joy, I remain your loving sister

Melody

(Mrs. O'Brien)

This was why they had heard nothing from her parents. They had never received the letters.

Vincent sank upon the window ledge. He leaned forward and put his face in his hands. "That is wonderful news, for your sister and Mr. O'Brien."

"Yes. It is hard to imagine her being a mother." It would be no hardship for *her* of course—with Mr. O'Brien's fortune, they could have as many children as they wished. Jane recoiled at the petty jealousy in her own thoughts. She had never desired a child before, so had no cause to envy her sister. Indeed, given Jane's history she had more reason to fear for her. A February confinement meant that Melody was six months along now.

Jane sat beside Vincent and looked at the letter again: Seventh of October. She counted the days to see how far Melody had been when she had written the letter and grew a little colder. It had taken over a month for the letter to arrive, and the roads would be worse now.

"Please include my regards when you write back." By the leaden weight in his voice, it was clear that Vincent's mind had already leapt ahead of hers. There would be no quick relief of their circumstances from that quarter.

"Of course." As much as she had wished for a book earlier that day, now Jane stared at the novel as if doing so would cause it to be something different. Even if they sent a reply today, they could not expect to hear from her family until January.

Fourteen

A Matter of Perspective

November in Murano was typified by heavy
rains without any of the charm of snow. Even
the incessant pigeons crowded under stone pilings and huddled in windows to avoid the rain.
Their fat grey bodies seemed like cobblestones
piled in every damp corner.

Jane had been caught by such a shower
on her way home, though speaking of their
single room as "home" was dispiriting even
without the rain. She pulled her heavy woollen
shawl, a gift from the nuns, over her head and
ran down the street. Without pattens to lift her
above the walk, the hem of her skirt quickly
became heavy and damp with rain. Jane
ducked into a small grocer close to their lodgings as the downpour increased too much to
ignore. Other passers-by crowded into a café

across the street to pass the time with a cup of coffee and a pastry.

The more wealthy simply rode through the rain in sedan chairs or upon the water in gondolas, leaving the task of getting wet to their drivers. In that moment, Jane would have been happy just to be able to afford an umbrella. Wanting even that, she must wait out the heaviest part of the downpour in the shelter of this small shop. Happily, she had some purchases to make for their dinner, so the time need not be a total waste.

Jane eyed the brace of ducks hanging from the ceiling with some longing, though she had not the slightest idea of how to prepare them. Simply the thought of warm duck, roasted perhaps, was enough to make her mouth water. She turned away from them, and from the rabbits hung beside them, and slipped past another customer to the dried cannellini beans. They already had rice and some onions in their room. She measured the beans into a small burlap bag and thought that she might go to the butcher and get a little rasher of pork fat to add to the beans for flavour. Vinegar, too. They were nearly out.

The thought gave her pause, that they had been here long enough to empty a bottle of vinegar. She almost had not purchased it, thinking that they would not be here more than a few weeks. She now suspected that they would have to spend the winter in Murano.

"You have to pay for that directly." The woman who ran the shop, a matronly widow with her hair pulled back into a severe bun, stood with her arms crossed.

"Thank you for the reminder, Signora Rotolo." Jane put the beans on the counter.

The woman said this every time Jane came in. Her son was a gondola driver and had received the notice from the *capo* about Jane and Vincent's travel restriction. He had passed the notice to his mother, and she, in a show of benevolent mistrust, reminded Jane of her want of funds every time she came into the shop. If her prices were not so good, Jane would have gone elsewhere.

"No credit."

"Have I ever asked for credit?" Jane's exhaustion spoke for her. "Have I ever short-changed you, or asked for any special consideration? Have I even questioned your prices? Do you, perhaps, think that I have forgotten that I am poor?"

Signora Rotolo's mouth hung open, and she rocked back a little upon her heels.

Jane realized that she had raised her voice and that the low hum of conversation from the other patrons in the shop had died away. Cheeks burning, Jane pointed to the bars of soap behind the counter. "A bar of the lavender soap, please."

It was absurd. She did not need the soap; she knew she did not. They had a small pot of soft soap that she had been given by the convent. But in that moment she felt that if she did not have a small treat, she would go mad. It had been so long since she had washed her face without it burning from the lye afterwards that she just wanted something nice.

And she wanted something that a poor person would not buy. She should not buy the soap.

The chandler put it on the counter and the herbal sweetness rose above the other scents in the shop. The square of soap in its neat, printed paper seemed unreal. Signora Rotolo

put the beans on the scale, without looking at Jane any further. "That is *lira sottile* of beans. Sixteen *centesimi*."

"Thank you." Jane counted out the coins from the little
change purse that one of the girls had given her. The soap
cost four times the price of the beans. She should not buy it.
"I am sorry that I raised my voice."

"We get thieves in. Not you." Signora Rotolo picked up
the coins. "Times are hard. I shouldn't have . . . You used to
be a lady, didn't you?"

"Yes." Jane bit the word off and felt that she might choke
on it. She tucked her purchase into her shopping basket. "I
used to be."

Heedless of the rain, Jane stepped outside, unable to
stand another minute in the shop with everyone staring at
her. She used to be a lady. Could Signora Rotolo have made
Jane's humiliation more complete? The phrase—"used to be
a lady"—as though she were a fallen woman. As though any
of this were her fault.

But it was. That was the thing that burned, and that Jane
struggled to accept or ignore or simply live with. As much as
she had tried to pretend that this was simply an adventure that
they would get past, the fact was that all of it was her fault for
trusting Signor Sanuto. Vincent had been ill at first, and then
later she had talked him into staying.

Why had she bought the soap? To prove that she was still
a lady?

Jane ran through the streets, dashing from doorway to
doorway through the rain. The long galleries that were so
popular in the region gave her a respite for a few hundred feet
in some places, but by the time she arrived at their door, she

was wet through. Jane paused in their doorway to wring the worst of the water out of her skirt and shawl. The heavy wool had kept most of it off her shoulders, but it stank of sheep now.

She climbed the stairs with her skirt clinging to her legs. The way up had never seemed so long.

The room was dark when she got in, and she was grateful that Vincent was out. What a foolish, foolish woman she was. Jane closed her eyes and tried to govern her emotions. The change in their circumstances did not materially change her. She was still a lady, though her peers might not recognise her current way of life. She was a lady and an artist.

"Should I light a candle?"

Jane shrieked and dropped the basket. Pressing her hand against her bosom, she peered into the gloom for her husband. As much as she was startled, she was embarrassed to have jumped like a schoolgirl. But still. He *had* been sitting in the dark. "Did I wake you?"

"No." His voice came not from the bed but from the window. He rose, and she could just make out his silhouette against the rain-splashed glass. "I just had not noticed that it had grown dark."

A match flared on the hearth, and he held his hand around the flame as he lit the candle. The warm light played around his face, making the shadows under his eyes more pronounced and catching on the grey hairs in his beard. Vincent had always looked older than his years, but emerging out of the dark, he seemed ancient. His shirt hung open and untucked. He wore his buckskin trousers, which were ill suited to the rain.

Jane glanced at the row of pegs in the wall. His other pair of trousers hung there, completely dry. "Have you been out today?"

"It is too wet for any tourists."

She realized that he had not gone out the day prior, either, or the day before that. Jane set her basket on the table and moved to stand in front of the fire, which Vincent had raked so that it provided almost no warmth. She pulled off her shawl and hung it on one of the pegs. Jane fumbled with the ties on her dress, which had drawn tight with the damp. "May I ask you to build up the fire?"

"Of course." He knelt by the hearth and began laying pieces of wood on the embers. Jane was unaccountably annoyed that she had needed to ask him. She knew that his spirits were low, but it would take little exertion to have the apartment warm for her when she got home.

"We can afford for you to have a fire, you know." Jane got the knots free and peeled the soaked fabric away.

He shrugged. "I was comfortable."

Comfortable? He had not noticed that he was sitting in the dark. Did he note that it was cold, or was he as insensible to that as well?

Jane's petticoat, too, was wet, so she pulled that over her head and hung it on the peg by the fire. Shivering, she took down her other petticoat, a torn one from the convent's rag bin. After mending, it served well enough. Jane pulled on the petticoat and her second dress as quickly as she could. There was a time when her wardrobe had a dozen or more dresses. Now she had two. But then, she used to be a lady. Now she had no need for more than one dress to wear and one to wash.

Washing. She was going to be completely self-indulgent and wash her face with warm water before she started cooking. Jane filled their one pot with water from the pitcher and hung it over the fire to heat. She walked back to the basket and fished out the soap she had purchased. The paper had become damp, which made the aroma of the soap more intense. "I bought some soap today."

"Soap."

"Lavender." She undid the spot of paste holding the paper closed, trying not to tear it.

"We have soap."

"We have soft soap." The smooth bar felt like silk, and it had been dyed to match its scent. "I needed a treat."

"I wish you had consulted with me first."

Jane raised her head in disbelief. Vincent still crouched by the hearth, coaxing flames from the wood. "I do not consult you on the other shopping I do."

"Those are not luxuries. We are supposed to be limiting our expenditures."

"I am aware of that. I walked home in the rain because we cannot afford a sedan chair or even an umbrella. I am wearing a mended petticoat. I know that we need to save."

"Then why spend money on a luxury?"

The fact that he so closely echoed Jane's own thoughts about the soap caused her anger at herself to boil upwards. It was only with great difficulty that she held it in. "It is a bar of soap, Vincent."

"But we *have* soap."

"I had a difficult day. I wanted something nice. I bought a *bar of soap*. With, I might add, money that *I* earned."

"Of course." He stood and dusted his hands, staring at the embers. If he had raised his voice, she would have felt perversely better, but it remained flat. It reminded her of nothing so much as when they had met, and he had seemed wholly composed of tightly controlled anger. "Of course, it is your right to spend your wages as you see fit."

"Yes. It is. And while we are on the subject, would it be too much to ask that you help with the household tasks when you are not working?"

"I *do* help. I take out the chamber pot, build the fire, and report our continued presence to the *capo di polizia*."

"And I cook, clean, and do the laundry and the mending, and then you rebuke me for buying a bar of soap. With money I earned."

His face became stiff, like a leather Carnevale mask. "Thank you for the reminder. I had forgotten what little use I was."

"Vincent, please. You are bringing in as much as—"

"I *was*. But now I am not, so we need to retrench, which is why the *soap* is something that I wish you had discussed with me before purchasing."

The argument had shifted while she was focused on her own hurt feelings. It was not the soap that was at issue, but the fact that she had earned the money. Vincent was not arguing with her, but with himself. Jane tried to calm him. "The rain will stop."

"It is November. Who is going to stand in the cold to watch a street performer?"

"But you are not just any street performer. You are brilliant and—"

"Brilliant?" His voice rose. "I stand there and no one cares." Vincent snatched a fold of glamour and divided it into five flames, which he tossed from hand to hand like a juggler. It was a prodigiously complicated weave. "Do you know why they came? Because I fainted one day and they were waiting to see if I would do it again. It does not matter how good I am, or how clever my illusions are. I cannot even support my wife."

This was the heart of it—the point around which Vincent kept circling. "But you do not need to support me."

"I know!" He took a shuddering breath and lowered his voice, still juggling the flames. "I know. You are well able to provide for yourself."

"For both of us. We share in this. There have been many times when you provided for me." The image of him sitting in the dark rose again before her. "It might help if you had some occupation to distract you."

"What do you think I have been trying to do? No one will hire me!"

"Not work, but something to occupy your time. To distract you."

Vincent laughed, a raw, angry sound. He added a sixth ball to those he juggled. "Like drawing? Or shall I take up needlework?"

"Why not? It helps with my understanding of knots. And you did offer, not so long ago, to stay at home if we had a child."

"It was a *jest*! Letting you support me is no different from those gamesters who burn through their wife's dowry and then live off her parents' pity and generosity."

"It is different in *every* way. We are in this situation not by choice, but by a misfortune of chance."

"And how is that different from gambling?" He dragged his fingers through the glamour, clawing the flames into a red haze. "My father was right."

"He was *not*. He would have you waste your talents—"

"Oh, and they are *so* useful. I am in perfect health now and *what good does it do*."

"Even if we have to abide the winter, my parents will eventually get my letters."

"What a conversation that is to look forward to. 'Good evening, Mr. Ellsworth. Would you mind paying two thousand pounds to get us out of debt? Oh, and by the way, we have pawned your daughter's wedding ring because without it we would be on the street. Could you pay for that as well?' God!" With his hand balled into a fist, Vincent turned and swung at the wall.

He checked the movement before the impact. Breathing harshly, he held rigid. Then he swore, twisted a fold of glamour, and vanished. A moment later, the sound of his breath cut off.

Jane stared at the spot where her husband had been, as though she could see through the *Sphère Obscurcie* he had woven. She still held the bar of soap in one hand. Trembling, Jane set it down on the table. He had never hidden from her like this. A very great part of her wanted to take up her shawl and walk out of the room to give him privacy. The other, larger part wanted to step forward and into the *Sphère*. Jane stared at the soap, willing herself to calm down and her breathing to slow. Soap.

And yet that was not what they had been discussing. Not at all.

Vincent was not angry at her. That was clear, in spite of his words. She had known that he was masking his distress, but had not realized how deeply it upset him to have her support them. Jane wet her lips and took another breath to steady herself. She walked forward, waiting for the moment when she passed within the *Sphère*'s influence.

She saw him before she could hear him. Vincent had slid down the wall to sit at its base with his knees drawn up in front of him. His head was bowed forward with his arms wrapped around it. When she stepped within the *Sphère*, his hands tightened into fists.

"Jane, please. Please." His voice was rough, as though it took all his power to force words out. "I am sorry."

She tucked her skirts around her and sat beside him. Jane stared across the room, trying to find her way through all the possible words to the ones that would make a difference. Everything she thought to say seemed as though it would hurt him more.

Jane slid her hand around Vincent's upper arm and leaned against him. His breath caught in a sound that might have been a laugh, or a cough, or a sob. Then he held utterly still again, not even breathing. Jane waited with her head against his shoulder as Vincent wrestled with himself.

She felt him let his breath out and then draw it raggedly in again. She waited as successive breaths passed, each a little steadier, until he lowered his hands. Vincent sniffed and gave a small laugh. "I have left my handkerchief in my coat."

"I have found that sleeves work well, in a pinch."

He chuckled—if Jane were being charitable—and wiped his sleeve across his face. "Muse, you are a wonder."

"I love you."

His exhalation sounded almost as if she had punched him, but Vincent wrapped his arms around her and rested his head atop hers. "I am so sorry."

"You have nothing to apologize for."

"You know that is not true."

"But I do not."

"We would be on the street if not for you. I have been a self-indulgent ass."

"You have been trying. It is not your fault that there is no work."

"No? I keep wondering if my success in England was due to who my friends were, rather than any innate talent. That is the problem." He stretched his legs out in front of him and leaned his head back against the wall. "I can tell myself that there is nothing shameful about our circumstances. I did not make wagers. We are safe. We are reasonably comfortable—if cold."

"But?"

"But . . . it seems that my father was right. If he . . . I was raised to believe that perfection was the only acceptable choice, and I . . . I have been failing—" His voice roughened again, and she could feel him fighting the emotion. When he spoke next, his voice was steady. "I have been failing for months. At glamour. At being a husband. At everything I set my hands to."

Jane slid her hand down his arm until she could intertwine her fingers with his. "Is your father more important than I am?"

"What? No."

"Then why do you persist in holding his opinion higher than mine?"

"I am—" His voice cracked into nothing. Vincent looked away, closing his eyes, and cleared his throat. "I will do better."

Jane rolled to her knees. Taking his face between her hands, Jane turned him toward her. "Vincent. You do not have to do better. You are already everything that I want. Whether we are living in a garret or Carlton House, I will love you. Stop letting that man punish you when you *have done nothing wrong.*"

He looked utterly unmoored. "But what have I done right?"

"Married me?"

The corner of his mouth curved upwards. "Yes." He flexed his hands, and then clenched them again.

"And your father is wrong. Glamour is a noble art, and *this will pass.*"

He nodded, as though he were trying to believe her.

Jane leaned forward to kiss him on the forehead. "My governess was forever saying, 'You will feel better if you wash your face.'" She paused, and then took a chance. "I have some soap."

Vincent laughed. The laughter grew beyond what her joke merited, and he leaned forward to rest his head on her shoulder. Jane folded her arms around him and held him while each ragged breath shook him. She had never thought that laughter could break her heart.

Jane had difficulty focusing on her charges at the convent the next day. She was tutoring Lucia in the use of glamour at the pianoforte. Though the girl had an admirable grasp of glamour, she could not hold Jane's attention. At every gap in instruction, her gaze turned to the stained windows and the rain that trickled down their exteriors. Vincent would be unable to busk again today. He had seemed somewhat easier in spirit after the soap conversation, and he had slept deeply that night, seemingly without a nightmare, but Jane did not feel confident that his spirits would remain lifted.

When she finished at the convent, she hurried home, pausing only long enough to pick up a loaf of bread from the convent kitchen. On the way up to the apartment, she slowed and tried to keep the stairs from creaking. At the top, she listened for sounds from the apartment that might betray Vincent's state. She heard a single, low curse.

Biting her lip, Jane pushed the door to the apartment open and stopped in surprise.

Glamour wreathed the room, creating the illusion of an orangery with glass walls opening on to a rolling English landscape. The orange trees arched overhead beneath a vaulted glass ceiling in the Gothic style. Their bed still stood in one corner, and though Vincent had done nothing to the furniture itself, its setting made it appear charmingly rustic. An inviting aroma of oranges, earth, and herbs drifted through the room.

Vincent stood over their small table with an onion in one hand. He had shaved. "You are early."

The earthy aroma, which mingled with the illusory oranges, was not the work of glamour—but came from the hearth. Their small pot bubbled with rice and beans. "Are you cooking dinner?"

He blushed and scratched the back of his head. "Trying, at any rate."

Jane set her basket down by the door. Even the floor had been worked over, so it appeared to be made of broad grey flagstones. She turned, slowly, to look at the whole glamural. It was still unfinished, but she could see the illusion it would be when he completed it. "Vincent, this is beautiful."

"You were right."

"About what?"

"When you said that I would feel better with some occupation. You were right."

Language fled from Jane's grasp. She could only cross the room and embrace him. His cheeks were smooth, and he smelled of lavender.

Their conversation after that was not in words, but was no less sincere for it.

When they parted from the embrace, Jane found her words. "Thank you."

Vincent cleared his throat. "I thought you would be out longer." He gestured to a shrub outside the glass wall. "I am not quite happy with the perspective."

Jane looked at her husband, holding the onion, then over to the cooking pot. She smiled at him. "From my perspective, everything is beautiful."

Fifteen

A Flight of Doves

Jane stood at the front of the choir as they finished rehearsals for the next service. She had grouped the girls in sets of three so they could handle the longer threads between them without strain. Sister Maria Agnes had been unfamiliar with the yoked technique that she and Vincent sometimes used to work at distances. It was similar to the Y-shaped stand that a glassmaker might use to steady a blowpipe but was composed of glamour. With it, a glamourist could treble the distance she could ordinarily reach. Using this technique from the choir loft meant that the girls could cause their flight of doves to pass over the congregation's head, instead of being confined to the space close to the choir.

Sister Maria Agnes had charge of the singers

and now stood beaming at the group. "Ladies, you have done very well today. I am very proud of you. Due to the rain, we shall take our recess in the warehouse before lunch." She looked to Jane, and nodded giving her space to speak.

"Thank you for your work today. Your coordination was admirable." She looked the glamourists over. The girls were all flushed, and more than one still breathed quickly. "Make sure to be careful on the stairs, and if you need to sit for a few minutes before going out, please do. It is better to be cautious than vain."

Laughing, they clattered down the stairs, but Jane noticed that some of the older girls stayed close to the younger ones and kept an eye on them. That consideration made her even more proud than the glamour they had created.

"It is a good group," she commented as she gathered up her sheet music.

Sister Maria Agnes nodded. "The Abbess reminds them that we are all equal in the sight of God, and, eventually, they start to believe her. Oh, but you would not want to be here at the start of a school year, when the wealthy girls first get mingled in with the 'pickpockets and thieves.' Poor Lucia . . . But, the girls from the street are often easier to mould than the finest lady."

"They know what they have gained, coming here." Jane tapped the edges of her music to straighten them.

"Oh, my dear, I did not mean to remind you . . . That is . . . I mean, your situation is not at all the . . . Except it is the same, I suppose." She sighed. "I should really blame this on my poor Italian, but even in German I can say the stupidest things. *Einen ziemlichen Bockmist verzapfen*—Lucia? What do you need?"

Her sentences ran so much together that it took Jane a moment to see that Lucia had returned to the choir loft. The girl bobbed a curtsy. "Pardon, ma'am, but Lady Vincent's husband is here."

Jane almost dropped the pages she was holding. Another letter must have come. Or Lord Byron was back. Or Vincent was injured. Or the apartment had caught on fire. Or, more likely, he just wanted to walk her home. She set the score down carefully. "Thank you, Lucia."

Sister Maria Agnes beamed and followed Jane and Lucia to the stairs. The long, winding stone staircase echoed with the sound of their footsteps in a peculiar syncopated rhythm. Jane was hard-pressed not to slip past Lucia and run. It was so hard to set a good example sometimes.

She rounded the last turn in the stairs and stepped out into the sanctuary. Vincent was standing by the front entrance of the small church, and his face lit when he saw Jane. Her knees weakened with relief. Nothing bad had happened.

Vincent carried her shopping basket over one arm and fairly vibrated with energy. "Can you come with me?"

"What is it?"

He hesitated, glancing at Sister Maria Agnes and Lucia, then gave a little nod of decision. "I saw the pirate captain."

"What!" Jane's surprise was so great that the idea of governing her tone did not even occur to her. The word burst forth like a flock of doves and echoed around the sanctuary.

The nun's exclamation was just as loud as Jane's, but in German—and, she was fairly certain, not entirely proper. She said something very fast to Vincent.

He replied, then spoke Italian for Jane's benefit. "Yes. He was disguised, but I am quite certain it was him."

"Dear Lord in Heaven—" Sister Maria Agnes appeared to suddenly remember Lucia, who stared at Vincent as if she were quite smitten with him. "If you will excuse us, dear. I think it is time for you to rejoin your sisters."

The girl clearly wanted to stay, caught by the romance of the words "pirate captain," but she gave another little curtsy and hurried out of the church. Jane waited for her to leave before voicing her next thought.

It seemed impossible that the pirate captain should have returned to Murano. Vincent had been distressed for so long that she was half afraid that he was imagining things. Jane studied him, looking for any sign of disordered senses. "You were—forgive me for pointing this out, but you were not fully conscious on the ship and saw the captain only once. Is there a chance you are mistaken?"

"I watched him as he searched your person. You may be certain that I marked his face very thoroughly. It was absolutely him, though he has trimmed his moustache and adopted to the clothing of a Venetian gentleman. But I doubted myself as well, so I followed him. Would you care to guess where he went?"

"Ca' Sanuto?"

Vincent shook his head. "He went to Signor Querini, who appeared to greet him most cordially."

They left their shopping basket with Sister Maria Agnes. She was nearly as excited as they were by what the appearance of the pirate captain might mean and, with their full approval, went to tell the Abbess.

As Jane and Vincent hurried through the rain, they speculated on the possibilities. It seemed likeliest that he had returned to Murano to ask Querini to make more *Verres Obscurcis*. Vincent explained that before coming to fetch Jane, he had followed the pirate captain back to a large private residence not far from the square where he busked. Unwilling to let him get away, Vincent had hired the Pulcinella puppet player to watch the palazzo and let him know if the man left the island, and then ran to find Jane. He said that he knew she would be vexed if he did not.

At the police station, Vincent held the door for Jane as they stepped into the vestibule. From there they entered the main office hall, and Vincent stepped up to the desk where *Gendarme* Gallo sat.

The *polizia* looked up, smiling, and set his quill aside. "Sir David, good to see you."

"Good afternoon. Is the *capo di polizia* in?" Vincent nodded to the office door, although it stood open and the office was clearly empty.

"Afraid not, but I'll tell him you came." He took up his quill again and drew the tally sheet toward him on which he recorded the Vincents' continued presence in Murano.

"Perhaps you might help, then."

Gallo raised an eyebrow at this break in routine. "Of course I would be happy to, if I can. What is the trouble?"

"I have seen one of the men who swindled us."

"What? In Murano?"

Vincent could hardly have seen the man elsewhere, as

they were not allowed to leave the island, but Jane held her tongue.

"Yes, sir."

The *polizia* frowned and wrote this down. "I will tell the *capo*."

"I—ah—thought that you might want to arrest him now."

"Is he disturbing the peace?"

Vincent narrowed his eyes. "Beyond swindling us, you mean?"

Gallo spread his hands as if helpless. "I have only your word on that."

Jane's nostrils flared at the insinuation. "Are you suggesting that we are lying?"

"Not at all. Merely that you might be mistaken, and I must leave all such decisions in the hands of the *capo di polizia*."

Vincent's teeth ground audibly, but he retained his visible composure. "And if the man should leave before the *capo*'s return?"

"Then that would be unfortunate." The *polizia* replied in an equally placid tone. "But I shall tell the *capo* as soon as he returns." He slid the paper aside and tapped it, as if in promise of his actions.

Jane stared at the paper. "Then . . . would it not be advisable to write down where and when my husband saw the man?"

The *polizia*'s complexion changed some at that, becoming paler, not redder with embarrassment, as one might expect. His countenance made it clear that he knew he had made an error. Jane knew with a sudden certainty that he would say nothing to the *capo di polizia*. Gallo recovered quickly, though, and pulled the tally sheet toward himself again. "Of course. Where did you say you saw the pirate?"

Vincent stared at him for a moment, no doubt struck by the same thing that Jane was. "I think it would be best if we waited for the Chief's return. When did you say he would be back?"

"Tomorrow afternoon." Gallo set his quill back down. "I would hope that you are not considering any actions for which I might need to arrest you. It would be a shame if you were to lose the freedom that the *capo di polizia* has so unexpectedly allowed you."

With a chill, Jane remembered that this was the officer who had found the promissory note in Vincent's pocket. It seemed to her that he had known, that he must have known it would be there. His current threats were very clearly those of someone who was in the employ of Sanuto.

And he had also known that the man who Vincent had seen was one of the pirates, without Vincent ever telling him. The same thought must have occurred to Vincent because he gave the *polizia* a short bow. "Of course. I will not take up any more of your time."

"It is no trouble at all." The *polizia* picked up the paper he had written the note to the *capo* on and put it in the drawer. He slid the drawer shut. "I am glad that we understand each other."

Vincent led Jane to the door. She could feel the restrained tension in his arm. When they were on the threshold, the *polizia* said, "I will expect to see you tomorrow with your usual report."

"Of course." Vincent opened the door, and they left as

quickly as possible without actually running out of the station.

A few streets away, Vincent directed them under a gallery and stopped. "Are we agreed that Gallo is in their employment?" He did not need to say who "they" were.

Jane nodded. "The question for me is whether the *capo* is as well."

"Either way, the *polizia* is going to alert them to the fact that we know they are here."

Jane straightened the cuffs of her coat. "Then we should see what we can find out before they do."

Vincent smiled and offered Jane his arm. "I love you. Very much."

Jane and Vincent hurried through the streets to the square. As they entered it, the Pulcinella puppet player stepped out of his booth, which he had set up under a colonnade. In spite of having a dry area around him, passers-by hurried past without so much as slowing.

The puppet player was a youngish man who was so exceedingly slender that he could have played Juliet in the days when Shakespeare's plays had been performed entirely by men. He was introduced as Signor Zancani. He nodded toward the building. "Two more men have arrived, but I've not seen anyone leave. 'Course, I can't see the canal entrance from here, but everyone who arrived on foot is still in the building."

"Thank you." Staring at the building, Vincent handed the young man a few coins.

Waving them away, Zancani said, "No, no. I didn't protest when you said 'hire' because you were in a hurry. If you want to do me a good turn, put a banner over my booth the next time the weather is nice."

"Why not today?"

He shrugged. "Because no one will stop today. I'm just here because I had some repairs to do to a puppet."

The Vincents thanked him and walked farther down the colonnade for a better view of the building that the pirate captain was in. It was an older style of home with a tall wall surrounding it and space for a garden between the wall and the palazzo. Lights were visible through the windows on the second floor, but none of the inhabitants stood obligingly near a window.

Vincent leaned closer to Jane as though his voice could be audible through the rain to those in the building across the street. "It occurs to me that they would recognise either one of us."

Jane nodded. "It almost makes me wish you had not shaved."

"I can grow the beard again, though it would not be fast enough."

"I said *almost*. Should we ask the puppet player?"

"No . . ." Vincent's voice trailed away and his gaze went distant, as it did when he was considering a theory of glamour.

"What? What are you thinking?"

Without seeming to hear her, Vincent took a step backwards, still staring into an inner distance. He pulled glamour and quickly wove a change in his hair colour from its usual dark brown to a steely grey. A full moustache now connected his side whiskers. He turned to Jane, managing the folds with a nearly invisible ease. If Jane had not known him so well, she would not have realized the effort. Only a very slight quickness of breath betrayed him.

"You are not thinking to confront them like that."

He shook his head, and the illusion stayed close to his person. "No. Just to see if Sanuto is there. I can pose as a messenger."

"Even if that were a good idea, you cannot seriously propose using glamour as a disguise."

"I can hold it for about half an hour, I think."

"For half an hour?"

"Likely longer, but half an hour I feel confident of." He had cleverly masked the places the illusion would likely slip in locks of hair so the movement seemed more or less natural. "I work glamour for longer periods of time on a regular basis."

"But not while walking with it."

"You recall Miss FitzCameron from your parents' neighbourhood and how she masked her teeth. If she could dance, why can't I walk with this?"

"She fainted constantly and could never speak while the illusion was in place. *You* are holding glamour over two areas rather than just one."

The smell of damp stone rose around them in answer to the rain. Vincent stubbornly continued to hold the grey hair and moustache while he stared at the building. "Have you another idea?"

What Vincent proposed was ridiculous on the face of it. To walk with glamour required a constant regulation of tension as the folds' relationships with each other and the ether shifted. Much the way sliding a line quickly through the fingers produced heat from friction, moving glamour took more energy than merely pulling it out of the ether.

It *was* possible to create small illusions and hold them, but not without risk to one's health.

But Vincent was right. They needed to know if Sanuto was here—or, if not, what the pirate captain intended—which meant that one of them needed to see inside. And yet Jane was uncertain what they would do with this information. "I do not know which worries me more. That you are thinking of going inside or that you are going to try doing it while wearing glamour."

Before he could make any further argument, a group of nuns walked past them. They wore a different habit than those of the sisters at Santa Maria degli Angeli, but it was enough for Jane's mind to offer a new possibility. "What about a *lointaine vision?*"

A *lointaine vision* was an invention of Vincent's that allowed an observer to watch something from a distance, even if there were obstacles in the way. Jane had used the fold only once, years earlier, to eavesdrop on her sister and the rogue who had attempted to seduce her. The glamourist could snake the folds around or over those things that blocked the view, and they carried sound as well. While there were other methods of carrying sight *or* sound, there was no other for carrying both. Its chief drawback was that it required constant management of the threads as they carried the sights and sounds from the thing viewed to the glamourist. Most significantly for their purposes, it retained the images of whatever was viewed through it. That had been useful when rescuing her sister, but since it was difficult to move the thread due to its length, there was little use for it in polite society. If they could convince the *capo di polizia* that the pirate captain was here, then a recording would certainly be of use, though they would have to bring the *capo di polizia* to the recording.

"Where would we cast the *lointaine vision* from?" He let the glamour masking his features dissolve, which gave Jane a measure of relief.

"By the wall. We would set a *Sphère Obscurcie* to mask us."

He shook his head. "The rain makes the outline visible."

"Really?" Jane thought for a moment, and could see why. "Ah . . . the offset of the raindrops would show. What if we were under shelter, then could we do it from here?"

Vincent cocked his head and measured the distance with his gaze. After a moment, he slowly shook his head. "I think it is too far to span."

"If we worked in tandem? We could try yoking it." If the children could pass doves over the congregation by working in teams of three, it seemed possible that two adults—professionals, at that—could span the gap between the buildings.

"I have become used to working alone again, clearly. Yes. Let us do that, Muse."

Jane and Vincent took up a station in the lee of a column, where the passers-by were less likely to stumble through their *Sphère Obscurcie*, and began to weave. Vincent stood in front, supporting the weight of the folds, while Jane fed the line out. The *lointaine vision* was a variation on *bouclé torsadée* in that both were a loop of thread coiled around itself. The difference was that the *lointaine vision* required leaving the loop open with a glamourist constantly feeding out the line and twisting it, while the *bouclé torsadée* was tied off. Even working in tandem, the energy to span the space across the street was such that Jane was glad they had chosen a spot next to a column, so that she could lean against it. Panting, Vincent once had to ask Jane to pause feeding out the line so that he could shift his grip on the yoke and lift it higher, to control the glamour's natural tendency to drift downward.

It took the better part of ten minutes for them to get the line into the lighted window. When they did, Jane gasped as the image shifted to show the room inside and the conversation became audible.

What she could see of the room was well appointed, but the *lointaine vision* was like looking through a tube. They could see only what was directly in front of its end. Jane did not see Sanuto at first, but she heard his voice clearly: "—tell you, one of the finest hunters I have ever seen."

"And did you win the horse?" The pirate captain sat in range of the *lointaine vision* on a low sofa. He was recognisable, though, as Vincent had reported, he had shorn his long moustaches and now wore the clothes of a Venetian gentleman. Beside him sat Biasio. Jane had another moment of shock at seeing them together, because she now realized why Biasio had seemed so familiar.

It was not that he had reminded her of Mathieu. "Biasio was the first mate of our ship."

"Are you certain?" Vincent hastily tied off the yoke so it would remain steady and came back to help her with the *lointaine vision* itself.

"Imagining the pirate captain with his moustache caused me to do the same for Biasio. I am quite certain." Jane shifted her grip forward on the glamour and let Vincent slide into place beside her. His fingers brushed the inside of her wrist as he took hold of the thread.

He grunted as he began to see and hear the room with her. "I still remember so little of that."

The men laughed at something that Sanuto said. Jane very much wished to see him, but he sat to the right of the room and only his foot, propped in front of him on an ottoman, was visible through the *lointaine vision*. The sword cane leaned against the low stool as though ready for use.

A fourth man stood at a sideboard at the far wall, pouring a glass of port. Jane recognised him as being the clerk who had supposedly handled their papers at the port. He lifted a glass of sherry and saluted the other gentleman. "As graceful a gambit as I have ever seen."

They continued to talk about the hunter and other admirable horses, and then conversation drifted to racing, but nothing incriminating was said, nor did they refer to Jane or Vincent. In fact, there was nothing to indicate that they were anything beyond genial colleagues. The glamour kept spooling out, and, even with Vincent's help, Jane's strength was beginning to flag. They knew that Sanuto was there, but nothing beyond that.

A knock came at the door to Sanuto's room. Biasio rose and opened the door to admit *Gendarme* Gallo. His hat was damp and his hair plastered against his head. The laughter ceased and the pirate captain sat up. "What?"

"Pardon the intrusion, signors." Gallo bowed to each man

in turn. "Sir David came to the offices today and said that he saw you."

"Saw who?" Sanuto shifted in his chair.

"Signor Coppa." He bowed to the pirate captain. At last Jane had a name for the man.

Coppa seemed entirely too silly to be a pirate captain— which, of course, he was not. But he also seemed too silly to be a rookster. Frowning, Coppa said, "Where? I avoided the square and their apartment."

"He did not say." Gallo turned his hat in his hand. "But I do not think he will be troubling you."

Sanuto leaned forward, his hand becoming briefly visible as he lifted his cane from its place. "Surely you were not fool-ish enough to imply that you were associated with us."

"He was going to go to the *capo di polizia*."

"And?" Sanuto sat back. "If he had, you would have told us, and we would have removed. Now . . ."

Coppa rolled his eyes. "Are we blown?"

"What about trying a MacGregor?" Biasio said. "You'd have to dye your hair again, Spada."

Spada? Which of the swindlers was that?

As if in answer to her question, Sanuto's voice rolled out. "Perhaps. Let's hear exactly what our friend said to Sir David."

"I . . . I told him that I hoped he would do nothing that would cause me to have to arrest him. And that I expected to see him tomorrow." Where his face had, before, been damp with rain it now had beads of sweat dripping from the brow.

"And?"

"And he wouldn't say anything else to me after that."

Sanu—no, Spada—said, "Go back. Say nothing else to him. If he brings it up again, imply that you work with the secret Carbonari society to reclaim Venice, but do not volunteer the information. Clear?"

"Yes, sir."

"Denaro? Pay the man."

Evidently, Denaro managed their money even when not pretending to be a customs clerk. He pulled out a handful of coins and counted out seven to Gallo. He bowed again to each of the men, and then took his leave. They waited until the door to their room shut, and then waited again until they heard the front door close.

As soon as it did, Coppa cursed. "Now what? Do you think you can still pull off a Hausman? I mean, they know we're here. I don't even know how. I swear I avoided all of the spots that either of them frequent."

"It is all right, Coppa. I think it is fairly clear that Gallo is not as steady a tumbler as we'd hoped." Spada tapped the ground with his cane. "Well, Bastone? Do you think you can make a *Verre Obscurci* without either of the Vincents?"

The apprentice, whom she had known as Biasio, hesitated. "Yes?"

"If they don't work, then he can at least fake it," Coppa said. "We'll be gone with the money before the Lombardy-Venetia buyers realize. Or simply blow town with their deposit."

"Short-term profit, gentlemen, is not as valuable as a repeat customer," Spada murmured. "That is why we are here. Coppa, any further thoughts on the location of the real spheres?"

Coppa shook his head. "None. And I am fairly certain that Querini was telling the truth, but we should perhaps have Bastone ask again when he goes to work with him. He knows him better."

Vincent made a startled intake of air at the same time Jane did. The real spheres? If they did not have them, who did?

Denaro humphed. "More and more, I think it must have been Gallo who made the swap. They worked when we first got them."

"Or they cracked in transit," Bastone said.

"Whatever the case, Bastone will have to make us a new one before the bidders come." Spada tipped his glass to the former apprentice.

"You don't understand how hard these are to make. I barely understand his papers."

Coppa narrowed his gaze. "But you watched them. That was the whole point."

"The folds were so thin. I only know they were using cold because they cracked a sphere the first night. I mean, it's like this . . ." His gaze went distant as he looked into the ether and reached for a fold. Bastone paused, gaze turning toward the window until he appeared to be looking directly at Jane. "Hullo . . . What's that?"

Sixteen

Tarot and Puppetry

The moment it became apparent that Bastone saw the thread of glamour they had pushed into the room, Vincent cursed. Jane hauled backwards to pull the thread out of sight, but Vincent held it firm. In the room, Bastone rose to his feet.

"He will see it." She tugged again, but Vincent's hands were in front of hers, and the thread did not move.

"He already has, but right now it is just a curious thread in the window. If it twitches, he will know someone is watching." Vincent slid his fingers into the thread and pried apart the two pieces. "Here, hold this side steady, but let it untwist. Then tie it off."

"What are you doing?"

"Making it look like it is the remnant of an

anchoring thread for a street illusion." He took the other end and let it begin to untwist. Taking a deep breath, he looked at Jane. "Do not worry." Then he ran, holding the thread, directly across the street.

To someone who did not understand the toll glamour could take, what he did might appear commonplace. To walk with glamour, even a single thread, was difficult. But this was a very long thread that had required two of them to support its length. And yet . . . he crossed the street, maintaining it by himself, and the end of the thread in the window did not move. Not at all.

As he moved, he fed the end he was holding back into the ether in a steady spool so that he was constantly changing the relationship of the thread to the ether, the thread to himself, and the thread to the yoke while keeping the end that stood in the window absolutely steady.

And he did all this while running.

He did this while fatigued from having spent the past half hour spooling out glamour.

Jane was therefore dismayed, but not surprised, when he attained the other side of the street, tied off the glamour, and sagged against the wall. Leaning against it, he turned and gave Jane a merry wave, but he was clearly fatigued. His breath puffed into the cool November air in great jets of steam. They rose into the air like a signal fire.

Vincent frowned and closed his mouth, curving his hands over his nose to mask some of the steam.

Jane tied her end of the glamour off, making sure not to let it move. The thread had uncoiled so that it no longer carried images from the palazzo. She looked up at the window without the benefit of the *lointaine vision* and was alarmed to see Bastone standing there. She shrank back, before remembering that she stood in a *Sphère Obscurcie*. She glanced across the road to see if Vincent's breath might be visible from the window, but he was no longer standing against the wall.

For a moment, Jane thought that he had cast a *Sphère* as well, before understanding that he sat, sagged against the base of the wall. Her instinct almost carried her forward, but she checked her flight before she stepped out of the influence of the *Sphère*. Bastone still stood in the window looking out, and would see her if she crossed the street. Though her every instinct urged her toward Vincent, she also knew his limits— better than he did—and knew that nothing worse would come of this than him becoming a little damp from the rain and the puddled water on the street. Still, it took an effort to steel her resolve and step back. She slid out of the *Sphère* and behind the column.

As she did, the puppet player was emerging from his booth. Signor Zancani motioned her back. "I will tend to him. Lest they see."

Biting the inside of her lip, Jane waited behind the pillar. It chafed to do nothing, but the puppet player was quite correct. The rain was a mere drizzle, and the overcast sky left more than enough light to see by, so she would be visible if she crossed the street now. Zancani darted across as though running for the door of the building next to the palazzo to escape the rain, but as soon as he was against the wall, and could trust it to hide him, he doubled back to Vincent.

Her husband was already stirring. With immeasurable relief, Jane watched Vincent accept a hand from the puppet player. The men made their way up the street, staying close by the wall. As they walked, Vincent seemed to recover his strength and rely less on the puppet player to steady him.

Jane forced her attention away from them and back to the window. Bastone was speaking to someone in the room, and seemed to have lost interest in the glamour. Had he been able to discern the spiral before they got it untwisted? It was similar enough to a *bouclé torsadée* that he might have recognised that someone was spying on them.

Signor Zancani paused at the corner and said something to Vincent. Her husband nodded and glanced at Jane, pointing at the puppet booth. She nodded in return as the men turned the corner away from her, guessing that they would circle through the streets to return to the booth and meet her there. Jane reached into the ether and undid the *Sphère Obscurcie*, taking care that the knot did not fray and call attention to itself. Keeping to the shadows deep under the colonnade, Jane made her way to the puppet booth and waited by it.

She divided her attention between the palazzo and the street. None of the men were visible in the window now, but she was as worried about the door, in case any of them should depart. More than that, her concern was for Vincent. In spite of her consciousness that his dizziness had been largely because he had tried to quiet his breathing after such an exertion, she would not rest easy until he was with her again.

It took some five minutes for Vincent and Signor Zancani to reappear at the far end of the colonnade. They had their heads close together as they walked, and were deep in conversation. At first, Jane caught only scattered words: ". . . need more than . . ." and ". . . you certain?"

As they reached the booth, Zancani nodded. "Of course." He pulled aside the brightly striped fabric of the back and motioned them inside. "It is not as elegant as your method of hiding, but the screen offers a good view of the street."

Jane followed Vincent into the little booth. It was dimmer than the exterior, though not so dark as she had expected. The gaily painted scenery had been done on a piece of thick netting. From the front, it showed a painting of a street in Venice, but they could see through it with perfect ease.

A trunk stood under one wall with a small sewing kit and a puppet upon it. The devil from the show lay with its wooden head tilted to the side so that a burn on the cloth body was visible. "Flash-paper accident," Zancani said, and scooped up the puppet and the kit and tucked them inside the trunk. He gestured to it. "Please, Signora."

"Thank you."

"And you, Vincent." The puppet player pointed to the trunk. "I know I said that you would make more money if you fainted, but I meant for an audience."

Vincent chuckled and seated himself beside Jane. "Zancani has agreed to help us."

"Help us do what?"

Vincent looked confused for a moment. "Regain our possessions, of course."

"Have you a proposal for how to do that?"

Her husband nodded, a slow light building in his gaze. "I have been thinking . . . They obviously do not have the wrong glass spheres. I think the *Verre Obscurci* will not work because of the rain."

"Ah." Of course. It had taken Jane and Vincent some time

to discover that the *Verre* required full daylight to work. It was only chance, really, that led to their first trial being outside on a sunny day, in such a way that made their use clear. If Sanut—if Spada had watched their experiments with the glass sphere at Ca' Sanuto and not understood that they required sun, then of course she could well imagine how it might seem that the glass had broken in transit. "How were you thinking to use this information? Shall we tell the *capo di polizia* or write to Mr. Hobhouse? We have names for them now, at least: Coppa, Bastone, Spada, and—"

"Denaro?" The puppet player shook his head. "Those aren't names. Those are the suits in the tarot deck."

"The what?"

Signor Zancani crouched by a small bag resting against the wall of the booth and pulled out a rectangular bundle wrapped in cloth. Unfolding the cloth, he exposed an elegant deck of cards. "I'm not above doing some fortune-telling from time to time, if that is what the audience wants. Here." He went through the cards and pulled out four. "Wands, Swords, Coins, and Cups."

Snorting, Vincent shook his head. "They are titles. Wands, or Bastone . . . for Biasio, who is clearly their glamourist."

"The pirate captain . . . Coppa, Cups." Jane leaned her head back, remembering the little clerk in the port office. "Coins. Denaro is the clerk."

"And Sanuto, their leader . . . Spada, Swords. That puts his sword cane in a new light, eh?" Vincent ran his hand through his hair. "Well . . . in any event, I have in mind something more personal than that."

The rain dripping on the street gave a false sense of

tranquillity inside the close confines of the puppet booth. Jane tapped her finger against her knee, considering Vincent's words. "You are thinking to beat Spada at his own game."

"Muse. For the past three months, I have thought of nothing else."

Jane slipped her hand into his. The prospect of regaining their possessions, of beating Spada, was deeply appealing, but the memory of how easily they had been fooled stayed with her. More precisely, the part that she had played in delivering them to him by being so trusting and not looking beyond the surface of any action. "As have I, but he is well funded and we are without resources. Then, too, he has a *polizia* in his employ. Clearly, he is prepared for us—look at the way in which Gallo behaved. The discovery might be something he had planned. I cannot help but think of how easy it was to spy on them and wonder if we are somehow playing into their hands again."

Vincent drew his head back and opened his mouth as though to retort. Then he closed it and shook his head, glancing toward Zancani. "You understand."

The puppet player raised his hands and took a step backwards. "Do not ask me to intervene. I will be outside." He ducked under the curtain before either could say anything. Jane was just as glad to see him go, though she knew he could hear them well enough. She paused and let her vision expand to her second sight, looking for any sign that someone was listening with less worldly means, but she saw no threads of glamour.

Running his hand through his hair, Vincent wet his lips. "Jane . . . We have an advantage, in that they cannot make the spheres work."

"So we overheard."

"But what reason would they have had to return to Murano? If their plan is to coax me into helping them resolve this, then they need me because the spheres do not work. If the spheres do work, then why would they need me?"

"Why did the pirates need to attack our ship? We did not understand the real reasons for that at the time, either."

He waved that aside. "It is not the same."

"We do not know that. All we know for certain is that Spada and his men are here. And how do we know that? Because you just happened to see one of them go to Querini's. Might that not have been their plan?"

"If he had passed through the square where I perform, yes. Absolutely, yes." Vincent's excitement drove him to stand, but there was nowhere for him to pace in the small booth. "But I was shopping—shopping at a *grocer's*. How could they possibly have expected me to be doing that?"

"A child watching the door of our apartment could easily report where you were going. Or perhaps the bait was intended for me."

Vincent shook his head firmly. "At a time when you are always at the convent? No. Look at the palazzo. I think they have been here for some days already. And who knows how long they will remain? We must act, and act quickly."

Jane crossed her arms, but the source of her discomfort was uncertain. Was it that she thought Vincent was mistaken and that they would be drawn even deeper into Spada's schemes, or was it that he was correct and she was simply afraid? Was her distress over their circumstances causing her to quiz every situation in which she found herself?

Jane did not want to live in a world where she could trust no one. Caution, yes, caution she had learned, but she hoped it would not dip into paranoia. She nodded slowly. "What did you have in mind?"

"I want to steal back the glass that Spada took and replace them with flawed spheres."

"Why bother replacing them? Why not just take them?"

"Because if we did, they would know that the *Verres* are gone, and that may drive them to try to re-create the technique. If they continue to think that it simply does not work, then it will go no further."

"They already think that they have the wrong spheres, and that is not dissuading them."

"But they do *not* have the wrong spheres. They will eventually understand the relation sunshine has to their performance."

Jane could see his point, but another obstacle occurred to her. "Where will we get flawed spheres? None of the glass-makers would work with us when we had funds. Why would they now?"

"They would not work with us because we wanted to watch. Now, we only need some balls of glass. We can hire an apprentice to make those."

Chewing the inside of her lip, Jane considered. She had seen marbles in glass shops, and they were inexpensive. The sort of thing they required had no design in it, and though larger by several fold, still might cost very little. That could work. "They still have the journal. We will have to steal or replace that as well."

Vincent did not quite mask his glee when she said "we." A

grin spread over his face. "Agreed. But we can make changes to it, so that if they try to re-create the technique, it will fail. The question is, how do we make a copy?"

"The scriptorium . . . They could duplicate it. But someone will have to go in to see what papers they have." She shook her head, not quite believing that they were seriously contemplating any of this. "This is madness, you know."

"It is. I am counting on that fact."

There was the gleam of excitement that she had been missing these past few months. That flare of inspiration was at the heart of her husband. Whatever the means, she was grateful to see the man she married coming back into his own. Even sitting in a puppet booth, she could see his mind working and putting together pieces of a plan, as surely as if he were plotting a glamural.

Her only concern—one that she would not voice to Vincent—was that they might not succeed. After watching him turn inward with despair over the past months, what would happen to her husband if they failed at swindling the swindler?

Seventeen

Lion in the Air

Jane sat in the window of the room they had secured across the street from the palazzo. They had used a little of the funds left from pawning her ring to rent the room, which Jane thought was rather a telling measure of Vincent's state of mind. Even with her heavy wool shawl wrapped around her, the want of the hearth was apparent. She had thought that their apartment was cold, but she had overrated its degree of discomfort. This room was little more than a closet and only the people crowded into it gave it any warmth.

Vincent leaned against the wall next to her, sketching a lion in the air in front of him. On the floor, Signor Zancani carved a puppet head. Each stroke of his chisel released a sweet resinous fragrance. Sister Maria Agnes sat with her rosary by the door, counting through the beads while she stared at the wall opposite.

On the other side of the canal, which Jane could not see from there, another room held Sister Aquinata and one of the other nuns, who were watching the palazzo's water entrance. For the past two days, all they had done was watch and discuss options. After talking over the possibilities for how to approach Spada, they realized that they needed more information. This had led to them watching the palazzo for two full days, in spite of Vincent's urgency, to see if there were any patterns that they might exploit.

Aware that they must also be under surveillance, Jane and Vincent returned to their small room each day at their usual time and tried to continue on as if the conversation with Gallo at the *polizia* station had truly confounded them. Vincent continued to check in at the station, but was denied every request to speak to the *capo di polizia*. He was uncertain if that refusal came from the *capo* or from Gallo.

Footsteps on the stairs caused them all to stop their activities. Vincent released the threads holding the lion. Zancani brushed the wood shavings to the side, and Sister Maria Agnes tucked her rosary away. Jane stayed seated, hardly daring to move.

The Abbess let herself into the room. The deep frown on her face told Jane everything she needed to know. She turned her face back to the street to continue her watch.

"He would not see me." Her words broke the silence that had held the room for the past hour.

Jane sighed, her breath fogging the window. She had so hoped that the *capo di polizia* was not involved, but if he would not speak to the Abbess, then that hope seemed in vain.

"Are you certain he knew you were there?" Vincent pushed away from the wall and drew out one of the room's chairs for the Abbess.

"Absolutely. His door was open, and I could see him clearly. Gallo went in to tell him. I could not hear them, but the *capo* looked up, made eye contact with me, and frowned." She shook her head. "I do not know what to think."

"It was worth a try." Jane had very much hoped that if the nun spoke to the *capo*, he could take care of the swindlers, but her last chance to keep Vincent from doing something imprudent had just evaporated. Jane had grown increasingly apprehensive about Vincent's state. While she understood his desire to best Spada and found it perfectly natural, the passion with which he threw himself into planning bordered on an obsession.

"So we will have to move ahead on our own." Far from being distressed, Vincent seemed almost excited by this news.

"I still do not see how we are going to gain access to the interior." From Jane's position, it looked as though their entrance was barred by the wall surrounding the building.

"I could make an attempt," Signor Zancani said.

Jane shook her head, but Vincent spoke the objection. "It must be either Jane or myself, in order to identify the papers and the *Verres*."

Turning her attention back to the window, Jane said, "The difficulty is that at least one member of the band is always at home. They keep inconstant hours and use both entrances indiscriminately."

"The servants are all local," Vincent said. "Might we do something with that?"

It was a small crack, but the only one that they might use to gain access. "Perhaps one of them could draw us a map of the interior? With that, we could at least narrow our search to the likeliest rooms."

The Abbess nodded. "I would be cautious about any who work there presently, but I can speak to the priest in this parish to see if there is anyone who has been released from service."

"There must be another way to enter." Vincent came to stand by Jane and stared across at the other building.

The Abbess joined them. "Perhaps it is time for us to ask them for a little charity?"

"Thank you, but no." Jane shook her head. "It is good of you to offer, but this is undoubtedly a precarious venture, and you have already done so much."

Her nostrils flared, and she lifted her chin. "They used my church. I do not take kindly to that."

"But they must also know that I am associated with you," Jane said, "and your visit to the *capo di polizia* will draw attention to that. Were you to call on them, even in the name of charity, it would be immediately suspect."

Some of the fight drifted out of the nun. She sighed. "I suppose you have a point. Well. Anything that does not harm my sisters or our charges is yours, should you need it. I will get a map for you, but I have no idea how you will get inside."

Vincent, who had been staring at the window, pointed to a grocer's boy who was trundling a barrow down the street. "Perhaps I could make a delivery?"

"We lived at Ca' Sanuto with Spada for weeks. They will surely recognise you."

Signor Zancani lifted his hand. "I can help with that."

As intent as Jane was on trying to stop Vincent from charging into danger, she found herself curious as to what the puppet player had in mind. "How?"

"Theatrical cosmetics." He grinned and lifted the puppet head. "Glamourists aren't the only ones who can create illusions."

While Signor Zancani was quite correct, there were tasks for which glamour was the best candidate. As a result, Jane now sat in what appeared to be Spada's library with the Abbess and Sister Maria Agnes, waiting for Vincent to return with Signor Zancani. Their footsteps echoed on the hollow wooden floor that lay under the glamour they had erected in the warehouse owned by the convent, which was used to give the girls a place for recess during rainy days. The glamural they had created would fool no one, but the hastily rendered structure gave them a better idea of what they would face when Jane went into the palazzo.

"You were right." Vincent walked through the wall, as if he were a ghost. The puppet player was close behind.

Jane jumped in her seat, in spite of knowing that it was a glamural. "I think you take a certain delight in that."

"You are adorable when you squeak."

"I did not squeak."

"Squeal?"

She humphed at him and looked to Sister Maria Agnes for support, but the little German nun was studiously going over her notes. "So we laid this out wrong when we created it?"

The room was a reconstruction based on the map and what they could see through the window.

Vincent shook his head and settled into one of the camp chairs they had disguised with glamour to represent the furniture in the library. His fatigue showed in the way he eased himself into the chair. The glamural was rough, but it was still extremely large. Jane felt it herself, and Vincent had worked even harder than she. "The hall upstairs matches the measurements. But it is not the same length."

Signor Zancani nodded. "It is a full ten feet shorter."

Sister Maria Agnes clapped her hands together and looked around the library, as if it could offer her some clue that they had not placed there. "Do you think there is a secret room, or is it simply a mistake?"

"Likely a mistake, given that our informant was not the most literate of maids," the Abbess said.

"I do not feel so certain." To Jane, it seemed more certain that Spada would have a hidden room in his palazzo for storing the spheres and other valuables. "It would make sense for Spada to install a strong room in the palazzo, and we know he has a glamourist on his team."

Vincent made a noise of agreement, continuing to examine the map as though he had not stayed up the past several nights studying them. "You will have to be prepared for both, I suppose." He scowled. "I do not like you going in alone."

"We have talked about this, love. You are impossible to disguise." Vincent had been forced to acknowledge that his height would be difficult to conceal. They also needed him outside for his ability to work glamour at a distance.

"With cosmetics, yes, but with glamour—"

Were they really going to have this conversation again? Her expression must have been clear, because Vincent cut himself off in midsentence and settled for a series of grumbles. She cleared her throat and sought to return them to the topic they had abandoned to discuss measurements. "Sister Maria Agnes, what is the word from Sister Franceschina and the other nuns in the scriptorium?"

The nun shuffled her pages to find a set of notes. "Sister Franceschina and her team say that they can make a duplicate. But given the complexity of the copy, they will need the journal for at least three days."

Jane grimaced. The chance of discovery was too great if the book was removed from the palazzo for that long. Assuming she could even find it when she went inside. Her chest tightened at the thought. "That makes it . . . difficult."

The group fell silent, recognising that she was right. Vincent tilted his head back to study the glamoured ceiling with a scowl. Sister Maria Agnes tapped her pencil upon her page of notes, and the Abbess removed her glasses to polish them. Moving his hands in a pantomime, Signor Zancani appeared to be trying to act out various scenarios with his fingers.

Jane pressed her fingers to her temple, trying to think. They needed to speed up the length of time it would take to make a copy of the book—or, rather, not an exact copy, but one in which certain key errors were introduced that would prevent anyone from understanding how the *Verres Obscurcis* were made.

Then she had an idea that might actually work. "Ah. There is a technique that glamourists use when multiple people are working on the same project, whereby a wall is broken into a series of squares. Each glamourist creates a rough framework within those squares, and then later the whole is tied together. Could each person from a team of calligraphers make notes about a portion of the page? Would that speed up the process?"

Sister Maria Agnes narrowed her gaze in thought and nodded slowly. "For the content, yes, but the handwriting—Oh! It is Sir David's. Of course. I see now, yes. Yes, that could work, indeed."

"Good." Vincent nodded with clear relief. His gaze went suddenly distant, then he turned to Jane with a lively interest that made her heart speed unaccountably. "Teams."

"What are you thinking?"

"A *bouclé torsadée*, but cross-woven with a lengthened pirl. It would only need a slight alteration to the rotational angle. Plus a *lointaine vision* running askance."

"Possible. But the distance?"

"Yoked and spliced."

Signor Zancani coughed and raised his hand. "Once again, for the puppet player?"

The nuns looked equally baffled, so Jane translated for her husband. "A *bouclé torsadée* ordinarily carries sound, but we can modify it to carry light instead. If we can work with a team of you, in the same way I had the choir girls use yokes with our dove display, then we should be able to span the gap across the street. Rather than trying to get the skein all the way across, Vincent and I can weave two shorter skeins and splice them. I can then hold the papers up to the *bouclé torsadée* so that Vincent can see them here in the closet room. Then he can run a *lointaine vision* through the *bouclé torsadée* to create an impression of the pages as I turn them."

Vincent nodded with the abstracted gaze of a man building a glamour in his head. Her husband had never appeared more attractive than in this moment. His idea would almost certainly work, and it would not require them to remove the journal from the premises at all. Then he frowned, tilting his head to the side. "No . . . no. It will have to be multiple *lointaines visions,* I think. After we finish, I can tie it off so that it plays in a loop and pause it wherever Sister Franceschina would like, but we can only have one page visible at a time."

Sister Maria Agnes nodded as she caught up with them. "And we need multiple nuns working on the copy to have it finished quickly enough. I have not used a . . . what did you call it? A *lointaine vision?*"

"It is an invention of Vincent's. I can show you the weave later."

"Can you move one after it is made?"

"If we keep it short and do not move it far." Vincent rubbed his forehead, scowling at the table as he thought. "Yes . . . that should work. We should make an extra journal to practise with."

"Agreed." Jane played through the scheme in her head to see how the pieces fit. "And then we need only to find a way to return to the palazzo to replace the journal with the forged copy. And replace the spheres with simple glass balls, though those will be harder to sneak in than the journal. And I will have to get them back out."

"I have an answer for that!" Signor Zancani perked up. "When I make your grocer's boy costume, I can give it a paunch so you can carry them in under your waistcoat. Padding only, the first time. Then replaced with the spheres."

"Excellent solution." At first Jane had been unconvinced that this plan could succeed, but as they talked through its problems, she found herself starting to believe that they might actually pull it off. "Let us hope that I can discover where the *Verres* are kept during my first—"

The unmistakable sound of a walking stick tapping against the floor cut Jane off. It accompanied the footsteps of a gentleman with an uneven tread, as though he walked with a limp. Jane looked to Vincent. He, too, appeared stricken by the sound. They had heard it so many times at Ca' Sanuto.

Sister Maria Agnes opened her mouth, but Jane quickly put a finger to her lips and shook her head. The sister subsided, seeming to catch the concern from Jane.

Vincent rose slowly and mouthed, "Spada?"

She nodded. That was her fear as well. It seemed likely that he had followed them to the warehouse, else they would have heard him sooner. In all likelihood, Spada had already heard Jane, as the walls of the glamural were immaterial. Jane had the instinct to flee, but there was no time to get the nuns out of the way before he entered the glamoured palazzo, and they *must* protect the nuns, in the hope that Spada did not know the extent of their involvement. What could they do?

Jane turned to Vincent, reaching for glamour to cast a *Sphère Obscurcie* over the nuns. He clearly had the same thought, and he gestured for her to keep talking while he carried it out.

Jane swallowed. What had she been saying? She could not mention the disparity in dimensions. What was safe? Perhaps some misdirection. "With luck, appearing as a cleaning lady will be regarded without suspicion and give me access to the entire palazzo." She could only hope that Spada had not heard the discussion of her actual disguise.

Vincent finished his glamour and vanished along with the nuns and the chairs. His voice carried out. "Yes, exactly so. And that will allow you to open doors for me while I am hidden by the new *Verre Obscurci*."

She breathed a sigh of relief that Vincent was following her lead. "It is fortunate that Querini was still willing to work with us."

A moment later, Vincent stepped out of the *Sphère Obscurcie*. He pointed to the outer wall, which the footsteps were approaching, and raised his eyebrows. Jane nodded. Yes. It made sense to confront Spada rather than letting him come into the illusion where their friends where hidden. Through the window, a gentleman had limped into view on the "street" they had rendered. He stood with his back to them, leaning on his cane, and stared at the artlessly rendered building on the opposite side of the street, which represented the building where Vincent would work glamour during their attempt to recover the *Verres*.

"I am particularly excited by the new effect," Vincent said. "The movement of the lion in Trieste inspired me to consider trebled weaves, and . . . huh." He stopped walking, clearly struck by an idea. Shaking himself, Vincent continued. "So, having a *Verre* that records movement should help in a number of ways."

Jane stared at him. What had he just figured out? Surely not how to record *movement* in glass, but *something* had just connected in his head. "Lord Wellington was delighted with the prototype we sent to him."

They had reached the wall now. Even though the glamural was rendered without detail, the walls still appeared solid. Vincent stood very close to her and bent his head to murmur, for her alone, "You are brilliant, and I adore you."

The heat from his body washed through Jane and left her breathless.

Her husband grinned and dove through the wall, vanishing as it appeared to close around him. The other man exclaimed, "Good God!"

In English.

Before she could follow, Vincent said, "Byron?"

Jane took an extra breath, and held it as she stepped through the illusion. After the terror of the past minute, it was deeply satisfying to see the great English poet jump backwards at her sudden appearance and yelp. Overcome with relief, she laughed with a sudden understanding of why Vincent so enjoyed appearing out of the walls.

The nuns appeared then, followed closely by Signor Zancani. Lord Byron looked doubly stunned. "My God—begging your pardon, ladies." He swept his hat off his head. "Vincent, what the devil—oh, this is going to be very difficult. What in heaven's name, perhaps?"

"I find that a simple 'what' followed by the question often suffices." The Abbess tucked her hands into her sleeves, all the wrinkles in her face conspiring to hide any sign of humour.

Jane covered her mouth to mask her smile, as the imperturbable Lord Byron opened his mouth to give a retort, and then closed it again. He bowed. "What? Is going on?"

"I was about to ask you the same thing," Vincent clapped him on the shoulder. "It is good to see you, but what are you doing here?"

"I got your letter. Letters, really. Damn—*Very*—*sorry* that I did not receive them sooner. We had left La Mira for a bit of travel and only just returned. I came straight back. Your landlord directed me to the convent." He turned to stare around at the glamural. "Is this Palazzo Utino?"

"You know it?" Vincent leaned forward eagerly.

Lord Byron nodded. "I went to a party there once, and then—" He cleared his throat and glanced at the nuns. "Shall we say that I had other reasons to visit for a while. Speaking of which, we shall have to settle your accounts."

Vincent had turned a little away and rubbed at the base of his neck, wincing. Jane realized that, to him, this would be a transference of debt rather than a clearing of it, and it would offer little relief. With narrowed eyes, he stared at the palazzo illusion. "Does anyone know you are back?"

"I came straight here. Why?"

"Because it occurs to me that it would be best if Spada et al still think we are without resources."

"Ah." Lord Byron cocked his head to the side and considered. "Well . . . there is a lady that I could—A friend that I could stay with."

The Abbess shook her head and tutted. "We know what you are, Lord Byron. Unless you plan on repenting, there is no point in pretending for our sake."

Lord Byron tipped an imaginary hat to her. "In that case . . .

Now heave' a lonely subterraqueous sigh,
    Much as a nun may do within her cell:
And à propos of nuns, their piety
    With sloth hath found it difficult to dwell;
Those vegetables of the Catholic creed
    Are apt exceedingly to run to seed.

"Is subterraqueous even a word?" The Abbess raised her eyebrow.

"Of course it is. A perfectly good word. Underwater caves."

Tilting her head with a look too innocent, even for a nun, she asked, "Then why not say that? It has the same number of syllables, and is easier to understand."

He scowled in a way that reminded Jane, with some amusement, of Vincent when affronted by an egregious example of poorly rendered glamour. "I will make allowances because English is not your native language, but you may trust me that the beats are in the wrong place. And 'subterraqueous' flows, while 'underwater caves' plods. And at any rate, it would have to be cavernous, which does not fit the metre at all."

"But cavernous is a real word."

"So is subterraqueous!"

Jane cleared her throat. "Could I ask you to offer us an opinion on a question about the interior of the palazzo?"

"Yes!" Lord Byron snapped. "I mean, of course, Lady Vincent. I would be glad to be of service."

"It occurs to me that you might know of a discreet entrance?" If Jane could avoid the disguise that Signor Zancani had planned for her, she would be delighted, whatever the source of that knowledge. She would much prefer to sneak in, if it were possible to do so.

"It depends. Do you swim?"

Jane shook her head. It would have been too simple to have him appear and offer an answer to their problems.

"So, barring a *subterraqueous* entrance, the service entrance is your best bet. I find that the kitchen staff in most homes are alarmingly easy to bribe." He peeled off his greatcoat and hung it over his arm, with the clear intention of staying. "What else can I help with?"

"Come inside, and I will show you the plans." Vincent turned the poet towards the wall and walked toward it with renewed vigour. Jane had hoped that she would be able to convince her husband to return to their apartment soon, but suspected that he would be up late talking to Lord Byron. As glad as she was to have his spirits lifted, Jane hoped he would not drive himself too hard.

Eighteen

A Flurry of Pages

Jane prodded the pad of cotton wadding in her cheek with her tongue. Her skin itched beneath the wool whiskers that Signor Zancani had glued to her jaw, and she had to resist the urge to scratch. The addition of spectacles helped further define her mask so that only her overlong nose was identifiable. Even that Signor Zancani had transformed by gluing a wart just below the spectacles.

She wore a suit of clothing acquired from a ragman, carefully padded by the puppet player to give her a paunch so it was an established part of her character when she returned with the imitation spheres. Jane ran a hand over the rough waistcoat and was briefly reminded of her time in Binché, when she had used her increasing figure to play a convincing man. She pushed that from her thoughts and focused on what she was about to do.

She stood around a corner from the palazzo with a barrow that they had intercepted from the local grocer. The delivery boy had been perfectly happy to accept Lord Byron's money in exchange for not having to finish his rounds in the rain.

Young Lucia rounded the corner carrying an umbrella and a shopping basket, as though she were a housemaid on an errand. She had been so proud when they had asked her to help. She stopped as soon as she was out of sight of the palazzo. "The Abbess says that all but the clerk just left the house."

"Thank you." They had planned to wait until some of the men left, but this was a better chance than Jane had hoped for. The only one left was the man least familiar with her appearance. She lifted the handles of the barrow and trundled it down the street, leaving Lucia to run down to the canal to carry the message to Sister Aquinata.

The sound of the barrow echoed off the cobbles and plaster, announcing her progress to everyone. Heads turned as she walked, but with no more interest than if it had been any other delivery man. At least, Jane hoped that was the case. She kept her attention on appearing incurious, which was no easy task. The barrow seemed to become heavier as she walked, and her arms burned with fatigue by the time she arrived.

At the palazzo, she entered the side gate and went to the service entrance. The delivery boy said that he always knocked, so she did the same.

After a few minutes, during which she was certain that one of the men would return having forgotten something, the door finally opened. Letizia, Spada's cook from Ca' Sanuto, stood in the door. "Where's Antonio?"

Jane tugged at her cap in greeting, using the motion to hide her astonishment. They had not seen her enter or exit the building since they began spying. Was she aware of her employer's activities, or simply an excellent cook that Spada kept with him wherever he went? Jane would have to work with the belief that the woman was fully aware.

Keeping her voice low and gruff, Jane uttered one of the Venetian sentences she had been instructed in. "Sick. I've your groceries."

Letizia gave no sign of recognising her, but stepped back and told Jane to bring the groceries in. Jane lifted the basket of squash from the barrow and tucked it under her arm. With her other hand, she picked up the three ducks they had ordered and carried them in. The wings kept catching on her fake paunch, and Jane was hard-pressed not to complete her disguise by cursing. She followed Letizia down a narrow passage to the kitchen and set the supplies on the side table. One of the local girls stood at another table chopping garlic and filling the air with its pungent scent.

Leaving the cook, Jane went back to fetch the remaining items. As she walked down the hall, she marked the door that led to the main house. It was not in view of the kitchen. In less time than she would have thought, she had the rice, chard, and asparagus inside. That left only the basket of oysters. Jane carried it in and set it on the counter.

She nodded to Letizia and went back down the hall as though she were ready to depart. Glancing over her shoulder, Jane slipped through the door into the main palazzo. Her heart beat violently against her chest. From their observations, it seemed unlikely that anyone should have reason to go to the side yard where the barrow stood, but she still felt all the pressure of time that its possible discovery presented. She stood in the dining room, a graciously appointed room with a row of windows looking out into the courtyard. Jane crossed the polished marble floor to the closest window. Grabbing a fold of glamour, she ran it up and out of the window. The glamour had no form or substance, and was visible only to the second sight. Vincent would be watching for it to know that she had made it indoors.

A moment later, a corresponding flash lit the roof of the building opposite. He knew she was there. Good. She waited a moment, till Vincent's signal flashed twice to indicate that, as far as he could ascertain, it was safe for her to leave the room. Jane dissolved her glamour in reply.

She went to the dining room door and eased it open, wincing as the catch clicked free. She peeked out and, not seeing anyone in the hall, crept across it to the room that their map indicated was a library. Turning the handle, Jane opened the door just wide enough to slide in, but forgot her fake paunch and was briefly stuck. Grimacing, she pushed the door wider and slipped into the room. She closed the door as gently as possible, but it still felt as though the catch clicking home was a gunshot. Jane waited by the door, breath held for the sounds of movement elsewhere in the house. She heard nothing.

Hurrying to the window, she sent up another flare of unformed glamour for Vincent's eyes. His flashed in return, and Jane turned her attention to the room.

Books bound in delicately tooled calfskin lined the walls, with gilt letters announcing their contents. Large, comfortable chairs stood by the windows and the hearth, waiting for readers. A library table stood in the middle of the room with some papers scattered upon it. For a moment, Jane had hopes that they might be related to the spheres, but it proved to be the drawings for a billiards table. Against the wall opposite the hearth stood a tall inlaid secretary. Jane began her search there.

Working methodically, Jane opened the top drawer and went through the contents as carefully as she could. She needed to find the papers without disturbing the other items. That drawer yielded nothing but receipts for various purchases, a washing bill, a bill for a new hunting rifle, and a program for the opera.

She felt at the back and the sides of the drawer for any secret compartments, but it was of solid construction and had no mysterious thicknesses. She slid the drawer back into place and moved to the next. It, too, had little to hold her attention.

The next drawer had a stack of letters, which all seemed to be personal correspondence. Jane turned through them, hoping to spy a code or some other tell-tale.

One with familiar handwriting caught her eye and nearly stopped her breath.

Why did Spada have a letter from her mother?

The contents of it seemed innocent enough. Her mother had written to a Mrs. Harrison, commiserating about her health issues, but comparison of ailments was usual in most of her mother's letters. Then Jane spotted a single sentence that had been underlined.

My eldest daughter and her husband—you may know them, I am certain, as Lady Vincent and Sir David, the Prince Regent's glamourists—will be separating from our party and going to Venice to visit—you will not believe this—to visit Lord Byron, the celebrated poet!

She sighed. Well . . . that explained how Spada had known they were coming, but she could not understand how her mother had come to correspond with Mrs. Harrison in the first place. Tempting though it was to take the letter, she placed it back in the drawer.

Save for that one letter, none of the drawers held anything that could be used to charge Spada or to shed light on the whereabouts of their belongings. Jane slid the last of the drawers back into place and stood, arching her back to ease the ache from leaning over the desk. Where next?

She glanced at the window to see if any signal from Vincent hung outside, but saw nothing untoward. If the papers were not in the library, then where? In a bedroom upstairs? Or in the second floor parlour they frequented. She disliked going up, since it would make leaving harder, and it would increase the chances that she would run into the clerk. But . . . she was inside, and another opportunity was unlikely to present itself.

Again Jane went to the window. This time, she shaped her glamour in an arrow pointing up, followed by a question mark, but kept both too attenuated to be visible except to someone watching for them. A moment later, Vincent sent two flashes, for yes.

Part of Jane had hoped for three, meaning no, but if the

way was clear, then she would take the risk. Jane crossed to the door. Moving with as much stealth as she could, she crept out of the library and up the stairs to the first floor. Her heart beat faster. On the ground floor she could claim to have lost her way, but here? A grocer's errand boy had no reason to be up here. The parlour at the front of the palazzo was off a long gallery, and Jane dearly wished that she could see the view from Vincent's window before opening the door. She had heard no footsteps or other sounds to indicate that anyone was moving about the building. Her palm slick with sweat, Jane opened the door and stepped into the parlour.

To her astonishment, Vincent's writing slope sat on a side table in plain view. For a moment she almost forgot to close the door, but she recovered quickly. Though she wanted to go to the battered oak travel desk immediately, she first needed to let Vincent know that she was in the parlour. Jane let her flare of glamour flash and kept her vision expanded to her second sight to see his response.

Relieved when he gave her the signal that it was safe to proceed, Jane reverted her vision to the mundane and turned to the desk. As she did so, she stopped with a gasp and deepened her sight back into the ether. One end of the room was rendered with glamour.

While the parlour appeared to end with a wall of green baize, a portion of it was actually a carefully rendered illusion. With her vision pushed fully into the ether, the illusion dropped away, leaving only the glowing strands of glamour that produced it. The folds and threads made a formidable tapestry composed of light, with trailing ends that remained attached to the ether. Woven through it were additional strings of glamour visible only in the second sight. Some she recognised as waves of sound tied into knots awaiting release. Others seemed to have no purpose except to confound the senses.

Now that she knew what to look for, it was obvious that a door in the far end of the room had been masked. It answered the question of why the measurements for this floor had seemed off. It was not due to the relative illiteracy of the person providing the map but evidence of a strong room. It seemed almost certain that the *Verres Obscurcis* lay beyond the glamour.

Equally certain: the glamural had alarms woven through it.

Jane surprised herself by cursing. There was little she could do now, but it would make their task much harder later. She took a moment to make certain that the rest of the room had no hidden surprises in it. A sofa stood in front of the hearth, which had a low fire. Raked as it was, it seemed likely that someone had been in the room earlier in the day and would return, but not soon. The chairs stood in comfortable groups, and a table held crystal decanters and the other accoutrements that a gentleman of fashion might require to be comfortable. Other than the wall of glamour, nothing seemed out of place in the room.

Which meant that, for the moment, Jane could concentrate on the contents of Vincent's desk. She had not seen it since it had been taken from him before the Battle of Quatre Bras. The lock had been broken at some point and not replaced. Jane opened the desk to the carmine leather slope. Lifting the lower lid, she found bundles of papers that appeared to have been neatly sorted. Labels in a quick, masculine hand marked them *non pertinente* and *riesaminare*—"Irrelevant" and "Re-examine." The "*riesaminare*" stack had letters from M. Chastain in Binché and Herr Scholes in Germany. Neither of them had any information about the *Verres*, though both men discussed glamour at length. The "*non pertinente*" stack contained lists of lambs and sheep, products of the code Vincent had used to deliver messages during the days leading up to the Battle of Quatre Bras. Jane's own notes were tucked into the stack, apparently unread, as though the mere fact that she was a woman rendered them worthless.

She turned through the pages and found only one where she mentioned sunlight. Tempting though it was to simply take the page, Jane carried it to the side table and drizzled some water from a carafe on the page, smearing the ink on the sentence in question. She blotted it with the inside of her jacket, then slid it back into the stack she had pulled it from and continued turning the papers to see if there was anything else that had been discarded as irrelevant and should be dealt with. Her name caught her eye.

A half-sheet of paper began:

My dearest Jane,

Muse. I am writing this because I want to talk to you and cannot. I love you and

He had been writing that in Binché, he must have been. On the paper below that, the ink was blotted and smeared as if Vincent had put the sheet away hastily. Jane very much wanted to take it out of the box and carry it with her, but she left it in its place and continued leafing through the pages.

Finding nothing else appertaining to the spheres, she closed the lower lid and opened the upper.

Here was Vincent's journal. Letting out her breath in relief, Jane marked its position and lifted it out of the box. The leather was smooth and well worn. She carried it to the window and set it on the sill in front of her. Jane spread her legs in her operating stance and took several deep breaths to prepare herself. She pulled a thin strand of glamour out of the ether and began to push it out of the window and across the street to serve as a scaffold for the modified *bouclé torsadée* they had planned.

There was no way she could hope to span that distance on her own. She merely needed to get the loop as far out as she could. The thread Vincent was spinning out from the other side would catch hers. It was not precisely a yoke, but it would serve a similar purpose. The yoke and splice had not carried the images with sufficient distinctness, so instead Vincent was going to reel her thread to his side of the street. In theory, at least. This had seemed to work most effectually during their trials, but the technique was new to both of them.

Jane's heart was racing faster than it should, and she barely had the thread six feet from her. It did not seem possible that she would get it over the wall at this rate. As she worked, she was trying to listen to the sounds of the house, but that split in concentration made it difficult to hold the thread steady and give it the twist it would need.

From the other side of the street, she could just make out Vincent's strand of glamour. They were keeping their work as close to gossamer as possible, so that only someone with their sight very deep in the ether would see it. But doing this meant that Jane was less aware of the house than she would like. Had she heard a sound, or was it only the thumping of her own heart?

Beneath the padding of her suit, sweat dripped down Jane's back. She had not calculated how much more quickly she would overheat in the disguise. Jane's hands trembled with the effort of spooling out the glamour till she was afraid she would drop it. She stopped, panting, and held the glamour as steady as she could. But if she stopped here, Vincent would have to span the gap farther than they had practised, which would not suit. She ground her teeth together and pushed the glamour out farther by another foot.

She should have drawn up a chair. It would do no good if she fainted while doing this. Jane stopped again, trying to slow her beating heart and calm her breathing. The whiskers on her cheeks itched with sweat. Jane closed her eyes and concentrated on staying upright. Only a little farther, and she would have it.

The line twitched in her hand. Jane opened her eyes to the welcome sight of Vincent's line hooked into hers. It was supported by a yoke wielded by two of the choir members, under the supervision of Sister Maria Agnes. She let Vincent draw her line back at his own pace as she fed it out to him. Even with his support, she still felt the strain of spanning that distance in her shoulders and back. The assistance made it possible, but not any more pleasant.

Through the line, she could feel the minute vibrations of her husband's touch as identifiably as if he were handling something fully tangible. Jane would know his work in whatever form it presented itself. He took the far end of the thread she had woven and tied it to his side of the street. With a sigh of relief, Jane did the same, anchoring it behind the window's heavy curtains. She ached, and sweat covered her brow, but it was done.

Jane picked up the notebook and opened it to the first page. Leaning against the windowsill, she placed the page in the glamour and held it as steady as she could. On the other side of the street, Vincent would be running a *lointaine vision* through the end of the *bouclé torsadée*.

As Jane waited for him to signal that he was ready for the next page, her breathing slowed and her heart rate returned to normal. Glamour flashed in the window. She turned the page, then held the book as steady as she could.

It would be wonderful to use this method to communicate at long distances but—aside from the difficulty in maintaining such a long thread of glamour—the *bouclé torsadée* required a clear line of sight from one place to another. Anything solid that intersected the thread would interrupt the vision carried through it. In most instances, it would be more efficacious to simply call out. Would it be possible, she wondered, to create something like this in glass?

The idea was worth exploring, at any rate, if they ever had the freedom to do so again.

Another flash and another page turn. The time passed slowly in a haze of flashing glamour and turning pages. Jane felt a curious mix of ennui and anxiety. It was tedious work, but each moment increased the chances of someone returning to the palazzo, or of the clerk deciding that he wanted to visit the parlour. And yet the more of the book they captured, the better their chances of passing the duplicate off as the real thing. The flash came again. Jane turned the page.

The flash repeated, four times in rapid succession. Mechanically, Jane began to turn the page again, before understanding what the additional flashes meant.

Someone was returning to the palazzo.

Nineteen

An Alert

The second curse of the day escaped Jane. She slammed the journal closed and stepped back from the window. She could not see anyone approaching the house, which meant that they must be entering by the canal side and were possibly already inside the palazzo. She hurried to replace the journal in the writing desk. Forcing herself to slow down, she set the journal on top of the papers with care, so as not to disturb them. Hands sweating, she closed the top compartment on the journal, and then closed the entire writing desk.

Footsteps in the hall. Men's voices. Jane sprang to the curtain to hide behind it, rejecting her instinct to reach for a *Sphère Obscurcie*. It was *almost* invisible to the second sight, but if Bastone was present, she did not want to chance him spying the weave, nor did she want to risk one of the men walking through the *Sphère* into her.

The moment she slid behind the curtain, she realized that it would not work. The paunch that Signor Zancani had given her belled the curtain out in front of it.

Jane stepped out again, looking for somewhere else to hide. Praying that they would continue on instead of entering the parlour, she made her way to the hearth. There was a chest near it that she might stand in the lee of, with a *Sphère* to assist her in hiding.

The door's catch rattled.

Stifling her third curse, Jane stopped where she was and wove a *Sphère Obscurcie*.

The door opened. ". . . most tedious opera I have ever seen." The pirate, Coppa, entered the room, followed by the clerk, Denaro.

"If you had read the review, you would have known not to go." Denaro headed for a side table close to the door that held crystal decanters and the accoutrements necessary for a gentleman's libation.

Jane stood five feet from the wall. If either of them decided to go to the rightmost window, they would walk straight into her. She wove another sphere to mute the sound of her breathing, then twisted the weave so that she could still hear them.

"Ah, but there is the lovely Marianna to consider. I so wanted to see her again." Coppa dropped into a chair and stretched his legs out in front of him. "Pour one for me, will you?"

Denaro poured another glass of brandy into one of the exquisite crystal tumblers. "She was not there, I take it?"

"No, alas. Her 'flower' kept her away." He stretched and put his hands behind his head. "I do so enjoy a good seduction."

"Yours or hers?" Denaro carried the tumblers across and gave one to Coppa.

He raised the glass in a salute. "Both, I hope. I can see why Byron was taken with her."

Jane had to bite the inside of her lip to keep her dismay silent. She did not want them to mean that Byron was involved, and yet . . . he had been away for the entire time that she and Vincent had struggled. What could keep him *and* the English consul from Venice for so long? And to return just as they were making their plans seemed suddenly suspicious.

"The boss doesn't like you flirting with her."

"Please. I'm *supposed* to seduce her." Coppa sipped his brandy and grimaced. "One of the more appealing ardours of the job."

"But not be seduced by her."

"What does it matter, if the result is the same? I have very much enjoyed occupying her time while he is out of town."

Did that mean that Byron was *not* involved? She was unused to living without trust, but found that her mind was more ready to mistrust Lord Byron than to believe that a man as worldly as he had been deceived by Marianna. It was safer to trust no one. Except Vincent.

She looked to the window, wishing for some sign of him or some way to signal him. He must be frantic with worry. For that matter . . . how was she going to get out of the room now that Denaro and Coppa were here? They appeared to be well settled for the evening, lighting cigars and continuing their conversation of seduction. Jane learned more particulars about the ways in which a man enjoys a woman's company than she had during three years of marriage. She came to a rapid understanding of what salty language truly consisted. It seemed impossible to be standing in the middle of the room and not have them know she was there when her blushes alone must give her away.

More pressing was the concern that the opera would eventually end, and then the other men would return to the palazzo. If Bastone entered the room, it was only a matter of time before Jane was discovered.

She turned her attention to how to exit.

Walking with a *Sphère Obscurcie* was difficult, but not impossible. She could manage a few feet with it before needing to stop. That would take her closer to the door, but . . . there was no way to open the door without its movement being apparent. Was there some way she could cause the men to open the door for her? What would make them leave?

The arrival of the other men, possibly. Or something related to their plot, which they were vexingly not discussing, could perhaps—Jane's stomach dropped as she realized the likelihood of Vincent trying something foolish to draw them away. She looked again to the window, wishing that she could signal to him. In spite of the singular focus he could display while working, he was not gifted with a deep supply of patience. If he thought she was in danger—which, to be fair, she was—he would come for her. Whether it was a pirate's stronghold or into a burning building, Vincent would—

She knew what to do.

Jane turned to the hearth. A burning building. If she masked the illusion within the *Sphère Obscurcie* while she was creating it, as Vincent had done with *The Broken Bridge*, she should be able to create a fairly convincing house fire. She just had to do it quickly. Then again . . . she did not need to create this illusion wholly with glamour.

Jane undid the *Sphère Obscurcie* enough to move it. By painful increments, she made her way to the fireplace, grateful for the rich Persian rug, which muffled her footsteps. There, she wove several clouds of smoke, which she pinned in place with a series of slip-knots. When she was ready, she could release them. They would fray and dissolve, leaving—she hoped—no sign of the glamour that created them.

Next Jane wove a small breeze, coming down the chimney, to fan the fire and push real smoke into the room. It was one of the few practical things glamour could do. As with all weaves, its effect on the corporeal world was faint, but enough for her purposes.

With those prepared, Jane undid the buttons on her shirt and pulled out the padding that made up the paunch of her costume. It was damp with her sweat. She pulled the wadding from inside her cheeks. The cotton had become soaked through with saliva. Wrinkling her nose, she put the wet cloth against her palm, then wrapped the padding from her paunch around her left hand.

Denaro and Coppa were still engaged in conversation, their backs to her, though their discussion had drifted to the racing gondolas kept by the owner of the palazzo and wagers about which one was fastest.

Jane wet her lips, sending up a prayer that this would all work. Then she plunged her left hand, swaddled in cloth, into the fire, and seized a small log. Even with the padding, the heat made her cringe. Moving as swiftly as she could, Jane set the rug afire. The cloth on her hand smouldered, and then its edge caught fire. Jane dropped the log and shook the cloth from her hand, adding it to the blaze on the floor.

Hidden by the sofa, neither man had yet noticed the additional fire in the room. Jane rose to her feet and walked with the *Sphère Obscurcie* so that it was as close to the door as possible.

From outside the palazzo, a great rumble of thunder sounded, loud enough to stop the men's conversation. Lightning flashed outside the window. Denaro said, "They'll have an unpleasant ride home."

"Perhaps they will stay in Venice," Coppa replied.

Jane could only hope that was the case. She edged closer to the door, pulling the slip-knots for the smoke with her. Before long she had to stop and bend over with her hands upon her knees to catch her breath before she could continue. Outside the thunder rumbled again, louder this time, and the flash of lightning came almost immediately. Jane straightened and wiped her face on the sleeve of her coat.

Her slow progress had taken her to within five feet of the door. She pulled the slip-knots, and the illusion of smoke added to the actual smoke in the room.

The men continued to drink and chat.

Truly . . . how long was it going to take them to notice that the rug was on fire?

Thunder rolled again, followed by an almost immediate flash of lightning. Jane turned to the window, only now noticing that the order was reversed. She should see lightning, *then* hear the thunder. It was Vincent—it had to be. But surely he was not throwing glamour that far into the air?

This time the lightning and thunderclap came simultaneously, terrifyingly loud and bright.

Denaro swore. "That sounded as though it were right on top of us."

In the distance, someone yelled, "Fire!"

Jane grinned. Vincent had set the exterior of the building on fire—or created an illusion of the same. Even separated by distance, their thoughts ran in the same vein. The call of "Fire!" was repeated.

Denaro sat up. "Do you think that's our—Fire!"

"Perhaps. Someone will come—"

"No, I mean there's a fire! Here!" He cursed and stumbled to his feet. "The rug, man! An ember must've fallen out."

Denaro leapt to his feet, spinning as though to make certain that he was not, himself, on fire. Denaro dashed to the side table and snatched a carafe of water off of it. He ran to the fire and tossed the water upon it. With a surge, the fire blazed higher.

"You fool! That's gin!" Coppa danced back from the blaze.

Outside, the cries of "Fire!" grew more frequent and more panic-stricken. Jane could not help but note that there were no subsequent thunderclaps. Denaro raced to the door and flung it open. Finally! He ran into the hall, adding his voice to the clamour. "Fire! Alarm! Fire in the parlour!"

Jane kept her eye on Coppa. He stood transfixed by the fire, but there was no telling when he would move. Jane took three deep breaths, gripping the thread of the *Sphère Obscurcie* tightly. She ran for the door with her gaze fixed upon the hall beyond. Dark spots swam in front of her eyes, and her heart felt as though it would burst. As the grey fog grew denser over her sight, Jane collided with the wall. She twisted the glamour into a knot and slid, insensible, to the floor.

The smell of smoke filled her nostrils. Footsteps ran past Jane. She held still for a moment, but the men who ran past did so without seeing her. Cautiously, she sat. The *Sphère Obscurcie* was still intact. She sighed with relief that her instincts had led her to tie it off as she fainted. Beneath her waistcoat, her heart still thudded, so she must not have been unconscious for long.

Smoke poured out of the parlour, and Jane began to wonder if their problem could be so simply solved. If the fire were not extinguished quickly, then perhaps the papers would burn up and the *Verres Obscurcis* crack.

Bracing herself against the wall, Jane rose to her feet. The hall pitched around her. She fixed her gaze upon a painting of a hunting scene on the opposite wall and waited for the dizziness to pass. She would not be able to make her way downstairs hidden by the *Sphère Obscurcie*.

For the moment, the hall was empty. Biting her lip, Jane listened for footsteps, but the activity seemed confined to the parlour on this floor. In the distance . . . well, she would have to be alert. Once she was on the ground floor, her presence would be easier to explain.

Holding her breath, Jane untied the *Sphère* and let it dissolve. She crept down the hall, feeling terribly exposed. The sound of her own footsteps seemed to echo in the hall, even louder than the shouting and crackling of flames. After a moment, Jane realized that it was not her footsteps, but someone else coming up the stairs. She shrank against the wall and wove a *Sphère Obscurcie* around her.

A slender young man with shockingly red hair came up the stairs carrying two buckets. He walked more slowly than Jane would have expected of someone in an emergency. At the top of the stairs, he peered into the first room, away from where she stood. In a hoarse whisper, he said, "Lady Vincent?"

Jane gaped in astonishment. As he turned, she recognised the profile of Signor Zancani. The red hair had so distracted her that she had not recognised the young man in his disguise. Jane dropped the *Sphère Obscurcie*. "Here."

He jumped and spun. "Oh, thank heavens."

"What are you doing here?"

"Giving you an excuse for being in the house." He handed her a bucket. "Your husband was certain that you could get out of the parlour on your own, but worried that you would be caught in the house."

"The rescue is welcome, thank you." She eyed the bucket. "We are watermen, here to quench the fire, I take it?"

"Just so." He nodded to the stairs. "Shall we go fetch some more water? Outside?"

"By all means, yes." It was a great relief to have someone else with her so that she did not have to creep through the halls fearing discovery. Even so, she was still so fatigued from her previous efforts that she was soon winded. When they reached the ground floor, the smoke was denser, which did not help. "Is that a real fire?"

"Mostly."

"You there! What is happening?" Spada's voice stopped them in the hall. He stood on the landing to the water entrance for the palazzo. Jane wished that she still had the padding on her belly. The itching of her whiskers became a sudden comfort as they stood between her and the swindler.

She tried to stand as though she were not alarmed by Spada's presence. This close, with his hair dyed black, it was impossible to understand how they had mistaken him for an older man when he had been Signor Sanuto. He had lines at the corners of his eyes, yes, but no more than a man of thirty. The limp, however, seemed real. He leaned on his cane and stepped towards them.

Signor Zancani raised his bucket in answer. "The palazzo was struck by lightning, Signor. It is on fire." His voice had risen and cracked like an adolescent's. "We're getting water."

"Fire?" he exclaimed. He tapped his cane on the floor, in a gesture that Jane recognised as him thinking. With a sudden curse, he turned to Bastone. "The Vincents are likely in the house."

"Surely not."

"All of us out, save Denaro? Then a fire. Check the parlour."

Bastone cursed and ran to the stairs.

Spada called after him. "Send Denaro and Coppa to me if you see them. I'll watch here." He leaned on his cane, frowning. From here, he could see the stairs and the front door. He also blocked the way to the water entrance.

Signor Zancani waved his bucket wildly. "We need to get more water, Signor."

With a grunt, Spada stepped back. Jane had to brush by him on her way to the water entrance, but he was looking past her to the stairs. They had to hurry before Bastone reported the second fire upstairs. It would, perhaps, have been better if she and Vincent had not had *quite* so much the same idea. She hurried down the steps to the water.

Signor Zancani dipped his bucket in the water and handed it to Jane, taking hers from her. She repressed a groan as she lifted the bucket. Her limbs ached with fatigue from stringing the *bouclé torsadée* across the street. With luck, the grimace would make her look even more masculine.

She and Signor Zancani made their way, water splashing, up the stairs and past Spada. He watched them go past, and Jane could feel his gaze weighing them. She felt the loss of the padding now. With every step she took, Jane tried to project manhood. Aged manhood, perhaps, but manhood nevertheless. Though she had wished all her life for a graceful stride, it now seemed all she could do to avoid mincing down the hall. The bucket of water helped.

Then they were past the kitchen and into the courtyard, where there was a small fire in the remnants of Jane's barrow. The flames had spread to the ivy covering the palazzo's walls. A line of people stretched from the fire, out the gate, and to the canal, passing buckets full of water to throw on the fire. Signor Zancani handed his bucket to the nearest man. "It's faster to go through the house to the water gate."

"Good thought!" The man clapped his hand on Zancani's shoulder and called instructions to the volunteer watermen who were working diligently to put out the fire.

Jane passed her bucket off, and in minutes the line reorganized itself to run through the house. In the midst of the change, she and Zancani slipped away.

Walking away from the palazzo, and from the apartment where the nuns waited, Jane finally allowed herself to take a full breath. "How did you set the fire? I thought it was glamour."

"Not everything needs to be. Sulphur matches." He frowned for a minute as if he had omitted something from his conversation. "Vincent's lightning sold it though. You should have seen it fork down out of the sky. Amazing."

She must have misheard him. To have the lightning appear from the sky, Vincent would have had to run a line of glamour up to . . . the sky. Jane swallowed, feeling suddenly ill, and certain that she had not misheard. "How is Vincent?"

Signor Zancani paused—not long, but enough that Jane felt every twist of his thought as he considered his reply. "He was alert when I left."

This was, Jane thought, not the heartening sentence that the puppet player must have intended, because it meant that Vincent had *not* been alert for some time before that. It took all of Jane's discipline not to change her direction and run back to the apartment where her husband was. It would do him no good if she led Spada there. Vincent was alert, at least.

Twenty

Fire and Water

Jane and Signor Zancani took a circuitous route back to the small room opposite the palazzo. In response to her questions, the puppet player related the events leading to Vincent's collapse as best he could. To get the sound and light of the storm to come from the right area, her husband had worked with the nuns to build a scaffold of yokes, atop which he placed his own glamour. Zancani was not well practised in the art, but he said that the nuns appeared shocked by its height.

Vincent had swayed after the second thunderclap. Sister Maria Agnes had stepped in to help, but the thread was so long that, even with it supported by the yokes, she had fainted after they performed the third thunderclap. For the fourth effort, he had worked the sound and light simultaneously, and fainted.

"Did he convulse?"

Signor Zancani shook his head. "No, but he was unconscious longer than I expected. Usually he wakes immediately."

"Usually?" Jane raised her eyebrows at that. One of Vincent's
great advantages as a glamourist was that he had tremendous
strength and stamina. He would have the occasional light-
headedness at the end of a long workday, but that was common
among professional glamourists. He had only passed out completely twice in Jane's time with him. She had fainted more often,
but, given the difference in their frames, this was not surprising.
"How often has he fainted, to your knowledge?"

"A handful of times at most. Usually when it was hot out.
And only for a few moments." Signor Zancani guided her
into a small alcove set back from the street. The back of it,
which had seemed closed off, took a little zigzag through a
courtyard and then led on to the street where the room was.

"And how long was he unconscious this time?"

"Ten minutes?" He shook his head and paused at the door
to their building. "I was changing into costume, so it may
have been less than that. He was alert after that, though."

Something in the way he said that made Jane wonder.
"Was he sitting up when you left?"

"Ah—no."

Jane opened the door and ran up the stairs. On the second
landing, she had to stop and lean forward to catch her breath.
Here she was angry at Vincent for over-taxing himself, and
she did not have sense enough of her own to remember how
much she had exerted herself. Bosom heaving, she proceeded
up the rest of the stairs to the third floor as quickly as she
could. Signor Zancani was not far behind.

The little hall outside the room seemed to be filled with nuns. Sister Maria Agnes was seated in a chair by the door and waved at Jane. She, at least, seemed none the worse for wear. On the other side of the door, Lord Byron sat like a guard. She hesitated upon seeing him, which he seemed to interpret as concern for Vincent.

Lord Byron rose as Jane came up the last few steps. "He is resting."

"How bad is it?" Jane kept her voice low.

"The Reverend Mother tended to him while he was sick—" He broke off, as if understanding that she had not known. The poet's concern for Vincent was so evident in his voice that it was difficult to believe that he had aligned himself with Spada. And yet, the swindler had also evidenced concern for her husband while impersonating Sanuto. "He only vomited, I think from acute dizziness. I have been in worse condition from drink, so I think he will be well if we can convince him to sleep."

Jane had no doubt that Lord Byron had indeed been deep in his cups on frequent occasions, but that was quite different from the toll too great an exertion of glamour could wreak on one. If Vincent had vomited, that meant he had been severely overheated. "Where is the Reverend Mother?"

"Here." The Abbess had been standing in the hall, lost among the crowd of black and white. "Lord Byron is correct. Your husband is stubborn, but should be well if he will rest and—"

The door opened. Vincent stepped into the hall and swept Jane into his arms. "Muse—thank God."

She huddled in the circle of his arms, thanking providence.

He was standing. His heart beat strongly against her cheek, even through her whiskers, with a steady and regular pulse. He would be all right. "I am quite well."

"Good." He stepped back and lost his balance. Vincent swung his arm out and caught the doorcase, steadying himself. All her relief fled. Vincent's face was ashen, with dark circles under his eye. His hair was matted to his head with dried sweat, and he squinted against the light.

"Vincent, you need to rest." Jane reached up to feel his brow. His skin was clammy to the touch.

"Later." He walked into the room, bracing himself against the wall with one hand. "We have things to discuss."

The Abbess exchanged a look with Jane that spoke clearly of her frustration and concern. Nodding, Jane followed Vincent into the room. It had the reek of someone's sick, which no cleaning would quickly lift. She did not see how he could even be standing. "There is nothing that cannot wait until tomorrow. You need to rest. For that matter, *I* need to rest, and so does Sister Maria Agnes."

Vincent gripped the frame of the bed and lowered himself to sit upon it. He kept his head level and his gaze fixed upon a point on the wall. "We need to speed up our plans. Their Lombardy-Venetia buyer is coming on Saturday next, and today is already Friday."

Jane took a step closer to her husband. "How do you know this?"

He looked uncomfortable for a moment in ways that had nothing to do with his physical condition. Then he shrugged. "I heard them talking. You left the *bouclé torsadée* tied off in the parlour."

A frisson of cold ran through Jane. She had forgotten to untie that one when she was trying to remove her other traces from the room. "Did Biasio see it?"

"Not yet. Though that is also a concern. For the moment it is fine, as I was able to untie it and change the spiral to carry sound instead of—"

"From here." Jane gaped for a moment. He had lost his mind. He had completely lost all sense of proportion if he thought that untying her end of the *bouclé torsadée* from here approached reasonable. To alter such a long thread on top of untying it was rash. The risks that he took with his health were indefensible. She clenched her hands into fists and fought for a level tone. "Ladies, gentlemen. Would you give me a moment of privacy with my husband?"

The Abbess looked immensely relieved. With a significant glance to Lord Byron, she pulled the door shut and left Jane and Vincent alone in the little room.

Jane struggled to present a measured composure. As much as she wanted to shout at him for showing so little sense, he was clearly ill. "I know that your plan requires tremendous effort, but I agreed to it because I thought it had some chance of success, without too much risk. Now I am not so sure. You must rest."

Vincent lowered his head to rest upon his hands. They trembled, as though palsied. "Jane, I will grant that I over-reached today, but going over our plan will not tire me any further. This is perfectly normal fatigue."

"This is *not* normal fatigue. Your hands are shaking; you cannot stand; you were ill. The only time—the *only* time—that I have seen you in this state was right before your collapse at Lady FitzCameron's. Do you think I want to watch you go into convulsions again because you are too stupid to admit that you have limits?" Jane would shake him, if she thought it would make him see reason. "You almost *died*, Vincent, and you have apparently learned nothing since."

"You are exaggerating." His voice was level, but he knit his fingers together so that the tremors were masked. "I have already admitted that I am tired, but the glamour I worked today was quite large, so that is to be expected."

"You had a collapse."

"I must tell you that it is extremely tiresome to have you constantly scolding me about my health when I am perfectly well."

Perfectly well? He was asserting that he was well when he was so dizzy that he could not stand. "I would not need to scold you if you would stop lying to me."

Vincent jerked his head back as though she had slapped him. Even that movement caused his face to pale. He closed his eyes and bared his teeth in a grimace. For a moment, Vincent breathed sharply through his nose, with his hands gripping his knees as though they were all that supported him.

Jane choked the urge to crouch in front of her husband to ascertain the state of his health. She already knew that it was poor, and the gesture would irritate him. And yet, watching him, she thought that this was something more than overexertion. "Signor Zancani told me that you have fainted a number of times while performing. When you asserted that you had recovered fully from your injury, that was not true, was it?"

"I cannot afford to be unwell."

"You cannot afford to kill yourself. If for no other reason than that it would distress me. Think of that, if you do not value yourself enough to take care." She crossed the room to sit next to him on the bed. "How badly are you still suffering from the concussion?"

His breath hissed out in an almost inaudible whine of protest as he prepared to lie to her, again. Then he sighed, letting his head loll forward. "It is irregular. Most days, I truly am perfectly fit. Other days, my head aches if I so much as look at glamour. Vertigo. Sometimes light hurts my eyes."

The evening when he had been sitting in the dark and they had quarrelled suddenly took on new shape. "Why did you not say something?"

"Because I was already pitying myself enough." Vincent relaxed his arms and released his grip upon his knees. "And there is nothing to be done, and you would worry and ask me not to work. And I was going mad."

She could not say that his reasons were invalid. "Chasing Spada is not worth your health."

"Walking away would kill me just as surely." Vincent spread his hands, as though to demonstrate that he was helpless in this, then clenched them when the tremors became apparent again. "It is not in my nature, Muse."

"I know." Jane rubbed her head, as though by chafing her scalp she could force her brain into a different configuration so that they could think of a plan that did not involve endangering Vincent. She stared at the door, where the pattern of light beneath it was broken by the shadows of feet. In a low voice, she asked, "Do you think they are listening to us?"

He looked at the door and nodded. "What will it take for you to feel comfortable moving forward with the plan?"

Her husband was the world's most impossible man. Unless she actually tied him to the bed, she doubted that she would be able to stop him from working. Even then, he would most likely continue to fret himself into a state. "I need you to promise me that you will not touch glamour for the rest of today, and all of tomorrow." Jane marked that off on her thumb and moved to listing on her fingers. "You must go to bed as soon as we finish talking here. Regular meals. Complete honesty about your health. Allow me to make the decision on when you need to stop working."

"I would never work again if that decision rested with you." He ran his hand through his hair. "I misjudged my limits *once* in the years that I have been working. Once. And the circumstances there . . . That was a unique situation. It will not occur again."

"What was unique? That you had been working for weeks without rest?"

"That I was showing off for a woman I wanted to court." Vincent took her hand and traced the spot where her wedding band should have been. "Please believe me, Muse, when I say that under normal circumstances I would have declined the request to perform a *tableau vivant*, or chosen a simpler subject."

Had he really almost died because he had been trying to impress *her*? The spectre of his convulsions still haunted her at times. He did not remember that night, or what it had been like to watch his back arch and his heels drum against the floor. The similarities between his countenance then and now were unmistakable. "And today?"

Vincent tucked in his chin and studied the floor. "I promised that I would come for you."

Jane could find no reply.

He lifted her hand and kissed her fingers. "Thank you for being concerned for me, but I knew the risk and was willing to pay it. I am not so poor a judge of my own health as you believe."

If he could see himself now, he would not make such an assertion. His face was grey with exhaustion, and dragged down as though he were ten years older than he was. Jane leaned against him. "So what do you propose now?"

"That I not touch glamour for the next day. Probably two. And that we let people back in so that I can explain the amended plan to them." A sudden yawn split his face, and Vincent covered his mouth, grimacing.

"And then we go back to the apartment to sleep."

"I think I need to stay here."

Just when she thought that he was being reasonable, of course he would refuse to go to sleep. There were times when getting Vincent to rest was like managing an infant. "Someone else can stay here to watch Spada."

"Yes, but—"

"You need to rest."

Vincent cleared his throat and looked away from her. "I cannot walk a straight line, Muse. I think I need to stay the night here. Or at least remain until the room stops spinning."

"Oh." Given that reason, it was difficult to protest. But if he would go to bed, no matter where, then she would be much relieved. "And you promise you will sleep?"

"I do not think I have a choice." He squeezed her hand

and covered another yawn. "Though I doubt it will reassure you, I feel terrible, but do not think I am truly unwell. Much of the nausea is due to the vertigo lingering from the concussion."

"It seems to me that Spada and his men have much to pay for."

"It is distinctly unpleasant." He rubbed his brow again, and his hand still trembled. *That* was not an effect of the concussion, she was certain. "Did I tell you that I think I have figured out how the lion in Trieste was done?"

"Are you trying to distract me?"

"Yes." He peeked at her from under his hand. "Is it working?"

She shook her head, but it was hard to maintain the stern expression he deserved. She was, in fact, curious about his idea, but the fact that his thoughts so quickly turned to glamour made her suspect that it would be impossible to keep him from working it.

"Truly? I could talk about trebled folds and spliced braids. The Romans could not have taken the time to render a lion between productions, so it must be a recording taken from two stations."

"Vincent . . ."

"Does the idea not intrigue—no, I see it does not. What if I said that I suspect the Romans used paired glamourists?" He sighed and lowered his hand. "Muse . . . may we call people back in?"

"Before you start, there is something that I should tell you about the room. It will affect our plans." She paused and reached for the ether to weave a bubble of silence. Just in case, it would be best if Lord Byron did not overhear her. Within the silence, she gave a hurried recital of what she had seen and overheard while standing in the room.

When she finished, Vincent rubbed his chin in thought. "Well . . ." He looked toward the door, as if he could see Lord Byron in the hall and ascertain his role. His voice stayed low. "Well . . . I do not think it is in his character."

"Regardless. Do we want to discuss our plans with him?"

"He is fickle, but I cannot think of him as being so utterly without honour."

"What of his affairs?"

"That is diff—" He sighed and looked even more miserable than his illness had rendered him. "I suppose it is not. Let us proceed, then, with caution and take into account that someone *might* betray our confidence."

"Like my mother." Jane winced, thinking of the letter she had found.

"Exactly so. Even if it is by accident."

"How do you propose we proceed, then?"

"By doing what I did to you in Binché. We do not tell them our whole plan."

"I cannot like that."

"Nor I. Have you another suggestion?"

Almost, Jane wanted to call the whole thing off and simply wait until January for her father to reply to her letter to Melody. That would be the safest and most prudent course. But even given Vincent's current state, she could see what it would do to him to walk away. "Do you still want to call our friends back?"

"If you will untie the silence."

She did so with some apprehension, but Vincent smiled, and though he was clearly still fatigued, that little smirk did much to restore her spirits. He raised his voice. "Zancani, you may come in."

The door opened immediately. The puppet player stepped in, followed not long after by the Abbess. With his red wig removed, his appearance was transformed. "So? You have kissed and made up?"

"Not while she is wearing those whiskers." Vincent squeezed Jane's hand. "But yes, thank you. Come in. We have things to discuss."

Jane rubbed the wool side whiskers and rolled her eyes. "I tried pulling them off, but . . ."

"Let me help. I have a good deal of practise with whiskers." The puppet player carried a small wooden box and knelt next to Jane. "Talk to us. Tell us your great plan while I restore Lady Vincent."

The Abbess crossed her arms and stood in the door. "And then you are going to bed. Both of you."

"Yes, madam." Vincent nodded. "You may be certain that my wife has made that very clear."

Lord Byron sauntered in and leaned against the wall. He wrinkled his nose. "Shall I open the window?"

"Please." Vincent winced, flushing. "And apologies."

"You should smell the inside of a puppet booth after a show. This is nothing." At Jane's side, Signor Zancani dabbed her cheek with something that smelled of brandy and tugged on the wool. It stung as he peeled it up, but it seemed to be releasing from her skin.

Vincent shifted on the bed, seeming uncomfortable to be

seated while women were standing, but he had enough sense not to rise. He rubbed the back of his neck. "Lady Vincent made some discoveries while in the palazzo that will require us to move faster than we had planned. Sister Franceschina, would you and the other nuns in the scriptorium have enough time to do the copying by Monday?"

The elderly nun studied pages of notes, which had quick sketches of the journal. "Yes . . . yes, that is possible. Written and bound by Monday."

They had not gone all the way through the book before Jane had been interrupted. She shook her head. This would not work. "What about the rest of the pages? It will do us no good to have a half-empty book."

"My guess is that they have only given close study to the pages concerning the *Verre Obscurci*." Vincent squinted at Sister Franceschina. "What if I write in the book after you are finished?"

That meant additional work for Vincent, when what she wanted most was for him to rest, so Jane proposed an alternative. "We are asking them to forge the other pages—why not these as well? I can tell them the sorts of things to write."

Sister Franceschina nodded. "We could likely do that, yes."

For a moment, it looked as though Vincent would protest that he was well enough, but he nodded. "Thank you. That would be a great help. And by Monday?"

Sister Franceschina turned through the pages again before giving a nod, but there was more hesitation there. "If the Abbess gives permission to burn extra candles."

"So long as you do not miss services or prayers." The

Abbess looked back to Vincent. "We will need all the prayer possible if this is to succeed."

"We have another problem," Signor Zancani peeled the top of the other side whisker free of Jane's face. "This Spada saw us in the hall, so the plan to regain the spheres will not work."

Vincent's brow furrowed. "Why not? Did he recognise Jane?"

"No, of course not." The puppet player looked affronted that the efficacy of his disguise would be questioned. "But she had removed the paunch. She is thus established for him as a slender man."

Jane closed her eyes, remembering the meeting in front of the water entrance. "I used it to start a fire."

"I was wondering."

"Can someone else go in to obtain them?" the Abbess asked. "It seems to me that our reason for sending Lady Vincent in the first place was to identify the papers, which she has done. And in the second, because her role would be established. But the spheres are surely easier to identify than the papers. Can we not send another?"

"The strong room," Jane said, her heart clenching with realization.

"Pardon?"

"The measurements for the hall were off because there is a strong room in the middle of the palazzo. To get inside will require a glamourist."

Here, the puppet player looked confused. "I thought that glamour was only an illusion."

"It is mostly an illusion." Vincent sighed and squeezed his

eyes tightly shut, as if the thought alone pained him. "A strong room is a room with corporeal locks that are masked by glamour. To undo the locks, one must first undo the glamour in order to see them. Undo it in the wrong order, and an alarm will sound. The illusion of noise is quite as effective as the real thing when creating an alarm."

Lord Byron cursed liberally, and the Abbess looked almost as though she would like to join him. Signor Zancani said, "That is unfortunate."

Squinting, Vincent nodded and grimaced. "I know. I do not like it either, but it will have to be either Jane or me, and Spada just saw her." Shaking his head, he stopped, took a breath, and turned to the puppet player. "Do you think you could make a French officer's uniform by Thursday?"

"I thought you said he was from Lombardy-Venetia."

"He is, but a French representative is due on Friday, and we can say he came early. Besides which, I speak French and not Venetian." Vincent's hand trembled as he lowered it to his side. "So, the costume?"

Jane started as she realized what he was contemplating. "You cannot be serious." He wanted to go into the palazzo as the French representative. "We have already discussed this. Signor Zancani has said before that he did not think he could sufficiently disguise you."

"I was not thinking of using cosmetics."

"Glamour?"

When he nodded, everyone in the room protested with a rapidity and vehemence that gratified Jane. She was not alone in seeing that he had pushed himself past the limits of what the human body could endure.

"Can you tell me another way?" Vincent lifted his head. Even as battered as he was, he appeared absolutely confident. The room silenced.

Jane searched for another option to get herself or Vincent into the palazzo. They could deliver a crate with her inside—which Spada would certainly search, and even then, how would she exit the property? Rob the house, under the cover of night—except that someone always seemed to be awake at the palazzo.

"You are unwell." It did not even begin to cover his condition.

Vincent looked grave and did not attempt to disagree, though she could not tell whether that was because she had made an impression on him or because he felt even worse than he was willing to admit. "I would not attempt it tomorrow, or even the day after, but we have close to a week." Jane drew breath to speak, but Vincent held up his hand. "And if we come up with another way to accomplish this between now and then, I will gladly give up the plan."

Lord Byron cleared his throat. "Forgive me, but what exactly is the plan?"

Vincent looked at Jane, as if to ask for understanding, then turned to the poet. "I am going to use glamour to make myself look like the French officer who they are expecting, with the goal of having them open the strong room and bring the *Verre Obscurcie* out. I should be able to swap the *Verre* and papers while inside, under the guise of examining them, so it will not require a second trip."

"But with the early arrival of the officer, they will be suspicious, surely." Jane could not begin to list the number of her concerns. Though it was something that they had discussed before, they had discarded it when the less dangerous plan had presented itself. "Spada knew the fire was set by us."

"Well, there *were* two of them."

She rolled her eyes. "Yes. But that means that he will now note and suspect *any* change in the routine."

From his place against the wall, Lord Byron shrugged. "So go at the time the officer is supposed to be there."

"And have two officers arrive?" Jane shook her head. "I do not see how that is better."

"Because it is fairly easy to make certain that an officer travelling some distance does not arrive on time."

The Abbess turned on the poet. "I will not be party to an innocent man being waylaid for the purposes of this plan."

"First of all, I sincerely doubt that a French officer has any innocence about him." Lord Byron cocked his head and smiled disingenuously. "As for his delay, I was not thinking of way-laying him so much as providing him with some companion-ship for the evening."

"Could you really?" Jane asked.

"My dear, I have tempted your husband to drink more than he ought to on—" He broke off when Vincent cleared his throat and shook his head slightly. Smiling, the poet flexed his hands, as though he were a pugilist preparing for a fight. "That is to say . . . a French officer? It will not be a problem."

Indeed? The poet had an undisputed reputation in this area, but she had not heard about his exploits with Vincent. She would have to decide later if she wanted to know about them or if it was best not to ask. Still, his offer would remove one problem . . . but only one. "Vincent, you said you could only hold glamour as a disguise for half an hour. That was when you were in good health, and I do not think that a week will restore you. Particularly if you are required to perform a second glamour as well, to unlock the strong room."

"It will not take long for them to bring the *Verre* out," Vincent protested.

The Abbess shook her head. "You are thinking like an Englishman. They will want to have coffee and talk about your travel. If you rush them, you might get them to open the strong room in half an hour, but you will not have time to complete the transaction and depart."

"What you need . . . is a distraction . . ." Lord Byron said slowly. Then he grinned and bowed his head to the Abbess. "If you would help, I think I can provide an excellent one, via subterraqueous avenues. Does the palazzo still have the racing gondolas?"

The water entrance would be perfect, if it were possible to get a gondola out without being seen. On land they might try a *Sphere Obscurcie*, but it would never work on water. "Wait— what if we had a real *Verre*, and used it to come in through the water entrance?"

"Where would we get that?" Vincent shook his head. "None of the glassmakers would work with us."

"Because they thought we were trying to steal their work." Jane turned to the Abbess. "But if we had someone to vouch for us?"

She straightened. "I will not lie, you know that. You would have to tell them what you are working on."

Vincent gazed at her, considering. Every part of his expression, from the set of his brow to the softness of his jaw, spoke of weariness. If it were possible to create a *Verre* by herself, she would, but it required two glamourists. If Vincent were incapable of helping, then it would also make his suggested plan impracticable.

Jane waited, giving him time to work through the problem on his own and to see that working a single thread of glamour was more possible in his condition than the madness of using it incessantly as a disguise. Eventually Vincent wiped his mouth and sighed. "All right."

Twenty-one

The Abbess and the Glassmaker

The following Tuesday, Jane and Vincent presented themselves at Signor Nenci's with the Reverend Mother. Jane had wanted to wait longer, but Vincent had pointed out that the glass needed time to temper. His colour was much improved, and to one who did not know her husband, he would seem to be in good health, but to Jane there was still a pinched quality to the skin around his eyes. When pressed, Vincent had admitted that light still pained him somewhat. The vertigo, however, had abated. He had been true to his word and slept through Saturday and well into Sunday. He had eschewed glamour entirely on Monday and pulled just enough from the ether on Tuesday morning to be certain that he could do so without any ill effects.

Though he had promised to alert Jane if any symptoms recurred, she was watching him closely and intended to stop their experiment if he betrayed any signs of fatigue beyond those that they had discussed. Assuming that Signor Nenci would even see them. The Abbess knocked on the door and folded her arms across her chest.

After a moment, the door cracked open and the same apprentice they had seen on their first visit poked his sweat-stained face through. His eyes widened at the sight of the Abbess. "Oh! Reverend Mother." He bowed. "What can I do for you?"

"I would like to see Signor Nenci." Her voice made it very clear that this was not entirely a request.

"Of course, come in." He stepped back, opening the door wider.

From inside, a familiar voice bellowed, "Tomà, what in the devil's name are you doing, letting a draft in!" Signor Nenci stomped up to the door with a deep glower. "How many times have I—Reverend Mother!" He cuffed Tomà. "Why are you keeping her outside in the cold?"

"Thank you." She stepped forward as though used to this sort of deference. Then Signor Nenci saw Jane and Vincent.

For a moment he looked confused, as though he recognised them but had forgotten from where, and then the memory came back with clear force. His face twisted as though he were going to swear, but he held in whatever comment he was about to make. Swallowing, he bowed to the Abbess. "I am afraid I need to ask your companions to wait outside."

"No . . . I do not think you do." She beckoned to Jane and Vincent, wrinkled face set in a mask of stern authority. "Sir

David, Lady Vincent, come with me, if you please." Without waiting for Signor Nenci's further permission, she walked through the door.

As Jane and Vincent followed, he bent his head down and whispered. "Why I am suddenly frightened of an old woman?"

She murmured back, "It is one of the compensatory powers of age. Wait until you see me in my dotage."

"You shall be a force of nature the likes of which the world has never seen."

"You are too kind." She stopped whispering, because Signor Nenci had shot her a look that carried much acrimony.

Once inside, she had the opportunity to look around Nenci's glassblowing factory and compare it with Signor Querini's. In spite of the fact that Querini's establishment was the newer one, this one spoke of modernity, with what appeared to be new ovens and working tables. A half dozen apprentices and glassblowers worked on creating goblets, bowls, and delicate candelabra. Nenci led them to a small office, kept separate from the rest of the factory by a low wall with windows looking out across the floor. He offered chairs to the Abbess and to Jane. Vincent, he let stand.

The Abbess steepled her fingers in front of her and nodded to Vincent. "Sir David has a business proposition I want you to hear out."

Signor Nenci scowled. "If it is to watch us work, the answer is no. Even for you, Reverend Mother."

The Abbess raised her eyebrows at Vincent and inclined her head.

Vincent inhaled and Jane could see him brace himself. "Am I correct that you guard your trade secrets carefully?"

Tilting his head to the side, Signor Nenci nodded. Clearly he had not expected this line of questioning. "Yes. Why?"

"Because we have a new technique and need a glassblower who will not share it."

Snorting, Signor Nenci dusted off his hands. "There is nothing that your English glassmakers can teach me."

"What about a glamourist?" Jane said, hoping to coax him to hear them out.

"Again with the glamour." He rolled his eyes, and it seemed likely that even the presence of the Abbess would not restrain his tongue for much longer.

"We can record it. In glass." Vincent's stillness was a sign of his tension, but she remembered when she had once thought this flat affect was due to unshakeable calm.

The glassmaker's brows drew together, and he glanced to the Abbess for confirmation. She nodded. "I have not seen it myself, but I have seen the work that these two can do, and spent enough time with Lady Vincent to be certain of her character. The other factor to consider is that Signor Querini worked with swindlers to try to steal the technique from them."

Signor Nenci wiped his mouth and stared at them for a long moment. He crossed the room and shut the door to the little office. "You said *tried* to steal the technique."

Jane said, "He has our papers and the *Verre Obscurcie* we created, but the swindlers do not seem to have an understanding of how they work."

He leaned against his desk and watched them closely. "How *do* they work?"

Vincent cleared his throat. "Do I have your word that you will not share it?"

"With the Reverend Mother as my witness, yes." He crossed his arms and waited.

"Glamour leaves a trail in glass. We can enhance that with the application of a gossamer-weight thread of cold. When the *Verre* is put into full sunlight, the light follows the path of the glamour and creates the same illusion." It sounded so abundantly simple when Vincent explained it that Jane could not understand why no one else had thought of it first. Though, to be fair, it did only seem to work consistently with the *Sphère Obscurcie*.

Signor Nenci straightened as Vincent spoke, with a look of intense concentration. "The illusion—what sort of thing can you produce?"

"So far, only this." He rapidly wove a *Sphère Obscurcie* and vanished. The glassmaker started, but did not exclaim. From within the sphere, Vincent's disembodied voice continued. "The glassmaker we worked with in Binché thought that it was because this weave had the same shape as the sphere we were trying to cast into. The challenge has been keeping it still enough while we are working. We have had only limited success with other weaves."

"Why a sphere?"

Jane frowned. "We thought that was the foundation of blown glass."

Nenci shrugged and picked up a bas-relief made of glass. His gaze had the intensity of expression that she associated with Vincent when he was planning a glamural. "For vessels, yes, but a slab sounds as though it would work better."

"A slab?" Vincent reappeared, shaking his head. "I do not understand."

"You pour the glass on to a working surface and use paddles to control the shape." Nenci's face twisted as though he were about to spit on the floor in disgust. "Querini did not even consider this, did he? Amateur. A slab, yes. Less movement, longer working time, and not hollow in the middle."

Jane's mouth fell open. They had been working with a craftsman, but this was an artist. Vincent seemed equally shocked, and ran his hand through his hair. "Can we try it?"

"Yes, yes! Come—no, wait." Signor Nenci stopped and looked at the Abbess. "If this works, I want to license it from them. Will you witness it?"

"In fact, we cannot license it." Vincent shook his head. "I am sorry, but I am bound by the Prince Regent not to teach the *Sphère Obscurcie* weave to anyone."

"But it works with other glamours, yes? It is only the sphere that was limiting you, I suspect." Nenci rubbed his hands together. "Yes . . . I am certain that is the problem. As I have no interest in invisibility, that should not be a concern. It is the ornamental aspects that I want. Imagine, a glass platter that will create a glamour for your dining room table, eh? If we set the slab in a larger piece of ornamented glass, then it can remain attractive even when the sun is not out."

"Um . . . and if we do not want to license it to you?" Jane asked, though in truth what she wanted was to go into the glass factory and try it straightaway.

"Of course you do." Signor Nenci waved his hand as if that was not an objection. "Your husband wants secrecy with this. I will offer you a ten-year exclusive contract, plus a share of income for sales of works created based on your technique. If it works."

Vincent shook his head, clearly as taken aback as Jane about the sudden reversal in the glassmaker's attitude toward them. What if he had been paid to learn the technique . . . ? But, no, they had chosen Nenci on their own. And yet, for all they knew, Spada had paid every glassmaker in Murano to learn the technique and give it to him. Even the Abbess could be an associate designed to make Jane trust her.

Was this paranoia, or caution? She looked at the glass-maker very carefully, searching his face for any sign of duplicity, though she was not sure how that would present itself. "Why?"

"Two reasons. No, three. One: Venice's glass industry is stagnating. If you give me ten years with this, then I can start to turn that around. Two: Other people will figure it out, eventually, but if I license it, Murano will have a jump." The glassmaker gave a smile that was closer to a sneer. "And third: Querini used to be my apprentice. With apologies to the Abbess, the devil take him."

On the last point, Jane had no doubt that his emotion was sincere, and it gave her a path back into clarity. He would have been a better choice to work with them from the beginning. Spada had not used him, then. And Jane suspected that the swindlers could not have used him as they had Querini, because Nenci was as dedicated to his art as they were to theirs.

They had found another partner.

Signor Nenci had cleared his apprentices away from part of the studio and erected a folding screen behind which they could try the technique. The Abbess settled upon a chair behind the screen to watch, confessing herself to be curious about the endeavour. Vincent removed his jacket, setting it upon a chair back near the wall. Jane wished that she still possessed a pair of buckskin breeches, but was not going to remind Vincent of the dangers of muslin at a furnace.

Scowling, Signor Nenci suddenly stopped in front of her, then shook his head. He leaned around the screen and shouted across the studio. "Rosa! I need your spare work smock!"

He then ignored them as he dragged a small metal-topped table from the wall toward the screen. The legs squealed against the stone floor of the glass factory, sending shivers down Jane's spine.

Vincent stepped forward. "May I help?"

"I want this there." He poked a finger at a spot in front of the furnace and stalked off to pick up a pair of wooden paddles. Vincent lifted the table, rather than dragging it, and carried it to the place that Signor Nenci indicated. "Rosa!"

"Coming, Papa." A young woman hurried across the glass factory with a black wool garment draped over her arm. She wore a similar garment, which was like a day dress that wrapped around to tie at the waist. It had long, closely fitted sleeves without any embellishments, and over it she wore a heavy leather apron.

He jerked his chin toward Jane and stomped over to the table that Vincent had placed. "Let her use it." Setting down the paddles, he adjusted the table with a steady string of curses.

The Abbess cleared her throat, which only made him curse more quietly.

Rosa rolled her eyes and beckoned to Jane. "Forgive Papa. He is a curmudgeon when he works."

"I am focused," Signor Nenci snapped.

"You see?" She held out the black dress to Jane. They seemed matched in height, though Rosa had a more pleasing plumpness than Jane. "Do you need help? I just wear it over my dress."

"Thank you." Jane took the dress. "My husband can also be a curmudgeon when he works."

Vincent frowned at her with a look that said that he could hear her, and also proved her point. He went back to rolling up his sleeves and conferred with Signor Nenci while Jane shrugged into the dress.

Rosa wrinkled her nose. "Men can be so peculiar about work."

"I can hear you," her father said, although he seemed a little pleased.

Caught by the fact that the young woman had a working smock, Jane asked, "Do you assist?"

Rosa gave an aggrieved sigh, as though she had answered that question many times. "I am a fifth-generation glassmaker."

"Oh—forgive me. I should have known better." Jane of all people should know what it was like to be an artist and face that presumption. She engaged herself with tying the lace of the dress. "And you wear wool to work in?"

Rosa nodded. "It does not catch fire the way muslin does, though it is rather warm. I use black because it does not show the scorch marks so much." She looked Jane over and gave a nod of satisfaction. "Do you need anything else, Papa?"

He shook his head, grunting, and waved her away. Rosa

laughed, as though used to his abstracted gaze, and walked off to leave Jane and Vincent alone with her father. He hefted the paddles and used one to point at the table. "I'll work the glass from here. Where do you need to be?"

Vincent took up a position opposite him. "Will this be in your way?"

Signor Nenci shook his head. Pulling on a leather glove, he turned to the oven, while Jane hurried to stand in front of Vincent. While she did, the glassmaker picked up a metal scoop and plunged it into the oven. He ladled out molten glass, then poured the glowing orange substance onto the table. "Wait."

Tossing the scoop into a container, he shook off the glove and began to use the paddles to shape the glass into a rectangle. For a moment, he concentrated on pulling the glass up as it tried to spread out on the table. Then he nodded. "Now."

Vincent reached into the ether and pulled out a fold of glamour, then let go of it. He coughed, stepping back from Jane. Concerned, she looked back at him. He shook his head. "It is nothing."

"Vincent—"

"The thickness was wrong."

Signor Nenci worked the paddles without looking at them. "Glass is cooling."

Vincent took his position again, reached back into the ether, and pulled out another fold. He began the weave for the *Sphère Obscurcie* shape, pausing for a moment to adjust the direction of the folds slightly to allow for the angle at which they were now working.

Jane pulled the lines of cold from the ether and followed

Vincent's path to strengthen its impression in the glass. Compared to working with the sphere, even one held still on the end of a pole, this was astonishingly simple. It took them only a little longer than it would to weave one without glass, and Jane was almost baffled when Vincent released the glamour. She did the same, with the sensation that it must not have worked.

Signor Nenci looked up at them as he stepped back from the table. A perfectly formed square sat on the table, and running through the middle of it, the faint occlusions of glamour. "Well?"

"That was easier." Vincent had a line between his brows as he stared at the glass. He rubbed the base of his neck, frowning. "How long before we can put it into the sun?"

Turning in place, the glassmaker looked around the studio, which was lit by slanted skylights in the ceiling. He snatched his leather glove off the floor and pulled it on. With a shriek of metal on stone, he dragged the table to the closest pool of sunlight. Vincent reached out to help him, then jerked his hand back, shaking it. Signor Nenci grinned. "Careful. The d——n thing's hot."

"Signor Nenci!" The Abbess stood to follow them.

He grinned. "Well, it is."

"I see." Vincent examined his hand, but did not appear to have burned himself.

Jane followed the men more slowly, hanging back so she could watch for the telling moment when the slab went into the sun—

—And Signor Nenci vanished.

"My God!" The Abbess raised a hand to her chest. "Ah . . . in heaven, hallowed be thy name."

"Eh? What?" Signor Nenci's disembodied voice came from the centre of the *Sphère*. To him, standing in its influence, the room would appear perfectly normal.

"Allow me." Vincent stepped into the *Sphère*, vanishing. "If you would go to Lady Vincent and then turn."

With a series of his habitual grumbles, the glassmaker stepped out of the *Sphère* and stomped across the floor. When he got to Jane, he stopped and turned. "Well?"

"Where is the table, Signor?"

His mouth opened as if he were going to make a sneering comment.

"Never mind the table," Vincent's disembodied voice said. "Where am I?"

For a long moment, the glassmaker simply stared openmouthed at the space where the table had been. Then he clapped his hands and began to laugh. "What else can we make?"

Vincent emerged from the *Sphère*, rubbing the base of his neck. "Let us find out, shall we?"

"We were only going to make the *Verre Obscurcie* today," Jane said.

"I did not expect it to be so easy." Vincent still wore a contracted brow. "We have time to try another."

"It is not the *time* I am worried about, but your energy."

Vincent scowled. "We said we would make three tries. It took only one, so why not see what else we can do?"

"You are rubbing your neck a great deal."

Vincent dropped his hand and sighed, stepping closer to Jane. He lowered his voice. "You know what this is."

"And you know why I am voicing my concern."

His jaw worked and he looked to Signor Nenci as if the

glassmaker would support him. Signor Nenci stepped away, studiously taking no notice of them. A loose thread on his leather apron consumed his attention. Vincent growled low in his throat. "I had thought you would wait until I had given you some cause for concern."

"It distresses me to see you acting unwell." She studied him, wishing that it was easier to tell when he was being honest about his health. "Would you tell me if your head was really bothering you?"

"After our conversation? Yes." Vincent held out his hand, spreading his fingers wide. No tremors were visible. "You see? I am perfectly well."

"Perfectly?"

"Adequately well, then." He rumpled his hair with real aggravation upon his face. "One more, Muse."

The Abbess watched them with her head tilted to the side. She had seen Vincent at his worst, and was no doubt wondering why they were even contemplating working with glamour now. Jane shared that. They had a working *Verre Obscurcie,* so there was no need to do anything else today. But Vincent looked so excited, and after months of his depression it was difficult to deny that sparkle in his eye. He did not seem the worse for wear, if she disregarded the hand that had rubbed the base of his neck. And truly, it was astonishing how easy it had been to cast the glamour into the slab of glass on the table. Jane was eager to see what else they could do. It was only the timing that concerned her.

But one more attempt could not hurt. Not really. "One more. And I mean one more *attempt*, not that we continue working until we create one more glass."

Vincent flashed a rare grin and spun back to Signor Nenci, then stumbled and took a step to the right to catch his balance. It was not much, but it was more than enough to show that he was dizzy. Jane put a hand under his elbow to steady him, in case it was worse than it looked. He jerked his arm free and pinched the bridge of his nose.

"Vincent . . ."

"I am—"

"Do not tell me that you are well." She glanced to the Abbess to see if she had noted Vincent's stumble. The nun had clearly seen it and was hurrying across the factory floor. "We have done everything here that we set out to do today. We are going home now."

"I was going to say that I appear to be a little light-headed, yet." He lowered his hand and glowered at the floor. "It is not enough to present a problem."

The Abbess stopped in front of Vincent and tilted her head up as if she could glare sense into him. "And if you lost your balance next to the oven?"

The look of anger and embarrassment that crossed his face was remarkable to behold. "That would be unfortunate, yes." Like a bear trapped between a trainer and his audience, Vincent turned between Jane and the Abbess. "Then I shall ask Signor Nenci to move the table farther from the oven."

Jane put a hand on his arm to stop him. Though they had discussed what she was going to say next, a significant part of her expected him to insist on staying regardless of any prior agreement. "When we were working with Querini, you made me stop when I was unfit and would not admit it. Do you remember? To pull me away, you said that you would stop working the next time I asked, without grumbling."

To his credit, Vincent only looked at the floor for a long moment, as though he were counting the tiles in the floor. Then he nodded, lifting his head, and gave a smile that was almost convincing. "Shall we go home?"

Not even Signor Nenci tried to convince him otherwise, for which Jane was grateful. When she got Vincent back to their apartment, she would find out how his health really was, when he was not putting on a show for the Abbess.

Twenty-two

Glass on Marble

Jane shifted over in bed and tried to find a more comfortable position. It was still dark out and she desperately wanted to sleep, but she had been tossing all night. Though they had worked hard on their plans, she was left with a lingering tension as she continued to think through all of the possible things that could go wrong today. Each time she answered one question, her brain would offer her another. Was Signor Zancani going to have the costumes ready? Yes, he had already shown them to her. Then would the nuns be in position to provide a distraction? Of course, they had already practised that. Would Lord Byron have any questions before they began? Probably.

As she rolled on to her back, the extra space in the bed told her that Vincent was not in it.

Jane sat up, holding the cover around her to ward off the cold. "Vincent?"

He stood at the window, a shadow against the dawn light. "It is raining."

Using the blanket as a robe, Jane crawled out of bed. The bare boards of the floor seemed almost cold enough to be the flagstones of Vincent's glamural. The glass walls of the orangery showed a still-dark landscape, but without any hint of the rain that appeared in the real window looking out over Murano. Low clouds covered the city, and rain drizzled down the walls of the city into the canals.

There was no possibility of a *Verre Obscurcie* working today, not even Signor Nenci's version. "Can we put it off?"

He shook his head. She knew that, of course. They had known that rain was a possibility when they went to bed last night. To wait increased the risk that the Lombardy-Venetia officer would arrive the next day and take all the *Verres*. They would have to use their other plan, then, and send Vincent in, today, as the French officer. "It frightens me, Vincent."

"You know I will be fine."

"No . . . I really do not. I know that *you* think you will be, but I want that faith."

Vincent turned from the window and wrapped his arms around her. "This will work, Muse."

And if it did not—oh, the things that could go wrong terrified her. "Just remember that I will come for you."

He smiled, and traced a finger down the side of her face. "That I know." Bending down, Vincent kissed her, first on the forehead, then the nose, and then her lips. His breath was warmth and life. Jane opened the blanket to pull him inside the small shelter with her. Vincent slid his arms under the cloth and down her back. Without effort, as if to prove that he was fit, her husband lifted her and carried her back to bed.

Standing with the nuns at their station under the gallery down the street, Jane adjusted the veil of her wimple to try to cover more of her face. The white cloth of the nun's habit covering her brow and the sides of her face did nothing to hide her nose. How could anyone fail to recognise her in this? Signor Zancani's ensemble had been more concealing, and even though this suited their purposes today better than dressing as a man would have, Jane kept wishing for the wart or glasses. The bulk of her costume got in her way, and with each movement she felt every lump and twist of the rope she had hidden within it.

Sister Aquinata elbowed Jane, while pretending to be paying attention to the girls they were professedly taking for an excursion. "A real nun does not play with her habit quite so much."

Dropping her hand, Jane blushed—which real nuns probably also did not do, or at least not to the extent that she did. The rain had lightened to a soft mist, but the clouds showed no signs of clearing. The driest path, however, was under the long galleries along the sides of the streets. They walked their charges under the gallery opposite the swindlers' palazzo. Signor Zancani had set up his booth there, and they planned to stop and watch the puppet show so that they were in place to provide some confusion when Vincent exited the building.

Other passers-by strolled through the streets, taking advantage of the temporary break in the rain to go about their errands. Jane watched the flow of foot traffic until she spotted the French officer. It was hard not to stare at Vincent, who she recognised only because she had helped him dress. The uniform had been cut to make him appear heavier than he was so that he could carry in the faux *Verres* for the swap. Signor Zancani had taught him to alter his walk to a more military bearing. With the gold trim on his uniform and the sword hanging by his side, her husband had quite the military swagger. Until the puppet player had forced her husband to walk with his chest out, Jane had not realized how much of the distinctiveness of Vincent's stride was because he led with his brow, his chin tucked into his collar, as though his mind were leading him forward.

Now Vincent's chin was held up.

Or, rather, not *his* chin, but the face of *Général de Brigade* Germain, which Vincent wore over his own features. The whiskers and hair colour had been altered by Signor Zancani so that Vincent had bushy white side whiskers and hair running to grey. Glamour altered the line of his jaw to give him jowls, and he had the bulbous nose of a man who drank to excess.

Sister Aquinata elbowed her again, and Jane dragged her gaze from her husband. A real nun would not stare at a man with so much longing. She sent up a prayer that Vincent would be safe. They were fast approaching the part of the plan that frightened her the most, when he went inside the palazzo.

The puppets. She must appear to be watching the puppets and making sure the girls were all staying with the group.

Sister Aquinata stood on the other side of their small cluster. At the end of this show, Sister Maria Agnes and the Abbess would take their place watching over the group. Jane stepped to the side until she stood upon the stone they had marked. From there, she was able to see the mirror that Signor Nenci had lent them. It hung on the puppet booth as though it were trimming, but angled in such a way so that it reflected the palazzo. She could see Vincent step up to the door and knock.

More significantly, she could hear. Jane had run a slender thread from the second-floor room down to the street to carry the sound from the *bouclé torsadée* that had remained anchored behind the curtain in the parlour at the palazzo. A casual passer-by who happened to stroll through the thread would catch at most a snippet of conversation from the palazzo but would be past too quickly to note it. If one stood in exactly the right spot, however, pretending to watch a puppet show, one could align an ear with the thread and listen.

Someone was in the parlour, because she could hear the quiet hiss of paper turning and the clink of glass on marble. Was that the sound of the *Verre* being set out on the side-board or simply a glass of brandy? No other clues came to identify which man, or men, were there, and it gave her nothing of the sound that happened elsewhere in the house. But she could see Vincent present his card—prepared by Sister Franceschina—and be admitted into the house.

A few moments later, the parlour door opened.

"Pardon me, sir, but *Général de Brigade* Germain is here to see you."

"Are you ready?" Spada. The glass clinked against marble.

"No, but I can fake it." Bastone. Papers rattled as he shuffled them. For a moment he appeared in the window as he crossed the parlour to the strong room.

"Then show him in."

The door closed.

Metal clicked. A lock? Another door opened with a faint hiss of cloth brushing cloth. Muffled, Bastone said, "Sometimes I wonder if the *Verre* never worked."

"Perhaps they were swindling us, you mean?"

"Exactly." His voice remained indistinct, as though he were in another room. "If Napoleon hadn't backed this, I would have voted for getting out long ago."

Spada snorted. "As would I, but . . . I saw the *Verres* work and used one myself, when the Vincents were out. They work."

"That is good, because they are not particularly attractive." Bastone's voice grew in volume as he walked out of what Jane assumed was the strong room.

The door opened again. A man with a gruff voice spoke Italian with a thick French accent, "Good afternoon, *messieurs*."

"General Germain." Cloth rustled as Spada stood. "Please be welcome. How was your journey?"

"It was good, *merci*." Footsteps sounded, and then her husband appeared in the window, as they had agreed. Jane could scarcely breathe, watching him. He would try to make them converse near the window in order to remain visible from the street. Vincent held two fingers in front of his chest to indicate that only two of the band of swindlers were in the room with him. "The weather is frightful today, is it not?"

Jane fidgeted with her rosary, considering. If there were only two men in the room, that meant that the others could be anywhere. It might not be safe yet to send the signal to Lord Byron to effect his subterraqueous entrance.

Spada said, "Alas, Venice in the winter is often like this."

Vincent raised a handkerchief and mopped his brow. "Now, where are these *Verres Obscurcis* that I 'ave 'eard so much about? Will you show them to me?"

Spada glided across the room to stand by him. "Of course, but let us first offer you something to drink. You must be parched from your journey."

"*Non.* Not at all. I would very much like—" He stopped abruptly and pressed the handkerchief to his brow again. "Will you be so good as to show me the *Verres?*"

"Are you quite all right?"

"Is no matter. Malaria left me—how you say—palsy sometimes." His image in the mirror was too small to make out the fine details. She could not see his hands shaking, but that must be what was happening. Jane's heart sped as if she were the one working the glamour.

"Spada . . ." Bastone stepped into view, with concern in his voice.

Vincent swayed. Spada took a step back in alarm as her husband's glamour ruptured into an oily spectrum and he crumpled to the ground.

Through the *bouclé torsadée*, Jane could hear Vincent's heels drumming against the floor and the sound that had given her nightmares: the short grunts of breath being forced from his body in convulsions.

Twenty-three

A Complicated Tapestry

She had known Vincent would convulse. The harsh edge of his breath bore into her head through the *bouclé torsadée*. Jane could not listen to that sound. Jerking her head out of the skein, she turned to Sister Aquinata. "Vincent is having a seizure."

The nun's mouth dropped open in horror. On the stage, the puppets stopped, Pulcinella turning as if in shock. Her voice had been louder than she intended, and all of the girls had clearly heard her. She had not meant to alarm them, but there was no time to worry about that.

Jane turned to the oldest of them. "Lucia, run to the river and tell Lord Byron to proceed, exactly as we have planned. Make sure you tell him to proceed *exactly* as we have planned."

Eyes wide, the girl nodded and ran down the street, pigtails streaming behind her.

Signor Zancani appeared from behind the booth, still pulling a puppet off his hand. Jane spared him a glance and said, "Nothing changes."

"What do you mean? If he is ill, everything changes."

"I am going after him. I will need a distraction to get us out, and we already have one planned. Use it." Without waiting for his inevitable protest, Jane ran across the street.

Behind her, she heard Sister Aquinata send another girl to tell the Abbess what was happening. Then the puppet play began again. Jane put them out of her mind. Her first objective—her only objective—was to get to Vincent and hope she was quick enough.

At the door, Jane sent up a prayer and shoved. It opened easily. Vincent's calling card fell out of the latch, where he had blocked the lock. Lifting the robes of her habit, Jane ran up the stairs, two at a time.

Coppa sat in front of the water entrance with a book, apparently guarding it. He looked up with alarm as she bolted up the stairs. "Hey!"

Jane ignored him, gaining the top of the stairs before he started up them. His footsteps chased her to the parlour. She burst into the room. Her feet echoed on the marble floor. The rug had been removed from the room, so Vincent would have landed on the cold stone floor. The *Verres* had been removed from the room, but for the moment Jane did not care about them.

Spada spun around. His brow furrowed in confusion, seeing only the robes of her habit for the moment. Jane charged to where Vincent lay on the floor, drenched with sweat.

His neck was pulled back in a tight arc, and tremors shook his body. Even though she had expected this sight, Jane stopped breathing in distress. She pushed past Spada and knelt at Vincent's side. "He must be cooled."

The confusion cleared from Spada's face. "Lady Vincent."

From the door, Coppa charged through. "Sorry. She slipped past me."

"I can see that." Spada leaned on his cane and limped forward.

Bastone stepped out of the wall as Jane grabbed a fold of glamour and wove it into a bubble of cool in an effort to reduce Vincent's temperature. She glared at Bastone, who halted by the strong room. "Help me. You know what is happening here. I need help with the cold weaves."

"I—That's really not my area." He took a step back, as though Vincent's condition were contagious.

Denaro stuck his head into the parlour. "What's going on?"

"The Vincents were attempting to steal our *Verres*. I think that settles the question of whether they work." Spada tapped his cane upon the floor. "Denaro, check the other entrances. I suspect that there will be another attempt to come inside. Likely the service entrance. That is how you came in before, is it not, Lady Vincent?"

"I need help." She loosened Vincent's cravat and pulled it free to help him breathe. If she thought overmuch about what was happening, she would lose her bearings. "Please. Overheating could kill him."

Vincent's colour was very high, but mottled red and white. Little bubbles of spit popped at the corners of his mouth. She kept her gaze fixed on her husband and let the sound of the swindlers' conversation wash over her.

"She's right. If he hasn't fried himself already," Bastone said.

She pulled another fold from the ether and laid it under the initial strand of cold. "Will you please, for the love of God, send for a surgeon."

"Why?" Spada paced around her, cane tapping against the floor. "Is there a benefit to helping you?"

Jane lifted her head and let all the loathing she felt for this man fill her voice. "If you want to know how the *Verre* work, then help me keep him alive, because if he dies, I swear to God that I will hunt you down myself and kill you."

He laughed, shaking his head. "Brave words from a woman trapped in a room alone with four men who have no reason to let her live."

"Of course you have a reason. Profit." Jane turned her head back to Vincent, shaking with rage. They would let him die. After all that she knew about Spada, she had still put some faith in his essential humanity, that he would not willingly kill someone. It had been a mistake. "If he lives, I will teach you to work the *Verres*."

"Not merely if we help you? But it is hardly our fault that he is in such a state."

"It is completely your fault." Jane pulled a third fold out and slid it beneath the others. Spreading it between her hands, Jane reached for Vincent's forehead and began to stretch the glamour over him.

"Nonsense. I did not force you to do anything. At every step of the way, you had a choice. You chose to let me pay for your ransom. You chose to let me take you in. You chose to let me help pick a glassmaker." Spada's voice was bewitching and reasonable. "You chose to send your husband here, knowing that he was over-taxed. His collapse last week was not enough?"

Jane bit her lip, knowing that he was right. She was surprised not that he had an informant in their group but that he admitted it so readily. She kept her hands sliding over her husband's form, under the layers of cooling threads atop him. As she passed down his chest, he convulsed and made a strangled grunt that alarmed her. She almost pulled her hands back, but kept laying the folds. The chill began to burn into her fingers as she worked. "And you are choosing to let him die. If you want working *Verres*, I would suggest that you make a different choice."

"Do you swear with the same fervour that you swore to kill me that you will show Bastone how to make a working sphere?"

She bit back the hysterical laughter that threatened to rise. They *had* working *Verres* but did not know it. "If Vincent lives, and is unharmed. Yes."

"I thought he had only to live?"

"Since I rather suspect that you will have no reason to keep either of us alive once you know the trick, then it seems prudent to stipulate." Jane shifted so that she could run a hand down each of Vincent's legs. The spasms were so strong that she could barely continue to work. Her own breath sped, as though to match his in tempo.

"Bastone. Help the lady." Spada limped across the floor. "Coppa, go for a surgeon. Quickly, if you please."

Jane suppressed her sigh of relief. This was only one obstacle surmounted, and it did nothing to lessen her concern for Vincent. Everything depended on how long it took Coppa to fetch a surgeon. She looked to Bastone. "Take these, if you please," indicating the folds she was holding.

"I—" He stopped in the process of kneeling. "Spada, where are you going?"

"To guard the door. I do not want any more surprises." He produced a key from his pocket. "You do not mind being locked in, do you?"

"Last time he set the room on fire."

They thought that Vincent had snuck in and not her? Jane kept her gaze on Vincent.

"If their roles were reversed, perhaps there would be some concern, but I do not think that will be a risk, given Sir David's condition . . . unless you are afraid of a woman?" Spada bowed, as if courtesy mattered, and stepped out of the room. He pulled the door shut behind him, and a moment later the lock clicked home.

Bastone gave a curse. "I always get left with the rubbish."

"Sorry to trouble you."

"What do you need." He dropped to his knees beside her with an aggravated sigh.

The urge to slap him was very strong. "Take these and keep them steady." She passed him the threads she had been working on in a sort of complicated cat's cradle.

He shuddered. "These are freezing."

"Well, we *are* trying to lower his temperature." Jane let her vision expand deep into the second sight to make certain that everything was in place. This was a complicated tapestry she was trying to weave, and her anxiety did nothing to help, but the lines of cold were clear. Jane pulled out another pair of folds, twisting them quickly around and expanded the bubble to contain the other threads. "I see that there is water on the sideboard. If you have the threads, I am going to dampen a cloth for his head before I lay in the next part."

"Go ahead."

Gathering her habit around her, Jane stood and walked behind Bastone as though she were going to the sideboard. She slid her hand into one of her voluminous sleeves to remove the truncheon she had hidden there. She had never been so glad to be undervalued because she was a woman.

Jane brought the club down on the back of Bastone's head as hard as she could.

Standing with her head outside of the sphere of silence she had just woven, the club landed silently. He doubled over at the impact, but did not fall. She raised the club again.

Vincent opened his eyes.

He sat up and punched the man. Bastone sagged to the floor in utter silence. Where Vincent had lain, an image of him remained, so that her husband appeared to be conjoined with a twin who twitched and jerked on the floor. Jane dropped to her knees beside him, entering the silent sphere. "Are you all right? That spasm terrified me. It was nothing we had practised."

"You hit one of my ticklish spots." He rolled Bastone over. "It was all I could do to keep a straight face. Did you bring the rope?"

"And everything else." Jane hitched up the skirt of her habit, under which she wore a pair of borrowed breeches. She had a length of rope wrapped around her waist and proceeded to remove it. "Spada is outside."

"I heard." Vincent took the rope and bound Bastone's hands. "I was able to watch Bastone open the strong room."

"Good." Though they had spent days planning for every variation they could think of, it was still a relief that this part of their scheme had worked. "I had hoped they would leave the *Verres* out, but did not think it likely."

Vincent nodded and looked down at the glamour of himself. He blanched beneath the remnants of his disguise. "I look awful."

"This is better than you were last week." The red and white splotches on his face were a result of Signor Zancani's craft. They had been hidden until Vincent dropped the glamour of the French officer. All that remained of *that* disguise was the white powder in Vincent's hair. The figure on the floor, however, Jane could not look at without feeling ill. It was too true to life.

He grimaced. "No wonder you were worried."

"I am only glad the lion technique worked."

"As am I." Vincent shoved a cloth into Bastone's mouth and began wrestling him upright. "Help me sit him up?"

Together they managed to get him propped up, with a pillow from the couch and used more the rope to tie him into a passable sitting position with his back to the door. Anyone glancing in would see Vincent still twitching, with Bastone sitting in watch over him.

It took only a moment for the two of them to create a recording of Jane, because the habit hid most of her movement anyhow, so the loop did not need to be long. It would not gain them much time, but with luck it would create some confusion as well.

With that arranged, they stood and went to where the strong room opening was masked by glamour. Vincent rolled his neck and flexed his fingers in preparation. Jane threw the *Sphère Obscurcie* around them, adding a second sphere to control sound. It would not keep the alarms from sounding, but it did allow them to talk to one another. "How is your head?"

"It aches, but I think that is from my 'seizure' more than anything." Vincent's gaze went distant, and he reached into the web of glamour. Tempting though it was, Jane did *not* expand her vision to the second sight to watch him. She kept her view on the door, waiting for Spada to look in or Coppa to return with the surgeon. If all went as planned, the surgeon would be Signor Zancani in yet another of his disguises.

To her corporeal eye, Vincent appeared to have his hands sunk into the fabric of the wall. His face was tight with tension and his eyes followed the path of invisible strings. He hissed at one point. Shaking his head, he pulled his hand out, then reached in again. Jane stayed as still as possible so as not to distract him, though she doubted that he could see her. His gaze seemed deeply abstracted. While he worked, Jane undid the neck of her habit.

Vincent twisted something inside the glamour, and a metallic click sounded. He let his breath out with a sigh. "Done."

"Thank heavens. I shall get the papers."

Nodding, Vincent stepped through the door. From her bodice, Jane pulled the journal that Sister Franceschina had prepared. Her habit had a truly astonishing number of places to hide things.

Vincent cursed.

Jane stopped with the book in her hand. What had made her husband curse? There was no alarm sounding. He stuck his head back out of the wall, appearing only from the shoulders up. "Muse, I need your help. It is a dark room."

"Shall I get a candle?" She tucked the book back into the belt of her habit.

He shook his head. "I was unclear. The room is glamoured to appear completely lightless."

"Oh . . . oh, dear." Even if they brought in a light source, their eyes would continue to perceive the illusion of darkness. "May I guess that there are additional alarms?"

"Almost certainly." Vincent pulled his head back through, and Jane followed.

The darkness inside the wall was complete. It seemed to press around her as though she had been buried. Jane opened the collar of her habit, trying to let in more air. She paused with her fingers at its throat and let her vision expand to her second sight. Glowing lines of glamour filled the space. Some of the lines pulled together into complicated clusters. Others stretched through the air without seeming to attach to anything.

She frowned, trying to sort out some order. "He was not inside very long."

"So they are close." Vincent sounded nearer than she expected.

Jane reached out until she found the fabric of his uniform, then followed it down the line of his arm and took his hand. "Perhaps we should not worry about setting off an alarm? We will be setting it off later, anyhow."

Vincent squeezed her hand. "But only after we have exchanged the *Verres*, to get Spada to open the door."

Gnawing on her lower lip, Jane considered the threads around them. "There must be a slip-knot close to the door, or he would not have been able to come in and set them down so quickly."

"So, perhaps these?" Fabric rustled.

"I cannot see what you are pointing at, love."

"Sorry." Vincent's hand dipped into the ether, and he wrapped a fold around his fingers so that they appeared to glow in the darkness. He pointed again at a set of threads close to where they stood.

She had only taken one step into the strong room, so these should be easy to reach from just inside the door. There was, in fact, a slip-knot. "Where does this . . . hm." Jane traced the line to a point where it snarled around some other fibres of glamour. It took her awhile to tease apart which one of the threads was the one that she wanted. It was sound. "No. It is an alarm."

"Should I exchange the journals? You are better at detail work than I am." Jane nodded. Then, remembering that he could not see her, she said, "Yes. Please." She pulled out the book she had slipped into her belt, then used Vincent's trick of wrapping unformed glamour around her hand so that he could see where to reach. "Here. Bring me the real one?"

His hand brushed hers and then found the journal. The shape of his glowing hand showed that he was gripping something, but not what. The book shifted in her hand as Vincent strengthened his grip. "I have it."

There was no need to keep him in the room now, no

matter how much she wanted him close. Jane let go of the book. "I will be as quick as I can."

Cloth rustled as he turned. Two footsteps, then silence. All Jane could hear was the sound of her own breath and the rustle of cloth as she moved. Even swallowing was overloud.

Jane crouched where she stood to examine a cluster of threads. One of them swayed a little apart from the others. Though not a slip-knot itself, it was tied to one. That thread traced back to . . . light. Good. She traced the line again to make certain that it was not tangled into something else, but saw nothing to trip her up.

As Jane reached for the thread, her fingers brushed something stiff, like a harp string. She stopped. Drawing her hand back, she strained to see what she had run into. It was so frustrating to know that there was light coming through the open door, but that glamour fooled her senses into believing the darkness. Did it matter, though? She knew that something were there. It seemed likely that if she pulled the thread of glamour, then the corporal string would trigger . . . something. An alarm. Or a trap.

But she was also quite certain that the line she had traced was designed to undo the darkness glamour. There must be a direction that one could pull the thread without running into an obstacle. Someone who knew the room would know that route. It was a cunning mixture of the tangible and the illusory.

Of course. Tangible and illusory. Jane chuckled as she stood and ran a strand of her own glamour out to the thread in question. Looping it through, she braced herself for an alarm and pulled.

Light flooded the room. She winced, squeezing her eyes shut against the sudden brightness. It was not that the room itself was bright, it was merely the contrast. Standing, Jane opened her eyes. The room was still only lit from the door, but that was more than enough to see the pitfalls that lay there.

Jane shivered at the lengths someone had gone to to protect the contents of the room. Had she pulled the strand of glamour and tripped the piano wire, she would have set off a small guillotine. A thief who did not know the safe path would likely have their hand cut off. There were bear traps on the floor, blades, and even a bucket of tar.

Wiping her face, Jane leaned back out of the strong room, and then stuck her head out of the *Sphère Obscurcie*. She waved to Vincent to let him know she was finished.

Vincent turned from the writing desk with a grin. Papers lay on the desk, where he had been sorting them. He hefted the book to show her that he had made the swap. Lifting the sleeve of faux glass spheres that Jane had given him, he crossed the room.

The lock rattled. Vincent stopped where he was and tucked the book under his arm. With his free hand, he wove a *Sphère Obscurcie* and vanished. Jane pulled her head back into her own *Sphère* and held her breath.

The door cracked open, and Denaro stuck his head into the room. He saw the tableau that Jane and Vincent had created and frowned. "He's still down?"

Bastone did not reply, of course. Jane pulled the truncheon out again, though there was no way she could cross the room swiftly enough.

"Mm-hm." The voice seemed to come from close to Bastone, but not from his lips.

Jane expanded her vision to the ether. Vincent had run a *bouclé torsadée* out of his *Sphère* and used it to provide a voice for Bastone. It would not work, though, if he had to produce more than a grunt. Jane ran her own line out as swiftly as she could, heart speeding. Why had they not had Vincent fall closer to the strong room?

"Where's Spada?"

The thread was *almost* in front of the image of herself. It would have to be close enough. "He locked us in. You cannot expect me to know his whereabouts. Now *please* do not disturb us. This is difficult work."

"But—"

"Sir! I am trying to keep my husband alive."

Scowling at the faux Jane, Denaro said, "Bastone, do you need anything?"

"Uh-uh."

"Fine. Tell Spada that I am looking for him, when he comes back." He pulled his head out of the room and shut the door. For a moment, Jane had a hope that he would forget to lock it, but it was short-lived.

She waited until his footsteps faded down the hall and then counted to ten before stepping out of the *Sphère*. Vincent let his drop, appearing with an inaudible, but very visible, sigh of relief that Jane echoed, nodding. He flashed an infectious grin, seeming to find these moments of terror exhilarating. He pointed to the strong room and raised his brow in question. She nodded in reply: Yes, he should get the *Verres*, since he still had the faux *Verres* she had given him earlier.

As Vincent passed her, Jane took the journal, which she would need later. She turned through the pages to make certain it was the right one, then opened her bodice to force the journal into her stays. Pressed against her skin, the book should stay in place while they were making their exit.

Jane tied the laces of her habit loosely, so she could reach inside when it was time to hand off the book. She hurried back to her place by the strong room door. Once Vincent was out, they could set the next stage of their plan in motion.

He poked his head out of the wall again. "Did you see what else was in here?"

"The traps?"

He shook his head. "The gold."

Twenty-four

The Subterraqueous Entrance

It took Jane and Vincent very little time to alter their plans to include the strong room. They had considered several different possibilities, depending on what happened in the palazzo. The simplest involved setting off the alarm deliberately and slipping out when Spada opened the door. The most complicated involved letting Spada think that their plan had gone horribly wrong, so that he would open the door. But everything began with the door opening.

They set about arranging the room to look as though Vincent had died and that Jane had lost her mind to hysterics. With short work, the glamour creating the illusion of Jane had been cleared away. Bastone, still out cold, had been laid on his side in an dishevelled fashion, with a bladder of fake blood—supplied by Signor Zancani—artfully dripping from his chest. The illusion of Vincent had been halted, so that it was no longer breathing. Jane shuddered just looking at it.

For her own part, Jane had the book ready and the bag of *Verres* slung under her habit. Vincent had dealt with the contents of the strong room. All that remained was to get into position and set off the alarm.

Jane leaned closer to Vincent and murmured, "Are we ready?"

He grimaced. "Yes, but I do not like it."

"Well, you can hardly have the hysterics if you are supposed to be dead."

"And I suppose you will only need to do it if more than one of them answers to the alarm, and probably not even then."

With Coppa out of the palazzo in search of a surgeon, they should have only Spada and Denaro to face. To improve their chances, Signor Zancani had volunteered to play the role of the surgeon and detain Coppa. Even so, they had taken the trouble to plan three different escape routes, depending on what happened when they pulled the alarm. Vincent liked none of them, because at least two involved convincing one of the swindlers to chase Jane out of the palazzo.

Jane stood on her toes to kiss him on the cheek. "As you so often reassure me, 'Do not worry.'"

"I begin to see why you dislike the phrase." But he handed her the handkerchief, which hid the sponge he had used to create his sweat-stained brow earlier. He hurried to his place by the door, drawing his sword as he went, then wrapped a *Sphère Obscurcie* around him to hide in as he waited.

Jane picked up a decanter from the side table and carried it to the strong room door, in case she needed something to throw in her "hysterics." She stepped into her own *Sphère,* setting the decanter on the floor. Jane took a breath, and put her hand into the glamour covering the strong room door. She grabbed every piece of glamour she could and jerked them out.

Trumpets blared with a flash of light that left her feeling blind and deaf. Neither was the case. Her body and mind was answering the illusion, even though it could not do any actual damage. The trumpets continued, sounding an alarm, which that made it feel as though her ears were bleeding. Jane shut her eyes involuntarily to clear her sight, but spots still swam in it. Oh, whoever had created this was very good. She rather wished they were not. She could not hear anyone coming over the noise.

For a moment she considered stopping the sound, but she was not certain what she would have done if Vincent really *had* died. She suspected that she would still be frozen over his—corpse was such an ugly word. Rather than risk getting caught unawares in the middle of the room, Jane prepared herself where she stood and rubbed her eyes to redden them. Still watching the door, she wiped her face with the handkerchief, drenching the headband of her coif as though she had been sweating heavily. Jane pinched her cheeks to make them red.

The door flew open, making her jump.

"Bastone?" Spada stood in the doorway. "What is—?" He cursed, spying Bastone's still figure.

Denaro shouldered past him and ran into the room. He dropped to his knees beside Bastone. "He is still breathing."

"But where is Lady Vincent?" Spada's gaze went to the writing desk, and his eyes narrowed.

Vincent had left it open after removing the journal. It should be shut, and Spada, seeing it and the papers on the table, could easily tell that it had been gone through. His gaze darted from there to the strong room, with the alarm blaring. Taking hold of his cane, Spada limped into the room.

He paused, taking a moment to look around him, but gave no sign of looking into the ether. After a moment, he reached back and shut the door to the hall. Wincing against the sound of the alarm, Jane bit her lip. So much for the hope that he would leave it open. Spada went to the writing desk and went through the papers there. He picked up the fake journal and his shoulders relaxed a little with relief. "She must still be in the room, or she would have taken this."

"Where is that surgeon?" Denaro rose to his knees to snatch a pillow from the sofa. "The bleeding must be stopped."

"Of course." Spada tapped his cane in thought. "Coppa went to fetch him for Sir David."

"Well, it's too late for the glamourist. She must have gone insane to overpower Bastone." He pressed the pillow to Bastone's chest, which only caused more blood to pour out of the bladder. Bastone moaned and stirred.

This would be a very bad time for him to wake up.

"But where is she?" Spada stopped with a page open and lifted the book. "Oh no . . . no." Leaning his cane against the table, he turned to another page, studying it intently. Then he grabbed a letter from the table and laid it on the book to compare the handwriting. Spada cursed. "That deuced woman."

"What?" Denaro snapped.

"It is a fake." Spada threw Sister Franceschina's carefully crafted book back on the table. He glared at the strong room. "I wonder if she got in there, as well."

"Leave it! Can you not see how badly Bastone is injured?"

"What do you expect me to do? Coppa is already fetching a surgeon. He will either arrive in time, or he will not." He cursed again and spun on the heel of his good leg, scanning the room. Jane had no idea if he had the aptitude with glamour to see far enough into the ether to spot her *Sphère Obscurcie*, and she chose not to find out. She picked up the decanter.

This was why they had planned for the hysterics. She stepped out of her *Sphère* and did her best imitation of her mother. Wailing, Jane threw the decanter at him "You killed him!"

"*Jesu!*" Denaro fell back on his heels at her sudden appearance. The decanter shattered beside him, glass flying everywhere.

Jane rushed toward the door, trying to keep up her keening. Spada snatched up his cane and chased after her. "Lady Vincent! Please be calm."

She grabbed a figurine and flung it at Spada, with an inarticulate scream. It was not far to the door. If she could get it open, then she and Vincent could both get out.

Denaro scrambled to his feet and ran after her. Jane evaded him, gripping her truncheon in her hand. Around it, she wove a sword like the one that Vincent wore. It would cut nothing and she could not carry it far, but it would suffice for threatening. Denaro danced back, his heel landing on a piece of the shattered glass. He slipped, falling hard.

Scowling, Spada twisted the head of his sword cane to draw it.

Vincent suddenly appeared, blade flashing toward Spada.

The swindler cursed and raised his cane. The sword was not yet fully drawn, so Vincent's blow came down on the wooden shaft. Splinters flew. Spada stumbled back, pulling his sword free of the cane.

Denaro's focus was split between the mad woman who was attacking him and the sudden appearance of a dead man. He scrambled back from the duel, putting the sofa between him and Jane. She let go of the glamour of the sword and made herself vanish.

"No, no, no!" Denaro scrambled to his feet. "Where did she go?"

Spada did not answer, being hard-pressed by Vincent.

Jane stepped three feet to the side, dragging the *Sphère* with her, then dropped it again, to run at Denaro. He threw a vase at her. Jane ducked, unnecessarily, as the vase went wide, and wrapped a *Sphère* around herself again. Denaro cursed, turning in a circle, as if she could have made her behind him.

Vincent lunged at Spada, who barely parried the attack. Jane then moved a few feet closer to Denaro, heart racing from nervous energy and effort, before she had to drop the *Sphère*. He was looking toward the swordsmen and did not see her reappear. Jane closed the last few feet, swinging her truncheon. The blow caught Denaro on the head, causing him to stagger. She hit him again, and he dropped.

Then the rhythm of the fight suddenly changed. Spada had parried Vincent's last blow and, with a curse, had begun to attack instead of retreat. He advanced steadily, no longer limping.

His bad leg, which he had favoured the entire time, was utterly sound. Without the limp, he was an even match for Vincent. The swords rang, even over the trumpets. Jane shook her head. They had not planned for this. Denaro rose to his knees.

Vincent wet his lips and took a step back. "Jane, run."

"I cannot—"

"Run!" He turned toward her, briefly, and the tip of Spada's blade caught him across the left shoulder, opening a patch of arterial red.

"Vincent!"

He stepped back, parrying the next blow, but slower.

Jane pulled the book out of her bodice and waved it at Spada. "You wanted this?" Then she lied. "The code to understanding it is in the list of lambs."

And then she ran, praying that greed would make him follow. Jane opened the door and fled toward the stairs. She paused at the top to make certain that Spada would leave Vincent. He had to follow her.

Spada burst out of the room. His sword dripped red on the marble floor. Jane gripped the book and ran down the stairs. Snarling, Spada chased her.

Straight into the arms of Coppa.

He appeared as startled as she was, and staggered at the impact. Jane twisted away from him, dodging past the other man, before recognising Signor Zancani who was dressed as a surgeon. Why were they here? The puppet player was supposed to detain Coppa.

Spada appeared at the top of the stairs, with Denaro behind him. "Grab her!"

Signor Zancani grabbed Coppa and swung at him. They tussled, weaving across the main entrance as though they were in a tavern brawl. The puppet player shouted. "Go, go, go!"

"Lady Vincent!" Lord Byron lifted himself out of the water into the nearest of the boats. For an absurd moment, all Jane could think was that she was glad he was fully clothed.

Which hardly mattered, when she had not been certain he would be there at all. Jane slipped past the fighting men and ran to the water entrance. Her skirts tangled around her legs, and she pulled them up, nearly losing her grip on the book. She flew down the stairs to the landing.

Behind her, Spada and Denaro wove past Zancani and Coppa's fight, bounding down the stairs to the water entrance. Lord Byron held out a dripping hand to help her into the gondola.

As she took his hand, the book slipped from her grasp, hit the edge of the gondola, and bounced on to the floor of the palazzo. Jane lunged for it. They could not have this book. Not if she wanted them to follow her out of the palazzo.

She snatched it and fell back into the boat. Lord Byron cast off, pushing the gondola out into the canal.

Behind them, Spada and Denaro clambered into the remaining gondola. It was longer than hers and wanted the little cabin.

"Is that one of the racing gondolas?"

Lord Byron nodded, face tight with concentration as he worked the paddle in the back. His lips were turning blue with cold. "I only got two scuttled." The boat slid through the water, houses flowing past. "How is Vincent?"

"Still in the palazzo." Spada and Denaro were not yet in view, which worried her. But they *had* left Vincent behind to follow her. That was the important thing. She did not let herself think about what might have happened after she left the room. None of which Lord Byron knew about. It came to Jane that he still thought that Vincent had been taken with a seizure. "His collapse was not real."

"The devil you say!"

"We knew Vincent would not be able to hold the glamour long enough, and also needed a reason for me to be inside as well. The Hysterical Wife seemed to be an appropriate scheme." She looked toward the palazzo, tucking the book back into her bodice. "It was safer if no one knew."

Behind them, the racing gondola edged out of the palazzo's water entrance, turning in a wide arc to point down the canal. For a moment, it appeared to just sit in the water with the two men in it. Standing, they worked the long paddles back and forth, and then the gondola began to move.

It surged forward, a wake rippling back from it. The distance between them closed faster than Jane would have guessed. A boom echoed down the canal. Lord Byron ducked and swore. "Are they shooting at us?"

Denaro lowered a hunting rifle, then took up the oar again to help Spada drive them closer.

"Yes." She had seen a receipt for this rifle when going through the library drawers and thought nothing of it. Yet another thing they had not planned for. "And they are gaining on us."

"With a racing gondola and two oarsmen, that is not a surprise."

In the boat behind them, Denaro took his hands off the oar long enough to load the hunting rifle again. Jane watched him so that the poet could concentrate on propelling the boat through the water. "He is aiming at us again."

"We will not make it to the church."

Another gunshot. Jane and Lord Byron both flinched. Surely they were far enough from the palazzo now. Vincent must be out. She glanced back as Denaro grabbed the oar again and they began to close the distance more quickly.

Jane replied, "If we turn down Canale di San Donato, then we can circle to our second escape route and abandon the gondola. The sisters are stationed there to wait for us. From there we can cross the Calle Angelo bridge and reach the church that way."

Lord Byron looked back and cursed. The only thing in their favour was that Denaro kept having to stop rowing to reload the gun. Even so, it did not slow them much, given how much faster their the boat was than Jane and Byron's. By now they had closed the distance to within twenty feet. If Denaro got the gun loaded again, it seemed likely that he would hit them.

He lifted the gun. Jane would have given almost anything for the sun to come out at that moment so she could use the *Verre Obscurcie*. She and Byron were all too visible, and trying to weave a *Sphère Obscurcie* at this speed would only result in the oiled light—

Which would serve well enough to obscure them.

Jane grabbed wildly for glamour, with no effort at artistry, only at scale, and let it dissolve into great oily swirls in the air. The glamour ripped and tore as she pulled it from the ether, shrouding them in coruscating rainbows. Denaro was close enough that she could hear him swear.

Lord Byron spared a glance back and gave her a savage smile. He crouched as low in the gondola as he could and still drive it forward. Sweating under her habit, Jane continued ripping glamour into shreds that filled the air between them and the other gondola.

A shot sounded. Chips of wood splintered off the cabin.

Lord Byron straightened and bent his back into the oar, counting under his breath. Jane frowned, wondering what he was counting, but that was all the attention she could spare him. Her arms burned from the masses of glamour she was throwing, but she dared not stop.

A pair of nuns stood in the street, conversing as if it was a normal afternoon. They looked down the street toward the palazzo in the direction that Jane *would* have been coming from if she had run out of the front door instead of the water entrance. The canal mouth was coming up on their right. Lord Byron showed no signs of turning.

"Do you see it?"

He nodded, panting like a glamourist now. "Thirty-two, thirty-three, thirty-four—Can make tighter turns. Hoping they can't—thirty-eight, thirty-nine, forty. Duck!"

Jane did, without questioning. As if he had been prompted, Denaro fired again. The glass window on the cabin shattered.

The nuns spun around at the gunshot. There was only a brief moment of hesitation before both nuns ran in different directions. One running along the canal beside them, the other up a side street.

At the last minute, Lord Byron cut his oar to the right, turning them into the side canal. For a brief moment, the buildings hid them from view of Spada's craft. A set of landing steps came down to the water not far from the entrance to the canal. The nun ran toward the steps, waving them to her.

Water splashed up the steps as Lord Byron brought the boat against the landing too fast, and too hard. The wooden side smacked against the stone with a jarring thud that threw Jane forward. Sister Aquinata ran from a side street to join her sister, and the two women helped Jane out of the boat. The moment she was clear, Lord Byron cast off again. "I will try to draw them away."

Jane did not have time for a thank-you. As she ran up the stairs to the street, the other gondola made the turn and coursed toward Byron's. He had no speed, as he was still pushing off from the wall. Spada drove his boat straight into Lord Byron's.

The poet dove into the water as the sharp prow slammed into his boat, splintering the side.

Jane ran.

Behind her, she heard shouting. Spada and Denaro had reached the landing stairs, and the sisters were trying every nonviolent means to slow them imaginable. She sent a silent prayer for their safety. If either nun were hurt because of her, it would be unbearable.

Then Sister Aquinata abandoned the nonviolent methods and produced a rolling pin from somewhere. She thwacked Denaro on his side, sending him tumbling down the stairs into the canal. Lord Byron swam toward the man.

Spada got past the other nun and reached the street. When they had planned this, Jane had not expected the need to work glamour on a moving gondola. The effort had left her winded even before running and now Spada gained on her steadily.

Panting, Jane reached the next intersection and a swirl of nuns flooded the street, each running in a different direction. Some stopped and ran the other way to create a mass of confusion. Jane blended into the chaos of black and white. She slowed to a walk and tried to calm her breath.

She glanced back. Spada fought his way through the nuns. When she reached the centre of the group, the Abbess spied Jane and fell in beside her. From behind them, Sister Aquinata shouted, "Hail Mary!"

At the signal, the nuns split into pairs, each of them walking briskly for a different door or street. From behind, they all looked the same. Jane and the Abbess headed for the bridge. As they walked, Jane pulled out the bag of *Verres*.

The Abbess took the bag from her, sliding it under her robe. "Sir David and Signor Zancani are safely out of the palazzo."

"Thank you." The relief opened the knot in her throat, and Jane was able to take her first deep breath since leaving

Vincent in the parlour. It was time for this charade to end. "As we had planned?"

The Abbess nodded. "We will see you at the warehouse." She split her path from Jane's and walked toward a church. It was not Santa Maria degli Angeli, but she would be safe there.

Jane did not pause, though. Her heart raced as she ran along the canal, as though she were still working glamour. That quick rhythm of her heart was familiar, but her legs were not used to the effort. Jane's pace flagged. She was only a few streets away from the bridge over the canal.

Jane glanced over her shoulder. Spada had stopped one of the other nuns and, cursing, spun away from her. He saw Jane, recognised her, and gave chase. She ran for the bridge, drawing him away from the Abbess.

A wooden sawhorse was set across the base of the bridge with a sign in Venetian. Jane slipped past it and pounded up the steep incline of the bridge. She stopped abruptly at the top.

The centre span of the bridge was missing. Through the gap, she could see straight down to the canal underneath. Had she been able to read Venetian, the sign would have told her that the bridge was under construction. Jane stood in the middle of the lane that should have crossed the bridge. She could hear Vincent's voice from the *Broken Bridge* shadow play: *This here don't go nowhere but to the canal.*

Turning, she faced Spada. He stalked up the bridge, carrying his cane. He gave no sign of needing it, but she was painfully aware that it contained a sword. His face was red with anger. "You have cost me a lot of money."

"I find that complaint ironic." Jane backed up, staying in the middle of the bridge, until she felt the edge. She held up the book. "Leave me alone, leave Vincent alone, and I will give this back to you."

"It will take longer, but we can decipher your technique from the *Verres* we have and Bastone's work with you." He walked closer.

"Then why chase me?" The drop to the canal behind her looked very far. "Stay back."

He unsheathed his sword. "I think you will find that it will be easier if you work with us."

"Stop, or I will jump." A threat that would be easier to make if she could swim. Jane held up the book. "And this goes with me."

For a moment he paused, and considered her threat. Narrowing his eyes, Spada shook his head. "You are not serious. If you wanted to destroy it, your husband would have burned it in the fire."

"My husband and I do not always agree." She drew her arm back to throw the book to her right.

"No!" Spada lunged for her.

She threw the book and stepped back, over the broken end of the bridge. Spada's hands closed over the spot where she had been, and the book dropped to the water below. A habit-clad body splashed into the water a moment later. The swindler dived from the bridge.

Jane, however, stood on a narrow board spanning the gap between the bridges. Sister Maria Agnes steadied her inside the giant *Sphère Obscurcie* that now covered them both. They watched as the life-size puppet Signor Zancani had made sank beneath the water, pulled down by the heavy cloth of the habit. The book floated on the water's surface, pages spread. Spada ignored "Jane" and grabbed the book, swimming for the side of the canal.

He crawled out of the water and opened the book. The sound of his cursing echoed off the walls of the canal as the ink ran across the pages and bled onto his hands.

Twenty-five

Puppets, Nuns, and Lavender

Jane and Sister Maria Agnes were among the last of their party to arrive back at the nuns' warehouse. When they stepped through into the echoing space, a cheer went up from the ladies assembled there.

Sister Aquinata hurried forward, wearing a smile that nearly hid her eyes. "We were starting to worry."

"We had to wait for Spada to leave the street." Sister Maria Agnes clapped her hands. "Oh! It was so exciting. You should have seen Lady Vincent facing him. She was so heroic!"

Blushing, Jane shook her head. "We could not have done any of this, were it not for you." She looked past the nuns for Vincent, but did not see him immediately. She reminded herself that the Abbess had said that he was safely out of the palazzo. Lord Byron sat with a blanket draped around his shoulders, pulled up in front of a brazier. Beside him, Signor Zancani had a piece of steak over one eye, but grinned when he saw Jane. "The puppet worked?"

"Beautifully. And the blood bladders, too."

"Come, come. I have some food for you." Sister Aquinata handed them each a bowl of warm polenta and beckoned them forward. Jane took the bowl, but all she wanted was Vincent. The sister beamed. "We want to hear all about it."

"Particularly since there were clearly parts of your plan that we were not privy to." The Abbess looked up from the bench where she sat, with Vincent.

Jane's husband had his shirt off, and the Abbess was tying a bandage around his left shoulder. He winced as she tightened the knot.

"Vincent!" Jane ran forward, alarm filling her throat.

"He is fine," the nuns said, as if in a chorus.

"It is a scratch, Muse." Vincent caught her hand and pulled her to sit beside him. Jane set the bowl of polenta on the ground, wanting to hold Vincent with both hands.

"I would say that it is a little more than a scratch," the Abbess said dryly. "But, yes, it is just a flesh wound, not mortal. And, yes, he will be fine, so long as he keeps it clean."

"I assumed the blood was from one of Signor Zancani's bladders!"

From his seat by the fire, the puppet player said, "He was supposed to present his right shoulder, not his left."

Vincent shrugged with the uninjured shoulder. "I was so startled that Spada had been feigning the limp even when we were not present that I turned the wrong way."

"Which means . . ."—the Abbess glared at him—"that you knew you would be fighting Spada. I want to know what your plan was and why you did not tell us. No more delays."

Vincent picked up his shirt and pulled it on over his head. "Well . . . Jane and I realized that the *Verre* from Signor Nenci would not help us, because of the want of sun." He stood and stretched, rolling his shoulder as if to test it. He turned from the Abbess to Sister Aquinata. "You mentioned food? Is there some of your excellent bread?"

She nodded with a smile and pointed to a trestle table a little to the side. It had bread, cheese, and bowls of polenta, which some of the nuns were already enjoying. Vincent thanked her and strolled toward the food table. Jane could feel the Abbess's impatience radiating from her. Casually, Vincent picked up a slice of bread and resumed his walk and his narrative. "Our problem was that the plan to disguise me with glamour was faulty because, as my wife correctly pointed out, I was not entirely well. At the same time, we were finding no simple way to go inside, so we decided to turn a fault into part of the plan." He cleared his throat. "Apparently, my work habits are well-known."

Lord Byron snorted.

Vincent glared at him, and the poet smiled mildly. Continuing his stroll, he walked round the nuns. "The idea was that I would enter, pretend to collapse, and use that to put them off their guard."

"But why not tell us? I was worried sick. We all were."

"Ah." Tilting his head, Vincent looked away from the Abbess and frowned. "That is very simple to explain. We knew that there was an informant. We did not know who it was. In fact, we owe you an apology, because we also misled you on a prior occasion. At Signor Nenci's we decided it would be best if I appeared in worse condition than I actually was."

She looked aghast at the implication. "Surely you did not suspect us."

Lord Byron raised his hand. "Actually, they thought it was me. Or my landlord's wife—which, to be fair, it was."

"Yes, and we were able to make good use of that to give them certain misinformation," Jane added, watching Vincent carefully. "But they knew things that Marianna could not have known." She expanded her vision to the second sight and looked where his gaze was fixed. Very faintly, if she pushed all view of the corporeal world from her sight, she could perceive the outline of a badly rendered *Sphère Obscurcie*.

The nuns gasped, and Jane popped her vision back from the ether. Vincent had disappeared.

A girl shrieked, voice echoing from nowhere. In the next moment, her husband reemerged from the *Sphère* with Lucia held under his good arm. She kicked and struggled in his grasp. His face was grave. "You were right, Muse."

Sister Maria Agnes dropped her bowl of polenta. "Lucia?"

"Let go! He's hurting me!" She thrashed, catching Vincent in the shin with her heel.

He grunted and hauled her over to the nuns. "Would someone mind . . . ?"

Sister Aquinata stood and walked over, her face going dark with anger. She took both of the girl's wrists in one of her large baker's hands and pulled her out of Vincent's grasp. "I am going to owe the Abbess penance for this, I suspect, but—does anyone have some rope?"

"Always." Signor Zancani set his steak down, revealing a very black eye, and pulled a bundle of thick twine out of his pocket.

One of the other sisters took the twine and helped bind Lucia's wrists and ankles. The girl fought them until Sister Aquinata shook her and said, "You do *not* want me to spank you."

The Abbess looked ill. "I would ask if you were certain, but it seems clear that it is true."

"We were not certain." Jane had wanted to be wrong, but as she and Vincent had lain awake each night, talking through their plans, it kept bothering her brain that Gallo had known which of the swindlers Vincent had seen. Nothing in their conversation with him had indicated which one it had been, and given that all four of the men were on Murano at the time, it could have been any of them.

"The only way for Gallo to have known which of the swindlers Vincent had seen was for someone to have run there from the convent to tell him. We had worried that it was Sister Maria Agnes."

"Because I am foreign . . ." The colour of her skin was left unspoken, but she tucked her hands into her sleeves.

Jane refuted that firmly. "Because you were there when Vincent told me. But Lucia was there as well."

Jane stood and walked over to the girl.

If Jane ignored the pigtails and the girlish clothing, Lucia's face was older than she first appeared. "You were on the ship, were you not? As a passenger?"

The young woman spat at her. The globule landed harmlessly on the floor between them. Jane shook her head and wove a bubble of silence around the girl, inverting it so that Lucia could not hear them, but they could hear her. Then Jane passed another bubble around her so that she sat in darkness. It was, perhaps, cruel to deprive her of her senses, but Jane was not inclined to be generous in that moment. There were yet things to discuss and she did not want to chance the girl carrying any further tales.

The nuns sat, stunned into silence. Jane turned back to the Abbess and spread her hands. "I am sorry. I thought that it was better to not include you in the full plan than to ask you to lie to her on our behalf."

"I see." The Abbess removed her spectacles and polished them on her black scapular. "If you were one of my charges, I would ask you to do some Hail Marys."

"I would be happy to do whatever you think fit." In previous years, Jane could not have imagined being so willing to participate in Catholic rites, but nothing seemed more appropriate to her now.

"And the rest of the plan? There were no troubles?" Signor Zancani put the steak back over his eye. "With obvious exceptions, of course."

Vincent nodded, rubbing the back of his head. "Reasonably so. But you have not told us about what happened to you."

"Yes. Why did you return with Coppa?" Jane asked.

"I was late to meet him and could not convince him to come into the 'office,' so I did my best to slow our return."

"Come now, man. You cannot tease us like that." Lord Byron pulled the blankets a little tighter. "What delayed you in the first place?"

The puppet player's eyes twinkled. "The thing I least expected. An admirer stopped me. Loved puppets. Wanted to know when my next show was."

"Could you not put him off?" Lord Byron asked.

"He was six. No. I could not."

"No harm was done." Vincent came to Jane and took her hand. "We accomplished everything we needed to."

Sister Maria Agnes sighed. "I am only sorry that you had to destroy Sir David's journal. Though that was *very* dramatic and exciting, and I suppose completely necessary."

With a smile, Jane undid the tie at the neck of her habit and reached into her bodice. From within her stays, she extracted Vincent's real journal. "It was a fake. The second fake, truly." Seeing the look of confusion in the nuns' faces, Jane continued. "Sister Franceschina's work was excellent, but we were afraid it would not be convincing. In case it was not, we had the journal she had made for our practise sessions."

"The one you dropped getting into the gondola?" Lord Byron asked.

"Exactly so. We had already doused it in water in advance, so I needed Spada to *see* it go into the water so that the damage was explicable, and so that he would stop chasing me. I tried to drop it at the palazzo and missed the water. The bridge was to be a last resort."

"It worked beautifully," Lord Byron said. "I could see it from where I was. It truly looked as though you had fallen into the water, even though I knew about *that* part of the plan."

A thought occurred to Jane. "What happened to Denaro? I saw you engage with him."

"A couple of *polizia* heard the shots being fired, saw the collision, and arrested him." The poet grinned. "I pointed out that he had also assailed a nun, which did not seem to please them. Which reminds me that we no longer have any reason to avoid taking care of your accounts."

Vincent compressed his lips and winked at Jane. She smiled, slowly. "Thank you. But it turns out that we no longer require assistance in that regard."

Jane and Vincent left the nuns to deal with Lucia, trusting their instincts on what to do with the young woman more than those of Murano's civil authorities. Lord Byron headed back to his apartments, where he planned to give notice and move to different lodgings. He invited them to come stay with him when they were finished with their obligations in Murano.

They went to the closet room across from the palazzo where they had spent the past week watching the swindlers. Signor Zancani had followed them as far as his puppet booth, which was still set up in the gallery facing the palazzo. He said his good nights there and began to take the booth down. It was too cold in the season to expect much traffic, and he had been invited to winter with Lord Byron in Venice.

For what Jane hoped would be the last time, they climbed the stairs to the small room and settled down to watch the palazzo. The real General Germain should be arriving there shortly to meet Spada. If Lord Byron was correct in his estimation of the French officer's state after the distraction arranged by the poet, he would have quite the bad head from an excess of wine. Vincent pulled up a chair in front of the window and held out his arm to invite Jane to sit on his lap.

"I will not hurt you?"

"Not so long as you stay on my right side."

She settled gingerly nevertheless, but took great comfort from the warm solidity of his form. "I am glad that I did not know the wound was real, or I should never have been able to leave the room."

"Mm." Vincent leaned his head against hers and inhaled deeply. "Have you thought about what we are going to tell your parents?"

Jane shuddered. "I am half hoping that we can beat my letter to Vienna, but I know that is unlikely."

"I will join you in hoping that—there he is." Vincent straightened in his chair.

Jane turned to the window and felt the absence of his body against hers as a line of cool down her side. In some ways, it was like watching Vincent walk into the palazzo again, except that this officer travelled with a small complement of soldiers. His aide knocked on the door.

After a few minutes, he knocked again, pounding so hard that they could hear it across the street even without glamour. The door cracked open, but not so far that they could see who answered the door. The Frenchman gesticulated with some passion. The door began to close, but the aide shoved his booted foot in it, and the officers forced their way inside.

Vincent set Jane gently to the side and stood. He leaned against the window, reaching for the *bouclé torsadée*.

She put her hand on his arm. "Shall I?"

"We can have this argument every day, Muse, but I would rather not." The words were irritable, but not his tone, which was buoyed by a laugh that seemed aimed at himself more than her. "Shall we trade off, so neither is fatigued?"

"What? Share a burden?" She moved in front of him. Given their comparative heights, that worked best for an operating position in their collaborations.

"Shocking." He murmured and slid his arms around her so that they could both hold the same line. Together they began to feed the line, carrying sound from the palazzo.

Staccato footsteps marched into the parlour. Cloth rustled as someone stood suddenly.

"General Germain, we did not look for you to arrive this evening," Spada said. "May I offer you something to drink."

"Yes, thank you." The French officer sat heavily in a chair. "I was delayed, for which I apologize."

"It is no trouble at all." Limping footsteps, interwoven with the sound of a cane. "I only regret that we may have to delay our exhibition."

"Is that so?" Cloth rustled again, and the officer humphed. "Why is that?"

"We keep the *Verres* in our strong room, but our glamourist is ill, and I cannot open it without him." Glass clinked and a liquid burbled into a glass.

"I find that disappointing."

"As well you should." Spada limped across the room. "I also find it disappointing, but I hope that tomorrow he will be improved."

"What is the matter, if I might inquire? Ah—thank you." Glasses clinked again. "To your health."

"He hit his head and is suffering from the effects of a concussion."

Vincent snorted. Jane could almost feel his smile through her back, or perhaps that was her own clandestine glee at the justness of Bastone's injury.

"I am sorry to hear that." He set the glass down on the wooden side table. "And the papers we gave you? What did you find in those?"

"It is very complicated, of course, but they have been useful."

"Messieurs, vous commencez à chercher!"

The men in the room began to move about. Wood slid upon wood as drawers opened and closed. Cabinets clicked open, then shut.

"Is there something I can help your officers find?" Spada's voice had a slight strained edge.

"Tell me more about the *Verres*. How many do you have?"

"Seven. But not all of them work."

Papers rustled. Wood scraped across stone as something heavy was moved. Then footsteps, quick against the marble floor. Paper hushed as a page was unfolded. The French officer growled and tapped the page. "Have you an explanation for this, Signor?"

Spada limped closer. Paper rattled as if his hand shook. "This is not mine."

"It is addressed to you, and seems to be a response to a letter offering to sell the *Verres* to Lombardy-Venetia."

"And yet I have never seen it."

"Have you seen *this*?" Another page brushed against

cloth, then unfolded. "No, no . . . I do not want to chance it becoming damaged. This is your handwriting, is it not?"

"No."

"Odd. The hand looks like the other letters you wrote to me. I thought the part in which you said—where is it? Ah, here—'The *Verres* do not work. Our glamourist believes that the Vincents' theory is erroneous on several points, but Bastone has a plan to trick the fat old Frenchman into thinking that they do' was particularly interesting." The paper was folded and put away. "It is very unfortunate that your glamourist is unwell. What a coincidence with our arrival, no? And what about our deposit? The gold we gave you to do this work?"

Spada gave a strangled sigh. "The Vincents. They broke in today and—"

"A glamourist and his wife? Not even a true military glamourist, no matter what tricks he might have, but an artist. Please. I find it far easier to believe that a swindler who was hired to learn a certain technique may have decided that it was easier to defraud his employer."

"I can promise you, nothing was easy about this job."

Other footsteps interrupted him. The French officer turned through pages in a book and grunted. "The pages of Vincent's journal that you reference in your letter . . . I find it curious that you knew that a *Verre Obscurcie* was impossible to make and yet you continued to request funds." He then spoke in French too rapid for Jane to follow, but it resulted in a flurry of movement in the parlour. For a moment, Spada appeared in the window, backing away. The sounds of a tussle followed, with an impact of flesh and a short grunt.

The men marched out of the parlour, leaving nothing but silence in their wake.

Jane and Vincent stopped feeding the line as though they were one person. Vincent folded his hands around Jane's and wrapped her in an embrace. "Does that sound as though Germain now believes that the *Verres* do not work?"

"I hope so." She sighed, feeling the last of her tension leave her body. "Those letters appeared to be persuasive."

Vincent kissed her on the cheek. "Spada should never have left me alone in the palazzo."

Jane turned her head to the side to kiss her husband. In so doing, she almost missed the front door of the palazzo opening.

Spada was marched out, his hands bound behind him. The French soldiers had Coppa and Bastone bound as well, though it looked as if Bastone was having trouble standing. The French officer strode down the street in front of them, with the fake journal of Vincent's tucked under his arm.

It was a beautiful sight. She sighed back against Vincent, revelling in the beat of his heart. "Do you feel uneasy about keeping his money?"

"Not in the slightest."

"Have I told you today how much I love you?"

"You may tell me again."

"I love you very much." An impish idea occurred to Jane, and she turned in Vincent's arms to regard him with the most solemn expression she could summon. "I had nearly forgotten. There was something that I overheard Denaro and Coppa discuss on my first visit to the palazzo, while I was trapped in the parlour with them."

"That sounds foreboding."

"Perhaps. It might require some exploration." Jane rose on her toes and whispered to Vincent one of the phrases that she had heard the two men use when discussing their adventures with the fairer sex. Pressed as she was against her husband, the effect of her suggestion was immediately felt. "Is that language salty enough?"

"Very much so." Vincent's voice was rough as he bent to lift her. His left arm slid under her knees, and he winced. Straightening, her husband looked a little abashed. "Let me take my wife's advice to not be stupid. Lady Vincent . . . I may need help undressing in order to explore this theory of yours."

"Rogue."

"Muse."

The closet room turned out not to be so drafty as Jane had thought.

They had fallen asleep on the little bed in the corner, both utterly spent after the exertions of the past week. Jane woke to the sound of the door shutting as Vincent re-entered the room, carrying with him the aroma of fresh pastry and two packets, one of which had clearly come from a baker's.

"Sister Aquinata will be upset that you purchased someone else's bread." Jane sat up, drawing the thin blanket around her.

"This is a glazed tart, not bread, so I hope she will forgive me." Vincent sat on the bed beside her, then shook his head and set aside the largest of the packets, which was giving off the tempting aroma. "I cannot wait."

"Is the pastry that good?"

He shook his head again and, with a smile, handed her the smaller of the two. "This is a belated anniversary present."

With a questioning look, which he answered only by an enigmatic smile, Jane took the package and untied the string that held the paper shut. Inside, covered in delicate printed paper, were three bars of lavender soap.

"One for each year." Then he slid off the bed to kneel in front of her. Vincent reached into his waistcoat pocket and withdrew a small gold ring. "Jane, Lady Vincent . . . will you do me the honour?"

As her husband slid her wedding ring back on to her finger, joy unfolded inside Jane as though the room had attained a sudden softening glamour. For the second time in her life, Jane accepted Vincent's proposal, and knew that she would always love him, for richer, for poorer.

With and without soap.

Twenty-six

Debts Paid

All that remained after the apprehension of Spada and his gang of thieves was for Jane and Vincent to repay their debts to the merchants of Murano. Vincent's tailor expressed his frank astonishment, but seemed quite willing to accept French coins and provide a receipt without question. He allowed Vincent to change into the clothing that he had repossessed and said he would send the remainder of the clothes to their lodgings.

Jane, likewise, found herself welcomed by the dressmaker and in short order reclothed. It was with some relief when Jane stepped onto the street with Vincent, once again in her travel pelisse and with a proper bonnet. Her husband offered his arm—his right arm—to her, and they stepped out in style. Other than his walking stick, which had some scars on the ebony shaft from where a sword had hit it, they presented a very attractive picture to those who passed.

It was remarkable how anonymous Jane felt while walking with her husband in respectable clothing, though in entirely different ways from only the day before. Was it truly only the day prior that she had felt eyes glancing past her because her mended clothing marked her as poor? Today the other passersby saw her, but as a fitting part of Murano rather than as a bit of refuse that they would prefer not to acknowledge.

Only one merchant remained unpaid, and it was a debt that required some conversation before they settled on a solution that satisfied all their requirements. They spoke to Signor Nenci about their idea, and he approved it with a gratifying vehemence. So they turned with eager steps to Signor Querini.

At the glass factory, Vincent knocked sharply on the door using the head of his walking stick.

Querini opened the door himself. "Where——" He recognised Vincent and attempted to shut the door.

He was thwarted as Vincent shoved forward and caught the door with his left shoulder. He grunted at the impact, but kept the door from closing. "We have business with you, Signor."

"No! I have no business with you. Not unless you have my money—and even then, I want nothing to do with you. Nothing, I tell you. Nothing." He was sweating, though the fire in his glass oven was out.

Jane looked past him and into his empty glass factory. "We have your money."

"You—you do?" He wet his lips and shot a furtive look to the narrow lane before opening the door wide enough for them to enter. "Mind the step."

"Where are your apprentices, sir?"

"That is no business of yours. I told you I want nothing to do with you, only my money." He crossed his arms over his belly and glowered at them. "Do you have it, or do you not?"

The man was odious, and Jane's stomach twisted at the thought of giving him anything. Vincent, with his peculiar sense of honour, had argued that they had agreed to his terms, and they did, in fact, have the object that they had hired Querini to make. The fact that he was an agent in a larger imposture was a concern, but Vincent felt that the correct thing was to pay the man the sum they had agreed to, no matter how much they resented it.

He pulled out his purse and began counting coins onto Querini's over-crowded desk. "I believe that is what we agreed to."

"We will, of course, require a receipt." Jane opened her reticule and removed a paper. "I have taken the liberty of drawing it up to save you some effort."

Scowling, he took up a stained pen, dipped it into the ink, and scrawled upon the paper Jane offered. "And then I never want to see you again."

"That is a mutual desire, I assure you." She turned to the second page for him. "And a copy for the *capo di polizia* as well."

With that signed, they turned to depart, taking no leave of him and sending no compliments to his family. He deserved no such attention. Only at the threshold did Jane pause to allow the part of herself that was vindictive a small measure of satisfaction. "I do hope that you enjoy the fruits of your labour."

Vincent closed the door behind her and offered his arm. They walked down the street without conversation until they reached a corner. Signor Nenci waited there for them.

"Well?" His tone was gruff, but his eyes twinkled.

"As we had planned." She handed him the paper Querini had signed without reading, which transferred his apprentices' contracts to Signor Nenci. "I would feel some remorse for tricking him, but his apprentices will be better served with you."

"Rosa's getting them settled in now." He folded the paper with surprising neatness.

"How long do you think it will take him to realize what has happened?" Vincent asked.

"About as long as it will take him to realize that no one local will buy glass from someone who was selling out to the French." Signor Nenci tucked the page into his coat and gave a wicked grin. "Murano is a very small town."

Even after paying off their debts, the remainder of the gold that Vincent had taken from Spada's vault came to more than enough to restore all of their stolen funds. By mutual agreement, the Vincents put the excess into the coffers of Santa Maria degli Angeli. The Abbess very pointedly did not ask where the funds had come from, but accepted them on behalf of the church with thanks. If any good was to come of Spada's ill-gotten gains, then Jane could think of no better choice than the convent's work.

The small garret where Jane and Vincent had spent the previous months no longer seemed so mean, with the addition of proper fuel for the fire and Vincent's glamour. Though, in truth, they were barely in it during the next week, as they spent the days at work with Signor Nenci. His daughter and one of his apprentices proved to be the best on his team at learning how to embed glamours in the glass. This prompted a discussion about whether the technique required both sexes to work. Jane found this a decidedly silly idea, and she and Rosa proved it by creating a *Verre Plat* of a vase containing a tulip of such delicacy that a living butterfly tried to alight.

The advantage of working with the slab method was that they could lay in several threads of glamour before the glass cooled too much to take an impression. Vincent speculated that they might eventually be able to stack the glass to create more intricate images, but that would require a different sort of planning to mesh the images.

Its disadvantage, aside from a dependence on sunlight, was that the images were utterly devoid of motion. Their attempts to record moving glamours failed, leaving only blurred impressions in the glass.

Jane and Vincent would gladly have stayed longer to continue experimenting, but they were keenly aware of the fact that Jane's letter was likely to have provoked serious concern in her family.

When they went to the *capo di polizia* to present their receipts for the debts owed, a small army of nuns went with them. To Jane's surprise, Signor Nenci offered to come as well. This precaution turned out to be unnecessary, as *Gendarme*

Gallo was not in that day. He had, it seemed, abruptly given notice and quit the island.

He had also apparently mislead the *capo* about the Abbess's reason for calling. On the day that she came, he said that she had wanted to know if they had seen the convent's goat, which he claimed had escaped. Of course, the *capo* had not seen it, since they did not have a goat, and had thus shaken his head.

With this misrepresentation cleared away and the weight of the evidence the Vincents were now able to produce, the *capo di polizia* had no difficulty in acknowledging that the Vincents were quite innocent, and apologized handsomely for detaining them in Murano. His consideration extended to walking them to the docks himself, to inform the gondoliers that they were free to go.

It was quite the procession to the docks, with the *capo di polizia*, the nuns, and the glassmaker marching with the Vincents. Some passers-by followed, simply because it seemed as though something of moment were about to happen.

At the dock, Jane exchanged many heartfelt embraces with the sisters, whom she had grown to adore quite as much as if they were blood relations.

Sister Maria Agnes bounced. "Oh yes! And in Vienna, you must absolutely go to the glamour orrery that the Franciscans did. It is a wonder, and you will love it." She said something in German to Vincent that made him laugh and blush a little. Jane made a note to ask him about it later.

Thrusting a bread-shaped wax paper package forward, Sister Aquinata just nodded, with her eyes suspiciously bright.

"You must write to us to let us know that you have arrived

safely." The Abbess took Jane's hands in both of hers, her wrinkles a map of smiles past and present. She opened Jane's hand and pressed a glass rosary into it. "I know you are not Catholic, but I want you to have this to remember us by."

Jane had to swallow back tears, but her deep gratitude showed in her voice, which she only barely controlled. "Thank you." The beautiful green and gold beads were already warm in her fingers. "We will be back to work with Signor Nenci."

That gentleman was speaking with much animation with Vincent. All his gruffness remained, but the act of working with the glassmaker had changed her perception of him, so that he seemed more like her husband in temperament than anything else. She deeply regretted that they had not worked with him from the beginning, more for the loss of opportunity than for the misfortunes that had ensued. The possibility of creating art, and not simply technique, charmed her.

The gondolier was ready to depart, and there was still so much to say that the only solution was to bid everyone farewell and leave much unsaid. However, Vincent looked at the assembled crowd and cocked his head. He turned to Jane and held out his walking stick. "Would you hold this a moment, Muse?"

"Of course."

Her husband flexed his hands and reached into the ether. With remarkable speed, he wove seemingly random threads of glamour together in a flurry of colour, then pulled a slip-knot, binding them suddenly together.

A dragon soared overhead, roaring its triumph to the skies of Murano.

The nuns, Signor Nenci, the *capo di poliẓia,* and all the

passers-by who had followed them without understanding why let out a gasp of admiration and applauded. And while they were distracted, Jane and Vincent boarded the gondola with full hearts and left Murano.

The open water in front of them was one of the most beautiful things Jane had ever seen.

During the entire month-long trip through Lombardy-Venetia to Bohemia, Jane had a constant fear that her father would ride past them on his way to Venice. When they pulled into Vienna at last, it was the twenty-first of December and the snow lay piled upon the streets. The lodgings that her family and the Strattons had taken faced on to Beatrixgasse and had large windows that let in the snow-filtered light. No heroine travelling in a chaise and four could have met with the surprise that awaited Jane and Vincent when they alighted and walked into the house.

Jane braced herself for concern and the need to allay her mother's fears. Instead, Mr. Ellsworth hurried out from the parlour and into the entrance hall with his arms spread in welcome. "Jane! Vincent! Oh, but it is good to see you. What a lovely surprise!"

"Oh yes, my dears, it is. If you had told us, I should have told cook to have a roast, and as it is I have nothing but chicken, which is not so nice after a long journey." Mrs. Ellsworth fluttered out into the entry hall. "You should have told us you were coming in time for Christmas!"

Jane glanced to Vincent, who had paused with his greatcoat half-off. His expression was guarded, but she suspected that his thought was the same as hers. It sounded as if Jane's letter had not yet arrived.

"Likely they *did* tell us." Mr. Ellsworth tucked his fingers into his waistcoat pockets and chuckled. "Your letter arrived, but it was so water damaged that we could not make out much except that you had *not* been attacked by pirates and that Lord Byron was out of town. Your mother was much relieved on both counts. Thank you for writing to reassure her."

Jane sighed with a great release of tension. She had never been so glad to hear that a letter had been mangled in transit. "Of course. I would never want to worry Mama."

"Such a considerate daughter," Mrs. Ellsworth cooed and took her by the arm. "But come in, come in to the parlour. You must be sick with cold, and you have lost weight. I declare. You will work yourself to death."

Jane's attention, however, was distracted by the entrance of Mr. O'Brien and Melody. Jane's sister was glowing, and very round. The graceful carriage that Jane had so envied was gone, though Melody still managed to make her increased figure somehow elegant. The two sisters' embrace was rendered unfamiliar by the change in Melody's situation, but was nevertheless heartfelt.

Jane was surprised to find that her cheeks were wet with tears.

"Oh, Jane . . ." Melody seemed to mistake the tears as sorrow for the child Jane had lost, which could not be further from the truth.

Shaking her head, Jane wiped the tears away. "No, no. I am so happy for you that it hurts." She squeezed her sister's hand. "You will be a wonderful mother."

By the smile this brought to Melody's face, it seemed to be the highest praise Jane could have offered her. "I am so glad you have come."

Mr. O'Brien watched his wife with a peculiar yearning joy that was captivating. She recalled the same look on Vincent during the few months when she had been expectant. Jane glanced at Vincent, who caught her gaze and returned it with a warmth that heated her through. It did not matter if it turned out that she could not conceive. Motherhood was not something that Jane was certain that she wanted, or could even achieve. Then again . . . Jane and Vincent might be in Vienna, and not working, long enough to let matters take their own course. Whatever happened, it would do nothing to change their regard for one another.

Melody led the way back into the parlour, where they settled in front of the fire and had good English tea while they caught each other up on their travels and the decision to return to Vienna. It seemed that Melody had not been plagued with the same upset to her stomach that Jane had faced, and was rather deeper into her term than she had thought when she wrote. Her confinement was expected in January.

"La! Only think! When we were in Trieste, I was—well, you know—and did not even know it. Is that not droll?" Melody ran her hand over her dress. "But am I not ridiculously large?"

"Oh, my dear, I was even larger when I was expecting you." Mrs. Ellsworth took out her fan and shook her head. "You will be larger yet, you will see."

Mr. Ellsworth cleared his throat and turned to Vincent. "I

say. I think we have been frightfully rude in not asking you how Murano was."

"Oh, yes!" Mrs. Ellsworth sat up in her seat. "Sir David, do tell us how you passed your time?"

Her husband, caught with his teacup to his lips, choked on any possible answer. Coughing, Vincent set the cup down on the mantelpiece and turned helplessly toward Jane. Then his gaze darted toward her mother.

Jane smiled, took a sip of her own tea, and rescued her husband again. "Our trip was entirely uneventful."

Afterword

Novels are not written in isolation, and I had a number of incredibly helpful people guide me through this one. I will thank them in random order, and hope, rather desperately, not to forget anyone.

First, of course, I must thank my editor, Liz Gorinsky, who was patient when my schedule imploded toward the tail end of the production process. She gives good notes and very gentle nudges. My agent, Jennifer Jackson, not only sells the books, she can talk me off the ledge when I am realizing that trying to write a heist novel is way, way harder than I expected it to be.

Speaking of heists, I would not have gotten through this without the help of my fellow pod-casters at Writing Excuses: Dan Wells, Brandon Sanderson, and Howard Tayler. We spent a lot of time trying to figure out how to structure things in novel form. Scott Lynch also was wonderful about sharing heisty tips with me. The tricky thing about writing a heist is that it has a very specific structure. One of its pieces is that there is a hidden plan within the visible plan. There is always a thing that appears to go wrong, but which was actually part of the master plan. That's easy in a movie because you are never inside the characters' heads. In a novel, particularly the fourth in a series with an established, tight third-person point of view, we're in Jane's head all the time. I could not lie to the audience, nor could I have Jane be in the dark. So I had to write the scenes to work for both the visible plan and the hidden plan, depending on the context with which you read them. It was a great deal of fun, and I cannot thank the gentlemen enough for their help in sorting out the elements that I had to have on the page.

Thank you to Noah Chan for suggesting the tarot card suits for the aliases of the swindlers. I put out a call on Twitter saying that I needed a set of four aliases for the 1817 version of *The A-Team*. My original plan had been to use commedia dell'arte characters for the group of swindlers but was thwarted by the fact that *il dottore* is a traditional character. I have a habit of inserting a *Doctor Who* cameo into each of the novels, and that meant inadvertently tying *il dottore* to the bad guys. It introduced levels of confusion I did not want, but I'll tell you a bit more about why I was unwilling to give that character up when we get to the "About History" portion. Suffice to say that the tarot suits were perfect.

Kelley Caspari helped me with the glass questions. She has

the handy combination of being a science fiction and fantasy writer as well as having trained in Murano as a glassmaker. She is the one who suggested the flat version of the Verre.

Gianni Ceccarelli answered my plea for some last-minute Italian help.

Paul Cornell helped me with some lines of dialogue when I wanted to make them more specific to a certain character.

My husband, Robert, is wonderful about letting me babble about the book at random intervals. He has a knack for asking the right question, even when he hasn't read the novel yet. I credit his truly wonderful parents with raising him right. Here I should note that though there are aspects of Vincent that are based on my husband, they have totally different back stories. Rob's parents are fantastic. Mrs. Kowal, in particular, gave me some valuable insight into Catholic nuns, which was much appreciated.

Thanks as well to my research assistant, Erica Bergstrom, who spent countless hours trying to find information about Venetian markets and fashion for me. Lynne Thomas tracked down what Venetian police officers were called, using her super reference-librarian skills. Librarians in general were wicked helpful. The staff at both the Chicago Public Library and the Multnomah County Library were amazing. Seriously, people, just wander into the nearest library and thank the librarian there for knowing all things, or at least where to find them.

My beta readers on this book were Amanda Jensen, Andy Rogers, Annalee Flower Horne, Bonnie Walker, Brent Longstaff, Callie Stoker, CEdison, Charlotte Cunningham, Colin Parker, Crystal Bryant, Donna, EngineersFalcon, Epheros

Aldor, Grant Gardner, Ian Miller, Jeff Evans, John Devenny, Jon Marcus, Julia Rios, Kassie Jennings, Kristin. Kurt J. Pankau, Laura Christensen, Lisa Bouchard, Liz Muir Busby, Maggie, Mary Garber, Micaiah Evans, Michael Simko, Peter Ellis, Susan Bermudez, Thom Stratton, Trey Wren, VicDiGital, and Wendy P.

My parents deserve specific thanks this year, because I had to review the copyedits over Christmas and they were very understanding about the fact that I just disappeared for hours and hours.

As usual, I need to thank Jane Austen for the inspiration. This time, however, she has to share that with Lord Byron.

And that brings us to our note about history.

A Note on History

I'll be honest, Lord Byron was not originally scheduled to appear in this novel. In the course of research, I read Andrea Di Robilant's book *Lucia: A Venetian Life in the Age of Napoleon,* and she mentioned that in 1817, which is the year in which the novel was set, Lord Byron was actually living in Venice. I jumped on it. I mean . . . a heist novel? With Lord Byron? This is not something you pass up.

Lord Byron was an inveterate letter writer. Those epistles have been collected in *Lord Byron: Selected Letters and Journals,* edited by Leslie A. Marchand. What was particularly helpful about this collection is that it had a selection of quotes broken down by subject in the back. Where possible, I've used Byron's own words for his dialogue, although sometimes I tweaked them to suit the conversation. He really did have a menagerie, by the way, including several monkeys.

The three poems he recites during the course of the novel are all slightly adjusted from the canonical version. I justified this in the book by pretending that he later wrote them down and edited them. I took excerpts from *Beppo: A Venetian Story* and *Don Juan* (Canto. 14). I also rewrote part of *The Prophecy of Dante* to be *The Glamourist*.

Because Byron was so diligent at writing letters and keeping a journal, it's possible to reconstruct a good timeline of his activities. The days that he leaves Venice in the book were days when he was actually gone. But . . . allow me to point out that Lord Byron was travelling with a man named Doctor Polidori, whom he often called simply "the doctor." There's a two-week period in which they are more or less unaccounted for. Anyone who is a fan of a certain time traveler will find it pretty clear what happened.

The only part of Byron's timeline that I moved was his swimming race against Mingaldo, although his commentary is close to verbatim from one of his letters. He swam in the canals often enough that I felt like I could get away with it.

The church of Santa Maria degli Angeli is a real church in Murano and had a teaching school attached to it. The nuns I have inhabiting it are entirely made up, though their order is not. Venice was a diverse city, even after the fall of the Republic. Because Italy had been part of the Roman Empire, and lay just across the Mediterranean from Africa, it had a high percentage of people of African descent. While I can't provide documentation that any of the nuns at this particular convent were black, it's not unlikely. The first documented black nun was Louise Marie-Therese in 1695 in France, and there are records of black nuns at other convents all through Europe. Vienna, in particular, had a large mixed-race population, which is why I chose it as the hometown for Sister Maria Agnes. When I first planned this novel, I defaulted to an all-white cast because that's what I'm used to reading in texts from the 1800s. The more research I did, the clearer it became that a homogeneous cast would not be historically accurate.

I was also surprised to learn that Venice had a number of female glassmakers. Until the fall of the Republic in 1797, the island of Murano was the predominant manufacturer of glass in Europe. During Napoleon's reign, in addition to sacking the city and looting the treasures. After that, to keep them in line, the newly formed kingdom of Lombardy-Venetia placed heavy taxes on the supplies needed for glassmaking, which created huge economic problems for the glassmakers. In addition to this, foreign glassmakers came and apprenticed, then took the techniques home with them. In the space of ten years, they went from having forty glassmakers to only three. Signor Nenci's studio was one of the few remaining glass factories in Murano. While I used his name and the name of his factory, the character who inhabits the name is entirely made up.

Not long after Jane and Vincent visited, Murano underwent a revitalization, and by the 1830s it had a thriving industry again. I like to imagine that it would have happened faster if the *Verre* had been real.

Yours,
Mary

Glamour Glossary

GLAMOUR. This basically means magic. According to the Oxford English Dictionary, the original meaning was "Magic, enchantment, spell" or "A magical or fictitious beauty attaching to any person or object; a delusive or alluring charm." It was strongly associated with fairies in early England. In this alternate history of the Regency, glamour is a magic that can be worked by either men or women. It allows them to create illusions of light, scent, and sound. Glamour requires physical energy in much the same way running up a hill does.

GLAMURAL. A mural that is created using magic.

GLAMOURIST.   A person who works with glamour.

BOUCLÉ TORSADÉE.   This is a twisted loop of glamour that is designed to carry sound or vision depending on the frequency of the spirals. In principle it is loosely related to the Archimedes' screw. In the 1740s it was employed to create speaking tubes in some wealthy homes and those tubes took on the name of the glamour used to create them.

CHASTAIN DAMASK.   A technique that allows a glamourist to create two different images in one location. The effect would be similar to our holographic cards which show first one image, then another depending on the angle at which it is viewed. Invented by M. Chastain in 1814, he originally called this technique a jacquard after the new looms invented by M. Jacquard in 1801. The technique was renamed by Mrs. Vincent as a Chastain Damask in honour of its creator.

ETHER.   Where the magic comes from. Early physicists believed that the world was broken into elements with ether being the highest element. Although this theory is discredited now, the original definition meant "A substance of great elasticity and subtlety, formerly believed to permeate the whole of planetary and stellar space, not only filling the interplanetary spaces, but also the interstices between the particles of air and other matter on the earth; the medium through which the waves of light are propagated. Formerly also thought to be the medium through which radio waves and electromagnetic radiations generally are propagated" (OED). Today you'll more commonly see it as the root of "ethereal," and its meaning is similar.

FOLDS. The bits of magic pulled out of the ether. Because this is a woman's art, the metaphors to describe it reflect other womanly arts, such as the textiles.

LOINTAINE VISION. French for "distance seeing." It is a tube of glamour that allows one to see things at a distance. The threads must be constantly managed or the image becomes static.

OMBRÉ. A fold of glamour that shades from one colour to another over its length. This technique was later emulated in textile by dip-dying.

NŒUD MARIN. A robust knot used for tying glamour threads. This was originally used by sailors for joining two lines, but adapted by glamourists for similar purposes. In English, this is known as a Carrick Bend.

PETITE RÉPÉTITION. French for "small repetition." This is a way of having a fold of glamour repeat itself in what we would now call a fractal pattern. These occur in nature in the patterns of fern fronds and pinecones.

SPHÈRE OBSCURCIE. French for "invisible bubble." It is literally a bubble of magic to make the person inside it invisible.

Reading Group Guide

1. Jane and Vincent suffer from poverty and great anxiety in this book. Have you ever been in danger of losing everything, actually had to start over, or known people in similar situations? How have you, or they, dealt with it?

2. Vincent and Jane's marriage is strained by their harsh circumstances. What in their behavior illustrates this, and how do they restrengthen their bond? Can you think of anything else they should have done, or of things that work for you that would NOT have worked for them, given their characters and circumstances?

3. Vincent and Jane put their trust in the wrong person at first, but eventually they do find

allies in Venice. How much do you think people take their cues from appearance and status today, as opposed to that period in history? What makes a person decide that a potential ally can be depended on for help, or decide to take a chance at helping somebody else?

4. For a few months, Jane and Vincent cling desperately to the hope of rescue by their relatives, unaware that their messages have gone astray. How have modern instant communications changed family interactions? In what ways is *Valour and Vanity* comparable to other heist stories, such as *Ocean's Eleven*?

5. Did you find yourself interested in learning more about glassmaking and the history of Murano? Many towns have glassmaking classes. What do you think it would be like to take one?

6. Lord Byron is a very vibrant character in this novel. Did you know much about his personal life prior to reading it?

7. In this novel, financial concerns require Vincent to engage in street performances of glamour, which is very difficult for him. Have you ever had to take a job that was emotionally difficult for you? How did you cope with it?

8. Travel in the early nineteenth century was very different from what we are accustomed to. Given the potential hazards, would you have ventured far from home?

About the Author

Annaliese Moyer

Mary Robinette Kowal was the 2008 recipient of the John W. Campbell Award for Best New Writer and a Hugo winner for her story "For Want of a Nail." A professional puppeteer and voice actor, she spent five years touring nationally with puppet theaters. She lives in Chicago with her husband, Rob, and nine manual typewriters.